Rising of Three

The Starseed Trilogy

Ashley McLeo

Meraki Press

*For my parents. Thank you for supporting and loving me.
I'm a lucky lady.*

Contents

Returning Cast

Lily Whiplark - Firstborn of the three, triplet, earth witch, healer, runner, and Terramar commune resident.

Evelyn Locksley - Second born of the three, triplet, water witch, siren, ceremens, and New York resident.

Sara McKinney - Third born of three, triplet, fire witch, ex-military brat, currently on sabbatical from her studies at Princeton.

Brigit McKay-Clery - Lily, Evelyn, and Sara's mother, earth and fire witch, blends amazing tea with herbs from her garden.

Aengus Clery - Lily, Evelyn, and Sara's father, non-wizard, and deceased.

Gwenn Dolan - Brigit's older sister, earth witch, Rena's ex-girlfriend, runs an internet business, and is a dead ringer for Lily.

Mary O-Byrne - Brigit's younger sister, water witch, siren, midwife, dresses eclectically, and is a dead ringer for Evelyn.

Aoife McKay - Brigit's youngest sister, fire witch, ceremens, runs Aoife's Apothecary in town, and is a dead ringer for Sara.

Fiona Fallon - Brigit's cousin, earth witch, healer, Lily's healing instructor, and college friend of Sonja Locksley (Evelyn's adoptive mother).

Nora McFadden - Brigit's best friend since childhood, skilled witch, prodigious ceremens, and Terramar intermediary.

Morgane Murphy - McKay family friend and triplet tutor, octogenarian, academic, and has a healthy disregard for societal restrictions. Brought Sara to her first adoptive mother and father, who perished in a car fire.

Rena Whiplark - Lily's adoptive mother, witch, Taurus, and matriarch of Terramar commune.

Annika Karlsson - Rena's partner, Terramar resident, witch, Swedish by birth, and dedicated yogi.

Selma de Avila - Terramar resident, married to Richard, chatterbox, Spanish, and siren descended from the sirens of the Odyssey.

Emily Harp - Terramar resident, empathetic witch, Texas born, and deceased at the hands of Amon, Empusa, and Lily.

Empusa - Oldest vampire in the world, daughter of Noro and Seraphina, twin to Amon, and deadly.

Amon - Oldest vampire in the world, son of Noro and Seraphina, twin to Empusa, and deadly.

Noro - Fata sent to Earth to prepare it for the arrival of the fata.

Dimia - King of the fata on Hecate, Lilith, Eve, and Seraphina's father.

Lilith - Sister to Seraphina and Eve, fata sent to scout Earth, mother, and first wife of Adam before his betrayal.

Eve - Sister to Lilith and Seraphina, fata sent to scout Earth, mother to Aya, lover of Noro, and second wife of Adam.

Seraphina - Sister to Lilith and Eve, fata sent to scout Earth, mother to Empusa, Amon, and Esther (the keeper of Seraphina's tale).

Hypatia - Guardian of Seraphina's tale before her abrupt death at the hands of Amon. Constructed a prophecy and re-wrote Seraphina's tale then hid it in space and time until the arrival of the three destined to save Earth from the fata.

Spells of Potential Interest

THIS LIST IS for those readers who are curious about the spells used in *The Starseed Trilogy*. Most of my spells are based off the Basque language, which is a language isolate having little to no similarities with other known languages. This list is not in alphabetical order, rather it is in the order in which the spells appear in the series.

- Solvo = Unbinds magic previously bound in a person.
- Hebeto = To dim, reduce, weaken, or blunt.
- Arma = Produces a shield charm.
- Flamarba = Produces a flame shield or gate.
- Flampila = Produces a fireball.
- Cludo = Closing or a barrier in mind magic.

- Inruo = Breaking in/intruding when using mind magic.
- Inruo ego = Sending memories into another's mind (Aoife's speciality).
- Candeo = To create a glow/light.
- Resipisico = To revive, regenerate, resurrect, reappear (waking the dead).
- Salus = The general healer's spell for health, welfare, and fixing of small injuries, can be additive but only to a certain degree. Does not work with every injury-vampire or werewolf bites for instance.
- Dedisco = Erases a person's memory.
- Volavari = To Fly/raise someone/something in the air.
- Islatu = To reflect.
- Aberro (for a person) = To deflect or throw back a person.
- Impingo (for an object) = Impinge, strike, dash, inflict, or throw back.
- Lotu = To bind a person.
- Dantza = To make someone dance.
- Birarazi = To make spin .
- Murr = To reduce or crush.
- Cogerba = "The ground-kissing curse" Forces people to the ground.

- Caeliter = Astral travel or space travel if you have a pneuma. :)
- Lascero = To tear, rip, break, claw, or mangle.
- Lascarma = To destroy a shied or other protective casing. Rip, tear, break, claw, or mangle.
- Clostium = To unlock.
- Pream = Blowing up something
- Serostium = To lock (a door).
- Dionean = A stunning spell.
- Mahasoka = Creates vine ropes.
- Benda = Like a bandaid spell it keeps wounds from getting infected. Preventative healing magic.
- Hercapto = Plants capturing a person. Ex. grass wrapping around a leg.
- Eginura = Conjures water.
- Finium = To halt your own spell (not someone else's).
- Argibeltza = The black light curse. Specific to fighting daemons because it swallows up the energy they've collected.
- Elkartaire = To pull air together, thickens the air. If the witch/wizard was strong enough (usually an air witch/wizard) this could create a shield of sorts.

- Homaire = To produce a compression wall of air.
- Motus = To move something.
- Bratu = A rotation charm that can rotate in any medium.
- Arimegin = A fata curse to rid the world of a fata pneuma who has done wrong for good (means "soul ceasing" in basque).

Spaceship Cleaner Needed
Sara

Sara padded softly along the creaky wood floor so as not to wake those still asleep. Stopping before the stone fireplace, she fingered the stocking stitched with her name before extending her fingers toward the wood laying in the hearth.

"Flampila," she whispered, and a bright orange ball of fire rolled from her palms to catch on the wood. Heat caressed her face. Sara sighed and pulled her fuzzy robe closer.

A toppling stack of papers on the dining table caught her eye as she rounded the corner of the hearth separating Fern Cottage's living room from the kitchen-diner. *Mary seriously came through,* she thought picking up The Guardian as her eyes roved over the dozens of other publications.

She spun on her heel, not ready to dig into current events, and set about making a cup of cinnamon spice tea.

Two hours later the table was littered with partially rumpled international newspapers and Sara's hands were black from the ink.

This isn't looking good. She chose a journal of questionable quality to skim next. An article on the second page jumped out at her and Sara stifled a laugh at the title.

Aliens Brand Woman for Spaceship Cleaner in Her Sleep

Sara's copper eyes ran down the words, widening as she took in the subtext of the article shaming a woman brave enough to tell her story, no matter how ludicrous it might sound.

Mrs. Leslie Leeteral from Hackney claims to have received an early Christmas present. One she isn't at all sure she wants. Unfortunately, like all tattoos we acquire once we've had a few too many drinks, this one is sure to stick.

The London native claims to have had a couple gins to celebrate her husband's Christmas bonus and gone to bed early the nineteenth of December. She had big plans to finish her Christmas shopping the next day and take herself out for a solo lunch and pint while her husband watched their three children. It isn't often you get alone time as a mum, so this part of her story, at least, we understand.

Unfortunately for Mrs. Leeteral, her night of rest did not go as planned.

She awoke with a start in the wee hours to find a ghostly figure leaning over her.

"He was massive, he was. Bright yellow too, like the sun. I thought he actually was the sun at first. Still asleep, you know. But then I saw how close he was and figured I'd be dead if the sun came in me room. Well, he saw he'd woken me and he came —*he flew*—closer, which had me in a right state as you can imagine. Me husband was working the night shift, and I was all alone, defenseless with the kids in the next rooms! I scrambled up as fast as I could and grabbed the lamp to fend him off. Bit stupid really. How do you fight a ghost with a lamp? Like I said, I didn't have me head on straight. He was inches from me when I realized I couldn't see through him and I thought to meself this can't be a ghost. When did anyone ever talk about a colored ghost? They're always white, ain't they? He had to be an alien."

At this point in the interview Mrs. Leeteral looks up at the sky and shivers.

"The alien came right up and looked at me. He had huge black eyes and a round, black mouth. At least I think that's what they were. He stared at me for what musta been ten minutes and then . . . He touched me."

Mrs. Leeteral pulls up her shirt sleeves to reveal muscular deltoids and a small, yellow tattoo that looks a bit like the moon.

"He marked me with this! Looks like the moon, doesn't it? I suppose that's where he musta been from. No idea why he marked me. Perhaps he was looking for a good cleaner? I've been in the business twenty years and you never hear of cleaners on spaceships. Musta gotten tired of living in all that filth."

There you have it, folks. The aliens are coming, and they need help cleaning up. Or perhaps Mrs. Leeteral should check her bank cards. One may contain a charge to her local tattoo parlor. Gin is a hell of a drink.

A small, nondescript photo of Mrs. Leeteral's mark was at the bottom of the page. Sara's chest fluttered wildly as she studied it. *Shhh, calm down. It's a photo,* she thought and her pneuma, the bit of fata soul she'd recently learned had been living inside her since birth, stilled.

It did look like the moon, and Sara could see how some would think the mark a misbegotten tattoo, too. But Sara knew better than to believe the mark was either.

If that reporter only knew how close Mrs. Leeteral was to guessing the truth, they'd be peeing their pants.

"How long have you been up?"

Sara jumped in her seat and directed her hands at the door.

Evelyn held up her palms. "Sorry! I didn't mean to startle you. But really, do you believe anyone is getting past Mom's wards?" She lifted an eyebrow and headed for the pot of coffee Sara had taken the liberty of making for whoever was up next.

Sinking down into her seat, Sara released a long exhale. *Of course I didn't hear Evelyn. She still doesn't weigh enough to make noise.*

"No, I'm sorry. I've been jumpy since New York. Even meditation has been hard. And no, I don't think anyone could get past Mom's wards, but what I think isn't always correct."

"Touché." Evelyn filled her cup with coffee. "What's all this?" She gestured to the pile of newspapers on the table.

Sara pulled a handful of newspapers closer to make room for Evelyn. "Papers. I asked Mary to drop them off a few days ago. It looks like she may have enlisted

Morgane's help, too. They don't carry all of these in the village shop. They're so we can keep in the loop."

"In the loop? Don't you think we're a little beyond what the average person knows?" Evelyn pulled out the heavy wooden chair across from Sara with visible effort.

She's not getting stronger as fast as Fiona hoped she would. Sara eyed her sister's lank blonde hair, skeletal arms, and ribs that were visible through her night shirt. At least her magic had returned a little. It was the first step. "There's no doubt we have more information on what's happening, but we're clueless as to what the fata are doing right now."

Evelyn scowled and looked into her cup.

"But these papers can help. Most of them are the typical drivel, but read this." Sara handed the page to Evelyn, who scoffed.

"You can't be serious. You know what this is, right? Or does this kind of crap not make it onto military bases?"

Sara rolled her eyes and pushed the paper into Evelyn's hand. "It does. Read it."

Evelyn opened it and her sapphire eyes skipped over the page, fast at first, then slower as she took in what it meant. "Well, shit. They've begun claiming people as their own." Evelyn set down the paper.

Claiming people. Sara shivered. "It appears that way. These papers are filled with all sorts of wild things.

Natural disasters which I'm sure are in no way natural, an increase in missing people all over the world, wild accidents or man-made structures failing. An entire highway in L.A. cracked the other day. The fissure was ten feet wide. They're blaming it on the San Andreas Fault but—"

"It's not that."

"Nope. This journal had the most obvious article. If this woman was claimed, she can't be the only one. She's probably just the only one willing to step forward, and this journal is crazy enough to print it."

Evelyn smirked. "My dad would die if he heard you call this rag *a journal.* You'd no longer be my 'level-headed, smart sister.' Too bad you're not interested in business. He'd hire you in a second. But you're right, none of these things are normal and that mark is definitely a fata brand. Even worse, it's not Dimia's or Noro's which means regular fata have started claiming." She sipped her coffee and looked around. "Where's Lily? She's usually up before me."

"She was up late last night texting texting a certain exuberant daemon." A lopsided grin spread on Sara's face lifting her freckle-spattered cheekbones.

A low whistle ran through Evelyn's red lips. "That girl has got it bad."

Sara shrugged off her robe. The fire had made the room toasty warm, and the tea had done the job of heating her insides. Even for a fire witch, it was hot. "She deserves it after the whole Liam/Amon catastrophe. When your first boyfriend turns out to be a psychopath vampire, you get a break on the second. From what Lily's told me he's the total opposite of Amon."

"Opposite personality wise. Looks wise, Alfred is a hottie, too. Lil must attract the tall, dark, and handsome types." Evelyn smiled a knowing smile. "Have you seen that letter he sent her? So sweet! He *really* likes her. Of course, that much was obvious when I met him. He was practically vibrating just looking at Lil!"

"When are you two going to get love interests of your own so you can stop gossiping about mine?" a groggy voice from the corner of the room mumbled.

Sara turned to see Lily, her wavy brown hair sticking out in all its bed-headed glory, smiling shyly at them. Sara pulled out the chair next to her and patted it. "I'm focused on other matters right now. Alfred's just so sweet it's hard not to talk about him."

"I'm off men for obvious reasons. The secrets of my siren talents and skills are at your complete disposal, sister dearest," Evelyn said, her tone grandiose.

A blush rose in Lily's cheeks.

Happiness becomes her. It's hard to imagine she's the same person from a month ago. Sara stopped staring and looked down at the papers on the table. Her oldest sister could only handle so much attention. She took the article she'd shown Evelyn and handed it to Lily.

"Yikes! You're laying it on her without coffee first? I'm getting a refill. Do you want any, Lil?" Evelyn stood up and made her way to Brigit's ancient coffee maker.

"Sure, thanks. Can you add cream until it's the color of a brown paper bag?" Lily turned to Sara. "What's this about?"

"Read it."

A minute later Lily set down the paper and sighed. "So, it's started already?"

"Looks like it. I've been online daily looking for clues, but you know how the Internet is. The term fata is useless. And mostly stuff about celebrities or conspiracy theorists who have a huge following comes up when I search aliens and magic. Nothing having to do with real witches or aliens, and if there is it's lost in the depths of the internet," Sara sighed with exasperation.

"Anyway, a few days ago, I realized newspapers might give more insight if I focus on smaller articles and not the front page. The smaller papers are generally willing to interview locals, even if they sound a little crazy, or report on smaller disasters to fill their pages. I asked Mary to bring some by."

Lily nodded and took the cup of coffee Evelyn offered. "I guess I shouldn't be surprised. The Acolytes worked fast last time—why would this time be any different? The new fata must be acclimating quickly to be claiming people already."

Evelyn joined her sisters at the table. "Or King Dimia ordered the few Eve brought over thousands of years ago to get to work while the other fata are becoming familiar with Earth's magic. That's what I would do. Like sending a scouting team out before an army."

"Did Noro ever let slip exactly how many came over?" Lily asked.

"No way. He's too secretive and smart for that. He didn't even tell Empusa or Amon who their mother was, remember? And they were his children and closest allies." Evelyn shook her head as if disbelieving her own words.

"To be honest, I only recall a couple dozen fata jumping through the portal, but I was also minutes from death. If my pneuma was any slower returning with the part of my mind she held to connect us through space, I would have been toast. There were hundreds of fata in The Crystal Palace, though. It was amazing—an entire palace made of gemstones and all those colorful fata waiting. I remember one in particular; it was fuchsia and looked a little scared of me." A thoughtful expression crossed Evelyn's face as if recounting her memories helped her unearth new information.

Her magic and strength are coming back slowly. It's

possible her memories are, too. "Let's hope you're right and only a couple dozen fata got through," Sara said. "That's still a lot but not compared to all the magical creatures on Earth. I don't like that we know so little about their magic or how to fight them. If there are hundreds, we could be in real trouble."

A New Kingdom
Noro

Noro swooped down the sloping hill through the frost-covered trees, his pace quickening as he approached the abandoned zoo. In the short time since he'd left the new fata of Earth to replenish their magical stores, much had changed.

Noro and his First Order Acolytes had furthered the fata cause more in two weeks than they'd managed for millennia. Infiltrating power systems, claiming humans, and creating a current of chaos to effectively undermine human confidence was a splendid start.

The humans won't need to worry themselves over their fate much longer. Noro flew faster and the largest hut in the park, King Dimia's personal quarters, came into view.

Learning that his first children, powerful beings

sculpted into exactly what Noro needed, had perished at the hands of Eve's sisters was the last straw. No longer would Noro make concessions for those magical creatures who did not welcome the reign of their ancestors. Nor would he hide in the shadows, skirting around weak humans.

No, he would use them as they used the land they were born to. The land they seemed to have little respect for. The same land that made them powerful. The land he would take.

No one born on Earth knew how sweet their world was. They'd never seen their home die as Hecate was dying. Never witnessed the plants and creatures within it wither to nothing. The magic fizzle from their souls.

Soon, the creatures of Earth would understand. And as humankind's power dwindled before their eyes, the fata would take up their reign.

The witches will pay for what they've done. If only Seraphina had consented to help, none of this would have happened. I would not still be called a fool. Fata would not dare gossip behind my back, even as I toil to make them powerful once more. I'll show them. He shot fifty feet above the trees and magic born of fury flew from him, splitting the tallest oak in the park like lightning.

No matter the amnesty Dimia promises I'll see to it

Amon and Empusa receive vengeance. Dimia does not yet understand how his daughters have changed. How their human blood has tainted the fata within them. How they are no longer his. But I shall make him see.

Three Circles Round

Lily

Lily pulled an extra layer over her head. It was the first day since returning from New York that she felt enough like herself to go on a run. *There's no way I'm not taking advantage of the free time, no matter how freezing it is out there.* Once their lessons started back up there would be little time to go on a long, satisfying run.

She opened the door. A shock of wind and rain slapped her in the face. Jumping outside before she could change her mind, Lily set off at a fast jog to work out the kinks. Rounding Fern Cottage, she caught sight of the lake and saw a blonde figure huddled along its banks.

Is Mary crazy? It's frigid out here!

As she neared her eccentric aunt, Lily caught sight of a book in Mary's hands and laughed. *She's reading in the wind and rain. Because that makes total sense.*

"Hey, Mary! What are you doing out here?"

Mary turned, and Lily's green eyes narrowed as her nostrils filled with her aunt's scent of grapefruit and rain. Mary was dry.

"Morning, Lil! Is everyone up, then? I arrived around seven and I didn't want to wake any of you, so I came out here to relax."

"You've been out in this for two hours?" Lily gestured at the inclement weather incredulously.

"Aye. I like the rain, the smell, the sensation on me skin, the sound, the fresh taste, all of it. Especially when it hits the water. It helps me think."

Lily blinked. She supposed it made sense, Mary being a water witch and all, but still. "Aren't you cold? Your sweater isn't very thick."

"I've set up a wee bubble 'round meself. Repels the rain and keeps me warm. Come see."

Lily moved to stand next to her aunt and sighed as her nose tingled with warmth.

"Aye, it's nice, isn't it? A shield charm with a weather-modifying spell inside, heat in this case. Useful if you're stuck out in the elements for a while, although they're quite draining. I'll need a big breakfast soon." She held up the book she'd been reading. "I'm about finished with the book Annika recommended. It's interesting, but I fear not useful for training you girls. I'll leave it at the cottage today if you want to read it."

Lily read the title—*A Guide to a Starseed's Time on Earth*—and lifted an eyebrow. "That sounds like an Annika book."

Mary's soprano laugh mingled with the sound of raindrops hitting the lake. "Turns out you three are far from the first people to experience this. There have been countless journals throughout time in which people claimed their soul was from elsewhere. Recent accounts, too. It sounds odd, but you can't say it's not true."

Mary was right. She couldn't contradict it. Not when Lily had a soul originating from another planet inside her, alongside her own human soul. Her pneuma fluttered somewhere around her liver and Lily sighed.

"You've gone and gotten my pneuma all riled up. I should go. She tends to stay still when my body is moving, so it's less distracting."

"Aye, like a babe. The motion rocks them to sleep." Mary paused. "I've been thinking, you three should name your pneumas."

"Sara already brought that up. I told her she should name hers Gertrude." An impish grin spread across Lily's face as her aunt chuckled. "See you later!"

She jogged around the lake and broke through the forest tree line. The scent of dirt and wet needles flew at her, soothing her with their familiarity. Unconcerned with getting lost, she took off down a random trail. Soon the only sounds she could hear were the blood pounding in her ears and the whooshing of air in and out of her mouth. In less than ten minutes she'd sprinted to the oak tree that had given her the clue to find Hypatia's book, now leafless in the cold winter air.

Lily slowed as she caught sight of a pair of black eyes gleaming at her from a hole in the tree's dense wood. Her heart stopped as the eyes grew larger and rounder. She squatted and shot a harmless tickling spell at the tree, ready to fight whatever was staring at her once it emerged from its hole.

A squirrel scurried out and Lily released her breath.

An animal, not a fata.

She kept moving, wanting nothing more than to put distance between herself and the memory of the day she'd gazed into Noro's dark eyes. Miles went by before an overwhelming urge to stop and gulp air stabbed her in the chest. Her stubborn streak persisted and instead she slowed from a sprint, run, jog, power walk, to finally a walk, her breath easing to normal.

Lily walked over to a stump and bent her foot at a right angle against the wood before leaning forward into the stretch. Sweat dripped down her face. Muscles, tight from days of inactivity, lengthened, making space within her. Only days ago, when she realized her body was no longer her own, did she grasp how precious that space was.

A moment alone. Lily placed her hand on her stomach. Only her breath moved there. *Maybe Mary's right and pneumas are like babies.*

She switched her feet and lifted her gaze.

"Goddess be," Lily whispered releasing her stretch and striding into the clearing. *Here I am, back where it all began. The unbinding site.*

Chunks of earth the size of small cars were strewn around the clearing before her. While the water had gone, the destruction it left was still visible. Fallen trees, including a couple massive downed sentinels at the edge of the clearing, marred the forest for miles. Only the strongest remained standing after the tsunami of Evelyn's magic. The fire pit, half frozen in the center of the clearing, was untouched and surrounded by a larger circle of scorched, blackened dirt. Lily's pneuma shot against her chest.

Ouch! So much for my alone time.

"Did you know this is where my magic was freed?"

Her pneuma danced within her.

"I guess so. Goddess be, that was exciting. Exciting and *terrifying.* Crazy to think how little I knew back then." She trailed off thinking of the way her magic had shot out of her, creating an earthquake and a fissure in the ground larger than a semitruck before flying back into her body with the speed of a freight train.

Since then, she'd grown used to seeing magic leaving her fingertips—though the way it spouted from her that first time, in the shape of a double helix, was an image she'd never forget.

Even back then we were getting hints. Everything we've done, it's all been about our blood, our DNA.

Her pneuma slammed against her sternum and Lily coughed. "What the hell? Are you trying to tell me you want out?"

Her pneuma rose in her torso, up and down, a nod.

Sharing her body with a being she didn't understand, a being who made Lily less connected with herself and the earth, was taking some major getting used to. Waking up in the morning, setting her feet on the ground and experiencing them rebound before they settled onto wood was disconcerting. Lily often wondered if she'd feel different about it if their pneumas weren't so airy. If it felt more like her body, grounded and hard.

Her pneuma swirled around her stomach, wrenching Lily back to the moment.

Alright! I'll let you out. Stop swirling around. You're making me sick. Fear accompanied her decision. Sara and Evelyn had each released their pneumas recently, but this would be the first time Lily let hers out since returning home. No matter how much she wanted her body back, the fear of losing her pneuma had been stronger. Lily sensed this had something to do with her realization that Lilith's pneuma, one of the original three fata sisters' souls, was inside of her. Lilith, the wanderer, the explorer, the one who had left her sisters. Therein lay the conflict. While Lily wasn't completely comfortable sharing her body, she also didn't want her pneuma, presumably one of their largest advantages against the fata, to leave like she had before.

"Caeliter," Lily whispered. Her lungs expanded, and she gasped. There was a sense of freedom for the first time in a week as a shimmering, ghostly green light flew out of her.

To Lily's surprise, her pneuma did not fly off into the woods but stayed floating before her "Aren't you going to explore? Isn't that what you wanted?"

"I wanted out. Not to run away." An airy voice filled the clearing, cracking from disuse but still imperious.

Lily jumped back and shrieked. "What the hell! You can talk?"

The green pneuma stared at her with round, black eyes. "How else do you think I understand when you speak to me?"

"But—why didn't you tell me?" Her voice was still high, disbelieving.

Her pneuma shrugged, an oddly human gesture. "Why didn't you ever let me out?"

Lily sighed. *Pneuma, one. Lily, zero.*

"I wasn't ready, I guess." Her eyebrows knit together. "Wait—if you can talk, why can't your sisters? Sara and Evelyn have let their pneumas out and neither reported a peep from them."

The ghostly figure before her shimmered and shook her head. Every second her pneuma stood before Lily, she was morphing from a blobby ghost into something more recognizably human.

"Their bond is not set yet. They'll speak when it is time. I will not rush that process by telling you secrets that are not mine to tell. You must understand, my sisters have waited thousands of years to meet yours. What is a few more days?"

"That's annoying," Lily replied.

Her pneuma smiled. It was so unlike Noro's smile, which resembled a lecherous wide "O." Lily's pneuma's smile looked nice.

Lily's shoulders softened at the familiar gesture. "You don't move like him. Or have the same shape as Noro. Is it because you're a pneuma and no longer a fata?"

Her pneuma stopped flowing and Lily sensed she'd said the wrong thing. "I'm sorry if I offended you."

"You have not. It was his name; I haven't heard it spoken out loud in years. You are right in thinking pneuma and fata are different. It is the difference between your soul and body. My fata body perished but my pneuma, my soul, remains. The contrast is not why I move differently, though; I'm simply reacting to your human-ness. Trying to make you more comfortable. Accessing relatable quirks. It will make our relationship easier."

"Oh. Thanks. It helps," Lily said, recalling the creepy way Noro moved. They stayed silent, staring at each other for a moment longer until Lily started walking and her pneuma followed. They'd made it another half mile into the woods when Lily broke the silence. "So, do you still go by Lilith?"

The pneuma pulled a face and Lily laughed. "I'll take that as a no. Do you mind me asking why not?"

"It is the name my father gave me. A name from another life and another place. I loved my old name, but it is time to take another, one of this world. Of you and this place. A name encompassing my experience here."

Lily nodded. "That makes sense. So, what is your name now?"

"It is not the right time to reveal that yet. I shall wait until your sisters have developed their relationships with mine. Once my sisters have been nourished, as I have, they will deem it time. You will know us then."

"Alright," Lily sighed. "You have a lot of secrets, you know that, right?"

Her pneuma turned to look at her, her black hole of a mouth stretched into a smile. "You have no idea how many, but you shall discover some soon enough."

Silence
Evelyn

"Your pneuma literally talked to you? Like with a *voice*?" Evelyn shot up from the couch. "What the hell! I've had mine longer and all she's done is shake around inside me."

She slapped her stomach and winced as the pain shot through her. "You've been holding out on me!"

"Mine hasn't said anything either." Sara pinched her rosebud lips together. "And we've spent hours meditating together. I wonder what made your pneuma open up?"

Lily shook her head, took off her drenched running jacket and shoes, and plopped down on the couch before the fire. "To be honest, I'm not sure. We got to the unbinding site and I could tell she wanted out, so I released her. The next thing I know, she's talking to me like it's the most normal thing in the world! She refused to tell me exactly why, though."

Evelyn's mouth fell open.

Sara shook her head. "But, I don't understand. Why hasn't that happened for us?"

Lily shifted on her seat. "My pneuma said you guys aren't there yet with yours. I won't lie, I don't understand what she meant, but she made it clear she's not going to spell it out. It's something you have to find out for yourself."

"What?!" Evelyn moaned. "This is so ridiculous. I—I can't. I'm going to go lie down."

Evelyn shut the door to her room and sighed out her frustrations. The blue and gold tones that Sara and Brigit had picked out soothed her nervous system as Evelyn allowed herself to melt into the wood. They had done a beautiful job at making the small, shabby single room feel like her. With a few personal touches, black currant room spray, photos of her parents and best friend, Vicencia, and soft Egyptian cotton sheets, Evelyn had done the rest. Now it felt like home.

It's hard to believe I thought they barely knew me at that point. I was wrong. Man, I wish I could stop being wrong.

Roman popped into her mind unbidden and she rolled her eyes. Thinking about him almost made Evelyn miss her captivity at Peacock Manor. When she'd been fighting to stay alive, she'd hardly thought of Roman at all. But as Evelyn had discovered since returning to Fern Cottage she'd only delayed her vexing feelings.

Currently, considering Roman made her head want to explode.

If anyone can see doing shitty things for the sake of their family, it's me.

Brigit had revealed the truth of Roman's situation, including his indebtedness to the vampire twins and their threats against his family should he not seduce Evelyn. At first, Evelyn didn't want to believe her mother, but she had to admit the story rang true.

If he hadn't sold me out, they would have gone after his siblings. Still, couldn't there have been another way? Besides breaking my heart? I wonder what he's doing now?

She sighed and flung herself on the bed, figuring if there was ever a time to spend a few minutes being angsty, it was now.

Two HOURS later Evelyn slammed the door to her room and strode down the hall.

"I take it you didn't have any luck getting your pneuma to talk either?"

Evelyn jumped.

"Geez, Sara! Couldn't you make a little more noise? You scared the crap out of me."

"Oh sure, I'll try to turn the pages more loudly." Sara raised an eyebrow and closed the novel she'd been reading. "If it helps, I didn't have any luck either." She patted the couch and Evelyn joined her.

"Sorry." Evelyn sank into the couch and the aroma of lavender that pervaded the cottage puffed up from the cushions. "That was dramatic and you're correct in assuming it didn't work. I expected it to be so easy after what Lily said and instead my pneuma floated in front of me doing the usual flips and stuff until I got frustrated and sent her away. Where is Lily anyway? I want to ask her exactly what she did again."

Sara waved her hand. "She's taking a nap. And don't bother. I already asked, and she gave me the same rundown as before. I've been thinking about it though and I guess it makes sense. Our pneumas are like living things inside us, with their own wills and desires. It's only natural they would choose to communicate with us on their own timelines."

Wish mine would hurry up.

Ever since Sara had revealed their pneumas were souls sent from another time and planet, making the triplets starseeds, Evelyn had wanted answers. She knew from the creepy nickname Noro had given her that it was Eve's pneuma, her fata soul, that had been recycled into Evelyn's human body.

While that was weird as hell, it also opened a lot of options for acquiring new information. After all, Eve was the one who started all this by letting Noro and seven other mystery fata through to Earth before the effort killed her.

"Don't you think it's weird that Lily got her pneuma to talk when she's the most uncomfortable having a pneuma?"

Sara pursed her lips and tilted her head. "I don't know? Her pneuma may have sensed Lily needed a more human form of communication and adapted to it. So Lily would accept her." Sara sighed. "But if that's the case mine will never show herself. We'll be meditating together forever."

"You have put yourself in a bind being 'in touch with your inner self' and all that," Evelyn teased.

"I see that now." Sara frowned. "What were you doing in there for so long? You couldn't have been trying to make your pneuma talk to you for hours. You don't have that kind of patience. Shoot, I only lasted an hour before I got fed up and sent mine out the window. If I'm honest I think she was as happy to be rid of me as I was of her."

Warmth spread up Evelyn's neck to her cheeks. "I was . . . oh hell, I was thinking about *him.*"

"Oh, processing. That's good."

Evelyn shrugged. "I guess. To be honest, I'm still conflicted. A part of me gets it. Roman did it for his family and if I can forgive anything, it's a man who does something shitty to help his family. Still, another part of me wants to bash his face in. He's the first guy I've been with in so long and as much as I'm loath to say it, I loved him. Now, not only do I have this rage and distrust rampaging through me, I also don't have closure."

Sara stood and stretched. "That may change soon. Mom told me our first wave of tutors arrive tomorrow. Alistair is supposed to be coming. Maybe he can help you through this? He was Roman's incubi mentor and knew him well growing up. Shoot, he may even know where he is now."

Evelyn's eyes widened. *Maybe Alistair can help. At least I can ask if what I felt for Roman was real.*

"I'm going to make a fresh pot of tea." Sara stood. "Mom blended a new peppermint green tea while you were gone and it's divine. Want some?"

"I'm good. Where is Mom anyway?"

"She ran into town with Mary to stock up on groceries and supplies for our lessons. Most people will be staying in the village, but they'll be eating meals with us between lessons. Mom wanted to be prepared and Mary thought she'd need help seeing as Mom's not a whiz in the kitchen."

"Smart." Evelyn offered a small smile and bit back her remark that there were some things you just can never prepare for.

Daemon Daze
Sara

Sara watched Lily leap joyously at Alfred as the daemon emerged from the frost-kissed orchard surrounding Fern Cottage. Alfred laughed moving the enormous bouquet in his hands to the side, so it wasn't crushed by Lily's body.

Alfred and Lily's kiss deepened, and Sara diverted her attention to survey the surrounding scene. Alistair and Brigit were revising what Brigit had termed "the syllabus" near the orchard. Celestine and Mary sat on a bench in the middle of the garden, pouring over Hypatia's book at Celestine's request. Gwenn and Eros, an elf from Lily's squadron at Peacock Manor, were sparring in the field. Gwenn's brown hair and Eros's chin-length, white locks whipped through the air as one worked hard to best the other. Caleb, a werewolf from the Battle of Peacock

Manor, sat with Fiona at the edge of the field watching Gwenn and Eros. Aside from the Samhain gathering, Sara had never seen so many people at Fern Cottage.

For sure never so many people who knew our foretold destiny, Sara thought. *With all this help, we actually have a chance.*

A flowery scent filled her nostrils. Sara tore her eyes from the fight to find Alfred standing before her with a nosegay of roses in his outstretched hands. Lily, Evelyn, and Brigit each had a bouquet too. *Talk about a charmer.*

"Welcome to Fern Cottage, Alfred." Sara took the bouquet and fingered the velvet soft petals. "These are beautiful."

"He even made sure the florist added witch hazel blooms to our bouquets. She didn't want to because she said they looked funny with the roses, but what does she know?" Lily's eyes danced with delight at her boyfriend's thoughtfulness.

Sara nodded. "I'm sure if the florist had known they were going to a bunch of witches she wouldn't dare say that."

"Especially not this group of ladies," Alfred agreed.

"Next time try to remember the rest of us," Aoife said, stepping up to join the group, her copper eyes sparkling with mischief.

Sara hid a grin as Alfred's face fell.

"I'm—I can't believe I did that. Next time—"

"She's teasing," Evelyn shook her head. "If you're going to make it in this group, you'll have to learn to deal with Aoife's sarcasm."

"Couldn't resist a wee poke, lad. I know her sisters and mother are the most important to impress. It's what these girls' father would have done as well. For future reference, I prefer chocolates anyhow." Aoife winked, and Alfred exhaled.

"Listen up!" Brigit's voice rang out over the large garden and field. "Now that everyone is here we can begin lessons. Girls, I've asked our tutors to come prepared with the strongest tricks of their kind so you're ready for anything. As not everyone fought each type of creature at Peacock Manor, we'll start with demonstrations. The demonstrations will show you the most effective way to battle other creatures. Now, let's put these flowers in water and get to work."

SARA'S SHOULDER hit the grass. She rolled to the right just as Alfred's jet of light hit the ground next to her and the air filled with the scent of burnt dirt. Sara picked herself up and glared daggers at the brilliant yellow glow Alfred gave off.

They'd been battling for only twenty-five minutes and she was already flagging. Days of inactivity around Fern Cottage had reduced her stamina, magical and otherwise. *At least I'm not Evelyn right now.*

After her abduction and the torture Noro had put her through, Evelyn was far from peak physical and magical condition.

A searing pain flew up Sara's arm, wrenching her from her thoughts. "Ahh!" she screamed.

"It's only superficial. A friendly reminder never to let your mind wander around a daemon."

It wasn't the first time Alfred had scorched her this session, but Sara was ready for it to be the last.

"Flampila," she murmured and hurled a huge ball of fire at Alfred. *We'll see how he likes a superficial burn.*

To her dismay, Alfred leapt into the air so that the fireball hit him straight in the chest and absorbed it. His chest pulsed a brilliant orange before the color dissipated, brightening his obnoxious sunshine hue.

Sara's mouth gaped.

"Not all daemons can do that, but I can." Alfred winked maddeningly.

Her mouth tightened. "Dionean!" The stunning spell flew past Alfred's shoulder where it hit the protective shield Aoife had set around them and bounced off.

Sara flung herself to the side as her spell came

charging back at her. Her pneuma spun around in her pelvic bowl and Sara placed a hand to her gut to calm it. "How the heck?"

"I decided you two were going a touch easy on each other, only using one spell at once. I inserted a reflecting charm into the shield. If you don't step it up, I'll make it permanent," Aoife threatened.

"What!" Sara's mouth dropped open.

"We're training for a war, Sara! No more nicey-nice. You too, Alfred. Now get moving or I'll send my own spells through this shield at the both of you."

Heat rose inside Sara and a flurry of spells preceded thought. Magic flew from Sara's fingertips faster than she could have imagined. Colorful language spewed from Aoife as the spells Alfred failed to absorb barraged her shield.

One by one, Sara watched Alfred take in her magic, transmute it, and shoot it back at her. By the time all his energy was expended, Sara was wheezing as though she'd run a mile.

"That's time!" Brigit yelled.

Sara's shoulders slumped in exhaustion. *Thank the goddess that's over.* She wiped her forehead with her sleeve and it came back soaked. *I'll have to ask Lily about that spell for beating a daemon. Using a spell will definitely be easier than sneaking up on one.*

"Nice sparring," Alfred complimented as though Sara hadn't been trying her hardest to injure him.

"Thanks." Sara forced herself to smile. *Every time I lose to him it's only making me a better fighter.*

"Just so you know," Alfred leaned closer to Sara. "I meant what I said. Not all daemons can do what I can do. I'm in the top ten percent of fighters, so whatever daemon the other side has is likely a pansy."

"Top one percent is more like it." Celestine joined them, a red-faced Evelyn trailing close behind. "He wins all the daemon tournaments in the states. Only Brutus from Bulgaria and Edgar from Scotland have bested you at Worlds, right?"

Alfred shrugged.

"And they're about three times his age. In a few more years Alfred will cream them," Celestine added, unwilling to let Alfred remain modest.

I fought the third best daemon in the world. Holy crap!

"I think it's time we head inside for a wee lunch and rest before going onto round two?" Brigit said, waving them all toward the house.

Sara sighed with relief and followed.

"Let me get this straight." Caleb, the werewolf Jane recruited as a representative for the triplets, set his fork down. "All these newspaper articles correlate to fata activity? Even this publication?" His aquiline nose wrinkled as he held up the tabloid with the article titled "Spaceship Cleaner Needed."

"That's one of the best ones," Mary replied. "Take it from someone who did years of research to find one book. Sometimes your answers lie in the most unbelievable places." Her blue eyes darted to the cottage floorboards where Lily had found Hypatia's book buried.

"If you saw the marks Noro branded into Evelyn you'd understand," Sara said. "The photo of that woman's mark looks very similar, but not identical to Evelyn's. Our theory is the fata, or at least the ones already here, have chosen a design to brand humans with. Then, when they're eventually out in the open, they can claim that human as theirs." She shoved another bite of gooey cheese sandwich into her mouth.

Caleb blinked and leaned back. "Damn. Have you told Jane? People going missing for a few days isn't unheard of in New York, but supernaturals should look out for their friends and loved ones."

"Not yet, but I will. You should tell your pack too, Caleb," Brigit said.

"This is all interesting information but I wonder

where the fata are right now? These articles are from all over the world, which tells me people everywhere are affected. But surely Dimia wouldn't let fata who are not powerful or fluent in the magic of this planet run free yet." Celestine, the only one not shoveling food into her face, paced about the room with an article in her hand.

Sara bit her lip. *Do we have any idea what they would or wouldn't do? Shoot, I don't even know what my pneuma wants to do, and she lives inside of me.* Her pneuma fluttered, tickling her full stomach. It was clear to Sara that her pneuma could interpret her thoughts, though she wasn't sure if that was a result of all the meditation she'd been doing to make contact with her pneuma or if it was just what pneumas did.

"You're probably right, Celestine." Evelyn nodded. "But don't forget there are seven other fata who have been here for millennia. Noro mentioned them when I was his hostage. This could all be the work of seven magically up-to-speed fata. And they can fly. Travel, even across continents and oceans, would be easy for them."

Celestine pursed her lip. "If we run with that line of thought and it's only a few fata doing all this branding and kidnapping, then there's a couple dozen somewhere hiding out until they become strong enough to venture into the world. If you were one of the weaker fata, where would you hide? I'd think they're together in a big group.

There is safety in numbers. It's why werewolves form packs, witches convene into covens, and humans amass in cities."

Sara tilted her head. *Where would I hide? Nowhere with lots of people, that's for sure.*

"There'd have to be an aspect of grandeur," Evelyn said.

"Why's that?" Brigit asked.

"I got the sense Noro likes luxury. You guys even said yourself that he chose a large room away from all the other rooms. And that manor! Sure, part of it was to impress me and to keep me off guard." Evelyn's face clouded as she recalled the night of her abduction. "I'll bet renting it out was Noro's idea. I would have gone to a less impressive place to be with Roman, and Roman would have known that. Hell, he could have taken me to that dungeon and I'd have stayed there with him."

At her side, Lily cringed noticeably. Sara nudged her, tilting her head in question, but Lily just turned and inserted herself in the conversation. "I'll bet Dimia wouldn't love the idea of staying in the middle of nowhere either. He's a king, used to being in the thick of it."

"The Crystal Palace, or at least what I saw of it with my pneuma, was in the middle of the kingdom and amazing," Evelyn agreed.

Her sister's strange reaction dissolved in Sara's mind

as research stemming from her grad school days bubbled up, filling her brain with options until she hit on an idea that felt right. "If I were Noro or Dimia, I'd hide my people in an abandoned but still glamorous site."

"Like old churches or castles," Mary said. "Many of which are remote and closed to the public. Yes, that would be brilliant."

"That begs the question," Alistair interjected. "How will we narrow down where the fata and Acolytes are? I'm sure all our minds went straight to European castles and churches, but all cultures have these sites. Noro has had time to investigate and I doubt he would choose flippantly." He raised his bushy, gray eyebrows to emphasize the great depth of their issue.

"We'll put out the call to sister covens," Gwenn said as if it were the most obvious thing in the world. "Ask witches the world over if they know of abandoned sites, sacred or beautiful, in their area. Bonus points if there has been any unusual brandings or kidnappings nearby. These girls didn't go public for us to do this all ourselves. We need to ask for help."

Sara nodded in agreement. Gwenn was right. The world was too big; they needed help.

"We'll brainstorm covens to call tonight." Mary nodded to Celestine, Alistair, Caleb, Eros, and Alfred. "We'll have more connections and can cast a wider net with you lot here. When the responses return we'll make a list of the top hits. From there we'll have to do the leg work."

"Which I'd be more than happy to help with," Celestine said and was seconded by Eros, Alfred, and Caleb.

"I could send my pneuma out, too," Lily suggested.

Sara sat up straighter. *Brilliant! Why only save our pneumas for battle?*

Brigit frowned. "Lil, let's see how your relationship with your pneuma progresses first. Learning how she fights best and how to defend ourselves from the fata should be our priority. I'm sure we'll have plenty of people volunteering to help. No need to send what could be your best fighting assets out into the world where there's a potential for losing them."

"I second that," Aoife said, rising to take plates. "Now then, we've had a long enough break. We should hit the field again before it gets too dark. Girls, grab a new partner and head outside."

Dating a Witch Is So Cool

Lily

SCRAPS OF PAPER littered the dinged coffee table as the creatures in Fern Cottage listed supernaturals they could call for help in some far-off corner of the world.

Since they had nothing to contribute in the way of names, Brigit set the triplets to preparing dinner for twelve. As the only one to grow up around a large group of people, Lily found herself nominated head chef. She reverted to a staple Rena, Annika, and Em prepared when it was the commune's turn to host the cross-country running team's spaghetti feed.

"Spaghetti and broccoli?" Evelyn quirked an eyebrow.

"Don't knock it until you try it," Lily said.

"Is it a cream-based sauce? Like Alfredo?"

Lily shook her head. "Red sauce."

Sara burst out in giggles. "Well, I'm not gonna lie,

that's strange, but I'm game. Come on Evelyn, I'll show you how to chop broccoli."

"I've seen how to chop broccoli, thank you very much."

Lily pulled three heads of tiny trees out of the refrigerator and handed them to Evelyn. She filled the largest pot with water and set the range to high. "I need to run to the bathroom while that heats. You guys can slice open the baguettes and smother them with butter and the minced garlic in the fridge. I'll be right back." Lily side-eyed Evelyn, who was cutting the leaves off the broccoli gently instead of chopping off the monumental stem in one go.

Oh whatever, it'll keep her busy while I try to corner Alistair.

Alistair was in the same spot he'd been in when the triplets started cooking: next to the loveseat with a sheet of paper in his hands and a pensive look on his face. Everyone else milled about near the fire, talking and adding names to the pile while Brigit sorted them into geographical areas.

Lily made a trip to the restroom first, so she didn't feel like a complete liar. She didn't really want to corner Alistair in plain sight of her mother and aunts, who were oblivious to her secret, but the present opportunity was too good to pass up. *As long as Evelyn doesn't notice, that's all that matters. It's been hard enough keeping quiet about finding Roman at the coven house. There's no way I can lie to her face.*

Lily made her way back down the hall and into the sitting room where she ignored Gwenn's inquisitive green eyes as she made a beeline for Alistair.

The old man glanced up from his list at her approach.

"Hello, Lily. We have yet to chat. How've you been since I last saw you? And how are dear Rena and Annika?"

"I'm good. They're good. Everyone's good. Can I ask you a quick question?" Lily's eyes darted to the fire. Gwenn was still watching.

Gwenn, while not as nosey as Mary or as pushy as Aoife, was the aunt Lily most jived with, and Lily had little doubt Gwenn sensed something was odd about this scenario.

"Of course." Alistair sat up straighter in his wheelchair and Lily inched closer.

"I know they discovered Roman in the basement of Peacock Manor. I found him tied up in a room in the Sisters of Salem coven house. He told me his story, how he loves Evelyn. Why was he there and what are they planning on doing with him? Have you seen him?"

Alistair sighed. "I'll admit for all my incubi skills I did

not foresee being asked about the same man twice by two women in one day."

"Evelyn?" *Goddess be, she's so much smoother than I am. I didn't even notice!*

"Precisely." Alistair set down his pen. "I'll be quick. Your aunt is watching us and something tells me you don't want others to realize you're apprised of Roman's situation. Roman is indeed still in love with Evelyn. I saw him once, when he stopped by the Sisters of Salem house to speak with Jane, who has been in close contact with your mother. While I'm not sure of his specific role, the boy was quite remorseful for what he did. I believe he'll stop at nothing to make it up to your sister."

"What did you tell Evelyn?"

Alistair raised a bushy gray eyebrow. "She needs to focus on herself. I told her no one has seen him. In a month or so, perhaps she'll be more amenable to hearing he works for our side, but for now Evelyn's anger towards Roman is as strong as her desire."

Lily nodded. So, Brigit was pulling the strings when it came to Roman. Just knowing that gave Lily a sense of calm. *I won't tell Evelyn I spoke with Roman. Not when Alistair thinks she still needs time to cool off.*

Lily's foot swayed beneath the table, hitting Alfred's.

He paused and winked at her before inserting himself back into the conversation.

Lily giggled. *We're legit playing footsie right now. How old are we?*

His foot hit hers again and Lily realized it didn't matter. *This is how new relationships should be: fun and sweet, not soul encompassing and heavy. I still can't believe I was in a vampire's thrall. Or that I killed him.*

As a healer, she'd been averse to taking lives at the Battle of Peacock Manor, preferring instead to spell her opponents and tie them up. For Amon and Empusa, however, she'd made exceptions. Their deaths had helped Lily come to terms with how she'd been used and to avenge Emily.

Brigit rose at the head of the table. "Thanks very much for supper, girls. It was quite good, if a bit unorthodox." She caught Lily's eye and smiled. "I believe we have a matter of business to attend to now that we're all sated."

More business? Heads tilted and brows furrowed around the table, mirroring Lily's confusion. They'd spent all day practicing magic and then compiling lists of supernaturals to enlist in helping them find the fata hideout.

"Christmas is two days from now. As a pagan meself, I'm aware many of you may be of another religious practice or simply not celebrate. However, the McKay clan is celebrating this year. We'd like to invite you all to join us for supper."

Why hadn't she thought of it before? The New Yorkers had rented rooms in the village until the New Year but spending Christmas day with them hadn't even crossed Lily's mind. She tried to picture a bunch of witches, a vampire, a daemon, an incubus, and a werewolf having Christmas dinner together.

Maybe that's why I didn't consider it, she thought with a giggle. *They aren't the types of creatures you picture having a nice family Christmas.*

"I haven't celebrated Christmas in years." Celestine's eyes twinkled. "I'm delighted by the invitation to dine with your family. May I bake something to bring?"

Oh, my goddess say yes. Lily fist pumped under the table when Brigit accepted Celestine's promise of what was sure to be an amazing baked good.

"Being Muslim I've never celebrated, though I've always wanted to experience it. I'd love to spend a supernatural Christmas with the McKay family." Alfred beamed.

Lily's heart fluttered, and she made a mental note to get Alfred a gift. *What if no one delivers out this far though? Where can I go in town?* She bit her lip.

Evelyn placed a hand on Lily's knee. "Don't worry, I've got everything covered. He won't miss a gift."

Lily tugged at her mind barriers and found them in place.

"I don't have to be a ceremens to see the anxiety roll across your face," Evelyn whispered. "Like I said, don't worry. I asked for a family Christmas even though no one here celebrates. The day will be memorable. It's my way of thanking everyone who saved me. Besides, I'm sure Alfred would be more than happy with a different kind of gift." Evelyn wagged her eyebrows and Lily whacked her shoulder.

LILY SLIPPED OUTSIDE, her face burning. It'd been impossible to join Alfred for a private stroll unnoticed. A titter of giggles rose as soon as the door clicked shut behind her and Lily sighed.

"Were you expecting any privacy during my time here, babe?" Alfred raised his eyebrow. White breath billowed from his lips into the night air. "Because I wasn't."

"No, I guess not." Lily grabbed Alfred's proffered hand and they strolled down the garden's stone path heading to the enchanted hedge that protected Fern Cottage from the rest of the world. She shot a glance over her shoulder in time to see Brigit closing the curtains in the living room. *Thanks for the privacy, Mom.*

Lily sucked in her breath as a flutter, like waves rolling up and down, began in her stomach.

"You OK, babe?" Alfred turned to her brows furrowed.

"Just a sec. I have to let my pneuma out. I think she wants us to have privacy."

"How do you know?"

"We talked yesterday. I told her you were coming and she said she may want to evacuate the premises for part of your visit."

Alfred's bottomless brown eyes grew round. "Talked? As in vocally? Why hasn't anyone mentioned this?"

"Because we're not sure how it happened. And I can tell Sara and Evelyn are bummed they haven't figured out how to speak to their pneumas yet. Especially Sara. She's so in tune with her body and has been meditating with her pneuma nonstop since they revealed themselves. I think she's taking her pneuma's silence personally."

"Do you think your pneuma will talk to me?"

Lily cocked her head. "I guess there's only one way to find out. Caeliter." A warm green light flowed, like steam from a hot cup of tea, out of Lily's chest and shaped itself into a ghostly human figure.

"Wow." Alfred's eyes bulged as he stared at the

emerald light on the other side of Lily. "Hi, Lily's pneuma. I'm Alfred." Alfred did a funny little bow.

"Hello, Alfred," the pneuma said and Lily leaned back in surprise.

"You're talking to him!" Lily cried. "She hasn't spoken to anyone but me yet!"

"I am." A small human-like grin spread on the pneuma's face. "We pneumas only speak when necessary. Talking isn't our true nature, you understand. We are intuitive rather than vocal beings. Our first conversation, my first in centuries, was quite tiring for me and I needed to regain my strength. I'll introduce myself to the rest of your family in due time."

"I'm honored," Alfred said.

"Thank you." The pneuma inclined her head. "It was good to meet you Alfred, Lily's paramour. I shall take my leave now. Lily, I will return in the morning, perhaps before you are even awake." Without further explanation, the emerald pneuma soared away, a bright green beacon against a black velvet night.

"Wow," Alfred said watching the pneuma fly away. When she'd disappeared, he turned to look at Lily. "So, I guess I'm your paramour?"

Lily coughed. "My pneuma is from a different world! Her vocabulary is tweaked. I'll tell her the proper term is boyfriend."

"No! I could get used to this whole paramour thing." Alfred's eyebrows danced up and down.

"I bet you could. Come on, let's keep walking. I can still feel my family watching us through the curtains."

They entered the orchard and Lily took the lead, pulling Alfred deeper into the trees. She had somewhere special to show him tonight.

"Did Brigit grow all this? She's an earth and fire witch, right?"

"She planted the seed like normal but her earth power accelerated the growth. That's why there are still plants in her garden thriving, even though it's practically freezing out. Most of the living plants are the ones required to make potions that Mom and Mary need when presiding over births. Mom says it isn't right to let all the plants live; the soil needs a break, too."

"My parents say the same thing but in a different way. You can't take, take, take. Sometimes everything needs to lay fallow, be by itself to grow."

"I can't wait to meet them one day. Did you tell them what I am?"

"They know you're a witch, but not one of the three witches fated to save humanity that everyone in New York is talking about. They can only take so much. Especially Mom, seeing as she's not a supernatural. Dad would get it but he'd worry about me hanging around you. He'd want me safe with them, and I wouldn't be able to stay away."

Their hands tightened around each other's as Lily pulled Alfred through to a small clearing in the orchard, a place where no matter how hard Brigit and Fiona had tried, not a single tree took root.

Until I came, that is, Lily thought gazing at the wonderland she'd created.

Vines thick as her wrist cascaded down the fruit trees and spiraled through their naked branches, creating a verdant curtain of privacy. Delicate flowers native to alpine regions carpeted the ground in shades of vivid blues, purples, and yellows. Along the rim of the clearing, a handful of petite lemon trees flourished in the dead of the cold Irish winter. It had taken a lot of extra spell work to ensure her hidden cove survived the cold while other trees in the orchard took their well-deserved rest.

"This is amazing." Alfred paused, crossed his eyes and breathed out through his mouth. "Hey! I can't see my breath anymore!"

Lily grinned. "This is my clearing. The place I come to when I need space and don't want to walk in the woods. I found it in late summer. Brigit said she never could get anything to grow here, but things grew for me. I've been working on getting it right and had to have Aoife come regulate the temperature for me when it got colder. It's about thirty degrees warmer in this circle than outside."

Alfred stepped to the edge of the clearing and fingered a thick vine, his long fingers caressing where it ended in a plush flower petal. "Dating a witch is so cool."

Small balls of light popped into existence, floating in the air around the clearing like lightning bugs. In the same moment, a tinkle of water falling from the vines and trees just outside the clearing provided background music.

Alfred's lips parted. "How are you doing all this?"

Lily shook her head. "As much as I'd like to take credit for that last bit, I can't. I think Sara and Evelyn may be behind this bit of witchery."

"Your sisters like me then?" Alfred inched closer, narrowing the space between their bodies.

"They do."

"Good. I plan on sticking around and want to be in good with all the McKay witches. You ladies are a scary bunch."

Lily laughed, but it died into a whisper of a breath seconds later as Alfred closed the space between their bodies to nothingness. He cupped her face, caressing it from cheekbone to chin.

Her heartbeat stopped, and air ceased to move in and out of her lungs. *He must be using magic on me.* But even as she studied the man before her, she knew he wasn't.

Alfred's dark eyes fringed in thick lashes, full red lips, and masculine jawline would be enough to garner any woman's attention. In that moment, his lips certainly had Lily's attention as they lowered slowly to hers and finally, touched.

Suddenly, Lily's lips were on fire. *She* was on fire, consumed by the feel of Alfred's lips on hers, the press of his hand on her back, his scent of cedar and soap. She pressed back and sensed the daemon's breath hitch.

Lightness overtook her. It was as if gravity had ceased to exist.

Alfred wrenched his lips from hers and crushed her to his chest. "Are you doing this?"

Doing what? Lily's head swam. She followed his gaze to find their heads level with the tops of the trees, a platform of grass, flowers, and vines growing upward beneath their feet, lifting them.

She couldn't help it, she laughed. "Probably. But I don't know how."

Brown eyes met green and Alfred beamed. "Like I said, dating a witch is so cool."

And the flames took her once more.

Snoopin'
Evelyn

How is it possible my Achilles is sore? Oh, that's right, I got the shit kicked out of me by a battle-hardened vampire yesterday.

Evelyn shook her head at the direction her life had taken and limped toward the aroma of bacon and hash.

"Morning, Evelyn!" Lily chirped as she glanced up from the frying pan.

Evelyn raised her eyebrows at Sara, who sat at the table reading a paper with a cup of tea in her hands. "Good morning. Someone's up early for how late they were out in the orchard last night." She poured herself a cup of black coffee and leaned against the counter, waiting for her sister to elaborate on her night.

"Alfred and I are spending the morning touring the village. He's swinging by in an hour to pick me up."

"Is that all we're getting? You know, Lil, Sara and I don't create a magical, romantic scene complete with fake fireflies and waterfalls for just anyone."

Lily plopped a few pieces of bacon onto a plate and grinned at her sisters. "Well, I appreciate it. If you must know, we had a great make-out session." Her smile spread impossibly further. "I even lifted us above the treetops without meaning to."

Evelyn let out a low whistle. "Damn, that daemon must be some kisser. I could see that, he's got super full lips."

Lily sighed and nodded. "He's skillful." She turned back to the bacon but not before Evelyn caught a blush spreading across her sister's cheeks.

"I'll bet," Evelyn snorted, snagged a piece of bacon, and popped it in her mouth. For the first time since her abduction she was actually hungry, and planned on taking advantage of the sensation. *I have a few more pounds to put on anyhow,* she thought and an image of her hip bone protruding in a way she found unnerving popped into her head. Evelyn shook it away, not wanting to go down that road again. It only led to bad memories. "How did you clear the morning off with Mom?"

"Your aunts and I decided to let the other supernaturals have a lie in after you went to sleep." Brigit breezed around the hearth and into the kitchen. "Alfred and Lily came inside right before everyone left. Alfred jumped at the chance to take our girl out."

Evelyn's shoulders loosened. *Thank the goddess. I'm so sore, I don't know if I could even handle sparring right now.*

"Instead, we're doing a true mock battle this afternoon. In the woods," Brigit said.

"Why in the woods?" Evelyn wrinkled her nose. "Why not the field? The woods are full of dirt and bugs. No offense, Lil."

Lily smiled dreamily, and Evelyn doubted she even heard her.

"Both places we've fought the Acolytes have been difficult to navigate. We can't count on the next altercation being in a place as wide open as a field. The forest adds visual impairment and obstacles to overcome. We'd rather be over-prepared."

"So, we're relaxing at home this morning then?"

"Mom and I are going out. You should come," Sara answered.

"But what if you ruin Alfred and Lily's date? The town isn't that big." Evelyn pictured the one main street in the village and the two groups trying to avoid each other. It would be almost impossible.

"Not in town," Sara replied. "We're going to Nora's house to see if we can find anything about where the fata are hiding out. There were so many calls and emails returned last night that we realized narrowing it down even further before we sent scouts to investigate the suggested sites would be helpful. From her letter, Nora proclaimed herself an Acolyte of Hecate, First Order, so she may have been party to important information."

Evelyn saw her mother stiffen in her peripheral vision. *The bitch's house.* Now that Sara mentioned it, Evelyn was surprised Brigit hadn't investigated Nora's place as soon as they returned to Ireland. *Then again, she's been sensitive when anyone mentions Nora's name. They were best friends for so long.*

Evelyn tried to imagine Vicencia backstabbing her the way Nora had. It was impossible. *I bet Mom felt the same way until it happened. She'll need support.*

"I'll go," Evelyn answered as casually as she could.

"Great. We're leaving straight after breakfast so we get back in time. Mary is meeting us there. She's a walking encyclopedia on ancient sites from all that research she had to do to find Hypatia's book. We're running to the market afterward for groceries. The others are planning on coming to the cottage by one o'clock for the mock battle," Sara finished, before straightening her paper and continuing to read.

Brigit's beat up sedan turned onto a narrow street boasting well-kept, single-family homes with colorful doors.

So modern. Evelyn eyed the new construction and compared it to the nearby local pub with its traditional thatched roof and worn walls.

"Is this a trendier part of the village?" Sara asked.

"I suppose you could call it that. It's a newer subdivision, that's for sure. Our town is small, so calling any area trendy is a laugh, but this is where many professionals live. They group together to mimic living in a city like Galway or Dublin but without all the noise and price. A lot of them commute into Galway a few times a week like Nora claimed she did." Brigit shook her head and frowned. "To be honest, it's changed a lot since I've been here last—more buildings. Nora usually visited Fern Cottage. I doubt I've stepped foot in her house for a year. Definitely not since you three arrived. Nora traveled most of that time. Now we know why."

Evelyn's eyes widened. *A lot can change in a year. Shoot, six months ago I thought witches only lived in fairytales.*

They pulled into the driveway of a smaller home with a bright red door. Two dead potted plants sat on either side of the door and a layer of leaves ignored since autumn covered the front stoop.

Mary was already there waiting.

"Here we are." Brigit killed the engine and fell back into the driver's seat, a tentative look in her eye.

Evelyn leaned forward, rested her elbows on the dashboard and pushed her mind out to detect any living being inside the house as Brigit had requested. She found nothing.

"No one is home. I don't sense any magic or wards in there either," Evelyn said, stepping out of the car.

Brigit nodded, unsurprised. No one had expected Nora to be home, but then, no one had expected Nora to betray her oldest friend either.

"You already checked inside?" Mary asked.

Evelyn nodded. That no one had been home for weeks, if not months, became more evident as they approached the stoop. A layer of grime covered the door's red paint and a tiny mouse hideaway nestled between the potted plant and the home's exterior.

"Where has she been living if not here? She acted as though she was home every few weeks." Brigit cocked her head. "Come to think of it, she often asked to stay the night. Said it was the wine but now I expect Nora couldn't bring herself to come here. It doesn't look like her place used to. She would never have let filth pile up, too house-proud."

Brigit shoved the spare key Nora had given her in the

keyhole and the front door opened with a groan. A faint scent of rotted fruit or trash fermenting in the can wafted out on a gust of stale air. Evelyn thought she heard the scurrying of a small animal somewhere inside.

Brigit flipped the light switch, but no light appeared. Apparently, Nora hadn't paid her electricity bills in quite some time.

"Candeo," Sara said. Three balls of light, gentler than fire but just as bright, burst forth from her hands and hovered in front of Brigit, bathing the room in a soft, yellow glow.

"Goddess be," Brigit murmured, two paces into the small entryway.

Evelyn's eyes widened as she followed her mother inside. She'd expected to feel nauseous when entering the home of the woman who'd helped give her up to the Acolytes. But the house was so unlike the put together Nora that Evelyn knew, she found it hard to believe Nora had ever lived here.

Shattered glass sprawled across the wood floor. Innards of cushions and papers covered everything. Remnants of food in various states of decay lay atop the few tables not turned over.

"It looks like someone got pissed off in here," Sara said biting her lip and pushing past Brigit, whose mouth hung wide open.

"Or went mad," Brigit said. "The old Nora would have *never* lived in this mess."

"Or both," Evelyn finished, eyeing the shattered glass. "I wonder if all this happened after Alexandria. She must have been *pissed* when their plan didn't work."

Brigit nodded. "We didn't see her for days after we returned. She told me she was in America but now, I think, she was performing damage control, ensuring her connection to the Acolytes was still in good standing."

Mary moved over to the table, on which sat a stack of leather-bound books.

"*Mystical Sites of Earth and Their Significance.*" Mary pursed her lips. "These may be helpful."

"Aye, sounds like it. Take them. You can geek out to your heart's desire tonight," Brigit replied.

The rest of the house looked like the sitting room except for Nora's bedroom. That room was cleaner than the rest but covered in maps with pins sticking into locales the world over. The pins had been repositioned many times, creating a swiss cheese effect in each map. Instead of trying to move the maps and risk losing pins, Brigit suggested they take photos with their phones.

"We can always come back for a second look if need be. Not like Nora will be here," Mary added, zooming in on a detailed map of Paris, which alone had five pins in it.

"What do you think the likelihood is that these are the

sites we're looking for?" Evelyn asked, leaning close to a pin stuck in the-middle-of-nowhere India.

"High," Sara answered, snapping her last photo. "The first map I saw focused on England and I know from my studies there are abandoned castles near a couple of the sites Nora pinned. There must be an intersection between the books Mary found and these pins."

Evelyn sighed as she took in the scope of what they were dealing with. "Noro's proud. He told me he would not allow his plan to fail. He wants glory for himself and the fata. It would be like him to choose a grand castle—bonus points if it has a dungeon to imprison people. He's all about impressing the new fata." She pointed to a map of Ireland she'd photographed. "There's a crapload of pins in this one, some close to here."

Mary sidled up to Evelyn and leaned in, their blonde hair mingled together, almost the exact same shade. "Goddess be, you aren't kidding." Mary squinted, the skin around her blue eyes crinkling as she studied the map. "I'm not sure what these sites correspond to. Ireland has many myths and legends, some of which may have attracted Noro to build a camp here. More research to do when we get home." Mary rubbed her hands together.

"Mom, let's upgrade your internet," Evelyn said. "From the looks of these walls, we may need the power of

Google in addition to a million books. And I'll go insane if I have to wait two minutes for every page to load."

Brigit groaned. "Your aunts and I are not tech savvy."

Sara grinned. "Well, it's a good thing you have us around now to handle tech. Let's grab those books and get out of here."

Matrix Ninja

Sara

SARA WHEEZED as she ran through the thick woods with the rest of the purple team. Glancing over her shoulder, she saw she wasn't the only one having trouble keeping up with Lily's "jog."

Evelyn looked ready to keel over, and the witchy version of capture the flag that was their lesson today hadn't even officially started. Mary wasn't much better, clutching her side as she ran, and their mother looked as if she already regretted the suggestion to mix their training up a bit.

"Lil," Sara panted. "Can you slow down? We're already out of breath."

Lily whirled around, and her mouth tightened at the sorry state of her group. "We'll never make it to the tree

I'm thinking of at this pace! Our hiding spot has got to be good if we want to win."

Sara refrained from rolling her eyes. *Maybe she shouldn't have bet Alfred a hundred bucks on the win.*

"Why you didn't bet him something free but equally *enticing,* I'll never understand. Then it's a win-win even if we lose this crazy game." Evelyn huffed as she caught up.

Lily pinked and Brigit came to her rescue. "That'll be enough of that Evelyn. Her mother doesn't need to hear such things."

"Maybe I should run ahead and hide the triquetra by myself? Morgane only gave us twenty minutes to hide it. I can get there and be back here by the time the game starts," Lily said. The iron triquetra that normally hung by the doorway of Fern Cottage, their team's "flag," was clenched in her hand and glowing the same vibrant purple color as the ribbons attached to everyone on their team.

"Good idea," Sara agreed. "We'll devise a plan and fill you in when you return."

Lily nodded and sped off at a speed Sara reserved for cheetahs and vampires. *Goddess be, she was holding back.*

"Well that explains her bottomless pit of a stomach." Brigit shook her head. "It's a good idea, though. The farther out the triquetra is, the longer it will take the yellow team to find it. If I were the yellow team I'd have Celestine or Caleb run ahead and hide their triquetra somewhere far off. Vamps and werewolves are always faster than witches."

"Let's not waste time. We need a plan!" Mary gestured for the team to gather around her. "I think sticking together in a large 'V' formation will work best. We won't cover as much ground, but I doubt we'll need to right away. I'll bet my sparkliest jumpsuit that the yellow team will opt for a wide defense first. They'll try to capture all our ribbons and move to offense only once our numbers have been diminished. Seems like something Aoife would insist on."

"By staying close together, we reduce their opportunity to pick us off and perhaps even pick them off with greater ease." Brigit considered her sister's plan further. "Bloody brilliant. It will also help keep Alistair out of our heads if we venture into his range. Aoife says a single mind is harder to latch onto in a group."

Sara had been wondering what Alistair could do to help his team as navigating through the woods would be impossible for his wheelchair. *Makes sense. Incubi can alter dreams, and I doubt they need to be in the same room to do so. I wonder how large his range of influence is?*

"Morgane should shoot off the starting mark any

minute now," Brigit said. "Did everyone ward their ribbon against summoning spells? If Aoife or Gwenn want our ribbons, they'll have to get close enough to snatch them with their own hands."

Everyone checked their purple ribbon and nodded. Sara was grateful the triplets weren't on a team by themselves against Aoife, Gwenn, Caleb, Celestine, Alfred, and Alistair. Not only because then the teams would be even *more* outnumbered than they already were, but she also doubted the triplets would have thought of practicalities such as protecting their ribbons from a summoning spell. The triplets would have lost so fast without their mom or Mary. No wonder they don't like letting them out of their sight.

Lily came sprinting back through the woods, her quick steps muted thanks to the silencing charm Mary had placed on all their shoes. "Done! The knot in the tree is so deep the triquetra disappeared when I put it inside. They'll never find it."

"Brilliant," Brigit said, and proceeded to fill Lily in on their plan.

"Like *The Mighty Ducks* with the flying 'V,'" Lily said.

Her analogy received blank looks and Lily sighed. "Never mind, Rich, Selma's husband, loves hockey. I must have watched that movie a hundred times. Clearly, we are not a sports family." She stopped talking and pointed to the sky.

Sara whirled about to see a shower of red fireworks.

"Morgane's signal." The red sparks reflected in Mary's large eyes. "It's time."

***

THEY MOVED like a pack of wolves sensing a camp of men and intent on a surprise attack.

If only our opponents had senses as dull as most humans. Sara kept her eyes peeled for Celestine, who would hear them coming before anyone else despite the silencing spell Mary had placed on their shoes.

She glanced over her right shoulder. Lily was twenty feet away to Sara's right, while Evelyn brought up the end of the "V" behind Lily. Brigit was in the lead, her sensing spells extending forty feet ahead of the group.

"The spell senses motion or magic before I can, including the yellow team's spelled triquetra so we'll know when we're close," Brigit explained when Sara asked about the faint white fog Brigit conjured from her hands and pushed ahead of her.

The sensory spell was simply another reminder that though the triplets had advanced by leaps and bounds, they were still relative beginners. There were many spells and enchantments their teachers wrote off as daily magic, useless in the triplets' fight against the fata. Sara supposed she couldn't fault them for teaching the most important, lifesaving spells first, not when their lives had already been on the line twice.

Brigit held up a hand and their "V" stopped.

A heartbeat later a massive gray wolf with a yellow ribbon tied to his fur charged out of the trees and rushed at Lily.

Fireballs flew from Sara's palm and Caleb, the werewolf, swerved right to avoid the onslaught.

Lily threw up a shield before the were had time to correct course and come at her again.

"Sara! Your left!" Brigit pointed.

Sara whirled about to find Eros the elf walking through the trees, an opaque shield in front of him and a triumphant smile on his face. *Dammit,* Sara cursed her instincts to protect Lily, which had left her side exposed.

"Lascarma!" Sara cried. Her spell hit Eros's shield, creating a six-inch gash in what looked like a solid, swirling white cloud before the elf. Sara's heart dropped as the gash healed itself before her eyes.

Eros smirked and narrowed the gap between them, his ribbon waving in the breeze off his slim right hip.

He won't fight until he has to. He's only trying to get close enough to take my ribbon.

Compared to witch magic, elven power was a blip on the magic spectrum. Most elves controlled only a single element. However, Eros was more like a wizard in the sense that he had control over all four elements but veered toward a specialty. Or in his case, two specialities: healing and air magic. It made Eros one of the strongest of his kind and an ideal elf for the triplets to train against.

Sara bit her lip. No one at Fern Cottage had a great proclivity for air, and it was the element she'd often ignored. Sara glanced about, seeing if anyone was free to help, and noticed Alfred had joined the fight, taking on Brigit and Mary at once.

Lil and Evelyn are busy with Caleb. I'm all alone. Here goes nothing.

Sara produced a blazing ball of fire and aimed it at the edge of Eros's shield, hoping to hit the elf's slightly exposed arm. It hit the shield instead and dissolved from sight. Undeterred, Sara shot a well-placed stunning spell next, aiming for the same exposed limb.

Eros's face tightened as he caught on to her plan and he yanked the shield to the side, covering him completely.

Dammit. He's quick.

Eros was five feet away now and Sara darted backward as far as she dared. She didn't want to have a fight at her back and front. It would leave her ribbon exposed.

He has to drop his shield if he wants to take my ribbon.

That's my moment. Sara widened her stance as if she were about to fire off a spell at any second.

Eros charged. Without breaking step, a tornado appeared from the top of his head, bent over his shield, and trapped Sara in a circle of whirling wind.

Dang. Didn't see that coming.

A fifteen-foot-tall tornado whipped around Sara, closing within inches of her skin. The smell of dirt and decaying leaves kicked up all around and filled her nostrils. Sara backed up and her short red hair lifted from her scalp. She shot a stream of fire into the tornado. It fizzled, unable to burn bright in the raging wind. Her shoulders fell as the wind spun around her, leaving only glimpses of Eros's maddening smile.

"Dionean!" Sara yelled, and her spell disappeared into the wind.

I need to get out of this damn wind tunnel. She looked up at the clear sky above.

A memory of vampires hopping over fire gates flashed in her mind's eye. She sucked in a breath.

Eros's hand was moving toward her now, preparing to take her ribbon.

Sara leapt into the tornado just as Eros's hand snatched bare air. Wind engulfed her, voiding her senses and stealing her breath as she rose higher in the tunnel.

"Volavari," Sara screamed into the wind, directing her

hands at herself and hoping this wasn't the stupidest idea she'd ever had.

Her body launched out of the wind tunnel and soared over the elf.

"Dionean," Sara cried, aiming her palms at Eros.

The elf crumpled to the ground, and Sara celebrated with a fist pump seconds before crashing into a tree.

"Sara! Wake up!" Lily's voice came to Sara as if in a dream and she opened one copper eye.

"What happened?"

"You pulled some real Matrix shit there. Jumped out of a tornado like a ninja," Evelyn said, kneeling to help Sara sit up. "And then you crashed into a tree."

"Eros! Did it work?"

"Aye." Mary smiled, and Sara saw her face was covered in sweat. "Once the other two saw Eros fall they retreated. Lil and Evelyn injured Caleb, but Alfred was fine, which makes me think their intent was for Eros to get your ribbon quick and easy. They picked up on the fact none of you are comfortable battling against air yet, but you managed."

"And we snagged Eros's ribbon!" Evelyn beamed and

held up a yellow ribbon. "He's walking back to the lake-side now."

"Here, take this," Lily said, pulling a vial filled with lime green liquid from her healer's fanny pack. It'd been a struggle to get the other team to allow her to have it, but Lily had put her foot down.

Sara downed the liquid, which tasted herby with a touch of citrus. Immediately her head cleared and a thrill ran through her as her heartbeat picked up. *Why drink coffee when we can have this?* Her body trembled, and Sara felt compelled to stand up and jump around. *Oh, that's why.*

"Your head isn't spinning or foggy, right?" Lily asked as she helped Sara to steady herself.

"Not at all."

"Good. I saw you hit the tree with your torso but I thought I'd check in case your head rebounded onto it, too. If you're fine, we should get moving before they come back. As long as we stay away from Alistair's sphere of influence, our teams numbers are equal now."

Sara took a hesitant step, and her feet rebounded off the ground as if she hadn't body slammed a huge oak minutes before. *Dang, this stuff is amazing.*

They continued walking, each on high alert and searching for the golden glow of the yellow team's triquetra. Sopping wet moss and mud sucked their feet down with each step they took.

Suddenly, the crack of a twig came from somewhere deep in the woods and their "V" froze. They stared into the darkness. Sara shivered. She couldn't understand why Lily spent so much time in the forest. Especially now that the leaves had fallen, the woods were pretty creepy.

"There!" Evelyn pointed behind them and everyone turned to see Celestine a quarter mile away, barreling toward them faster than any human could run. She was carrying Aoife on her back and even with Celestine's supersonic speed, Sara could make out the huge shit-eating grin on Aoife's face.

"She's having way too much fun with this," Mary muttered, shaking her head.

"Aye, she is." Brigit rolled her eyes. "You three take Celestine. Mary and I will deal with our exuberant sister. Remember, no fire. The deal was trap Celestine and she'll surrender her ribbon." The words were barely out of Brigit's mouth when Celestine skidded to a stop before them.

Aoife leapt off the vampire's back and stuck the landing. "Always wanted to do that," the fire witch boasted before Brigit and Mary shot simultaneous spells at her.

Celestine lunged at Evelyn, who shot a stunning spell at the vamp. It hit, and dazedness rippled over Celestine's face, then vanished, before she'd even landed on the ground.

Holy crap, Mom wasn't kidding. Vamps recover fast.

Evelyn, her chest heaving from the effort she was exerting, tossed up a shield a millisecond before Celestine's hand darted out to take her purple ribbon. The vampire's hand hit the shield and she pivoted to Lily.

"Lotu!" Lily cried, darting back into the trees.

Celestine swung left and the body bind curse hit a tree in its path.

Sara rushed behind Evelyn's shield. "Keep your shield up and we'll try to catch her from behind. When you're close enough, tell Lily mind to mind to create a shield, too. I'll run out last and cast one. We can combine them and trap her."

"What do you mean when I'm close enough? I'm there now, Lily's mind barriers always leak when she's stressed."

Sara sensed a whiff of strong magic fly from Evelyn. She glanced at Lily, who nodded emphatically as her eyes caught Evelyn's. Sara and Evelyn advanced together, closing the space between themselves and Celestine. Sweat poured down Lily's forehead and Sara guessed her sister wouldn't be able to hold off Celestine's advances much longer. The vampire was too fast and nimble. They needed to immobilize her.

"Tell Lil to force Celestine to the ground. I'll help. If we hit her numerous times our spells will be more effective. Then we can trap her between our shields and the ground," Sara instructed Evelyn.

As soon as Sara heard what Gwenn called "the ground-kissing curse" leave Lily's lips, she jumped out from behind Evelyn's shield and joined the fight.

"Cogerba! Cogerba! Cogerba!" Sara rattled off three ground-kissing curses in a row, hoping one would strike the light-footed vampire.

Two curses hit Celestine simultaneously, forcing her to the ground.

"Cast a shield before she can throw it off!" Sara yelled.

Her sisters complied and three transparent, bluish shields pinned Celestine to the ground.

The vampire gazed up from her supine position on the dirt and ripped her ribbon from her side. "I surrender. Nice, job girls. If fire had been on the table, I would have been toast—or ash, I suppose—a long time ago."

Triumph bloomed in Sara's chest a split second before a familiar, herbaceous scent of holy basil filled her nostrils. She turned to find her senses had not misled her. Gwenn had joined the battle against Brigit and Mary while the triplets fought Celestine. They were laying the defense on thick, which made Sara wonder if they were near the other team's triquetra. "We'll release you once we've beaten the rest of your team. At least you'll be safe beneath the shields if fireballs fly."

Celestine shrugged and pushed a finger against the shield that held her. "Whatever you say. I'm not going anywhere."

The triplets rushed off to join a new battle.

Like a Drowning Mermaid
Evelyn

Evelyn leaned against a tree and wiped the sweat pouring from her brow. *Holy shit, is this real?* She rubbed her thumb against the yellow ribbon in her hand, Aoife's ribbon. It had taken an ungodly amount of energy and five witches to take down Aoife and Gwenn, but the purple team had finally prevailed. *I bet running a marathon is easier.*

Mary joined her at the tree, her scent of grapefruit and rain intense after the fight. "You alright, love?"

Evelyn took in her aunt's disheveled state. Tattered leggings, singed leg warmers, and a gaping hole in Mary's favorite "sporty" jacket revealed just how hard her aunt had been working. "Fine. Needed a breather, that's all," Evelyn lied. She didn't feel fine. Her legs shook as though they might fall off, but she didn't want anyone else to know that. Since her abduction, they'd babied her enough. And Evelyn hated feeling like she wasn't strong or good enough.

"You lot should move out, so the purple team can find your triquetra and finish this," Brigit teased Aoife, Gwenn, and Celestine, who had yet to move on.

Despite just losing her ribbon, Aoife appeared smug. "We'll see who prevails. We've still got a daemon, a were-wolf, and an incubus on our side."

An incubus? But he can't make it out here.

"We'll be waiting by the lake," Gwenn said, shooting Aoife a warning look. "See you in a few hours."

"Aoife seems confident. We must not be anywhere near their triquetra," Lily said as soon as Aoife, Celestine, and Gwenn were out of sight.

Evelyn shook her head. "You're thinking of it wrong. Alistair is no help to them this deep in the woods, but Aoife still mentioned him. Does no one else find that telling?"

Brigit's eyes grew wide. "You're right. Alistair must be the triquetra's guardian! They knew we'd assume Celestine would run it out, the goddess only knows how far, so they did the exact opposite."

"Aoife's idea to be sure," Mary muttered. "Having us look all around the forest but hide the triquetra right where we started would give her a right laugh. Too bad her pride gave her away."

"All we have to do is get to their triquetra before they get to ours," Brigit beamed. "Alfred and Caleb are still able to search the woods for ours, but if they're smart, they'll have sent one of the lads to help Alistair now that their numbers are diminished. I'll bet it's Alfred guarding their triquetra. If I were on the yellow team, I'd use Caleb's nose to find ours."

"So, it's us against a werewolf's nose," Lily said, her tone downcast.

"We best get moving then," Mary said, turning and disappearing through the trees without another word.

THEY WERE HALFWAY to the lake when Evelyn spotted a yellow beam of light circling high in the sky. "What the hell is that?" She pointed upward.

"Shite!" Mary cursed. "Alfred's set off a signal for Caleb. Probably Aoife and Gwenn got back and warned him. We have to hurry."

"Crap," Evelyn muttered as everyone broke into a run. Soon her legs were quivering with every strike against the ground. *I doubt I'll even make it back to the lake.*

Caleb will come across me collapsed on the ground and take my ribbon, easy as you please.

"I see a glimmer of water," Lily yelled over her shoulder fifteen feet ahead.

Evelyn's eyes followed her sister's gait, strong and able as she jogged through the forest. *I can't wait to be strong again—* "Oh shit! Mom!"

A gray blur shot out of the trees, snagging Brigit's ribbon and darting toward the lake with the purple ribbon waving from his mouth.

"That wolfish sneak!" Brigit shook her head, looking down at her bare hip.

As if in response, a joyous howl came from somewhere ahead of them and Brigit narrowed her eyes.

"There's no point in me running with you now. I'll meet you at the lake. Be on the lookout for that bloody werewolf."

Five minutes later they exited the forest to find the entire yellow team waiting for them at the lake's edge, huge grins plastered on their faces.

Lily charged, engaging Alfred in a duel right away. The other two members of the yellow team, Caleb and Alistair, remained close to the lake, waiting for the purple team to make their move. Evelyn assessed Caleb in his wolf form before shifting her gaze to Alistair sitting self-assuredly in his chair. *What have they got up their sleeves?*

"Evelyn, can you help Lily while Sara and I take the other two?" Mary asked after a quick glance down at Evelyn's shaky arms.

Heat crept up Evelyn's neck at the acknowledgment of her weakness. *No! Just get over it,* Evelyn chided herself. *So, Mary gave me a two-on-one fight. It's not like Alfred's a picnic to spar with.* Evelyn glanced at Lily, huffing and puffing, dark tresses flying around her red face as she battled her boyfriend. Alfred, in comparison, looked fresh as a new raindrop.

"Got it."

Alfred beamed as Evelyn joined her sister.

Ugh, even when Lily and he are fighting he's happy.

"Dionean." Evelyn's stunning spell flew at Alfred, whose dark eyes widened as he leapt backward to catch it. She frowned. She hated that daemons could turn her own power against her, that she didn't have full control.

A hailstorm of spells rained from Lily's fingertips, meeting Alfred's beams of yellow in the space between them and colliding like fireworks.

Evelyn threw up a shield, her head turning to avoid the blowback. *What the hell?*

Brigit was at the edge of the forest behind her, waving her arms and pointing at the lake. The next instant Evelyn witnessed her mother's body stiffen, her limbs snap to her side as someone body bound her. *But she's out already!*

Evelyn's head swiveled and she saw Gwenn, all the way across the lake wagging her finger at Brigit. *She was trying to tell me something.*

A beam of light slammed into Evelyn's shield, tossing her into the mud surrounding the lake. The stench of rotted reeds filled her nostrils and Evelyn gagged as she broke the suction between her skin and the mud.

"What were you doing?" Lily panted when Evelyn joined her behind her shield.

"Sorry! Mom was trying to tell me something and your lover boy blasted me!"

"Probably about Sara," Lily fired a spell at Alfred and Evelyn turned to see Mary still battling Caleb while Sara stood at Alistair's side, her purple ribbon in his hand.

"Why is she so still?" Evelyn asked, her eyes widening at the strange scene.

"Alistair has her enchanted." Lily threw up a shield as an unrelenting spray of yellow light flew at them. "Don't you feel it? He's trying to extend his reach into my mind. I've been pushing him back the whole time, which is freaking exhausting."

Alfred spewed out another spray, and Lily, not missing a beat, lowered her shield.

"Argibeltza," Lily screamed, sweeping her arm wide. The black light hex, the only curse known to be fully effective against daemons, shot from her hands. It swallowed up the sunny beams before they could collide with her shield but failed to hit Alfred. Lily jerked the shield back into place, preparing for Alfred's next onslaught.

Evelyn, however, had stopped paying attention to Alfred. She'd never experienced that. Or had she? Evelyn did a quick scan of her brain and stood up straighter. There *was* someone there. *Holy crap! Alistair is trying to break in.*

She felt inside her head again and sensed it once more. The subtle push on her skull, the faint tingle rushing through her body as Alistair's energy manipulated her body chemistry. She hadn't noticed it before with all the other stimuli around. No, the incubus was not ignoring her and going after Lily. He was trying hard to put them all in his thrall. And failing. *Let's see what happens when I do this.* With one swift kick of power, she shoved Alistair's influence from her mind.

The incubus doubled over in his wheelchair, a cry of pain escaping his lips.

Evelyn watched with glee as Caleb's wolfish head turned for only a second to make sure his teammate was safe. Unfortunately for the yellow team, a second was all Mary needed to pull the wolf's ribbon from his neck, disabling Caleb, and rush to Alistair's side to steal his ribbon, too. Mary had just demolished two-thirds of the yellow team.

"Arma," Evelyn said protecting herself and Mary as Alfred released another shower of yellow light.

"Thanks for that," Mary said, joining Evelyn and Lily. "Those bloody daemon sprays are unpredictable. Let's finish this. I can help Lil beat Alfred, but you'll have to get the triquetra. I can't swim with this cut." Mary held up her left arm and Evelyn recoiled at the gash on her forearm.

"I have no clue what you're talking about." Evelyn's body shook as Alfred hit her shield again, this time with a laser-focused beam of light.

Mary's eyes widened. "Their triquetra! It's at the bottom of the lake!"

Evelyn whirled about. Sure enough, a dim yellow light rose from the lake's dark depths. She shook her head wondering how she'd missed the glow when she stood at the water's edge just moments before.

"Did you try to summon it?" Evelyn asked daring to hope Mary had forgotten that summoning spells existed as she took in the thick layer of muck on the water.

"What kind of question is that? Aberro!" Mary shot a deflecting spell at a beam of light headed straight for Lily. "Of course I did! The lake's impervious to magic. The yellow team made sure someone had to retrieve it manually. Now, quit wasting time with questions, we're all exhausted. Go finish this, Evelyn."

Evelyn sighed, already not looking forward to her task, and ran to the water's edge. Her face, covered in dirt and sweat, stared back at her as she looked into the black pool and kicked off her shoes. *Why the shit hasn't this lake frozen yet? That would have stopped them from hiding the triquetra in freezing cold water. Dammit, I hope there's nothing creepy crawly in there. No! Don't think about it!*

Evelyn took a deep breath and dove in. Her breath flew from her lungs as liquid water enveloped her. With twenty long, expert strokes born from many hours at sea with her father, she was at the center of the lake. Treading water, Evelyn tried to catch her breath, stolen equally from the cold and the exertions of the game, as she peered into the dark water, trying to locate the triquetras position before diving.

A twenty-foot dive at the most. I've done it before. I can do it again. Sucking in air, Evelyn dove before she could talk herself out of it. She was halfway down when she realized she must have misjudged the depth. *How is such a tiny lake so deep?* She propelled herself downward, straining her muscles to their breaking point. Her ears popped. Ten more pulls and she'd be there.

Then, as if she were a buoy, Evelyn's body floated away from the triquetra. She pulled with all her might, pausing the ascent before lurching upward once more. Going against reason and her will, Evelyn rose until her

her head broke the surface. The frigid air hit her and she shook all over. To make matters worse, her pneuma was going crazy inside her, adding to the onslaught of sensory input and threatening to send Evelyn into a state of blackout.

Stop that! You pulled me back up with all your crazy fluttering. I have to get the triquetra. It's a short dive, I'll be fine.

She dove again, harder this time, desperate to be done with the mock battle and back in front of Fern Cottage's huge fireplace.

Her pneuma went ballistic once again, racing up and down her body, pushing air from her lungs and pounding against her throat. It took all of Evelyn's remaining energy to ignore her pneuma and swim deeper, closer to the triquetra.

I so don't have time for this. You're fine. We're not in danger. Just exhausted.

After struggling for every kick and pull forward, Evelyn made it to the bottom of the lake and clasped the triquetra in her hand, victorious.

Her pneuma pounded against her lower ribs so hard it felt like a bus had hit her. Evelyn gasped and lake water tasting of decaying reeds spilled into her mouth. Her pneuma swirled faster in her gut and Evelyn's head spun. She would pass out if it didn't stop.

I have to let her out or I'll drown, Evelyn thought, unable to even push off the bottom, the sensation was so overwhelming.

Caeliter. She watched, dizzy to the point of vomiting as her pneuma shot out of her. Black spots swam in Evelyn's vision. She pushed off the bottom weakly but didn't rise. *Someone help,* Evelyn thought, sure she'd never make it to the surface before passing out.

"I'll help you," her pneuma spoke, her voice flowy and lyrical, before floating under Evelyn and pushing her body to the surface.

The Drunken Duck

Sara

SARA HAD BEEN UP since the small hours considering what she'd seen and heard yesterday. How Evelyn had appeared out of the lake clutching the triquetra, sputtering water from her lungs and screaming at her pneuma. How the bright blue pneuma had spoken back. How Evelyn had been too wrecked to even swim back to the shore and Mary had created a current to carry Evelyn to the lake's edge so they could pull her out. How after being warmed by the fire for an hour or so, Evelyn finally told them what happened at the bottom of the lake.

As the only triplet still restricted to "yes" or "no" answers from her pneuma, Sara couldn't help but feel jilted. She threw back the covers. Her feet hit the ground and she padded over to her meditation altar, where she spent the first twenty minutes of each morning.

And for what? She worked so hard at trying to listen to her body and the alien soul living inside her wouldn't even talk to her? Sara pushed down the annoyance rising within her, lowered onto her massive meditation cushion, and fingered the red material.

Mary had found it for her when they were redecorating the bedrooms to better suit each triplet's taste. Her fingers traced the beadwork Mary had personalized the side of the cushion with. Usually, Sara would find the line of beads rounding the cushion gaudy, clashing with her preferred color palette of red, yellow, and orange, but not this time.

Red, blue, green, red, blue, green, red, blue, green. The beads covered the entire side of the cylindrical pillow. The order was perfect, and the more Sara looked at it, the more she loved it. Not so much the colors, but the thought that went into it, the literal act of sewing Sara in with her sisters.

Somehow, Mary had sensed Sara's desperate need to belong despite her attempts to put on a happy face and cover up the constant ache growing up neglected had left in her. Though it was just an object, Sara had to admit that the cushion helped—especially in the days when Lily had been furious at Evelyn and subsequently Sara for refusing to express the same anger.

Her altar, filled with photos, candles, a couple colorful

crystals, and a tiny figurine of Ganesha, the elephant-head Hindu god, stared back at Sara, soothing her.

As a researcher of marginalized women throughout history, Sara was wary of religion. Still, even though she wasn't Hindu, she loved the stories portraying Ganesha that she'd learned from her yoga studies. As the remover of obstacles, patron of arts and sciences, scribe, and god of new beginnings, Ganesha's tales had helped her through sticky parts in her life.

Sara closed her eyes and took five elongated breaths in and out. She'd spent hundreds of hours practicing breathing to calm her nervous system. It usually worked right away, clearing her head and sending a rush of awareness through her body. This time it didn't.

Instead, the image of Evelyn rising from the lake clouded her mind.

She sighed. It was going to be one of those sessions. Letting go of her expectations, Sara shook her stiff shoulders to loosen them and allowed her mind to wander where it would. *Some days you get the bliss, some days you get the monkey mind.*

Today was definitely the latter.

What if my pneuma never speaks to me? What if I started out strong but my sisters will surpass me in power? What if studying and reason won't help me this time?

Sara bit her lip and dug her fingers into her thighs.

She'd always prided herself on being bookish and smart. It was a constant that defined her childhood, something no one could take from her. Her grades had been her ticket off base away from her passive-aggressive adoptive family and into the hallowed halls of academia. Intelligence had always counted for a lot in her life.

But Lily and Evelyn seemed so surprised. When Lily came out of the woods she didn't even know how she'd gotten her pneuma to talk. And Evelyn was trying not to drown. How can such a profound act be so unintentional? It doesn't make sense! Ugh, maybe I need to go walk in the woods or take a swim in that freezing cold lake.

Sara's eyes popped open as the image of Evelyn surfacing the lake ran through her mind once more.

No freaking way. Lily is an earth witch, Evelyn is a water witch. They were both immersed in their element. Does that mean—?

Her pneuma rustled around inside her and Sara's stomach dropped. She looked at the clock and saw she'd only been on the cushion for five minutes. Five minutes and a revelation. That was a record. She rose, knowing there was no way she would finish her practice today.

Laughter tinkled in from the kitchen and Sara's heart softened at the sound of a Christmas Eve morning she'd never experienced—one full of love and family who actually wanted to be together.

There was no need to tell them now. She didn't want to ruin everyone's Christmas with the thought of her standing in a fire to get her pneuma to talk. She could wait a couple days, at least she thought she could.

"WE'RE HERE, LADIES," Alfred said, pulling into a parking spot, getting out, and rushing around the car to open all their doors. "The Drunken Duck is around the corner."

Sara mumbled a thank you, still a tad annoyed her sisters had forced her to come. She'd been nervous all day thinking of what lay before her and wanted nothing more than to burrow in her bed, considering how to bring it up to everyone else.

Unfortunately, Lily and Evelyn were having none of that, not when their mother had agreed to let them out of the house alone for the first time. Well, partially alone. Sara could already sense the wards Mary had set around the pub hours earlier, and she suspected her fun-loving aunt hadn't left after performing her task.

Warm air stung Sara's cheeks as they stepped inside the pub. It was old and looked it, with smoke-stained walls, huge beams in the ceiling, and colored lights strung all around the edges to brighten the place up. The smell of beer and fried food pervaded the room. A band sat in the corner before the hearth. Traditional Celtic music, heavy on flutes and accordions, provided ambiance for dancing. The music ran through her, lifting her mood and blurring her worries.

Mary was in the far corner by the band. Having already set wards around the pub for protection, she was now kicking back, laughing, and having a pint with a group of friends. She waved when they walked in and blew them a kiss. Sara's lips lifted at her aunt's flamboyant red and white Christmas outfit.

A group of middle-aged men eyed their group. One man had already approached Mary and was pointing back at them. Another group of younger men smiled from a long table. It seemed they were in for a night of either getting hit on or asked if they were Brigit's daughters.

A hand waved high in the air and Sara spotted their friends in the corner, each with a pint and a smile on their face.

"Hey, Dan," Evelyn purred as they sauntered past the table of young men Sara had noticed.

Dan, a handsome man with dark hair, leered at Evelyn, proud he'd been singled out.

"Hey, Evelyn. Would you and your friends care to join us for a pint? We'll make room." Dan pushed the friend next to him over to squeeze four more onto the table.

"I'd love to boys, but we're meeting a group over there. Save me a jig, won't you?" Evelyn lowered her lashes and Sara smirked as Dan's jaw dropped.

"They're all yours, beautiful," he said, recovering his swagger as best he could.

"Thanks. Talk later." Evelyn sashayed to the corner table and half the eyes in the pub followed her.

"Getting in some siren practice?" Sara whispered.

Evelyn shrugged. "Aoife told me Dan is crazy into himself the first time I came here. Since then, I've always made it a point to target him. Helps to bring him down a little when he can't have what he wants." She lifted one corner of her lips in a wicked smile. "Plus, it's fun."

A laugh escaped her and Sara's shoulders loosened. *Is that the first time I've laughed today? Man, it felt good.*

Sara slid in between Eros and Caleb. "Thanks for inviting us out. It's good to be out of the house."

Lily shot Sara a look of surprise and Evelyn raised her eyebrows.

"What? Geez, you two, I'm not a hermit nun."

Caleb howled with laughter and patted her on the back. For a werewolf, a species of supernatural known for being tough and brutish, it always surprised Sara how soft Caleb's touch could be.

"Sorry!" Evelyn held up her hands. "I've never heard you talking about going out. It's a nice surprise that you want to let your hair down. In fact, I want to reward you. First round, or whatever round you guys are on, is on me!" Evelyn waved over a waitress with jet black hair and tanned, olive skin.

"What's the lightest beer you have?" Sara asked.

The waitress listed off a few light beers and then leaned closer and grinned at Sara as if she was sharing a secret. "But if you're wanting a real Irish experience, nothing's better than a frothy Guinness on a cold winter's night. People our age don't drink them as much anymore but me granddad loved his Guinness and I do, too." The waitress placed a sassy hand on her hip and winked.

Sara's face burned. "Sure. I'll try it," she said barely able to meet the girl's probing gaze.

"If you don't like it, it's on me. I wouldn't want a sweet thing like you to suffer through a drink she didn't like." Sara watched the waitress saunter away full of confidence and pizazz.

An elbow jabbed Sara in the side and she turned to find Evelyn wagging her eyebrows. "I'd say someone has an admirer. You should go talk to her!"

"Stop!" Sara swatted her sister away. "She's working, and I don't have time for a relationship, or whatever, right now."

Lily cocked her head. "Is that right?"

"You and Alfred are different. You're both supernaturals and fighting together. I don't sense magic of any sort coming off her. Can you imagine starting a relationship with a human right now and having to lie about what you're doing?"

"I second that," Evelyn said, a small scowl on her face. "When I thought Roman was human it was so hard keeping things from him. I hated the secrets, but didn't want to put him in danger."

Surprisingly, Lily's eyes grew wide and she bit her lip. *Is that news?* Sara thought, confused by her sister's reaction.

"Still," Evelyn proceeded. "I'd never say *flirting* with humans is out of bounds." Evelyn wagged an eyebrow at Sara.

"Well, I do," Sara replied. "What if there are spies still watching us and I put someone in danger just by taking an interest in them?"

"Now then," the waitress purred as she appeared with their drinks. "I find it hard to believe a sweet lass like yourself would put anyone in danger. You look like a lover, not a fighter."

Evelyn smirked. "You'd be surprised. Do you have a moment to sit with us?"

Sara glared at her sister.

"Wish that I could, but as you lot can see the entire village is here tonight," the waitress sighed. "Another night, though?" Her gaze shifted from Evelyn to lock on Sara.

Sara nodded, and the waitress beamed. "Brilliant. Well, I best be off. Let me know how you like that beer, love."

Lily laughed. "Evelyn, you better step back! Sara will set you on fire in front of everyone!"

"If it gets her talking to that sweet waitress then so be it. She needs to loosen up," Evelyn said.

"Don't you two think you've tortured Sara enough?" Alfred said.

"This coming from the man who wouldn't stop hitting on me in front of my family the day we met?" Lily scoffed and whacked him on the arm.

What she wouldn't give for a relationship like theirs. But not now. Not when Sara had bigger things on her mind. A vision of walking into fire rose in Sara's mind and she picked up her beer and took a swig. It was, to her surprise, delicious—milky with roasted coffee undertones. That hot waitress knew what she was talking about.

"I don't know about the rest of these guys, but I'm super freaking excited about Christmas dinner tomorrow. Your mom was so great inviting us all. I'm stoked to see the witchy decorations Mary was going on and on about yesterday. A werewolf Christmas is the same as a human Christmas unless it falls on the full moon." Caleb's eyes shone as he spoke, triggering chuckles from everyone at the table.

Sara nodded. "She's thankful you're all here helping. Mom likes having a full house."

Aoife told her as much when they were training one day. How different Brigit was since the triplets had returned home. While Sara couldn't be sure, she got the sense that before their mother had been living a half life. A life consumed by working out the prophecy and what her daughters had to do with it.

Distracting herself from her misery, just like me with my books. Sara frowned and took another swig of beer.

"Way to bring Sara down again, Caleb." Evelyn rolled her eyes. "Now I'll have to call that waitress back over to lift her spirits."

"Why are you sad, Sara?" Celestine asked, the concern evident in her voice.

Celtic Christmas music swelled as the table fell silent, all waiting for Sara to respond. She bit her lip. *May as well tell them.*

"It's the pneuma thing. Lily and Evelyn have both talked to theirs but mine is like a mute."

Eros placed a comforting hand on her arm, his eyes

leveling with hers knowingly. "I get the sense you've figured out how to do it?"

Sara gaped. "Are you insinuating you *know* how? Why didn't you say something last night?"

Eros nodded. "As soon as Evelyn came out of the water I realized. I thought it best you work it out on your own. I figured it wouldn't take long."

"Super great that you two have figured something out. Can you stop being so cryptic and let the rest of us in on the secret?" Caleb asked.

"To get their pneumas talking my sisters released them while immersed in their primary element. I have to do the same."

Evelyn and Lily gasped

Caleb winced.

Alfred and Celestine remained calm, though their eyes grew wide.

"You have to be in fire to release your pneuma? But that's crazy!" Lily exclaimed. "It's not fair! I only had to walk in the woods and Evelyn swam in a lake! Sure, the lake was cold, but there's no comparison!"

Sara took a huge drink of beer. "Still, it makes sense. Nothing else I've tried has worked and I just have a feeling it's what I need to do."

"Have you told your mother?" Celestine asked, her voice somber.

"Not yet," Sara said. "To be honest, I'm surprised she hasn't brought it up."

"I'm not," Celestine said. "No mother wants to picture her children in pain. She may have made the connections deep in her soul but has been unconsciously ignoring it. Brigit won't like to hear it, but you must tell her. You'll need everyone's support if you are to have the courage to do this."

Sara nodded and downed her beer.

Love and Secrets Muck Up Everything

Lily

Lily's head swam as she stumbled into Alfred's hotel room.

"It's like pints never stopped coming to the table. I swear I only ordered two." She giggled and collapsed onto Alfred's bed.

Alfred perched on a chair by the door to untie his shoes. "I think Mary had something to do with that. I must have seen twenty people ask her about you three. I bet Mary requested they not bug you, so they showed old-fashioned Irish hospitality and sent beer instead."

"The bill was low," Lily shrugged. "I'm sure I'll regret the pints tomorrow. But it was such a fun night!"

The mattress sank as Alfred sat down next to her. He smelled of cedar and soap. "At least you don't have magic lessons tomorrow. You can recover then."

His fingers traced her jaw, dropped down to her sternum, followed the curve of her collarbone and trailed down her arm where Alfred intertwined his fingers with hers. "Do you think Sara will be OK? I don't think she even heard Caleb's story about running wild through New York and almost getting put in the zoo. And I'm positive he only told it to cheer her up."

Lily shook her head. "We'll all be feeling terrible tomorrow. And, knowing Sara, she won't be able to stop thinking about releasing her pneuma in a freaking fire."

Alfred shook his head. "Speaking of pneumas. Is yours here?"

"Nope." Lily looked up from lowered lashes. "I released her when we left the cottage. I wasn't sure if you and I . . ." She trailed off.

Alfred eased himself next to her and propped up on his elbows. He laid a hand on her waist.

Lily shivered as electricity shot through her. "No using your power on me," she teased.

But her words drowned as Alfred's lips brushed hers, silky and strong all at once. A fire burned deep inside her as their lips explored each others. Alfred inched closer, his hand drifting from her waist to cup her cheek. He pulled away and Lily opened her eyes to find him staring at her.

"God, you are beautiful. If I could look at you all day, I'd be the happiest man alive."

Her heart stopped as she stared at the man before her. A strong, good man who was hot as hell. "You're pretty attractive yourself," Lily whispered. Her hands trembled as she gripped his muscular arm. *Is tonight the night? Am I ready for this? I should have asked Evelyn if she had any tips.*

Alfred sat up, took her hand, and lifted her torso to level with his.

Lily's eyes widened. Had she done something wrong?

"As much as I want to, Lil, I don't think tonight is our night. I want our first time to be special. A night you'll never forget or regret. I don't want you to be nervous. And I definitely don't want it to be in a shabby hotel room." Alfred's cheeks pinked.

A wave of disappointment washed over her, but she tempered it by grabbing his hand and shifting closer. "No matter where we choose, our first time will be special because it's with you. I'm falling in love with you, Alfred, and I'm willing to wait." Her heart soared as his brown eyes brightened. "I'm not going to stop you if you want to make it extra special, but please, no cheesy love-making music."

Alfred leaned forward, his lips seeking hers. "I'll keep that in mind, beautiful," he murmured.

Lily slipped inside the cottage and quirked her head, listening. It was quiet, everyone was asleep. She took off her boots and went to get a glass of cold water before turning in. Rounding the hearth corner into the sitting room, her hand flew to her heart.

Brigit sat on the couch.

"Shit, Mom, you startled me!"

"Sorry, Lil. I only wanted to make sure you made it home safe," Brigit patted the spot next to her.

Lily raised her eyebrows but took a seat anyhow.

"Your sisters said you were out with Alfred? Where did you two go?"

Lily's eyebrows rose. *Are we really going to have this conversation? I'm twenty-one!* She leaned back as casually as she could manage, hoping to convey that she was worldly enough not to have this talk. "We were at his hotel."

"Hmm," Brigit stared into the unlit fireplace. "You know I like Alfred, right? I see the way you two look at each other. I can't blame you—he's a good lad, and a woman would be mad not to find him attractive."

Lily's stomach sank. "But?"

"But, I want you to be careful. Falling in love is a powerful thing. We have a job to do, Lil, and it's great that Alfred wants to help. Like I said, he's a good lad. Any other time I'd be ecstatic for him to court my daughter, but right now I worry your attraction puts you in danger." Brigit sighed and looked Lily straight in the eye. "We're in a battle for our lives, for a free world, and love can muck up your reasoning. Look what happened to your sister."

Instinctively, Lily shot up from her chair. "That's so unfair! Why invite him over here then? Why say something now? It was no secret we've been talking day and night since the Battle of Peacock Manor! If you didn't want the relationship to deepen, you shouldn't have invited him to the cottage!"

Her mother winced. "Alfred is one of the best daemon fighters in the world. I'd have been mental not to accept his help. You three need to learn from him so you can become stronger witches. The more you learn, the safer you are, and your safety is my top priority. As for your relationship, I suppose I didn't expect it to progress so fast. I expected you to be hesitant after Amon. I wasn't considering your big heart, how once you love, you love easily and fully. Most of all, it was an old lady's error. I'd forgotten what it was like to be young and in love. Like I forgot with Evelyn." Brigit dropped her brown eyes to her hands.

Lily's throat tightened but she wouldn't give in to the emotions her mother was stirring up. Not when her mother had mentioned Evelyn. The timing was too perfect not to ask the question burning in the back of

Lily's mind for weeks. "You say love mucks up our reasoning? Fine. I get that. But you know what else mucks it up? Secrets."

Brigit's eyes rose to meet her daughter's bright green ones. "Secrets?"

"I know all about Roman, Mom. I found him at the safe house and talked to him. Why didn't you tell any of us you found him? And what do you plan on doing with him?" The questions rolled off her tongue.

"You haven't told your sister, have you?"

Lily shook her head.

Brigit exhaled. "Good. I wanted to tell you all. Evelyn first as she'd be most sensitive to it. But she's not healed physically yet and I couldn't bring more pain down upon her. Please understand, Lil. I promise I'll tell Evelyn when the time is right, and I'll tell you what's afoot now if you still want to hear it."

Celestine's words from earlier that night came flooding back to Lily.

No mother wants to picture her children in pain.

She sat back down.

"Since you talked to Roman, I won't go into how we found him, but the circumstances lent credence to his story. Why would the Acolytes throw someone on their side into a locked room? Still, I couldn't trust him at first, so I kept him tied up. To be honest, he was a good sport. I expect he felt he was paying a penance for betraying Evelyn. Anyhow, he's free now and roaming New York."

Lily's mouth fell open. "What if he runs into the Locksleys! They'll skewer him alive for his part in what happened."

"They've been informed he's working for us now. Roman is no longer involved with Locksley Enterprises. In such a large city it's unlikely they'll bump into each other. James and Sonja weren't pleased, but they understood. As the other side has Nora, a well-informed spy, we needed one, too."

"He's a double-agent?"

Brigit nodded. "He found Nora. Told her that I hurt him a bit and now he's committed fully to their side. When she asked about his feelings for Evelyn, and why he tried to help her escape, he said he was over her. Claimed to be already enchanting dozens of other beauties in the city. Nora bought it and now he's in New York working with the Acolytes. Unfortunately, he's only received grunt work so far. I'm hoping eventually they'll let something important slip around him."

"Wow. That's brave of him to return as a spy. Considering what they did to Evelyn, and they needed her alive, I can't imagine what the Acolytes would do to someone who betrayed them. How are you talking to him without us knowing?"

Brigit held up her cell phone. "I know it's hard to believe, but I turn this thing on from time to time. We've been texting, and I call when you three aren't around."

"Thanks for telling me. Can you promise to tell Evelyn soon, though? I don't want this to cause another rift in our family. We're all doing so well now." Lily's stomach tightened at the thought of her sister and her not talking. It was the last thing she wanted after they'd lost so much to get where they were.

"I promise, love. I only wanted to wait until she was healthy. I hoped by then I'd have enough information to justify keeping in touch with Roman. The boy's already made it clear once I tell Evelyn about him, he wants to speak with her. At this point, I'm protecting both of them." Brigit sighed. "Now that we have no secrets between us what do you say we go to bed? Tomorrow's a big day."

Another secret—Sara's hypothesis of how to speak with her pneuma—popped into Lily's head and she bit her lip. *It's not my secret to tell.*

Lily kissed her mother on the cheek. "You're right. See you in the morning."

A Pagan Christmas
Sara

"THIS ONE'S YOURS, SARA." Brigit beamed and handed Sara her stocking.

"Mom, this is too much," Sara said as her arm dropped beneath the weight of her stocking. "How did you get all this stuff in here without us noticing? Aren't we supposed to be pagan or something?"

Brigit's eyes watered and Sara sighed.

How am I supposed to tell her I want to walk into a bonfire when Mom's been tearing up over stockings all morning?

"Even pagans can use a day of celebration filled with love and cheer. We'd have done Christmas when you were little anyhow seeing as your father was Catholic. And it's not too much. Your aunts and I have been picking things up here and there since you three arrived in June. I suppose we thought it good luck. We've missed twenty Christmases of spoiling you three and have loads of Christmas magic to make up for."

"I'd say you've got the magic part down." Lily stared up at the twinkling lights Brigit had enchanted to hover inches below the cottage ceiling.

Sara's eyes landed on the smallish fairy bush in front of the fire. Brigit had unearthed and potted the bush after many assurances to any fairy who might be listening that she would replant it the day after Christmas. The fire's light caught ornaments resembling rubies, sapphires, emeralds, diamonds, orange topaz, aquamarine, and peridot twinkling on its branches. Sara fingered the peridot-hued bauble representing Gwenn and the copper topaz that screamed Aoife. Her fingers trailed through the branches and knocked off an ornament. Sara cocked her head.

"Who does this one represent?" Sara asked, holding up the smoky gray ornament.

Brigit smiled a sad smile. "Caught on to my color scheme, did you? That one's your father. I couldn't bear to leave him off. He loved Christmas so much."

"I like how you paired yourself as his opposite. Smoky quartz and diamond, they're beautiful together. A contrast and a team." Evelyn came closer to admire the bush.

Brigit pinked. "I couldn't decide what to do for meself so I chose the easy way."

"It's gorgeous, Mom." Lily pulled Brigit's stocking from the wall. "Now, what about your stocking?"

Brigit's eyes widened and watered again. "You three didn't have to put anything in mine. Christmas presents are mostly for the children."

"Not in this family," Lily said, pushing the stocking into Brigit's hands.

Sara grinned at the look of shock on their mother's face.

They all sat down and poured out the contents of their stockings.

Sara gushed over the new mala bead necklace Evelyn gave her, the wild essential oils Lily had requested Rena send from their Terramar stock, and a book titled *Magical Arts of Egyptian Witches Throughout History* from her mother.

"Bahati mentioned you seemed interested in their magical heritage," Brigit said.

"It's perfect!" Sara agreed. Her adoptive mother always bought Sara gifts she would never use, like makeup pallets and subscriptions to fashion magazines. "It's the most thoughtful gift I've ever received."

Brigit beamed and pointed at the haul in front of her. "I can't believe you three. I have such generous daughters.

Evelyn, thank you for this lovely necklace." Brigit opened a robin egg blue box and pulled out a necklace with ruby, emerald, and sapphire gemstone pendants.

"And Lil, these soaps and balms are to die for. Rosemary and mint are two of my favorite scents. I'll have to put a standing order in with Rena to ship it year-round."

Finally, Brigit picked up the mug personalized with her daughters' and sisters' faces. "I'll never take my tea out of another mug again. It's my favorite, Sara. Goddess be—you three certainly know how to spoil me. Thank you, girls."

"Likewise," Sara said. "When are Aoife, Mary, and Gwenn arriving? I assume we'll have to wait for them to finish opening all those?" Sara pointed to the pile of gifts on the ground.

"Aye, we'll wait," Brigit said. "I asked them to give me until eleven, so they should be here within the hour. Mary—probably sooner, she's excited to spend Christmas with her nieces for the first time. She may even try to actualize her vision of dressing you three in matching outfits today. She went on and on about tutus when you were still in my belly."

Brigit smirked at the horrified looks on the triplets' faces. "I wouldn't worry, girls. Where is she going to find tutus big enough around here? What do you say I make us some breakfast and you three get ready? The rest of our guests will get here at one and we wouldn't want to be in our pajamas when Mr. Perfect arrives, would we, Lil?"

BRIGIT HAD BEEN RIGHT ABOUT one thing.

Mary brought matching gifts.

Sara counted her lucky stars that Mary had opted for sweaters instead of tutus. In fact, Sara actually liked what Mary had chosen for her. The sage green wasn't bright or crazy, as was often Mary's prerogative. It fit her well and complemented Sara's copper eyes and red hair. For once, she felt as striking as her sisters, rather than strangely pretty.

They opened the rest of their gifts in a whirlwind of paper and hugs of thanks. Sara had never received so much for Christmas in her life. As she stared at the pile of sweaters, yoga leggings, witchy books, crystals, and even her own Book of Shadows to write in, a lump rose in her throat.

How did I get so lucky to have all these people who actually want to be with me?

Brigit's smile grew wider as the day progressed. "What do you girls say you move all your gifts into your rooms? Aoife, Mar, Gwenn, take yours to your cars, and someone clean the rest of this mess up. I'm planning on a full house for dinner. Morgane and all the New Yorkers are coming by soon. It'd be nice if they had a place to sit." Brigit glanced around the piles of paper and boxes in the sitting room. "I still need to hop in the shower and get dressed. Everyone else looks good, but I'm still a right mess." Brigit retreated down the hallway.

Sara's heart thumped hard against her sternum. *Now's the time. We've had our magical Christmas morning and now I have to spoil everything.*

An elbow nudged her shoulder and Sara looked up to find Evelyn standing beside her. "We got this. You should tell her before dinner, so she can prepare. It isn't right that the New Yorkers know and not Mom."

Sara grabbed a handful of gifts as props and sped down the hall after Brigit. She opened the door to her room, tossed the gifts inside, slammed the door shut, whirled about, and gasped

Brigit stood in the middle of the hallway, robe on and shower cap in hand, looking at Sara with a look of puzzlement.

"You're in a right state."

"I need to talk to you, Mom. Alone."

Brigit's brown eyes widened, but she said nothing. Only nodded her head toward her room. "Everything alright?" she asked shutting the door behind them and sitting on the end of her bed.

Photos of the triplets above Brigit's bed jumped out at Sara. She bit her lip hard. If it hadn't been for that damned prophecy, her life could have been so different. She'd have been surrounded by family who loved her. Had Christmases like this every year. Known her father. Sara sighed.

Brigit cocked her head. "I take it that's a no. What's wrong, love?"

The bed sank as Sara took a seat by her mother, who as always smelled comfortingly of cinnamon and lavender. "I've been thinking about how Lily and Evelyn can both talk to their pneumas, but I still can't."

"Oh, Sara, don't worry about that today." Brigit laid her hand over Sara's. "We'll figure it out. I know it can be hard being the odd woman out, but you'll get there."

Sara's heart clenched. She'd come to expect her mother and aunts' loving gestures. Still, sometimes when they caught her off guard, Sara reacted as she would have if her adoptive mother had shown her affection: startled, shocked, even confused.

She cleared her throat. "Well, that's the thing," Sara's voice cracked. "I think I've already figured it out. It won't be pretty."

"Pretty?" Brigit asked, a line forming between her brows.

Sara took a long inhale and an even longer exhale,

hoping to calm her nervous system. "Remember how Lily was on a run in the forest when her pneuma spoke to her? And Evelyn was swimming?"

Brigit nodded, though the pieces didn't seem to click. Sara suspected Celestine was right. Brigit was blocking the revelation that would only bring her angst.

"Those are both their primary elements. If I want my pneuma to speak to me, I'll have to be immersed in my primary element, too."

Brigit's hand flew to her mouth. "No, that can't be true. There's got to be another way."

I've ruined the best Christmas ever. Sara's heart sank as tears filled her mother's eyes.

"I don't think so. I've tried so many things, and we both know I'm more in tune with my body than Lil or Evelyn. That's why I don't think it's what I can do that's the missing piece. It's where I am, the environment, meeting her halfway. Believe me, I don't want to do this either but I have to try, and I want to do it soon. I don't feel right lacking this connection to my pneuma. It could be critical to our success."

"How soon?" Brigit looked smaller than when they'd walked into her room.

"Today, if you'll let me. I don't want to wait and today is ideal since Fiona will already be here. I'll need a good healer afterward." She didn't want to think of the excruciating pain awaiting her. Even if she stood inside fire for mere seconds, there would be damage. That was the nature of fire, instantaneous and all-encompassing.

Brigit nodded and turned her head to gaze upon the photos hanging above her bed.

Evelyn as a teenage prom queen. Sara as a chubby, ginger-haired toddler. Lily decked out in running shorts lined up for a race. All photos people had sent to Brigit over the years. Photos she'd cherished.

"Well," Brigit said after several seconds of silence. "I always knew this Christmas would be a memorable one. I'll call Fiona to make sure she arrives with her healer's bag."

Christmas Phoenix
Sara

THE ROAST and potatoes sat heavily in Sara's stomach as she watched Alfred, Eros, and Caleb stacking logs for the bonfire.

Am I up for this? She shivered and pulled her blanket closer.

After Brigit told her sisters the plan they'd set to work, sketching out a map of a bonfire that Sara could stand in and exit from quickly if the process allowed for it. She was sure her pneuma wouldn't come out if she stood next to a fire, or even in a tiny one that licked her legs. She'd already tried to think small using a candle the night prior —a drunken idea that seemed brilliant but only resulted in four blisters on her hand.

No. Sara was positive she needed to be engulfed in

the flames. Like Evelyn had been drowning in water and Lily, the luckiest of all, had been deep in the forest.

If only I was an earth witch.

Her pneuma jumped inside her and Sara yelped. Smoke tickled her nostrils and understanding dawned on her. The men were done; the fire was lit. *It was always the flames for you, wasn't it? Well, when we can finally talk, I'd love to hear why. Because there are a million other ways I'd have preferred this to go.*

"Psyching yourself up?" Lily asked coming up behind Sara.

"Ha. I guess you could call it that."

"I would. It's what we'd say in running and what you're about to do is more strenuous than any race I've ever heard of. How long do you think it'll take?"

Sara shrugged. "I'm hoping it will be fast, but something tells me I won't be able to do it until the flames are all around me."

There was a flash of light. The flames had caught on the larger logs and were fanning high into the night sky. It was time.

The cottage door slammed shut and her mother, aunts, Evelyn, Fiona, Morgane, and Celestine marched out. Only Alistair was missing, having asked for a ride back to the hotel after dinner, claiming such sights did not sit well with him.

"If I didn't know any better, I'd say this is the finale of a witch hunt," Brigit said.

"There'd be a lot more cheering and foul vegetables being tossed about if that were the case." Morgane, the triplets' occasional teacher and spunky octogenarian, joined Sara. Her velour outfit shimmered in the fire's light and brought a smile to Sara's face. She loved when Morgane visited. They were both scholars of the occult and could geek out on this kind of stuff all day.

"I'd be an unlikely target anyhow," Sara added. "Not being an elderly woman living alone, a successful businesswoman, or a healer. Or worse, all three. My red hair might grab some attention, though."

"I'd be in a right pickle then, wouldn't I?" Aoife said.

Sara nodded. As a redhead and a successful apothecary shop owner who dared to live alone, Aoife would be a prime target. "Luckily, you're a ceremens. You'd persuade them and run away. I'd never have worried about you during any witch hunt in history."

Aoife's copper eyes glinted with the fire's light. "Aye, me either. Nor would I have worries about you, wee one."

Eros approached the group of women. "The fire is as high as it's going to get. We're ready whenever you are."

Brigit sucked in a breath, but Sara ignored it as she stood. Drawing it out wouldn't make this any easier. She ran her hand through her hair. *Good thing I'm not a huge hair person.*

"I have a hair tonic that allows it to grow back fast, Sara. It will be the easiest bit of healing. Remember to hold your breath so you don't do irreparable damage to your lungs. Are you sure you don't want the skin protectant I brought? It won't stop the fire from burning you but it will slow it." Fiona's large brown eyes begged Sara to take protection with her.

This must be torture for a healer to see a person intentionally hurt themselves.

"No thanks. I don't want to give my pneuma any reason not to speak. I'll do it with no protection like Lily and Evelyn. That way if it doesn't work I'm not compelled to try again. I only want to do this once."

Fiona sighed. "Thought you'd say that. I brought everything I can think of to heal you but still, be quick."

Sara nodded, and a flurry of arms covered her.

Evelyn and Lily gripped her the hardest. "Be as fast as you can—don't fight her. Then, get the fuck out of there," Evelyn said.

Lily nodded, her eyes misty. "We're releasing our pneumas in case they can help coax yours out faster."

Brigit hugged her tight, her breath hitching in her throat. "Do what you must. We stand behind you. I love you, my brave little fire witch." A damp kiss brushed

Sara's cheek. When Brigit released her, a single tear ran down her face before she could wipe it away.

In true Aoife manner, her words were more chilling than hopeful. "Fire's a right awful thing to command, wee one. We can control it, use it, and sense it in our blood, but we'll never truly be master of it no matter how much our soul craves it. Remember that when you step into the flames. Give yourself over. Let it transform you. Don't fight it. Then, get out."

She'd needed the hugs Mary and Gwenn gave her after that. The men patted her on the back, each looking guilty that they'd been the ones to build the bonfire she was about to step into. Caleb cracked a nervous joke and then stared down at the ground. Sara loved her new friend more because of his awkwardness. Morgane was next.

"If this doesn't work, we'll implement a shutout. Kick that pneuma to the curb until she starts talking! She doesn't know how good she has it, but once she's gone a night or two out here, she'll be begging to come back and live inside you."

Weak chuckles filtered through the air. Sara gave Morgane a grateful smile for lightening the mood.

Her last hug was for Celestine. "I will watch from back here but please know I am with you and wish I could be closer to the flames."

Sara understood. She wouldn't want Celestine too

close anyhow. One spark and the vamp she adored would die.

"Thank you for bearing witness," she said and before Sara could distract herself further, she turned and walked toward the fire.

SMOKE DANCED in Sara's nose, filled her lungs, and constricted her airways. Hot at a two-foot distance, her skin already burned and her fingers trembled, begging her to use them, to create a pathway through the crackling flames so she may enter unharmed. The dress Sara had chosen, hoping it would keep the flames from hugging her skin when she exited the fire, fluttered in the cold winter breeze like the fire before her.

Contrary to every other being in the field, her pneuma whirled about excitedly inside Sara.

She wanted to tell it to stop, that she had enough sensation, and to calm down. Instead, she used her pneuma's energy for fuel and stepped forward.

Flames licked at her feet the second Sara entered the circle of fire, the skin, muscles, and bones not yet on fire, though they would be soon. *Get in the center, then retreat inside to push out the pain for as long as possible.*

Three more steps and she was there, in the tiny center of the circle Alfred, Caleb, and Eros had constructed.

All Sara needed to do was stick her foot out and the thin fabric atop the rubber sole would catch. The heat smoldering inside her shoe would become nothing but energy consuming energy.

Sara shook and a bead of sweat rolled down her face. She blinked the sweat from her blazing eyes and commanded her foot to move a millimeter toward the flames, to start the burning. Her foot didn't budge.

Luckily, it didn't need to.

A breeze found its way through the fire to catch on her dress, igniting the cotton in a second. Flames ran up the fabric and the skin of her back sizzled with heat.

Sara bit her lip and squeezed her eyes shut. The metallic taste of blood seeped onto her tongue as she swallowed a scream.

Her pneuma was dancing now, like the flames that surrounded them.

The joyous dance contradicted how Sara felt as flames engulfed her. Her insides were nothing but smoke by this point. Red, juicy blisters rose on her back. She didn't dare peek down at her feet, which she feared were nothing but ash at this point. The stench of burned hair filled her nostrils. A wailing sound sliced through the night and Sara realized she'd started screaming.

Now, I have to do it now. I can't withstand much longer.

"Caeliter." Sara's lips trembled with the effort of the single spell.

Her pneuma pounded against her chest but didn't leave. Instead, she swirled inside Sara who thought she might pass out at any second.

The flames surged higher, setting Sara's breast aflame. Her hands flew up to beat out the flames, but the inferno didn't stop there. Before she could even put out the fire on her chest, Sara's hair caught and the bottoms of her ears shriveled.

Why not? Come out! Caeliter, Sara thought again, no longer able to breathe, let alone speak.

Once more, her pneuma pounded against her chest, stilled, and then shot up her neck, straight between her eyes. An enormous pressure pushed against the inside of Sara's eyeballs.

What the hell? Sara's eyeballs threatened to bulge out, to become fuel for the bonfire. She didn't want to open them but the pressure from within was growing too great. She'd prepared to lose hair, have disfigured skin, weaker lungs, even a stunted gait, but Sara had never imagined losing her vision for this. *If I go blind, I'll kill you.*

She opened her eyes. Fire was everywhere, including

her pathway out. Voices rose outside the flames and Sara knew her family was discussing when to intervene.

Caeliter! Sara thought again, all patience gone with the skin of her back. *Get the hell out!*

Her vision tinged cloudy red and her pneuma seeped out of her eyes. Sara had the profound impression that a pressure valve was being released through her head though it did nothing to minimize her searing nerves and shaking body. Her heart cracked open and head tilted back. For the first time since she could remember, her body felt free, new, like a phoenix reborn.

Above, the moon, a crescent in the sky shone down upon her, and it too was red. Everything was red.

Suddenly, her crimson pneuma was before her, brighter than ever before. She expanded and glittered as if Sara wasn't there.

Is she smiling? Sara swayed on the spot. *Did it work?*

"H-Hello?" Sara stuttered and collapsed into ash.

The Human Zoo
Evelyn

"Has she woken up yet?" Evelyn asked as Lily entered the dining room on tiptoe.

A long sigh flew from Lily. "Not yet. Fiona is still in our room sitting up with her. There's not much else to do besides apply burn salve until she wakes up." She gestured to the mass of papers before Evelyn. "What are you reading?"

"Morgane brought a bunch of papers Sara requested from Dublin. As she's out, I'm playing Sara. I even lit a candle and om'ed a couple times this morning to get into character. Except I did it from the comfort of my bed. These floors are too damn cold to be sitting on. I don't know how Sara does it. Anyhow, now I'm catching up on world news and trying to spot sketchy things the fata may be behind."

Lily raised her eyebrows in amusement. "First off, Sara has a huge cushion she sits on so her butt doesn't freeze. Secondly, did you find anything interesting?" She filled a mug with coffee.

"Not yet, but I'm only through about half. Morgane brought one of every major world journal. There's even one in French, the crazy old bat. Can anyone here even read that? I bet she was just having a go at us. Want to help?" Evelyn handed her sister a stack of papers as she sat down, before diving back into her own.

The usual headlines popped out at her. War, famine, some new tech company going public, an oil company losing money, artificial intelligence conspiracies, the stuff Evelyn used to devour every morning during her days at Locksley Enterprises. Back then she'd been looking for weaknesses in the market, new areas to exploit, or clients to contact. Now she was looking for something different.

Evelyn flipped to the culture section, the odor of paper wafting over her. She rolled her eyes at the article displayed front and center. *For shit's sake. Who cares who wins "England's Best Pie" contest? What is this crap?* She tossed the journal aside and grabbed the next on the stack. Her heart stopped.

On the front page was a headline that chilled her bones.

Residents of Paris Woke Up All Bearing Identical Tattoos

Imagine waking up days before Christmas with a gift you aren't sure you wanted. Now imagine that gift is inked on you for life. For two dozen Paris residents, that's exactly what happened.

Evelyn stopped reading as her eyes latched onto a photo at the bottom of the page. A photo of a navy star, a twin to the one she bore on her own right inner thigh. She resisted the urge to hurl the paper across the room.

"Well, shit."

"What?" Lily asked, leaning forward in her chair.

"Noro, he's branded people in Paris as his. Look."

Evelyn pointed to the picture and Lily skimmed the article.

"Wasn't there a blown up map of Paris in Nora's house? I swear I saw one in Sara's photos." Lily asked when she was done.

"I don't remember, but we were all taking photos everywhere so that doesn't mean much." Evelyn pulled out her phone and flipped through the pictures on it, stopping suddenly when she reached a map of France. "Look! There's a pin in Paris on one of these photos." Energized, she kept scrolling through her photos and finally came upon a map of the city of Paris, blown up and detailed just as Lily had described. Her eyes latched onto a prominent red pin in an ocean of green. She zoomed in. "Lil, Google the Vincennes Woods. There's a pin in it. What comes up?"

Lily pulled out her phone, her fingers flying over the keys and eyes running down articles.

"It looks like it's old royal hunting grounds converted to a public space with tons of things to do: a horse racing track, pathways for biking and walking, a Buddhist temple, an old castle." Lily paused and cocked her head.

"And?" Evelyn prodded.

"There used to be a human zoo there in the early twentieth century. One of those creepy, messed up exhibits back in the old days when Europeans were fascinated with people from Africa and the Middle East. It's abandoned on the edge of the park now but one of these articles has photos of tons of buildings that still stand there."

A human zoo. I bet a few of the disappeared people are being kept there. That has to be it. It's Noro's style to treat humans like animals. The name alone would appeal to him. I bet they have it warded with magic to deter humans.

Evelyn stood up. "Do you want to wake Mom or should I?"

Brigit set the phone it in its cradle. "The Paris covens haven't noticed any unusual activity in their city. Most asked if I wanted them to send anyone to investigate the area tonight. I declined for now."

Celestine nodded in agreement. "No one should investigate until they have been briefed. I can go and prepare the Paris covens, if you wish?"

"Me, too." Caleb raised his hand. "I'm ready to kick a little fata ass. Pay them back for taking my best pack mate from me." The werewolf cracked his knuckles. The sound of popping bones echoed through the cottage.

"I'll go, too," Alfred said.

A sharp inhale came from Evelyn's left and she knew without looking it was Lily, already worrying over Alfred's heroism. *Boy, you're dating a healer, not a warrior.*

While Evelyn appreciated big gestures and acts of heroism from the men she dated, Lily was a different story. *Forget Roman, wherever he's hiding. I need a guy like Alfred.*

Brigit nodded. "I'll call the covens back and ask for volunteers to accompany you. You can fill them in when you arrive in France. The fata haven't been here long, so I don't expect they've strengthened their magical reserves yet."

Celestine nodded. "I still have a few vampiric acquaintances in Paris I can ask to join us. From what I remember the zoo is at the far reaches of the Vincennes Woods. It would be good to have a local show us the best way to approach without being seen, if that is even possible. I think I shall return to my room in the village to make my calls and plan. Caleb, would you like a ride?"

"Better than running all the way into town. I think I scared a little old lady half to death the other day when she spotted me transforming from wolf to man in the woods." Caleb gave a sheepish shrug, and the pair slipped out of the cottage.

Alfred, seeing Lily's distress, grabbed her hand. "Let's go for a walk in the orchard."

"That was settled quickly," Evelyn said as soon as she and her mother were alone.

"Aye." Brigit rubbed her temples and turned to fill her coffee mug for a third time. "We should be ready for something like this at any time. Clearly, Celestine is. I suppose that's what happens when you've been alive a couple hundred years."

"And the boys just want action."

"Hmph. Caleb is a werewolf so yes, the action is appealing to him, but Alfred is volunteering for a different reason."

"To be the hero in Lily's eyes?" Evelyn asked, curious to see if they were on the same page.

"No, the lad's smarter than that. He'll go because there's a chance his involvement will spare your sister harm in the future."

Three, Three, Three
Sara

I SURVIVED. The words came to Sara before she'd even cracked her eyes open. She rummaged around inside of herself, searching for her pneuma. She wasn't there. Pushing her torso off the mattress, Sara sat up. Something moved at the side of her bed and she yanked her blanket up to her chin.

"Sorry," Fiona said. "Didn't mean to startle you."

"It's fine," Sara replied loosening her grip on the blanket. "I should've expected you would be there. How bad do I look?"

Fiona quirked an eyebrow. "Why don't you see for yourself?"

It was the last thing she wanted to do, lift the blanket covering her to see burnt skin, or worse, no skin. As she couldn't feel anything at the moment, Sara guessed she'd deadened her skin's nerve endings. She was no healer, but she had witnessed how Lily cringed and whimpered after she dove through a flame gate to kill Amon.

I don't feel anything like that.

Slowly, she lifted the blanket.

"What the heck?" Her voice filled with wonder as her eyes took in the smooth, pale skin of her legs and her intact feet. Her eyes latched onto a few red spots here and there. Nothing a little burn salve couldn't fix. Her gaze lifted to meet Fiona's, demanding answers.

"When you collapsed, your pneuma rushed over you to protect you from the fire until Aoife could run in and pull you out. Your pneuma healed the worst of your burns then. Only a few areas will need spot treatment. I've been rubbing ointments on them while you slept. Your body hair is gone, but most of the hair on your head is fine. One side got burnt. My tonic can fix that."

"Wow," Sara murmured. "I didn't see that coming."

"You and everyone else," Fiona replied with a smile. "I'll go tell the others you're up. They're anxious to see you."

Sara leaned against her headboard. She closed her eyes and stretched her memory to come up with a time-line of Christmas night. She remembered walking into the fire. Smoke filling her lungs, the fire burning her skin. Her pneuma going crazy inside her, pain, searing feet, and fear that her eyes would bulge out of their sockets.

What the hell was that about? My pneuma has never left my body so violently. Or taken so much time to do so. I could have died in there.

"I would not have allowed that. I was simply relishing in the tribute given. I have not savored the power of fire for so long."

Sara stiffened and her heart stopped at the voice—airy, strange, yet resonating in her bones as familiar. Slowly, she opened her eyes.

Three ghostly figures glowed against the backdrop of the curtains—emerald, sapphire, and ruby, shining with a brightness Sara had never seen. The red pneuma rearranged her round facial features to match something resembling a human smile.

"You're talking! But why are my sisters' pneumas here?" Sara's face fell. She'd been dying to know the being living inside her better. Sara had so many questions to ask about her pneuma's past, her own past.

One, specifically, she couldn't wait any longer to know the answer to. A question she'd wished to ask her pneuma alone, but supposed she'd simply have to make an exception for Seraphina's sisters. The Fern Cottage was small and alone time, sparse.

"Was it you or me who started and saved me from the

car fire which killed my original adoptive parents?" Her shoulders tightened with every word. The question had burned in her since she'd learned she may have been the one to cause it. The idea that she may have been the one responsible for throwing her life into the chaos and misery it became later was almost too much to bear. Sara knew the question was a coin toss, it could go either way. Still, if there was the option of closure, of knowing she hadn't been the progenitor of her own misery, she'd take the chance.

The red pneuma's black orbs gazed back at her as if she could read Sara's very soul. Softly, she spoke, "The crash was entirely an accident, the fire too. You are not to blame for killing those people. As for who saved you, that was entirely your magic, not mine. It was a loophole your mother placed in her binding. Not until very recently, when you released me, was I freed and able to perform magic of that magnitude. Fear not Sara, you are at fault for none of what happened to you in the past. I'm sorry I could not save you some pain in your younger years."

Sara's breath left her lungs as she fell back into the headboard. The guilt she'd been carrying for her inability to save her first adoptive parents did not instantly vanish, but perhaps, in time, it may. She opened her mouth, another question on her lips but the red pneuma stopped her.

"We'll get our time together and I'll answer any personal questions I can," the red pneuma assured her. "Now, however, it is time for everyone to know the truth."

"They'll be here soon," Lily's green pneuma said, floating forward. "I sense Lily approaching. We knew they'd want to check on you before we told our tale. Your mother is welcome to listen, too."

Like anyone could stop Mom from being here.

"True enough," the red pneuma said.

"You can read my mind?" Sara asked, not at all bothered by the idea. The thing had lived inside her, witnessed her entire life; she figured it had an all-access pass.

"In a way," Seraphina's pneuma reincarnated answered. "It's more like we have a psychic connection. One I can access as I am more versed in magic than you are."

There was a creaking sound and Lily, Evelyn, and Brigit rushed through the door only to stop dead in their tracks.

"There they are!" Evelyn cried out.

Sara cocked her head to the side.

"Our pneumas. They've been missing since last night."

"You should sit down," Sara answered. "I have a feeling they're about to tell us something huge."

"THE MORRIGAN," Brigit whispered. She fell back in her chair. "You're telling me you three were the goddesses Morrigan of this isle? The goddesses of war, fate, and sovereignty? That this has all happened before? That my daughters house the same pneuma, the same fata souls, the Morrigan triple goddess once did?"

Sara's pneuma nodded her head.

They're putting in so much effort to be human. Our mannerisms can't be natural to them. Not when we're solid flesh and blood, and they're . . .

"Air and ether," Sara's pneuma finished. "No, human mannerisms are not natural, but you three are human so communication is easier if we adapt."

"Let me get this straight," Evelyn said, her voice high. "You three have been reincarnated through generations of witches at various times, living in conjunction with the witch's human soul. However, this is the first time all three of you were reborn together, as triplets, and also released? Isn't that a huge fucking coincidence?"

"Quite huge," the sapphire pneuma agreed. "As we said, the only other time we were reborn together was here, on this very isle. It is a place where magic runs deep. It seems fitting we were to be reborn here again."

"The goddesses of sovereignty, war, and fate reborn,"

Brigit whispered again and shook her head. "Yes, it seems quite fitting, considering the situation we are in."

Lily gripped her mother's hand and turned to her own pneuma. "We've done everything you wanted, including Sara nearly killing herself. Now it's time to tell us about you. At least your names. It would make communicating to and about you three easier, so please, can we make one part of this easy?"

"Tributes, what you did by immersing yourselves in our favored elements, is not only an act of devotion but a binding contract between two parties. Engorging my sisters and I with our element of choice is a blood sacrifice of sorts. It enhances our psychic connection with you, which will surely be useful, and for that, we do not apologize. It needed to be done." The green pneuma paused for a second.

"However, I could have told you more of myself before, but I thought adding stress to your mother was unnecessary. She, at least, would recognize the name I now claim as part of the Morrigan. It's a name which inspired great fear or devotion on this isle, depending on the circumstances. I will claim the name from the time I was with my sisters and we fought together, as three and one. My name is Badb."

"I," the sapphire pneuma floated forward to Evelyn, "am Macha."

Sara stared at her red pneuma with wonder. Like her mother, she, too, had heard many of the mysterious tales surrounding the Morrigan, the Phantom Queen—apparently queens—who at times intervened in battles to sway the outcome.

There were many different accounts throughout history and mythology regarding the Morrigan. Most scholars could not even agree on the basics, such as if the goddess was one being, three being, or one goddess with three faces. The correlating names for the goddesses were an even larger stretch. Having their pneumas clarify this academic mystery gave Sara a thrill. "Does that mean you're Nemain? Or another name?"

Her pneuma winked.

Once again, Sara was stunned at the care they took to use human gestures and contort their perfectly round facial features into patterns recognizable to her eye. *They did have a whole other lifetime of practice.* She thought back to Seraphina's tale when the original fata sisters lived as humans. *Or a few lifetimes I guess. Wait—?*

"But what about the prophecy?" Sara asked. "If you three have been reborn together once before, why didn't you fulfill it then? You must have been strong if you were the Morrigan. Why is this happening to us? That used to be so clear but now that you've introduced the idea of multiple reincarnations it's not."

Nemain smiled at Sara. "The same prophecy appeared during our first ever triplet rebirth, the lifetime in which we grew up to become the Morrigan. The difference between then and now was in the way our mother back then interpreted the prophecy. As your own mother often says, choice plays a key role in magic. Our mother at that time, also a witch, chose not to send us away as the prophecy instructed. As a result, the witches we lived inside did not become as ingrained in the wider world of humans as you have. Like many witches we spent our early days living on the edge of town, learning our mother's cunning ways until we surpassed her in skill. Our human shells and their own souls were well versed in magic already. Add in the magic we brought as pneumas living side by side with their human souls, and the witches we lived inside became powerful indeed. We performed what humans call miracles, and people sought us out. Soon enough, we became revered as goddesses. I'm sure Noro realized we were reborn at that time but he chose not to fight us."

"We had a bit of a reputation to be frightened of," Macha remarked.

Nemain, the red pneuma, nodded. "People of that time believed deeply in magic, prophecy, and fate. Hence, they believed in us. It was not as opportune a time for Noro to capture us. Not like now, when humans think little of magic. Noro has never been one to work harder than he must and no one in their right mind would have attacked the Morrigan at that point in history—not with a pack of Morrigan-worshipping Celts at their back."

"But no one even knew about us until two weeks ago," Sara murmured. "We made ourselves vulnerable to Noro by staying a secret."

Brigit hitched in a breath.

"Mom, what's wrong?" Sara asked, startled.

"This is all my fault then," Brigit croaked. "If I'd kept you with me like the Morrigan's mother did with her daughters, raised you as witches from birth, you'd never have been so vulnerable. This would never have happened to you three. Nora was right in her letter. I interpreted the prophecy wrong. My mistake cost us a lifetime away from each other and a greater chance that the fata will win."

"No freaking way!" Evelyn exclaimed. "'*Three, three, three, shall it be*,' even that points to the fact it *should* be us. I always considered it a weird ra-ra cheering thing, but no. It spelled it out, the third coming of the three would fight the fata. Not Seraphina, Eve, and Lilith when they first came to Earth. Or Badb, Macha, and Nemain, though it seems like warrior goddesses would be more qualified. It was always meant to be the third coming of the three! The third time the original sisters' pneumas walked Earth together! You were fated to take the prophecy literally, Mom. To give us our own lives, ingrain us in a larger worldwide culture, and yes, make us weaker than we should be so that Noro felt safe enough to come out and fight. Someone has to deal with this, right? We have every motivation to want to beat Noro and Dimia. We have people we love to protect, personal vendettas, a stake in this that he cultivated himself."

"Three has always been a magical number," Sara added. "And this is the perfect time in history for Noro to make his move. Barely anyone believes in magic any longer. To swoop in now, when no one has protected themselves against it, makes sense. Think of all the claimings and kidnappings that have been happening. If those people had set up wards or used protective herbs, they might still be safe."

"It's like you always say, Mom, magic is about choices. You chose to protect us and give us people all over the world to love. You created protectors of humanity," Lily said, placing a hand over Brigit's.

Brigit sniffed, looking unsure but grateful for her daughters' words.

Lily cocked her head and looked at Badb, her pneuma. "I still have one question though. How is it possible that with all the generations of humans born, you three have only been reborn at the same time twice? It seems like the math is off."

Badb nodded. "A good question. We were usually reborn in different parts of the globe. Often my sisters were worshipped as goddesses of other cultures which I would not learn about until later. The variance of the human life cycle was another factor that separated us. One would die young and go to the realm in-between deep within the earth to lie fallow while one was being born. We always recognized each other through tales but were rarely fated to be together, let alone be born as sisters or triplets. As you know, that is rare. This rebirth was our third time born as triplets on Earth. The first time was through a portal, a metaphorical rebirth on a new planet and birth of all magical beings here. The other two times were during our birth as the Morrigan and now." Badb paused and glanced at Brigit.

"But more importantly, this was the first time we were born to a mother inclined to believe the prophecy, a mother willing to see it through, and *finally* to beings willing to set us free. It all had to align, making the chances slim. When we were the Morrigan only half the stipulations were met, and as my sister explained, Noro was not willing to risk his life's work when we were already so strong."

Sara sucked in a breath. As a historian, she'd long

since realized her life was intertwined with people of the past, all part of one continuation of the cycle of life on Earth. Still, nothing she'd studied or imagined had been like this. "So, my question is how are we going to become as strong as the Morrigan and kick Noro off this planet?"

Nemain's black, round eyes met Sara's. "You've already begun."

Coming to Terms with My Life
Lily

"Here, try my new blend of burn salve," Lily said, joining her sisters in the sitting room.

Evelyn raised her eyebrows. "Are you saying yours is better than Fiona's? The student has surpassed the teacher?"

Lily blushed. "No. I just want her to try it."

Sara took the jar. "I'm sure they're both great. I'm lucky to have two healers around who can help me with the last pesky burns."

Lily nodded and gave her sister the once over. It was true, Sara didn't look as if she'd walked into a bonfire. In fact, she looked better than Evelyn, though her wounds were newer. Lily's gaze shifted to her middle sister's hips, which were finally rounding once more. She wished she knew how to accelerate Evelyn's healing. Evelyn caught her staring and Lily averted her eyes quickly.

"So, has anyone's pneuma—sorry—have Macha or Nemain returned yet? Badb is still out." *It'll take a while to get used to these weird names.*

"Why couldn't they have chosen more modern versions? Like Marj, Nina, and Beth?" Evelyn said, mirroring Lily's thoughts and rolling her eyes. "I mean, whatever, I guess I should be happy to have a name for the soul living inside me half the time, but Macha? It sounds like a tea. And no, she hasn't come back yet."

Lily chortled. It did sound like tea.

"Nemain either," Sara chimed in. "I suppose they needed sister time. It's the first instance when they've been together for centuries. Imagine that. Living in bodies, knowing your sister's soul is out there or in the realm where souls go to wait for a body. I wonder if they were always in witches' bodies or if they sometimes got stuck with a human?"

That would suck. Lily burst out laughing at the thought. Until recently, she hadn't known she was a witch; now she couldn't imagine going back to being a regular human?

"What's funny?" Sara asked.

"Oh, nothing. Just coming to terms with my life," Lily

answered dramatically. "When they spoke of souls recycling from the Earth to different people that sounded a lot like reincarnation. It's kind of all coming together, you know? Different beliefs of different cultures?"

Sara nodded. "It makes sense that their souls would create beings with exceptional talents, like the Morrigan. So many heroes and heroines of different cultures could boil down to the same three souls." Sara's face lit up. "I should get a mythology book and try to figure out who they were!"

"Or just ask the thing living inside you which god or goddess it was embodied in," Evelyn drawled. "No need to be an overachiever here Sara. We've already got enough to figure out. What's on the docket for today, anyway?"

"Seeing as Alfred"—Lily's heart clenched as she said her boyfriend's name—"Celestine, and Caleb left this morning for Paris, we're back to focusing on witch magic this morning. I think Alistair said he'd stop by to train, too. Then pneuma lessons in the afternoon."

"Thank the goddess one of those will be easy. Even if being around Alistair reminds me of Roman, I'll take dealing with that incubus any day. Sussing out incubus magic is one of the things coming easy to me now," Evelyn said.

Lily cringed at the mention of Roman's name and

caught Sara's curious glance. She was about to turn away, run into the kitchen for coffee, anything to avoid Sara questioning her and Lily having to make up a lie to cover up her knowledge of Roman, when she heard their mother coming down the hall. Her shoulders loosened.

"Morning, girls. Ready for our big day?" Brigit breezed into the kitchen-diner, her auburn hair wrapped in a towel, and headed straight for the coffee pot. "Besides their aversion to iron, we never knew much about how to kill a fata, but today that all changes! Now that Badb, Macha, and Nemain are spilling secrets we'll get answers fast."

A great conversation: By the way, how do we kill all your old friends and family from your home planet? Then again, will they even care? They seemed kind of detached from the idea of being fata after so many human reincarnations.

A side-by-side image of Noro and Badb filled her mind. One was mysterious, yet kind. The other was cold and ruthless. Lily's shoulders tightened and she bit her lip.

Goddess be, please don't let Alfred run into him.

"Are you still upset that Alfred left?" Sara asked.

Lily sighed. Though not a mind reader like Evelyn, Sara had always been perceptive to Lily's moods. And there was no doubt Sara had been awake when Lily returned to their room that morning sniffling after saying a tearful goodbye to Alfred.

She shook her head. "No, I understand his reasoning. His powers could come in useful there. If he's able to pick up vast quantities of fata energy, maybe we can study it. But it's dangerous. What if I never see him again?" Her eyes dropped with her voice and Lily felt vulnerable in a way she never had before.

Selma had never even gotten Lily to talk about guys she was crushing on, but with the McKays and her sisters, it was different. They'd been there when Lily learned her first boyfriend was a vampire. They'd seen the effect Amon had on her and witnessed Lily kill him.

"Especially since you two still haven't done it. To lose Alfred without that experience would be a tragic loss," Evelyn said.

"Evelyn! Have a little compassion!" Sara whacked Evelyn on the shoulder, though her lips turned up.

"And please, remember your mother is right here," Brigit said. "Do I need to leave the room? I'm still not ready for this part of motherhood."

Evelyn held up her hands. "Hey! The guy's hot. If his attention to detail in other areas is any indication, he's probably great in bed, too. Sorry, Mom, it's the siren in me."

Brigit rolled her eyes, but Lily was grateful that Evelyn had lightened the mood.

I can't go around feeling sorry for myself that Alfred's gone. He's an adult, he made a decision, and I have important things I need to deal with. It's not like he's going to stop me from running into battle either. He'll come back, I know he will. They all will.

No More Secrets

Sara

Sara flung herself on her bed, exhausted. *Two lessons down, one to go.*

Their pneuma had returned just after breakfast and requested they begin lessons in late afternoon, so they'd started the morning working with Alistair. As he had when they played capture the flag, the incubus had taken over Sara's body and mind with ease. Lily, well practiced in mind barriers by now, had performed marginally better, though it was Evelyn who had excelled.

According to Alistair, Evelyn had the perfect combination of powers to battle an incubus, not to mention a motive never to fall under an incubus's thrall again. Sara sighed. She wasn't nearly as competitive as her sisters, but she still loathed being the worst at things, especially activities reliant on being in touch with her body and mind. She was *supposed* to be the best at that.

The bedroom door opened and Lily shuffled in, covered in dirt and splashes of potions.

"Did Gwenn or Fiona keep you late?" Sara asked, sympathy in her voice.

As a result of poor communication, both Gwenn and Fiona had shown up for Lily's midday specialty lessons. Thus, while Sara was contentedly playing with fire, Lily had been subjected to practicing intense earth magic spells and healing spells at a frantic pace.

"What? Oh, no, I was talking to Alistair."

Though she could not see her sister, who was hidden by the long divider that ran the length of their room, something in the way Lily spoke pinged in Sara's brain. Memories from the early morning lesson she'd tried to bury resurfaced.

Lily and Brigit stiffening or twitching whenever Evelyn probed Alistair for more information on Roman, which had been often. It was clear to everyone that Evelyn wanted to make sure Roman had not made her look a fool when she was under his influence. It was only after many assurances from the incubus that Evelyn ceased her questioning. Only then had Lily and their mother relaxed. Sara sat up and leaned her back against her headboard.

"Lil?"

"Yeah?" Lily poked her head around the divider as she struggled to put on a clean pair of pants.

"Is something up? You've been acting weird whenever someone mentions Roman. You practically flinched every time Alistair mentioned his name today."

Lily paled and inched behind the divider.

Sara's eyes widened. She knew there had been something strange going on. "Lil, come on! Aren't we past the stage of keeping secrets?" Sara asked. She hated secrets, especially ones her family kept from each other, including her own. Every secret was a jab to the gut reminding Sara she still didn't fully belong, that they weren't a cohesive unit yet.

A sigh came from the other side of the divider. "You're right. I'll tell you but you have to promise to zip it until Mom says something." Lily emerged, her hands shoved deep into oversized sweatpants.

"I promise."

Lily inhaled a deep breath and spoke rapidly on her exhale. "Mom found Roman in the manor when we rescued Evelyn. He was at the Sisters of Salem house and I stumbled upon him. They're still in touch and he's working as a spy for our side." She bit her lip.

Holy crap.

"You two realize Evelyn will be pissed that you kept

this from her, right? She'll have every right to be mad and Evelyn is not above holding a grudge."

"I know!" Lily placed a hand atop her head. "Mom didn't even know I'd seen him. I only told her after I came back from hanging out with Alfred the other night. They found Roman locked in a basement room. He attempted to break Evelyn out of Peacock Manor and failed. Mom didn't think Evelyn was ready to digest the news while she was at the safe house. She was way too weak and would have wanted to rip him a new one. Mom's making one of Evelyn's favorite meals for dinner. I'm hoping that's a sign she's planning on telling Evelyn tonight."

Sara shook her head. She couldn't disagree with Brigit that Evelyn had been too weak to hear news of Roman at the New York safe house. "Let's hope so. Are you going to come clean when she does?"

"I hated keeping that secret and we're in a good place now. I have to come clean," Lily admitted.

Sara sighed. While her life with her adoptive family had been lonely and full of neglect, at least it hadn't been so complicated. "You two make it hard for me sometimes. All I wanted my whole life was a tight-knit family and every time there's a fight or secret between you guys it affects me. Aside from all the issues we're facing together, it's not like I don't have my own problems. I act all calm and peaceful most of the time, but I came here with issues, too. It's time for both of you to step up to the plate and work together while I work on myself." Sara surprised herself as the words flowed from her mouth.

Lily's eyes widened. "I didn't know you felt that way. I guess I thought you liked being in the middle? It sounds kind of dumb to say that. Who would like to be a peacekeeper all the time?" Lily sucked in a breath. "I'm sorry, Sara. I'll try not to put you in the middle anymore. If you need to talk about—whatever you need to talk about, I'm here." She paused to study Sara. "I mean seriously, though! You seem like you have your shit together!"

Sara smiled and relaxed onto the bed. A weight she'd been carrying around had been lifted from her shoulders. Finally, she could breathe and consider herself for a minute. Her past, and how it was affecting her feelings integrated into her present. How she fit in. "We all have our own junk to work through—some just do it more quietly than others, and I'm not ready to talk about it yet. I'm going to take a power nap before our next lesson, OK?" And with that Sara rolled over and closed her eyes.

How to Kill a Fata
Evelyn

"Now that we are rested and accounted for, we'll begin. Today, we cover the basics of how to defeat a fata," Badb, Lily's green pneuma, proclaimed as soon as Macha had joined them from doing huge corkscrews in the sky.

Evelyn had an inkling Macha hadn't wanted to return because of her.

I guess I did treat her like crap today, not letting her out until the last minute. Ugh, what's wrong with me? Just because I'm not in total control of myself doesn't mean I should treat her like a slave. Am I that desperate to feel empowered again?

Badb floated forward an inch, her diaphanous green form shimmering. "As you can see, my sisters and I comprise two substances: air and ether. Air keeps us grounded on this plane. Ether allows us to access the plane beyond where we may rest safely when the body we inhabit dies. In the plane beyond we live as a soul until a suitable new body comes along that we may claim. When we were whole fatas we lived as air and ether, too, but in different proportions. Regarding fata biology, they are susceptible to that which they are most familiar. Therefore, if you want to kill a fata, your best option is air magic."

Bodies shifted all around. Air magic, the magic the triplets lacked. Magic their mother and aunts lacked, too. There was even a shortage of air magic in their coven, the coven of Ilargia. It was an element they rarely trained with, preferring to stick to their strengths. Evelyn rolled her eyes. Of course it would be like this.

"That poses a problem seeing as none of us are gifted in air. Mary has the most, but I'd hardly call her an air witch," Brigit said.

Mary shook her head vehemently.

"I thought as much," Badb said with a nod. "Water witches have a greater proclivity to air than fire or earth witches. No one knows why. I have often thought it is because water comprises hydrogen and oxygen, molecules also found in air. Water witches are familiar with these molecules in their liquid state and that familiarity helps."

Macha flew forward. "It's no surprise none of you are gifted with air as most air witches were murdered early on. It is an activity which has kept Noro and the seven other fata I brought over in my first life on Earth occupied for years. They knew creatures gifted with air to be dangerous, so they sought to end them. Still, the gene has persisted, but with fewer air witches to teach the new ones, they rarely become as strong as in early days. None of you are natural air witches but you have tremendous skill and us as your teachers. My sisters and I are probably the best trainers of air on this planet, being made of the element itself."

"So, besides training with all sorts of different creatures and our specialty element lessons, we'll be taking on a whole new element?" Even with Badb's reassurances that water witches had an easier time with air, Evelyn felt exhausted at the mere thought.

"It appears so," Brigit said.

"Aren't you worried that when we learn air our magic may go astray and hit you?" Lily's voice cracked, indicating she was certainly concerned about such a mistake.

There was no other word for it, Macha smirked. "I cannot wait for the day you are strong enough to do that. My sisters and I susceptible to air, yes. However, as our body chemistries are different from that of a fata's, it takes a great deal of skill to tweak the air to become deadly enough to end us. In truth, only a fata would know how to accomplish such a feat. I believe it is—and will *remain*—

far beyond your capability." Macha's dark eyes bore into Evelyn's.

Evelyn bristled, recognizing Macha was deliberately trying to rile her up, getting back at her for earlier. Part of her wanted to accept the challenge, though she had no desire to kill any of the pneumas.

Lily, however, looked profoundly relieved.

"*However,* there is a second method to kill fata which is much easier. One that would work on a pneuma should you cut deep enough, and a technique Lily has already used." Badb's green glow intensified as she pulled the group back on track.

"Iron, while not topically lethal to fatas like it is to the fae, is still a valid means of killing fatas," Badb said. "One only need to plunge the iron deep enough into a fata to puncture its inner pneuma. Once the pneuma is destroyed, the fata as a creature will cease to exist, just like if a human soul was destroyed all that remained of the human would vanish, save the memory of them. They are analogous structures, the pneuma and the soul. One must go very deep, though, past the pneumatic membrane to the core of the fata. If you nick the membrane but do not puncture the pneuma, there's a chance the pneuma will survive, as Seraphina's did."

"So, if I had pushed the trowel in a little deeper Noro might already be gone?" Lily asked, her voice pained.

Nemain nodded. "It is the same method Noro used to kill my fata body. Luckily for me, my pneuma, that is to say my being as I am presently, escaped before he could puncture further than my pneumatic membrane. I can't be sure, but I am almost positive he transformed the most superficial layer of his arm into iron. How he did it without injuring himself, I have no idea."

"We need weapons then, like from a blacksmith. Are those even around anymore?" Evelyn furrowed her brows. "Or maybe guns? Guns are easy to get in America but what about here? Do iron bullets exist?"

"We can get guns but none of us have ever handled one. As for iron bullets, goddess only knows. Have you three handled a gun?" Aoife asked.

The triplets shook their heads.

"Well then, I don't expect we should add shooting to the long list of things to learn. Shooting a gun well, without hitting anyone on your side in battle, is harder than it looks. Especially when your opponent can fly. A trigger is easy to pull when you're scared. We don't want any mistakes," Aoife said.

"The blacksmith is not a bad idea, though," Brigit mused. "We should get fitted with iron-tipped weapons as a fallback to magic. Sharp ones to use for close-range battle as Lil did with Noro. Something like a dagger. They'll be useful against other creatures, too, and if we order enough, our supernatural kin who do not have the proper magic to kill a fata can carry the extras."

"Excellent idea, but for now, let's begin with air," Badb said. Her black eyes shifted to Evelyn. "Now, Evelyn. You've come into contact with Noro. When he touched you, what did it feel like?"

Evelyn stiffened. Yes, Noro had touched her. "Coupled" with her, as he called it, and while it had been nothing like human sex, it had been bad enough. Every time she thought about it she wanted to puke.

"That time it felt like tiny tornados brushing my skin."

Macha turned her body to face Evelyn slightly.

"But there was another time, too, when I'd first arrived. I tried to hit him with a rock, but his body flowed out of the way, like a water balloon in your hand. When he slapped me afterward, it was like a board across my face. There wasn't even a minute between the actions, but it seemed he was able to pick his consistency?"

Badb nodded. "That is typical of a fata. They can choose to be more or less solid, similar to how air can be thicker or thinner with altitude. What types of spells would you suggest using against Noro now that you know what he's made of?"

Evelyn's lips parted. She hadn't expected a pop quiz. "Is there a hurricane spell? To rip him apart?"

Sara stepped forward, her face flushed with excitement. "Is it possible to mold air into other weapons? Like a knife so you could puncture the fata's skin? Mimicking the trowel Lily used but made with magic?"

Nemain smiled and floated toward Sara. "Molding it into weapons takes great finesse but it is one of the most foolproof ways of killing a fata. Individual molecules of air are invisible to fata, though they can see variations in thickness when air moves together—a gust of wind, for instance. Witches can see this, too, though the air must be much tighter. If the air is pulled together tight enough, as it would be to mimic an item, it will appear hazy to a witch's eye."

Badb nodded. "A hurricane may work as well, Evelyn, though I don't see any of you trying that soon. To manipulate air on that level would be exceedingly taxing."

Evelyn wracked her brain, desperate to come up with a brilliant air idea.

"Could you knock it out with a wall of air?" Lily asked. "I met a witch at Peacock Manor who could knock people out with the sound waves of her scream. Is that possible?"

"That," Badb did a strange little jig, "is what we are working on today! It is a beginner's air spell as it does not take much fine-tuning. Today you shall start with building and moving a wall of compressed air across this field.

Eventually, you'll be able to trap a fata with air, then crush it against the ground."

Evelyn became aware of her nails digging into her palms and loosened her grip.

Whatever, let them come up with the brilliant ideas. It's execution that matters and I refuse to fall short at that. Not when it can save my life.

EVELYN COLLAPSED on the ground an hour later, completely spent.

"Try again," Macha instructed, her sapphire color dark and demanding.

A groan escaped Evelyn. *Payback is a bitch.* "Fine. I'll try one more time, but after that I need food. A large glass of wine, too. My body feels like it may break at any second."

For the first time since the start of their lesson, Macha's eyes met Evelyn's. "I can see you are not exaggerating. Your body is running low on nutrient reserves and your magic is near the point of exhaustion."

"You can see when I need to eat and how low my magic is? That's an unfair advantage."

"I did live inside you for twenty-one years." Her tone

indicated she still hadn't forgiven Evelyn for keeping her captive all morning.

Evelyn bit her lip. "You know, I am sorry about not letting you out. I'm having issues with not controlling my body. I mean look at me." She pulled up her shirt and pointed at her protruding hip bone. "I've just started gaining weight back. Being out of control is not something I'm used to. I promise as long as I'm awake, I'll let you out whenever you want from now on."

"You have no power over whether I stay or leave in your sleep anyhow. That power applies only when you are conscious," Macha replied, her tone haughty.

Evelyn quirked her eyebrow.

The blue of Macha's face deepened, and she flew to Evelyn's side. "It appears we both have things to learn about the other. I, too, dislike not being in control. I was once revered as a goddess. Now I am to live inside a mortal being for half my life? Can you imagine that?"

"I never considered it," Evelyn mumbled.

"Nor had I considered how you would feel sharing your body. In the past, people were honored to share their body with me." Macha did a convincing impression of a human sigh. "We will need to work on meeting each other halfway."

"Yes, we will." Evelyn offered her pneuma a small

smile and rose off the damp grass, glancing around at the group as she did.

So far, only Mary had created a single wall of air. She was now working on whipping up two and sweat poured off her cherubic cheeks with the effort. Lily had managed a few smaller tornados and Sara a gust of wind. Neither of which, according to Badb, would be useful in fighting a fata. Evelyn's competitive streak flared. Except for their incubus lesson, she'd been the weakest triplet for weeks and she was over it. She wanted to be best at something, dammit.

"You are close. I can feel it. Remember," Macha said, floating closer to Evelyn, "you have an advantage here as a water witch. Start with visualizing the molecules of air in front of you. Then envision them coming closer together. Do this as you invoke the spell. In fact, don't use the spell for a wall of air, break it down into two. Pull the air particles closer to each other and then ask them to build a wall. Breaking it down is slower, but you will get the feel of air better."

"The spell I've been trying won't work without the visualization and a precursor?" Evelyn asked.

Macha shook her head. "It will, eventually, but none of you are skilled at air yet. Badb called the homaire charm a starter spell, and it is, for an air witch. As a water witch, you will have to work harder. Your sisters harder still. Visualizing your intention will help you bond to the air."

Magic is all about intention and choice.

How often had Evelyn heard Brigit say those words? *Too often, and it seems they still haven't sunk in.*

She closed her eyes and took a deep breath, paying extra close attention to the fresh, chilly air flowing in and out of her lungs. Trying to picture a thousand particles dipping in and out of her body. Then she moved outward, to ten feet in front of her and imagined dots of all different sizes flying about. As she pictured the dots in her mind's eye, a sense of control bloomed within her, a certainty that she could manipulate them. Evelyn opened her eyes and while the dots were not there, she felt them as though they were.

"Good, now pull them closer together," Macha whispered.

She knew the spell, having done it once before when she formed a tiny ball of air to use as a distribution method for calling Macha back to her from Hecate. Sure, this was more air than she'd ever worked with, but Evelyn understood the concept was the same.

"Elkartaire," Evelyn said. The air *thickened* into a haze before her eyes. She gasped. It held no shape and moved sporadically, but it was a start.

"I take it that means you can see it? That's a sign it's

ready. Now, envision the air spreading and straightening into a rigid brick wall, a form you can actually use. Only when you see it in your mind's eye should you use the second spell."

Evelyn's sapphire eyes widened as she zeroed in on the thick layer of air before her, smoothing and transmuting the amorphous shape into a brick wall in her mind.

"Homaire." Evelyn whispered the spell Badb had taught them, and suddenly the air shot into place creating the wall she envisioned.

I freaking did it! Her concentration faltered, and a hole formed in the wall.

"Concentrate!" Macha demanded. "Now, if you want to impress your family," she glanced at the rest of the witches, none of whom had noticed Evelyn's victory, "you will move this toward them."

Evelyn smiled a wicked smile. A feat which minutes ago seemed impossible now felt simple. "Watch this."

She held her hand out before her. "Motus," her magic connected with the wall, creating a magical joystick. "I'm coming for you," Evelyn whispered and shot the wall of air straight at Sara.

"Another spoonful, please," Evelyn said.

Brigit ladled more savory stew into Evelyn's bowl with a smile. "Someone worked hard today. I'm pleased your appetite is up, makes me think you're healing faster." She chuckled. "Also lets me know my cooking isn't as bad as Mary suggests."

"Not bad, Brig, though you could do with broadening your horizons. How 'bout I show you how to make a nice curry one day?" Mary said, her eyes alive with hope.

"I don't fancy my bedsheets smelling of curry." Brigit wrinkled her nose. "We'll have to get our fix when we go to the city."

"Because that happens so often," Mary muttered.

Evelyn barely heard the sisterly banter, transfixed as she was on her mother's single comment about her health. *I was the only one to move a compressed wall of air all the way across the field and I'm still a weakling? When are they ever going to think me strong enough?*

She shoved a spoonful of stew into her mouth and sighed. It was no Michelin three-star restaurant, but Evelyn had to admit, her mother made a damn good stew.

Evelyn blinked as Lily, who'd already inhaled her bowl, stood and went back for seconds. She watched her sister's lean muscles contract as she moved to the pot and ladled four more spoonfuls of stew into her bowl.

Evelyn glared down at her food.

No one ever doubts Lily or Sara and I'm far more robust. Well, usually I am.

She glanced back up and saw Brigit had joined Lily and they were whispering.

Are they talking about me?

Self-consciousness got the better of her and Evelyn decided it was time to tell her family their tiptoeing around her weakened state was bugging her. She couldn't live this way anymore.

"Hey, Lil. Mom. Can we talk?"

Lily jumped away from Brigit, a guilty look on her face

"Uh, sure," Lily said, shooting a covert look at Brigit.

"I want to get something off my chest," Evelyn said.

Sara and Lily bit their lips and Brigit sighed. "Funny you should say that, Evelyn. I have something I need to tell you, too."

Evelyn's blood froze. *Are my parents safe? Were they taken? Or claimed? Oh, crap. What if they hurt Vici?*

She sat up straighter, trying to regain control of the emotions and thoughts running through her. "You go first. Is it my parents or Vici? Are they safe?"

Brigit's mouth fell open. "Nothing like that! Something else I've been meaning to tell you. Try to think of what I'm about to say in terms of strategy. The Acolytes have spies, well-placed ones. We thought it best if we had a spy, too."

Evelyn cocked her head.

Brigit continued. "We found Roman locked in the basement of Peacock Manor. He was weak, bitten all over by vampires, and had another man with him. The person who found them thought they were both hostages. We brought Roman back to the Sisters of Salem safe house and he recuperated. I found out who he really was there. I told him he had two choices: be turned in to the Supernatural Union or join us as a spy. He chose the latter. He—"

Evelyn interrupted. "You're telling me Roman was in the same house as me . . . a few doors down for a whole week and no one told me?" Her voice was hard, cold, demanding of an answer.

"We wanted to, Evelyn, but you—"

Evelyn cut Lily off. "You knew?"

"I—I stumbled across him when we were there. A day before we drank your blood." Lily's voice shook as she spoke.

Evelyn's head swiveled to Sara. "Did you know?"

Sara shook her head. "Not until last night."

She turned back to Lily, who was now pressing her lips together so hard they'd turned white.

"Why didn't you tell me? After all we've been

through? Were you still trying to get back at me for not returning to Fern Cottage right away?"

"No!" Lily choked out. "I wanted to tell you, but like Mom said, you looked so sick and had been through so much, I didn't want to hurt you more. You could barely sit up, let alone take your anger out on Roman. Plus, after I talked to him I wasn't sure what to do. "

"You *talked* to him?" Evelyn roared. "The man who betrayed me. The one who stood there while Noro tortured me? What on earth could Roman have to say that would necessitate you sitting there and having a nice chat with him?"

"Evelyn, please," Brigit's brown eyes were pleading. "If you want to blame someone, blame me. Your sister stumbled across him, helped him out for a minute, and left. She's been conflicted about finding Roman this whole time. It should be me you're mad at. I decided not to send Roman to the Supernatural Union. I questioned him and recruited him for our side. And I'm the one who's been receiving his intel this whole time."

Evelyn shot up from her seat. "So Roman is free and talking to my mother when he gets the chance. I can't believe this." Water shot out of the sink as her anger skyrocketed,

Mary flicked a hand to turn it off.

Evelyn had forgotten her aunts were there, but now

her eyes roved over them. They looked guilty. Of course they knew. Her mother would never keep something like this from her beloved sisters. If only Evelyn could say the same for her sisters.

You mean the sisters who risked their lives for you? a voice said in the back of her head. She deflated a bit. Fine, there was that. And yes, a spy for their side could be useful. Nora proved that much.

Still, I'm so fucking tired of being treated like I can't handle things.

"I hate hearing this. It's like you can't trust me." Evelyn shot her hand out as Lily opened her mouth. "I know that's not true, but it's how I feel. I'm also over being treated like I could break at any minute. You guys have to let me in on things. Let me practice and fight as hard as Lily and Sara. Otherwise, what use am I? I refuse to be the weak link in our chain."

Evelyn sucked in a breath. "Sara must be rubbing off on me because this would never have happened so fast before, but I forgive you for keeping this from me. Having a spy is to our benefit. But *no more* secrets or lies. I'm going to my room. I'll see you in the morning." She picked up her stew and pushed back her chair to leave.

Evelyn was halfway around the hearth when she stopped. "One more thing: I want to see Roman as soon as possible."

Worrywart

Lily

Lily rustled the paper she'd been skimming and sighed.

Sara lowered her newspaper. "If you don't want to help, you don't have to."

"It's not that," Lily said, giving up and setting the journal down. It contained an article on a dying Paris suburb near the Vincennes Woods. The handful of residents still living there seemed to have given up on their tiny town and evacuated without a word or forwarding address. No one knew where they'd gone.

Sara claimed it smelled of fata interference, but Lily wasn't sure. Maybe they'd grown tired of seeing their once vibrant town decay around them? Stranger things had happened, like Evelyn's reaction the night before. Or her boyfriend texting her that morning to say he was venturing into a zoo built to cage humans back in the day and searching for aliens. That about took the cake.

I wish he took his phone with him. What are the chances that fata are sensitive to electronics?

"What is it then?"

Lily blinked. "What?"

"Why are you acting so dramatic this morning?"

"Oh. Do you think she forgave us?"

"She said she did," Sara answered.

"Yeah, but do you think she really did? Four months ago Evelyn would hold a grudge against me if I simply did a spell better than her. This time I hid something *huge* from her. I deserve for her to be mad at me." Lily understood why Sara was so calm. She'd only known the secret of Roman's existence for a few hours.

She's not to blame like Mom and I are.

"You're right. You would deserve it," Evelyn said sweeping into the room.

Lily stiffened. She'd been so in her head she hadn't even heard her sister coming.

"To be clear, yes, I forgive you for reals. Let's be honest, I can't afford to be mad at any of you. It's a waste of energy, and like I said last night, I'm trying hard not to be the sucky one. So, if you still feel the need to make it up to me, you can do so by helping me strengthen my magic."

More sparring? Is she serious? That's the last thing I want to do. Lily's muscles groaned, and her bones popped as if in agreement.

"You want to add another round of lessons?" Lily asked. "And you want me to help you? I mean, it's not like I'm the best fighter here." She hoped she was misunderstanding Evelyn.

"That's exactly why I need your help." Evelyn approached the table and took a seat across from Lily as if they were in negotiations. "Why would I ask Sara first? I'll start with you, learn the sneaky moves you've thought up to make up for your lack of fire and unwillingness to kill. When I've learned all I can, I'll ask Sara. Then, Mary, Gwenn, and Mom. I'll ask Aoife last, seeing as she's my elemental opposite and the best fighter of the group. If I can best Aoife, then I'll ask a pneuma to fight me. I wonder which one is the best fighter?"

Lily tried not to be offended that Evelyn had placed her on the bottom of the fighting totem pole. *She's not wrong. I've always preferred healing to fighting.* She switched tack. "What about running out of steam? Aren't you worried you'll deplete your power before our pneuma lessons?"

Evelyn waved her hand. "Nah. As long as Alistair is the only one here, our morning lessons will be with him. If there's one thing I've got down, it's throwing off an incubus's thrall. For me, it's more like I have two lessons a day."

So, it's me who will be exhausted. Well, I guess I deserve that.

"Fine. We'll have to practice before Alistair comes by, though. There's no time in the schedule otherwise. That means getting up early." Lily raised her eyebrows. Of the triplets, Evelyn was the last out of bed every day.

"Done," Evelyn leaned back in her chair. "Do either of you know if Mom called Roman last night? I was serious when I said I wanted to see him. If there's anyone I want to be mad at, it's him." Her lips tightened.

Sara shrugged. "She turned her phone on and texted someone but didn't tell us who it was."

"I'll ask her when I see her then."

Lily shook her head. Evelyn was on the warpath to get shit done today.

"What about Alfred and the rest of the scouting team? Has anyone heard from them?" Evelyn's sapphire eyes pivoted to Lily.

A long sigh escaped Lily's lips. She supposed it was inevitable she'd be thinking about Alfred all day. Her fingers twitching to look at her phone, waiting for his call, his voice, reassuring her that he was safe and sound.

"I got a text early this morning, saying they'd be out for the day with the scouting team. They're not taking phones with them in case a fata can sense it. The human zoo area is warded. A wizard from a Paris coven told Alfred he doubted anyone had been by there in weeks because of how the wards were set."

"He'll be fine, Lil," Sara said, grasping Lily's hand before biting her lip, clearly conflicted. "I guess there's really no good time to share this. Look what I found." Sara lowered the paper she'd been reading to the table and pointed at an article.

A moment of silence fell over the room as they read the article. With each word, Lily's heart sank further. A bridge had collapsed under mysterious circumstances, this time in Florida, killing ninety people.

"So, after a couple days of rest, the fata are on the move again," Evelyn said her lips pursed. "I believe Noro could go that far but the rest of them? No way. They were so weak looking when my pneuma saw them on Hecate."

"I agree. I still think this, and all the rest of the destruction we've read about, is the work of the seven other fata who have been here for years. It's in their best interest to continue wreaking havoc everywhere while the new fata accumulate power. Otherwise, no one will fear them when they emerge and claim responsibility."

Lily's stomach sank. Sara was right. Her mind whirled.

We can't be everywhere at once. Hell, at this point we

wouldn't stand a chance against the strong fata anyhow. Goddess be, I hope we can get up to speed fast.

204

New Year's Day
Sara

Beams of light peeked through the curtains of her room as Sara rose from her meditation. She changed quickly, shivering in the cold morning air. A peek around the divider to the other side of the room confirmed Lily was making good on her word and had risen early with Evelyn to get in an extra round of sparring.

Last night Sara hadn't been so sure her sisters' early morning practice would happen. Not with the amount of wine Lily had downed between trying to have a good time and glancing at her phone to see if Alfred had made contact. An uneasy sensation settled in Sara's stomach. *I hope Alfred calls—anyone calls—today. We should have received word by now.*

The scouting team had been out of touch for three full days. It was a length of time Sara would have found relatively short for someone to worry about a person, especially one she didn't live with, in the past.

Back then she would have claimed the person needed space, that three days was nothing—the same excuses her adoptive family used when Sara left for college and found her connection to them trickle to practically nonexistent. All things she had learned to say to keep others at arm's length over the years.

But they know we're waiting to hear from them. They must have camped out in the park. Scouted more.

She walked into the sitting room. Judging by the cold hearth, Brigit was still asleep.

"Flampila." Sara produced a ball of flame in her hand and rolled it into the hearth, then threw a handful of kindling at the flames to feed them. They caught and began dancing, warming her face and chasing the winter chill from Sara's body.

She strode around the hearth into the kitchen. No papers sat on the table yet, which wasn't surprising considering how late her mother and aunts had stayed up last night. Mary and Gwenn's shrill laughter was still ringing through the cottage at three in the morning.

There was no coffee in the pot, so Sara set about making it, savoring the quiet ritual. The cottage was overflowing with the aroma of freshly brewed coffee when the front door creaked open. Lily and Evelyn ran in, rubbing their hands together.

"You're back early. Usually, you train for another hour." Her eyes widened as Lily waved and ran down the hallway without another word. A second later, the bathroom door closed.

"It's so cold out there I swear I thought my ass froze off for a minute. I had to turn around to check it was still there." Evelyn rushed to the fire and presented her backside to it. "Lil puked and wanted to brush her teeth. I doubt she comes back out for a few hours. She needs sleep."

"Dang, that stinks," Sara said pouring Evelyn a cup of black coffee and handing it to her.

Evelyn shrugged. "New Year's Day ritual if I ever heard of one. This is the first New Year's Day I've woken up feeling good in a while. I could get used to it. What are you doing?"

"Puttering around. Thinking."

Evelyn nodded knowingly. "They should be back, shouldn't they? Not hearing from Alfred may be more the reason why Lily's sick, though the wine didn't help, I'm sure. She even brought her phone out to spar. Left it lying on the grass screen up. It looked like she had a twitch with the number of times she looked at it."

"Almost makes me wish we had morning lessons

today. Not that I enjoyed being at the mercy of an old man's spell, but it would keep our mind off things."

Evelyn smirked. "Stop being so dramatic. You got better. Remember, Alistair said he and Roman," her lips tightened, "are the strongest incubi he knows of. You should be fine if you come across a weaker one."

"I suppose so," Sara said. It rankled that she was no longer the best at everything. Lessons with Alistair had gotten marginally better the more Sara practiced, but her air magic hadn't progressed at all. Evelyn, on the other hand, excelled at both subsets of magic. While Sara told herself she wasn't jealous, she would give a lot to be in the same boat as her sister.

"If you want to try again, I'm sure Roman will put you in his thrall whenever he shows up," Evelyn said in a forced, casual tone.

"Has Mom mentioned when he's coming?" Sara asked. There was no way they were getting out of talking about Roman now. Sara had a sneaking suspicion the upcoming reunion between Roman and Evelyn had sparked a maniacal magical fervor in Evelyn. She didn't want Roman to see her as weak.

"Not a date, but soon. Mom says he had to stay for some New Year's Day event the Acolytes were having. I hope he comes before the scouting team. I don't want any more of an audience than necessary when I give him a piece of my mind. I've already considered a few—non-injurious—spells I'll use on him. Enough to scare him a little but not leave a mark for when he returns to spy."

Sara shook her head. *Maybe there's a teensy bit more to it than not appearing weak.*

The cottage door opened.

"Morning, girls." Mary entered the kitchen-diner, filling the small space with her fresh scent. Her arms were laden with newspapers.

Sara thought she looked tired but not bad considering the amount of wine consumed last night.

"Morning, Mary. Thanks for bringing those by. I wasn't expecting any of you for a few hours," Sara said as Mary tossed the papers on the table.

"Aye, Aoife and Gwenn will have a lie in but I'm here to wake your mother up. Today is the start of the new year. We have plant collecting to do in the forest. Fiona's already trudged out there. The number of wild weeds and herbs earth witches like to gather on New Year's Day is bloody mental." Her finger floated in a circle around her ear for emphasis. "So, they asked for my help. Plus, they knew I'd be able to function. Aoife and Gwenn always refuse it, but I drink Fiona's hangover potion no matter how foul it tastes. That and I built up a tolerance in me younger years."

"Wait! You're telling me there's a potion to cure hangovers! Why don't witches sell this? They could make millions!" Evelyn's eyes threatened to bulge out of her head.

Sara smirked at Evelyn's business savvy, even in this new world of hers. "You'll have to tell us some of your stories one day, Mary." She loved hearing her mother's and aunts' stories, but Mary's stories were by far the most entertaining.

Mary chuckled. "When you're older."

"Deal." Sara sat down at the table and dove into what had become her morning routine—hunting for fata in the pages of world papers.

SARA DRAGGED herself away from the hearth and into the wind and howling rain. She shivered. Her body and magic were flagging. Aoife had been too hungover to mentor her, so Sara spent New Year's Day working with Mary, Evelyn, and water, her elemental opposite. Working with water for too long always left Sara bogged down as if she were drowning. With fire it was different. With fire in her hand, she was fully alive.

I should play with fire a little before our pneuma lessons to get the juices flowing.

Nemain shimmied up and down inside Sara. She

grinned at the sensation and opened her palm. A fireball flamed to life inside it, warming her hand and heart. *Ahh, that's better, but more would be nice.*

"Flamarba," Sara said and a flame gate rose around her from the damp grass.

Nemain fluttered wildly.

"Geez, fine. Caeliter."

Nemain burst out of Sara's chest and flew into the fire, her diaphanous, red body blending into the orange dancing flames. After a couple spins around the flame gate she flew out, toward Sara, her black hole of a mouth spread into something resembling a human smile. The sheer happiness her pneuma exhibited pried a grin from Sara.

Suddenly, shouting from far in the field met Sara's ears. She turned to see Fiona, Brigit, Mary, Evelyn, and Lily waving to get her attention. Macha and Badb shimmered nearby.

"Time to go, Nemain," Sara said, letting her flame gate drop and sizzle on the wet grass below. She regretted its absence immediately.

Sara ran as fast as she could to the shelter of the large shield her mother, Fiona, and Mary had become adept at creating for their lessons. Despite the cold of the season, air lessons were held outside. Fern Cottage was too small for ever-growing compression walls of air and flying air spears.

Predictably only the two water witches of the group, Mary and Evelyn, had managed to create a wall that appeased Badb, the pneuma slave driver of the Morrigan trio. Now, they were creating two walls at once, while everyone else still struggled to materialize one.

In an effort to improve her air magic, Sara had even consulted the McKay grimoire only to find there hadn't been an air witch in the family for over three hundred years—Florence Newton, whose ghost they had met on Samhain, being the last one. Florence's spells were as difficult as the Morrigan's spells. In the end, Sara decided only to work on what their pneumas wanted them to learn and focus the rest of her energy on bettering her battle skills.

"Hey," Sara said to the crowd as she rushed below the shield, Nemain joining them only a second later, a red blur in a gray Irish day. Sara's eyes darted to Lily, who looked loads better than that morning, though still pale. "Feeling better, Lil?"

Lily nodded. "Fiona gave me a bunch of herbs to eat. They helped a little. Next time though, I'm preparing that damn potion I learned about today. I never want to go through a day like this again." Her eyes shot to Fiona, who shrugged.

"I offered the elixir to everyone. Not my problem if you all were too far gone to listen."

"When did Badb return?" Sara asked.

"Thirty minutes ago," Lily whispered. "She's a little testy that I got drunk last night. Said there was no way she would return to a temple so defiled. I'm avoiding her as best I can."

"A good idea," Nemain agreed and flew to join Macha, who hovered on her own while Badb circled the shield, checking its efficacy.

Badb circled back and Sara swore she looked different from the day before. Tired. *I guess they really need their recuperation time inside us.*

"As none of you can use air walls well enough to kill a fata, that is what we will work on once again. If by some miracle someone manages a perfect wall, they will move ahead to creating a weapon out of air. My sisters and I will instruct as you practice. Begin." Badb floated off, away from Lily.

Sara turned and quirked a brow at Lily. "No pep talk today. That's different."

"I know." Lily's green eyes followed Badb. She bit her lip. "I guess everyone needs their sleep. Goes to show what we do affects them a lot."

"Yeah. Well, see you after lessons. Good luck." Sara walked away to claim a spot. Once there she widened her feet and bent her knees in a natural fighting stance. Her magic sparked inside her, begging to be released as fire once again, and she sighed, wishing she could give in to the flames. *Not right now.* The fire calmed down, though it still simmered in her blood, ready to be called on should air fail her.

"Homaire," Sara said half-heartedly, not expecting much more than a constriction of the air before her. Something too vague to be called a wall, and too obvious to be nothing. A half spell as all her others had been.

Instead, her breath hitched in her chest as a small wall, thin and bending in the middle, formed before her. Sara walked forward to touch it. Aching to touch the air she'd called, to finger its pliable form and prove to herself *something,* no matter how subpar it was, had actually happened. Her fingers trembled, an inch away, when an earth-shattering scream ripped through the evening air.

They're Strong

Sara

Sara whirled to see Lily, a blur of black leggings and flapping red jacket, sprinting toward the orchard. Her eyes tracked Lily's trajectory, latching onto a blonde figure walking through the trees, carrying a man with raven dark hair.

Celestine and Alfred!

Sara set off toward the duo. By the time she got there, Lily was already running her healer's hands over Alfred.

The daemon's cheeks were collapsed in and slashes ran across his high cheekbones. One leg dangled as if too painful to move. He smelled foul, unwashed and dirty. Worst of all, bloodstains had seeped through his shirt, telling of the destruction below.

What the hell happened? How did they get across the borders looking like that? She peered into the trees behind them but did not see their companions, Caleb and Eros. Sara's stomach tangled into knots.

"Lil, we need to get him inside to assess his injuries. Lessons are over!" Fiona called back to the pneumas, who unlike the witches had not rushed over.

Sara tried not to judge their pneumas' absence. They had been the Morrigan in another life and had probably seen many men like this, or worse.

"Mary, run ahead with me so we can prepare a cot for Alfred." The next instant Mary and Fiona were off, sprinting toward Fern Cottage.

"What happened?" Lily's voice was edging on hysteria.

"The fata," Alfred said. It was clear speech was uncomfortable for him. "They're strong already. Much stronger than we thought."

Sara's jaw tightened. *A fata did this? Not a crony?*

"Let him lie down first, Lil." Brigit peered into the woods behind the daemon and vampire as if she, too, were looking for Caleb and Eros, before shooing everyone toward the cottage.

"Careful when you lie him down," Fiona instructed. "His ribs may be broken."

"Undoubtedly." Celestine waved Lily to the side and lowered Alfred on the cot.

Fiona knelt with her knees on a cushion.

"May I cut off your shirt?" She held up a pair of scissors.

Alfred shrugged and his eyes narrowed in pain. "Not like I'll be able to wear it again."

Fiona grabbed a handful of the bloodstained shirt and pulled the fabric up. Sara shuddered at the sound of dried blood ripping off Alfred's skin, but Fiona didn't even blink and proceeded to cut the shirt down the middle and pull each half to the side. Slashes—some deep, some shallow— marred Alfred's creamy brown skin.

"Looks as though you received lacerations on your sides and back," Fiona murmured, her face inches from Alfred's skin. She wrinkled her nose. "Most aren't deep but there are a few concerning ones. And something smells funny. May I lift you up?"

"Celestine carried me for miles. Nothing can be worse than that."

Lily placed her hands on Alfred's side, waiting for Fiona's instructions on when to lift.

"Not like that. I know Celestine was as gentle as she could be but some of his wounds look nasty. Notice the faint blue tinge around them? That's not natural, and I'd rather not touch them for risk of further contamination. Step back," Fiona instructed, and Lily removed her hands.

"Volavari," Fiona said.

Alfred rose a half foot off his cot.

"When you use a levitation charm for healing, you must be gentler with it than when in battle or normal everyday use. Visualize your magic going through a hose. Kink the hose down before you perform the spell, slowing its flow, so the patient doesn't soar into the ceiling." Fiona scooted closer to examine the bluish liquid oozing from Alfred's wounds.

"Bratu."

Alfred rotated at Fiona's command, enabling her to get a better look at the wounds that ran along his side, without touching him.

"I'm like a pig on a spit," Alfred joked.

No one laughed. They were too entranced by the blue pus seeping from the gashes running the length of his side. Lily's hand flew to her mouth; her green eyes were wide and brimming with tears.

It's a wonder he's not unconscious. Sara shook her head, taking in the carnage and swallowing repeatedly to keep her lunch down.

"It was a fata," Celestine said from where she stood in the back of the circle with the pneumas.

"I figured as much." Fiona lowered Alfred back to the cot. "I've never seen wounds like this. It's why I'm hesitant to touch him. Did the fata transform its limbs into blades as Noro did in Hypatia's book?"

Celestine nodded. "I was fighting off another. Unfortunately, not being a witch and being unarmed meant I was running from it uselessly." Her lips flattened at the memory of being unable to fight off an enemy. "I saw Alfred fighting with all his might. He was trying to get away in one piece while the creature slashed at him. He fell, and the fata loomed over him to deal a final blow just as I broke loose of my adversary. I scooped him up and rushed through the park. The fata did not follow, thank God for that." Celestine crossed her chest in the Catholic manner.

"Thank you for saving him," Lily choked out.

Fiona nodded. "Will someone hand me my healer's bag?"

Brigit rushed to the entryway where Fiona kept her healer's supplies for times such as these.

"Thank you," she said as Brigit handed her the large leather bag. "Now, if you lot don't mind, Lil and I appear to be in for a night of experimental healing. I'll call if we need anything, but for now, what we need most is space."

<hr>

RASPBERRY TEA STREAMED from the pot. Water and brown bread were shuttled to the healer's corner before the rest of the group convened in the kitchen-diner.

Brigit took her seat as a cry of pain flew across the

sitting room. She winced. "Let's be as quiet as we can. No one needs the extra stress right now. Thank you for bringing Alfred, Celestine. If anyone can heal him, it's Fiona and Lil. Now, where are Caleb and Eros?"

Sara's heart rate quickened as the vampire's eyes closed. When she opened them pink ringed the outskirts of her bright blue eyes.

"Caleb is dead. He didn't transform into a wolf fast enough and they came upon us so quickly." Celestine wiped her eyes, coloring the back of her pale hand pink. "Eros pulled his body away into a thicket of trees, but we had to leave him there while we fought. Eros and I went back later and found his body. Someone had manhandled him further. Eros is trying to find a way to get Caleb back to New York, to his family, without human intervention. It is proving difficult to transport a body that far. Smaller planes, like the one Alfred and I took, ask fewer questions for the right price but they won't risk a longer flight."

Everyone around the table was quiet, but not surprised. They had all expected something of the sort when Celestine and Alfred appeared alone. A hot tear fell down Sara's cheek. Caleb's quick grin and habit of walking around half transformed for laughs ran through her mind. *He's not the first to fall, nor will he be the last, but dammit, I'll miss him.*

"I'll call my father," Evelyn's voice cracked as she said

the words. "He'll send his jet. Caleb helped save me. My dad will do anything in his power to get Caleb's body to his family."

"Thank you," Celestine inclined her head. "I'll relay that message to Eros."

"Can you tell us what you saw? Clearly, things are worse than we thought," Mary said, her eyes puffy from crying.

Celestine nodded. "Much worse. We spied on the zoo for almost an hour before they spotted us. I'll admit, staying hidden was a feat. The fata were flying overhead every few minutes. We saw them playing with their magic, testing it. They had strong wards up and weren't concerned about attracting the attention of humans. They're not as weak as we believed. Most appeared strong, perhaps not as strong as Evelyn claims Noro is, or even as strong as one of you, but *not* weak."

The vampire drew in a shuddering breath. "I'm afraid, we've underestimated them. The ones who fought us were few in number, only six or so, and they were stronger still. I believe they were of the original seven Eve brought over. Their power seemed to flow from them effortlessly. If the rest are like those seven anytime soon, we are in trouble."

"How many were there?" Brigit asked.

"I'd guess there were fifty total," Celestine said and

glanced at Evelyn. "It seems you may have brought over more fata than you thought. It's understandable, seeing as you were in no condition to count them as they traveled through space to here."

Evelyn's mouth fell open. "Th—that's possible."

"There's one more thing you should know," Celestine said, her voice grave. "There were humans there. About one hundred as far as I could tell. I suspect they are some of the claimed. They looked slow, sluggish, as they often look after a vampire has taken too much blood. They walked around the zoo in a daze."

"The suburb that disappeared," Sara breathed. "I bet it's those people."

"We have to do something about this. We can't let the fata hold people hostage," Mary said.

"I agree. We could mobilize an army like we did at Peacock Manor. It will take longer as we'll need far more people, but we could do it," Brigit said.

"I'd advise against that," Macha said. It was the first time any of the pneumas had spoken since seeing Alfred's wounds. "In fact, I would like to go first and scout once more. Unlike Celestine's group, I can make myself invisible so the fata will not know I am there. I can spy on them for a time and report back with how they are progressing. Remember, this is a new species on your planet and every fata's magic develops differently. We will need to know their strengths before you take a full army in."

"But—" Evelyn looked taken aback. "What about our lessons? And you being out of my body for so long? Won't you like . . . die?"

Macha's stance, hard and business-like, softened. "My sisters will stay to continue your lessons. There is no point in everyone going when you have much to learn. I will have to inhabit animals as I go to survive, but it will be worth it to gather information. I have sins to atone for still. This is my task."

"You have atoned for your sins, sister. If you had not, we would not be together," Badb said the words as though she'd repeated them many times.

"It is nice you believe that, sister. If only I did."

Therapy
Evelyn

When Evelyn awoke the next morning, she was not alone.

Macha fluttered in her chest, reassuring her. Her pneuma had stayed with Evelyn last night rather than go exploring with her sisters as was often the pneumas' prerogative. She would need all the energy she could collect from Evelyn's body if she were to survive the trip to Paris and not dissolve into the ether.

Was this really the best way to keep informed of what was going on? Why wasn't sending another scouting team better? Preferably, one that didn't need to worry about inhabiting animals to store up energy. One she wasn't bonded to.

An image of Caleb's smiling face flashed in her eyes.

Evelyn pulled the thick comforter closer. *Then again, maybe Macha going is for the best. Can she get injured?*

Evelyn bit her lip. *Is she offering to go to get away from me? I thought I was getting better at not controlling her.*

A hammer struck the inside of Evelyn's sternum and her hand flew to her heart.

Shit, that hurt!

"Caeliter," she murmured and the sapphire pneuma flew out of her mouth with her breath.

Macha did a couple circles around Evelyn's single bedroom as if working out the kinks in her airy body before landing, human-like, on the bed. "Good morning."

"Morning."

"You are uneasy with my decision to spy. Worry not, Evelyn. I am a being nearly as old as human life on this planet. The worst that can happen is I dissolve into the ether. It would be nothing compared to what you went through."

"I guess I don't understand why it has to be you? You were a goddess once—why can't you delegate someone to go for you? Aren't there a few souls from your past who would be happy to go if you asked?" Evelyn was aware she was grasping at straws with that last one.

Macha opened her mouth wide and released an airy laugh.

Evelyn's brows furrowed. She hadn't known pneumas

could laugh. Aside from when she'd needed Macha at Peacock Manor, she'd kept the ethereal being at arm's length, interacting only during lessons, weirded out and fascinated with Macha all at the same time. It was like the start of Evelyn's relationship with Lily all over again.

Why do I do that with those I need to be close with, but can bullshit network with anyone? But Lil and I got there, which means Macha and I could, too, if she would stay.

Macha's bout of the giggles ended and she looked at Evelyn with soft, black eyes. "To start, I never ceased existing as the Morrigan. I simply dove back into the earth after my body died and waited for a new one. Thus, I am still technically a goddess and that is why I must do these things alone. When you are at the top, you cannot delegate your most difficult tasks to anyone but yourself. Think of your father."

Her father's slate gray eyes and slim, wolf-like stature flashed in Evelyn's mind. Memories of James staying up all night at the office, going through page after page of boring legal briefings to protect those who worked for him, denying board members and close family friends personal gains so that *all* his employees would receive healthy bonuses. Macha was right. Her father wasn't a god, but he acted as a person responsible for others' welfare should. As Macha was.

She tried a new tack. "But why can't Badb or Nemain

go with you? Do we need both to teach us? I'd feel better if you weren't alone."

"I wouldn't," Macha said. "Assuring the safety of my sisters is what I want. As I said, I am atoning for my previous sins, at least to a small degree. Without my selfish actions millennia ago, the reality of earth would be different. You'd have grown up here, in this house, with sisters, aunts, grandparents, a father, and a mother. You would not have to put your life on the line, nor the lives of those you love. Noro would not have touched you."

Evelyn's eyes filled with tears. She'd thought about that potential past Macha spoke of many times. Wondered who she'd be if she'd grown up here.

All this before coffee. It's gonna be one hell of a day.

"I understand, but I don't regret my life. Whether I ever meld the two families like Lily has done, we'll see. Still, it's enough for me to be a part of both, separate but equal." She sucked in a breath as Macha nodded. "There's one thing I want to ask you about before you leave. Maybe you won't know the answer, but I figured you're a goddess so you might."

Macha's dark black eyes widened and she levitated herself to sit by Evelyn's side.

"You mean to ask me about Roman, do you not? If what you felt was real?"

Evelyn blinked. Was she that transparent?

"Of course, you are not!" Macha replied, reading either Evelyn's mind or her body language, she wasn't sure. "I have lived inside you your whole life and was with you during your time with Roman."

Evelyn blushed.

"Do not be ashamed. Your actions with him were nothing but human. Raw, open, trusting, *loving* humanity at its best. Though I did not understand them in my first life here, as a fata, I've come to value those traits. They are the same traits Noro despises." Macha glanced out the window and Evelyn's gaze followed.

A streak of green and red ran through a sunrise of pink and orange straight for the cottage. Badb and Nemain were returning home.

Macha sighed and turned from the window. "I was always envious of their bond when we were fata, even on Hecate. It is part of what drove me to act as I did. I wanted a bond such as theirs and hoped I might find it with Noro. I did not, but you may have with Roman."

Evelyn's sapphire eyes widened. "But he betrayed me."

"He did, to save his family from Empusa's and Amon's fangs. I suspect you would have acted much the same if either of your families were in danger. The real question is can you see beyond what Roman did to you? See all the way to the man he is: A man willing to give up his world for those he loves?"

"You mean . . . me?" Her mind wandered back to her talk with Alistair.

He, too, had told Evelyn that Roman loved her when she asked. It was information she'd taken with a grain of salt. The incubus had been Roman's mentor, after all; perhaps he wanted only to believe the best of his protege. Macha, however, had no such personal ties to Evelyn's ex.

Macha nodded. "He loved you. It was clear in his body chemistry when you two were near each other. It was more than incubi magic, but he also made the wrong choice giving you up. In a way, you two are alike. Giving up one world for those you love. You have made that decision twice. Once when you came here and stayed. Again when you stayed in New York to help your family with disastrous consequences. Both times you were giving up a world, letting someone down. It is up to you to decide if what Roman did is unforgivable or not. I suspect you will only know when you meet him again."

Healing of All Sorts
Lily

"You didn't have to wake up so early to watch over me. You and Fiona both need more rest. I'll be fine for a couple hours," Alfred whispered.

Lily shook her head. "Your wounds are of an unknown nature. What kind of healers would Fiona and I be if we left you alone? Pull down that blanket."

Lily didn't feel the need to mention she'd actually been up for hours, watching the minutes on her phone tick by in the darkness until she was sure Fiona would not tell her to go back to bed. At five in the morning, she ventured out into the sitting room. By that time Fiona had been more than happy for Lily to relieve her. While Alfred slept, Fiona filled Lily in on how she was going about figuring out how to heal Alfred's wounds.

"I've diagramed his major cuts and applied different

salves to each," Fiona had explained. "Some are cures for known conditions, others are experimental. None seem to do him harm, nor are they working miracles. If you apply a salve of your own creation, document it on the diagram I've drawn of his body."

Lily glanced at Fiona's healer's grimoire now. She'd seen the leather-bound book Fiona carried with her dozens of times, though she'd never been permitted to write in it. As she flipped to the page Fiona had flagged, Lily wished it hadn't been this catastrophe that granted her the privilege of making her own mark on the grimoire.

She sighed, taking in the illustration. Alfred was little more than a tube with limbs, splattered with lines on the page. *Maybe that makes it easier to be objective this way. That, or Fiona is a terrible artist.*

"It's never a good sign when your doctor sighs like that. Fiona was positive about my prognosis. What's up, babe?"

She gave Alfred a soft smile and took his hand. Fiona always tried to put on a happy face for her patients. She'd have to work on that.

"At least none of your wounds look worse," Lily said, avoiding the question. *Or smell like you're rotting from the inside any longer.*

Alfred hummed, catching Lily's ploy. "This is not what I expected we'd be doing when I got back. I pictured running in the countryside, riding horses through the woods, and visiting Galway." He paused. "I should cancel those reservations today. There's no way we're making them now."

"You booked us a getaway? But . . . did you ask Mom? She's been so cautious about us leaving without her or our aunts. Remember when they warded the village pub for us?"

"Are you kidding me? Of course I asked your mother. No way do I want any of the McKay witches coming after me."

Interesting. After Mom's warnings about falling too deep for Alfred, she was still willing to let me go away with him?

Lily gripped Alfred's hand tighter, rubbing her fingers along the callouses. "That's sweet. Thank you, but you're right. We should cancel the trip. There's no way you're going anywhere, and we'll have plenty of time together right here."

"Not as romantic as I'd been hoping." Alfred wagged his eyebrows and Lily giggled.

Oh, if only that could have happened.

"Not at all." She leaned over and kissed him. "Now hold still. Fiona's diagram of your body is amateur, and I have to make sure I'm not putting this salve on any part she's already treated. We're trying to figure out what works best with your wounds topically. Goddess knows we may need this remedy again, so we have to be sure."

"Yes, doc, I'll be quiet," Alfred closed his eyes and leaned his head back into the cot.

She released his hand and brought her finger to the pages Fiona dedicated to Alfred's case. The salve Lily had concocted of tansy, hags taper, and monarda was a novel one. Each of the plants was used for antibacterial, expectorant, and healing purposes but never in this combination before. She had to be careful with it. She didn't want to place her salve on a cut next to anything it might react badly with.

Scanning Fiona's notes, Lily found no obvious clashes. Good, she'd put it on the worse-looking cut then. She glanced up from the page and found Alfred was no longer relaxing but watching her.

"Watching you and Fiona do what you do is amazing. It's more than magic, it's science. Ragnar, the lead healer in my coven, is nowhere near as meticulous as you two."

That's why Fiona wouldn't let Ragnar come near any of us when we were healing in New York, Lily thought, though she said, "Thank you. That's a huge compliment."

"Plus you're hot when you're in healer mode. All serious and working. I mean damn, babe." Alfred fanned himself with his hand.

Lily laughed. "Calm down, Casanova. I need to apply

this. After, I'll make you something to eat? How's that sound?"

Alfred laid back once more, his face split into a smile.

She cleaned his wound and applied the salve, which smelled unpleasant but was nothing compared to the odor of Alfred's wounds. After she was done, Lily placed her hand inches above the wound and whispered, "Salus."

The charm did not, as it had so often done, heal the wound before her eyes, but then Lily hadn't expected it to. If it were that easy, Fiona would have healed Alfred already.

Salus was a great charm for everyday cuts, scrapes, bruises, and with enough effort behind it, some larger injuries. Magical wounds, however, were more difficult.

She finished by propping Alfred's torso up with a few pillows. "What do you want for breakfast?"

"Eggs and bacon, or whatever they call it here. Some hash on the side? I'm starving."

"You got it." She kissed him softly. As she walked into the kitchen her lips turned up at the corners as Alfred whistled, two long and low notes, behind her back.

***

Lily scrambled four eggs and fried a few strips of bacon. She poured off most of the grease and used the rest to cook up the frozen hash she'd found in the freezer. When the hash finished, she pulled out a jug of premade green smoothie, which Fiona had left in the fridge with a note proclaiming it was for Alfred, and filled a glass.

"Smells amazing," Alfred groaned.

Lily handed Alfred his plate, which he immediately dug into. Smiling she placed his smoothie on an end table and removed her own breakfast from where it balanced on her forearm. "I'm glad you think so because I'll probably be making you this same thing for a few more days."

Alfred stopped eating and sat up straighter.

"What? Did I say something wrong? Is the food bad?" Lily asked, glancing down at her plate.

"It's not that. The food is perfect. It's just . . . I've been thinking, Lil."

Lily's gut plummeted at the tone of his voice but she stayed silent, waiting for him to continue.

Alfred's velvet brown eyes bore into her. "Once I heal, I need to get back to New York."

"Your parents want you back," Lily said sadly.

"Yes, but that's not why I need to go back. Fiona filled me on what's been happening. Your lessons with the Morrigan. How you're working with air and not having as much success as you do with other lessons."

Lily frowned.

"Fiona's words not mine, babe," Alfred said. "Anyway,

she also told me the Morrigan's reasoning why fata killed off air witches and wizards. It got me wondering if we had any in the New York coven and you know what? I can't recall one air witch or wizard in our coven. If what the Morrigan says is true and air witches were persecuted, that's a good reason to stay hidden. Our coven is huge, in one of the largest cities in the world, and we don't have a single air witch? So, I started to think if I'd ever heard of an air witch in any other New York covens. I came up blank, but that can't be true. They have to be there. New York is home to every type of person imaginable. There has to be at least one air witch, and where there's one air witch, there's likely a secret network." Alfred lifted an eyebrow.

Lily set her plate on the table. "If we can find more air witches, we stand a greater chance against the fata." She shook her head. "You're right. They may hide from all other magical creatures because they've been warned of persecution against them."

"And if they learn others are fighting to rid Earth of their persecutors, I bet they'll want in on the battle."

Lily grabbed Alfred's hand, excited by the revelation even as her heart dropped at the idea of him leaving. "You're a genius. I have only one request. I want a night alone before you leave. It doesn't have to be a huge trip. A night in town would do."

Alfred's eyes shone but before he could answer the sound of creaking floorboards broke the spell between them. Lily turned to find Evelyn standing at the edge of the room. Instead of the usual smirk she wore whenever she caught Lily and Alfred being mushy, her mouth was set in a downturned line.

"Sorry. Pretend you didn't see me," Evelyn mumbled, her voice scratchy as if she was holding back tears.

Lily shook her head as her sister attempted to disappear around the hearth. "Wait a second, Evelyn. What's wrong?"

"Nothing, I—"

Lily patted the ground next to her.

Evelyn sighed. "Fine." She joined Lily and Alfred, her eyes fixing on Alfred's manhandled chest before darting away. "How are you? Is Lily taking good care of you?"

Alfred nodded. "I've been under the best watch all night."

"Are you going to tell us why you sound like you've been crying?" Lily extended a hand to take Evelyn's.

Evelyn let out a long exhale. "It's been a rough morning. Macha still wants to scout the fata and I'm worried about her going. I haven't been the best host body but being separated that long . . . it seems wrong."

Lily gazed into Evelyn's deep sapphire eyes and lifted

a corner of her mind barrier. *But that's not everything, is it?*

Evelyn bit her lip. "I asked Macha about Roman. I know what he did was terrible, but when I was talking to Macha, who apparently knows me better than I know myself, I couldn't stop thinking I'd have done the same. If it was my mom and dad, or one of you. I mean, I've destroyed men's lives for a lot less. It made me more sympathetic. Not that I've forgiven him or anything."

Evelyn turned to face Alfred. "I feel weird asking this. Being the resident man expert and all, I should know, but I'm not a guy and I need advice. From everything you heard, do you think Roman loved me?"

Lily's gaze traveled between Alfred and Evelyn. Both looked uncomfortable.

"Well," Alfred paused, as if not sure how to proceed. "I've never met Roman, but I can see how his choice would be a hard one. Between choosing your family or the girl you think you love?"

He glanced at Lily and their eyes locked. "All I know is I love my family, too, but there is no way I'd give up Lily. I'd have figured out another way. There's a chance he did. It's possible his backup plan was to save you and escape and that's how he got locked in the basement. Honestly, I think you won't be able to sort out anything until you see him again." Alfred shrugged his shoulders.

Evelyn sighed through her nose. "Thanks guys. I'm gonna go grab coffee."

Lily bit her lip as she watched her sister go, her tall frame still a touch too thin for its proportions. Lily couldn't help but wonder if it wasn't the emotional turmoil or lack of closure in Evelyn's relationship with Roman that was keeping her from healing completely.

For her sake, all our sakes, I hope Roman comes soon.

Family

Sara

"Good morning." Celestine called, letting herself into Fern Cottage later that morning. She waved at Sara and Evelyn, perched on the couch, before making her way over to Alfred. The daemon looked peaceful, not pained by his many injuries, thanks to a sleeping potion laced with painkillers Lily had given him after he'd eaten the breakfast she made him. "How is he?"

"A little better, though none of the salves we've concocted are working miracles," Lily sighed.

Celestine wrinkled her pert nose. "I was never the healer you and Fiona are. In my days as a witch, we knew far less about the body than we do now, but I had a thought last night. Knowing what we know of the fatas' sensitivity to iron, perhaps adding iron granules to the salves could be beneficial? It may weaken the fata magic remaining within him."

Lily's eyes widened. "That's a great idea. I'll go call Fiona and see what she thinks. Excuse me." She rushed out of the room.

The vampire watched her go. "I hope it works. Alfred's parents have been calling me. They want him back."

She turned to Evelyn. "Speaking of parents. Caleb's family sends their thanks for use of your family's plane. Caleb's body landed in New York this morning without issue. There's a small funeral planned for him soon."

Evelyn bit her lip. "It was the least I could do."

Brigit walked around the hearth, hands and forearms laden with four plates. "Morning, Celestine." She set the plates on the coffee table and offered Evelyn and Sara forks. "Where'd Lily get off to?"

"To call Fiona," Sara answered, before stuffing her mouth full of sausage. "Celestine had a great idea for a salve for Alfred."

"That's grand." Brigit cut the food on one plate, presumably Alfred's for when he woke, into smaller pieces. "Anything else new?" She eyed the vampire.

Celestine shook her head. "I've been fielding calls about what's happening over here. You should reach out to Jane soon; she'd appreciate an update. Keeps talking about how she wants to hop on a plane to be closer to the action."

Brigit opened her mouth to speak just as the phone rang. "I'll get that. It's probably Jane sensing we were speaking of her. She has excellent intuition," Brigit said, an amused look on her face as she walked back into the kitchen-diner.

As soon as Brigit was out of sight, Lily rushed back into the room, her tired eyes shining with hope. "Fiona agrees it's a great idea. I'm going to crush a little iron into a salve I made to test it." She glanced at her food and made her way to the table covered with salves, a new spring in her step.

If Lil is giving up food, you know it's got to be a great idea. Sara stuffed a huge bite of potato into her mouth and rose to join the crowd forming around Alfred.

In Sara's unqualified non-healer's opinion, the daemon didn't look much better. Alfred's exposed arm still oozed a constant stream of blue pus that made Sara shiver.

She observed as Lily pulled a salve out from a shelf, opened the glass jar, and set in on the table. She plucked a smaller jar filled with metal balls from her ingredient shelf and extracted a single iron pellet.

Sara stared at the pellet, sizing it up against the mortar and pestle Fiona and Lily kept close at hand. She wondered how on earth Lily was planning on crushing the iron. It would surely take forever with the stone tools meant primarily for plants and seeds.

"Murr," Lily whispered the crushing spell before Sara had a chance to voice her question and the iron pellet reduced to a dark sand. Lily took a pinch of iron between her fingers and flicked it into the salve jar. Finally, she opened a drawer, produced a thin glass rod and stirred. The moment the iron disappeared into the cream she stopped. Using the glass rod, Lily dabbed a small amount of salve on a rough part of Alfred's exposed arm.

Sara gasped. The result was as startling as it was gross. Pus, blue as the sky and smelling of moldy fruit, shot out of Alfred's skin like a volcano pulling from the deepest recesses of the earth. It landed on the wood floor with a sickening splat, dotting the cot's undercarriage and Lily's shoes.

"Ugh, that's disgusting." Evelyn covered her mouth as the pus continue to leach from Alfred's body. "Is it ever going to stop?"

At least a cup of the goop covered the ground beneath his laceration. Alfred had so many cuts that if the same thing happened to all of them, he'd end up a sack of skin.

"It's slowing," Lily replied.

"It must have been highly pressurized," Celestine

noted as the pus slowed to a trickle and stopped a minute later.

Lily nodded, her face inches from the cut, inspecting it. "I'll wait until he wakes up to do it again. That way I can ask him how he feels. Does the site already look a little better to anyone else, though?" She moved her head out of the way.

Sara agreed, the gash looked smaller already. Now the wounds just needed to close. A feat, judging by the number of slices across Alfred's body, that would be difficult on its own.

The sound of footsteps alerted them to their mother's presence. "Did it work?" Brigit asked, rounding the corner. She stopped short as her eyes latched on to the mess of blue pus on her floor and raised an eyebrow.

"Sorry, Mom. I'll clean it up. It seems to have worked but I'll wait until he wakes up to try again." Lily said. "He didn't get a lot of sleep." She glanced back at the plate of food on the coffee table. "And I'm starving."

Sara shook her head, unsure she'd be able to finish her breakfast.

"Was it Jane?" Celestine asked once they settled by the fire.

"It was. She agreed, Alfred should go home as soon as possible. But that wasn't all she wanted to inform me of." Brigit twisted her torso to face Evelyn. "Roman contacted their coven the other day. He says he didn't want to wait any longer to see you."

Evelyn stiffened.

Sara's heart clenched in response. It dawned on her that both her sisters were going through a lot at the moment. *They've given so much. I wish I could take their pain away,* she thought watching Evelyn bite the inside of her cheek.

"I know this will be a lot for you, honey, so let me know what you want to do and I'll tell Jane," Brigit said. "She says he is ready to leave as soon as you say the word—"

"Tell him to come soon. Tomorrow if he can. Make it after Macha leaves so I have time to pull myself together again. I need to put all this shit behind me." Evelyn rose unsteadily as if the news had thrown her off balance. "I'll have Dad send the jet."

"I don't think that's necessary. Your father shouldn't be bothered and Roman can pay his way. He has a lot to make up for." Brigit frowned.

"Isn't that the truth? But whatever gets him here faster is what I want. If that means Roman is freeloading on my family jet, so be it. Whenever he comes he'd better be prepared to explain himself. Excuse me, I have a lot to think about." And with that Evelyn turned and sashayed from the room.

Sara watched her go, her copper eyes darting only momentarily to their mother's fierce gaze as she followed her middle daughter's movements.

So, this was what it was like to be a part of a real family. A turbulent mix of emotions Sara had no way of recognizing gushed up from deep within her. It was what she had always wanted. What she had craved, and what, despite the McKays' warmth and support, felt just out of her reach.

How is it possible I still feel like I'm not quite enough?

Plans and Practice

Lily

"Your wounds are healing nicely." Fiona peeled a layer of gauze with extra absorbent maxi pads attached from Alfred's shoulder. The pads were likely the only reason Brigit's rug was not covered in colored pus. "We'll send you home with extra salves and the recipes so your healers can mimic them. It would be good to stock up before another altercation arises."

Since the first application, Fiona and Lily had been experimenting all day with adding iron to other salves, none of which Alfred claimed hurt him, though all produced an explosion of pus. Fiona postulated this was because the iron was helping to expel fata magic alongside with the usual bodily fluids and cells.

"Thanks, Fiona. I want to get back home and do my part. Where better to find air witches and wizards than a huge city like New York?" Alfred pushed himself up with an effort.

Lily sighed. *He wants to help,* she reminded herself. Alfred had told her again and again that the sooner this was over, the sooner they could be a normal couple.

"I agree," Fiona nodded. "New York seems to be a hub of helpful supernaturals. In fact, Brig said Jane and a delegation from your coven will arrive with Roman tomorrow afternoon. Evelyn requested it be after Macha leaves, and I don't blame her. The girl acts tough but it's a lot to handle. The delegation is hoping to learn air magic and spar with our girls."

Fiona glanced at Lily before shifting her gaze to Alfred. "If you're up for it by tomorrow morning, you can take the Locksley jet back to New York. There's no way you'll be fully healed, that won't be for days yet. However, the sooner you leave, the sooner we can find air witches."

Lily shot Fiona a look and Fiona shrugged as if to say, *"You know he'd have come up with it on his own anyhow."*

"That'd be perfect," Alfred said, grasping and squeezing Lily's hand. "As much as I'd like to give Roman a piece of my mind, it's more important I make it to the city fast. My mom is not pleased, and I'll have obligatory family time before I can scout."

Sorrow that Alfred was leaving her, pride that he wanted to stand up for Evelyn, and guilt at keeping him from his family warred inside Lily. She took her conflicting feelings as more proof that she'd found a good guy.

"Don't worry about Roman. He'll get what's coming to him," Lily said confidently. Evelyn had been steely and silent all day, which Lily figured couldn't bode well for the incubus.

Brigit rushed into the room.

"You alright, Mom?" Lily asked taking in her mother's frazzled expression.

"Aye," Brigit said. "I forgot I had packages waiting for me in town and the shop closes in forty minutes. Just running down there to see if I can make it before they close. I'll miss the start of your pneuma lessons. Shouldn't you be getting out there with your sisters soon?"

Lily ignored the question and sat up straighter. "Are they the weapon prototypes Evelyn ordered?"

Brigit nodded. "The post office wouldn't let Aoife pick up the boxes. Said they needed my signature. What a time to become a stickler for the rules, I said. Anyway, I'm off." She ran out the door, through the garden, and disappeared into the orchard abutting the hedge that closed Fern Cottage off from the rest of the world.

"That's so freaking cool. I wish I was learning to fight like a ninja," Alfred said.

Evelyn had commissioned a blacksmith in London to

create an array of smaller, more wieldable weapons designed for each triplet's measurements. Whatever they were disinclined to use, their mother, aunts, Fiona, or anyone else on their side would claim.

"Speaking of learning," Fiona shot Lily a look. "You really should be getting outside. Sara and Evelyn went outside a half hour ago."

"Fine, I'm going." She leaned over and kissed Alfred on the lips. "I'll see you later."

Lily pulled her hood over her head only to have it blow right off. She shivered as the cold seeped into her bones. *You'd think growing up in Oregon I'd be used to the rain, but Irish winters are a different beast.*

Running toward the shield, Lily could see the wall of air Evelyn was moving with ease across the field. A rush of heat warmed her cheeks as Lily ran through the confines of the shield charm. *Thank the goddess Aoife set a heating charm.*

"About time!" Gwenn teased from her side of the vast enclosure. "We were about to come separate you forcefully. Thought perhaps Fiona had stepped away for a mo' and you took advantage of the fact?"

Lily blushed, though she doubted anyone could tell with how red her cheeks were from the rain. "Ha, ha. I was just checking on him. Why don't you clowns move over so I have room to practice?"

Two HOURS later she trudged back across the muddy field alongside her sisters and aunts. Sara, Lily noticed, had developed a limp. Evelyn had performed the best, but even she looked disheveled as Badb had pushed her to work with three air walls simultaneously. In fact, the only beings who appeared happy were Badb and Nemain as they flew off over the trees into the dimming daylight.

Good riddance, Lily thought, happy not to see Badb again until she returned to say goodbye to Macha, who had disappeared beneath Evelyn's skin as soon as lessons were over. Air magic hadn't gotten the least bit easier.

How in goddess' sake am I ever going to master it?

To an outsider, the hours of practice would appear like little more than a group of women hanging out in a field. A minute of Evelyn hovering an inch above the ground, her chest heaving with exertion as air billowed beneath her, had been the pinnacle.

While Lily felt disappointed she wasn't experiencing the same gains, she didn't dare complain. She'd witnessed Evelyn's face light up as she hovered above the damp grass, and Macha's elation. Lily knew exactly why both felt the joy they did: Evelyn's magic was returning with force, growing stronger by the day.

Her progress will be a great way to surprise Noro when we meet again.

Lily bit her lip. Maybe it was better that Alfred was leaving soon. She needed to be spending her time practicing, rather than sitting at his bedside.

Although she knew it to be true, her heart broke at the thought of not being near him all the same.

Farewells

Evelyn

HOT WATER STREAMED over Evelyn's frozen body, washing away the mud and chill. The marks Noro left on her skin had healed, though the claiming brands on her inner right thigh remained—a navy star and a white swirl glowing up at her, taunting her every time she braved taking her clothes off. She hated the sight of them and dreaded the day she was intimate with someone. How would she explain the markings to someone if they weren't a supernatural?

Shutting off the water, Evelyn grabbed her towel and wrapped it around her body, tucking in a corner and creating a tight white dress of sorts. She wiped off the foggy mirror and looked at her face, pleased with the fullness in her cheeks that seemed to have reappeared overnight. She was wrapping her hair in another towel when a shout of excitement burst from the sitting room. Evelyn cocked her head to listen.

Mom's back with the weapons!

She pulled the bathroom door open and steam billowed out. "You can't open those without me! I ordered them!"

A guilty hush overcame the excited voices. "Well, hurry up! We won't touch anymore as long as you're out here in two minutes," Lily shot back.

Evelyn liked how they sassed each other now and didn't take it personally. It reminded her of her relationship with Vicencia.

She got dressed in record time and ran down the hall. The boxes Brigit had retrieved from town were open, though only one weapon—a delicate, short spear—was unwrapped.

The blacksmith went above and beyond for a prototype. Must have wanted to impress me, Evelyn thought eyeing the Celtic knots and crows the smith had etched on the spear's side.

"This is the Sara-sized spear," Lily said, holding it out for Evelyn to see. "The blacksmith organized them by wrapping colors because we ordered so many. His note says the other two wrappings hold larger weapons."

Evelyn reached for the largest one, the spear made for her, and unwrapped it. The iron was cold in her hands and the tangy scent of metal puffed up from the wrappings. Etchings of crows and wavelike Celtic markings, similar to the ones on Sara's spear, leapt out at Evelyn.

"You didn't tell that smithy anything about us, did you?" Brigit asked her gaze shifting between Evelyn and Sara's spears.

"No," Evelyn answered, her brows furrowed. "Why do you ask?"

"Because this smithy seems to have sensed something. Was he Irish?"

Evelyn cocked her head. "I didn't ask but his accent wasn't clear British. Maybe a mix?"

"If you talk to him again, ask. These carvings make me think he's Irish and respects the old ways. The knots should be familiar to you as they would be to any tourist that walked down a high street in Dublin. However, it's the bird that interests me. A crow is the sign of the Morrigan."

"No way," Evelyn breathed. "Let's open the rest and see what he came up with!"

Once everything was unpacked, Evelyn couldn't believe the array of weapons before them. The sitting room looked like a medieval war room.

Each type of weapon had a tag attached to it, informing the witches what it was and how to use it. Evelyn gravitated to a club. It had a slender wood handle topped with an iron ball dotted with spikes, the largest of which was at the apex of the club. The label identified it as a morning star. Evelyn eyed the many spikes and imagined them slicing her leg open as she fought. It was perfect for puncturing a pneuma membrane, but impractical for running with.

She moved on, her eyes catching on a war hammer a foot long with an intricate iron handle and curved pick. Evelyn hefted the hammer. The swirling inlay of the handle fit the contours of her hand like a glove.

"The horseman's pick. A weapon of Islamic origin used by cavalry during the Middle Ages in Europe," Evelyn read off the label. She lifted it a few times. Running with this would be easy. The pick would definitely puncture a fata and the hammer end was useful, too.

Especially if I run across Felix. Perfect for bashing his sadistic werewolf skull in.

Sara fingered a small, sharp dagger that looked light and wieldable.

A stiletto, Evelyn thought, the name popping into her mind from some hidden depth without her reading the label. The weapon Lily held was harder to place but resembled the morning star that had initially interested Evelyn but with larger diamond-like protrusions narrowing into a deadly point rather than small spikes.

"What is that, Lil?" Evelyn asked.

"A flanged mace." Lily spun the two-foot-long weapon in her hands. "The note says back in the day they tore through armor. I figure a fata will be easy compared to that."

True that, Evelyn thought, running her hand over the pick end of her war hammer with a smirk.

THE CLOCK in Brigit's living room chimed nine o'clock, an unwelcome reminder that Macha was leaving soon. A thump inside her chest echoed the ding—Macha, making sure Evelyn heard the clock sounding their agreed upon hour.

"I heard it," Evelyn mumbled. "Caeliter." She opened her mouth wide for Macha to exit.

The sapphire pneuma shimmered before her a moment later. Her face was arranged in a human smile, a gesture that had once freaked Evelyn out, but as of late she'd come to appreciate.

"It appears that as soon as we developed an understanding of each other is when I am set to leave," Macha commented.

Evelyn nodded, not in the mood to pretend she was pleased with what was about to happen.

Macha floated closer, invading Evelyn's space. "I want you to know I'm proud of your progress. Your air magic is strong. Besides continuing to practice, the best you can do is help your sisters grow strong, too. What is it humans say? See one, do one, teach one?"

Evelyn bit her lip, pushing back the annoyance that arose whenever Macha read her mind with such ease. *I should beg her not to leave. Now's my chance.*

"And you know that is not possible," Macha replied as if Evelyn had spoken. "We need someone to act as a scout and gather information. My sisters and I are the logical choices and I will not let them go in my stead."

Evelyn sighed, understanding where Macha was coming from. "We should go out to the sitting room to wait for them, shouldn't we?"

Macha nodded and followed Evelyn from her small room, down the hall to the sitting room where Lily, Sara, Brigit, Alfred, and Mary sat waiting.

"Thought you might want the extra support," Mary said when Evelyn locked eyes and went to sit next to her favorite aunt.

They sat there together in silence, no one knowing quite how to proceed. Evelyn's eyes roved over Lily, who looked exhausted from their lessons that afternoon. *Macha was right. She needs major help with air.*

"Do either of you want to work on practicing with air

for our morning sessions? I can help you out if you like. We could play with our weapons, too." Evelyn tried to sound nonchalant but Macha's wide pneuma grin undermined her tone.

Lily's green eyes widened. "You mean, instead of sparring? Yes, anything besides that!"

"Maybe not totally omitting sparring," Evelyn said. "We could work on air for half an hour and then spar or practice weaponry the second half hour? That way we get everything in."

"Sure, I'll take it."

"I'm in, too," Sara agreed.

"I'm proud of you girls. You've all been putting in so much extra effort," Brigit commented.

"Seriously," Alfred said from his cot. "You three are like gym rats but with magic.

Evelyn laughed. "What a charming comparison."

"It should be," Alfred replied. "When I go back, I'll make sure everyone knows how hard you're working and will pressure them to do the same. If everyone else worked half as hard, we'd have this war in the bag."

Suddenly, two beams of light—one red, one green— shot through the window above the loveseat.

Alfred gave a start, throwing the thick covers off.

"Apologies," Macha said to Alfred. "My sisters have poor manners."

"We forgot he was staying there." Nemain whirled to a stop next to Sara. "And we were in a hurry to see you off."

"It's all good," Alfred said looking a touch embarrassed as he pulled the covers back over his naked chest.

Badb approached Macha. "We come bearing gifts for your journey, sister. A gift I hope will help keep your strength up while you are away from the body that houses you."

The body that houses you? Evelyn pursed her lips together, unsure how she felt about such an impersonal title.

"A gift?" Macha's dark eyes lit up.

Badb hovered above Macha and twisted in midair, wringing herself out as if she were a towel. A shower of water fell upon Macha, some of it landing on Evelyn.

"What the hell was that?" Evelyn asked, brushing the water from her arm.

As if I'm not wet enough in this rainy ass country.

Brigit replied. "The Morrigan was a water goddess. Some streams and lakes of this land were holy to the people who worshiped her. It's said the Morrigan blessed those waters and hence, they are enchanted. This must be from one of those streams."

"Correct," Macha said, her black eyes shining with pleasure. "My sisters know I favored the water from this stream. Something in its composition endeared it to me. Perhaps because it ran from an underground cave beneath a budding stalactite, which reminded me of a beautiful rock formation on Hecate. I'm really not sure why."

"Our gesture is more one of goodwill and binding us together than mystical beliefs of the past," Nemain added.

They're making it clear they want her to come back. Evelyn's annoyance softened. She hoped Macha could read those signs, too.

"I thank you for your token, dear sisters. Shall we be off?"

"We are to accompany Macha as far as we can before parting," Badb said, answering Lily's silent question. "And yes, the time has come."

Macha whirled to face Evelyn. "Remember what I have taught you and pass it along. While I redeem myself, you must show the people of this world how to fight for what is theirs. Be the leader you've been striving to be your whole life in your old world."

Evelyn inhaled as her pneuma's airy limb reached out and touched her third eye.

"If you experience a vision, do not fret. It is because I have opened myself to you. I am leaving a bit of my essence as you did with your mind the first time I was freed. It is my way of sharing information with you," Macha said.

"Thank you for everything."

"You're welcome. And thank you for sharing your body, housing me for years without your knowledge. When I return I hope I am still welcome."

Evelyn nodded, unsure she'd be able to speak without her voice cracking.

"Until next time, Evelyn."

Then, without another word, three pneumas shot out the window.

As Evelyn watched the colored shooting stars grow smaller in the night sky, a profound sense of loneliness washed over her. For the first time in her life, she wished someone else was there to hold her up.

A Go-Between

Sara

"Let's start by the lake," Evelyn said as the trio neared their usual practice spot, evident by the trampled grass and areas where the ground had been burnt black.

"The lake? But we can't secure a shield over water well and that may be dangerous if our magic goes out of control." Lily jolted to a stop. "Or *can* you secure a shield over water now?"

Sara tilted her head, her copper eyes boring into Evelyn. Lily was right—the natural fluidity of water made it tricky for all but strong water witches to hook and secure a shield to its surface. Mary was the only one at Fern Cottage skilled at such a feat, but Evelyn had been progressing quickly in the last few days. Had she learned?

"I wish. No, but since water links naturally with air, both having hydrogen and oxygen in them, starting with water may help. If anything, water is easier to see." Evelyn shrugged.

Why didn't our pneumas think of this?

Sara shook her head and was glad Nemain appeared to be resting inside her and hadn't heard the unfair comment. It was like asking a master to explain the basics of their craft. Masters rarely thought too hard about the fundamentals, especially when in the flow.

Not to mention our pneumas don't always think like us.

That much had become plain in the short time their pneumas had been speaking to them. While the witches and pneumas strove toward the same goal and their pneumas attempted to mimic human facial and vocal expressions, their methods of communicating and working often differed.

"Smart," Sara said, suddenly aware Evelyn was waiting for a response. "What gave you the idea?"

"Macha has been giving me tips on how to break down air spells into smaller ones. I think you need baby steps, too. It's too big of a jump to go from earth to air or fire to air. Getting to know water can be a baby step, then you can move on."

Breaking it down into more manageable parts. It was so obvious Sara wanted to smack her forehead. *Thank the goddess Evelyn figured it out.*

SARA FED the flames more fire magic as she watched Lily push around her second air wall of the day with glee. She was weary from working with water for the last hour and had been happy to pause and warm herself. Fire was a delight to work with after the heaviness of water.

Lily is killing it with that air wall. So why am I still having so much trouble with the first baby step?

She glanced at the fire before her and winced, the answer staring her in the face. While Lily worked, Sara had reverted to what was comfortable. She sighed and stepped away, already yearning for the heat from the flames.

"Eginura," Sara said, bidding a stream of water to shoot from her hands. "Volavari."

The second spell caught the stream of water before it hit the ground and lifted it to float before her, like a giant raindrop. She touched the water, molding it into a near perfect circle. Sara recalled Evelyn's words to describe water. They were so different from Sara's description of fire but were filled with the same passion.

"Water is ever-changing. You can control it for a time but never truly master it. To be honest, I don't even try to anymore. I'm simply the guide. I let it move where it will, carving its own way, like a river winding through a moun-

tain eroding rocks. I trust water will work with me, teach me, protect me, and I meet it where it is. Let water go, trust it, and it will listen."

Sara eyed her own perfect sphere. She was putting a lot of effort into keeping the massive raindrop in place. Far more than when she produced fireballs, which held the same spherical shape. She was doing exactly what Evelyn claimed not to, trying to control completely, instead of trusting. She relaxed her grip a touch. The water expanded, undulating on its own into an oval, then a knobby sphere, and back to a circle.

"Sorry," Sara whispered to the water. "Fire witch habit. We always have to be in control, or else we'd light ourselves on fire." The water did not respond but the calm flowing through Sara indicated she was doing something right. *Let's run with this.*

"Motus," she murmured, and the shifting parcel of water moved with her toward Evelyn and Lily.

"That's the first time I've seen you look comfortable playing with water." Evelyn beamed at her.

Her sister was right. It was the first time Sara *felt* comfortable with water magic. "Your speech from earlier sank in. I love fire but I've learned to be stringent with it, always keeping it contained. Otherwise, it can cause major damage. I'll have to undo that learning when I work with water."

"True, but don't underestimate water." Evelyn swept her arm to the side.

A wave rose with a roar from the lake, twenty feet high in an instant, causing the lake to shrink to half its volume. Sara and Lily watched as Evelyn pushed the wave into the forest. The water collapsed on a sapling, bending it in half, nearly snapping the young, thin wood. The scent of wet dirt flew at them as the water receded back into the confines of the lake.

"Water can cause damage, too," Evelyn finished.

Sara nodded, unable to turn her eyes from the tree that Lily, looking scandalized by Evelyn's actions, pushed magic into, strengthening it from the inside until it stood tall once more.

"I didn't mean to insinuate that it couldn't," Sara offered.

Evelyn shrugged. "I'm not sour. It seems to be the consensus that fire is more destructive than water. Especially when we're so focused on fighting other creatures, vampires in particular. Fire was the first thing we learned to fight with, right? And for good reason. Fire was our best weapon for a long time, but against the fata it's useless. What you hold now, however, isn't."

Sara cocked her head. "I couldn't do what you did with this tiny ball. Perhaps I could fling it hard at someone, but that wouldn't work as a weapon against a fata either," Sara said, trying to work out what her sister was talking about. She knew Lily had used water to escape from Amon's grasp once.

A smile split Evelyn's face. "Probably not, but you're a fire witch holding water. You already have a relationship with the water in your hands. Are you able to maintain that relationship if you used a bit of your natural power? Apply heat to the water."

Sara's mouth dropped open. It was so simple. Basic science. Apply heat to water and you get a gas. Why hadn't she thought of that? A pang of guilt hit her as the answer came. *Fire witch supremacy complex. Water didn't come easy so I did the minimum, held it at arm's length . . . story of my life.*

"That ball of water looked so much like the little fireballs you carry with you for heat. It's what gave me the idea," Evelyn said, interpreting Sara's dropped jaw correctly. "If you use fire to get to air, something familiar to bring you to something unknown, you may keep the relationship you built. Try it. Remember not to confine the water too much as it's transforming. Let the water expand as you apply heat. I bet it'll stay with you."

Sara called forth the fire magic within her and let it trickle out through her fingertips. The heat seeped into the air surrounding the water and permeated the undulating aquatic globe. The yearning to light a fire in her hands hit her, sharp and hot, but Sara held back.

It was fire's nature calling to her, always wanting to burn bright and devour everything in its path. Minutes passed, the fire magic beating against her skin, begging to fly free. Still, Sara stayed strong, pushing tiny increments of heat into the water, waiting for the slightest change.

Suddenly, steam appeared, hot and misty in her hands.

"It's working!" Sara exclaimed and a candle wick of a flame caught on her finger. She cut off the excess fire and concentrated once more.

The work was painstaking, but soon enough, a ball of energized air hovered before Sara. It was larger than the water, as was the nature of heated gas, but remained contained in the loose boundary she'd defined. She beamed at Evelyn, who stood back with her arms crossed.

"Now, try flattening that air out into a wall," Evelyn spoke with an undeniable tinge of pride in her voice.

"Homaire," Sara uttered the spell and the bubble of gas flattened into a thin wall. A wall more solid than the one other time the spell had almost worked for her. Her wall would never do for trapping a fata, but it was there. "Wow. You're a great teacher, Evelyn," Sara whispered, amazed.

"Thanks. When you're in business, you often have to

look for loopholes to accomplish the impossible. All you two needed was a loophole." An easy grin spread across her face, raising her pink cheekbones high. "And I have to admit, it felt so good to boss someone around again."

Lily coughed at her side. "Don't get too used to it."

Laughter trickled from Sara. Her wall of air shattered as her concentration waned. She didn't care; she could make another.

Horseman's Pick, Flanged Mace, and Stiletto

Lily

LILY GRIPPED her mace as she strode out to the field flanked by Evelyn, Sara, Mary, Gwenn, and Morgane. Since they'd opened the weapons, she'd been anxious to try her flanged mace.

"If I've read accounts of battles, fights, and torture, then Morgane has read a thousand more. I bet she could help us with stance and holding them if she has time to come to the cottage," Sara had said the day before, after a failed weaponry practice. When she'd called the elderly witch to request her presence at Fern Cottage, Morgane let out a whoop loud enough for the rest of them to hear through the phone.

As soon as she'd walked through the door that morning, Morgane had inspected the remaining packages and claimed her weapon. She'd chosen the stiletto Lily had passed on when they picked their weapons. Morgane had sheathed the stiletto in a scabbard and beamed, looking as if she'd been waiting for this day all her life. Knowing Morgane's quirky nature, Lily thought perhaps she had.

"Alright, ladies, let's see what you five are made of," Morgane said as the group slowed to a stop midfield. She pointed to Sara. "You first."

Sara unsheathed her stiletto and held it so tight her knuckles turned white.

"At least you're holding the thing like you aren't scared of it. The only problem is if you hit another blade, yours will deflect back into your face. Loosen your grip, shake out your arms and legs. You want to be strong, fluid."

"You know that from reading historical documents?" Lily asked.

"What do you think people wrote about back in the day? Tending the farm? Paper and ink were precious and only used to honor those able to pay for the privilege, like conquerors, or to glorify God. Occasionally, you'll find a description of the torture of someone who did not believe in praising either, but that's rare. That, and I've been to a fair few historical festivals in my day where there was a combat area for those who own armor and weapons but rarely get to use them—an impromptu tourney of sorts.

The onlookers get to throw fruit at the loser. It's all in good fun."

Lily pursed her lips to keep from laughing at the mischievous look on Morgane's face.

The old witch walked down the line, giving tips to enhance their control over their weapons. The subtle tip she gave Lily altered her stance and grip entirely, changing the mace from something awkward to a second appendage.

"Imagine a fata coming at you. Kill them," Morgane instructed and began walking around as they followed her orders, occasionally taking the weapons from their hands to demonstrate. All eyes watched in awe as Morgane hefted Gwenn's ax with her thin arms and sliced through the air as if she'd done it a thousand times.

"Lily, take a break from swinging your mace and work on thrusting it from your body in different planes. The tip on the top is perfect for puncturing a fata's skin. Any skin. They didn't place it there for nothing, my girl."

Lily did as Morgane said and saw what she meant. Thrusting straight up was different from hurling the mace through the air in front of her. The increased range was a game changer, and if she was honest, a little awkward. She would have to practice both.

Morgane nodded her approval and moved on, getting to each witch before gathering them in a group once more.

"You all have the basic motions down for your appropriate weapon. Now, let's see how you fare with an opponent. Gwenn, please step forward."

No way are we actually fighting each other. What if one of us slips up? Lily cringed at the thought of having to heal her sisters or aunts from an injury she'd inflicted.

"Could you grow a tree and animate its limbs? It will serve as our first, more solid opponent. Then we'll move onto working against something more fata like."

Gwenn's green eyes lit up and a second later a tree shot out of the sodden ground, spraying dirt and grass everywhere. The fresh aroma of spring rolled off it in waves as it unfurled its new branches and leaves. The tree grew to six feet high and stretched and flexed its branches as though it were a person.

What a show-off. Lily snorted watching her aunt play with the tree, creating thick, knobby knots of muscle where a bicep would form on a person.

"Perfect, a volunteer!" Morgane shoved Lily toward the tree. "Use your mace to beat the tree. If you puncture the bark, we'll count it as a win. No magic."

She made her way to Gwenn's creation, which was still preening for the onlookers. Lily had to admit, the tree was magnificent. Only when Lily was closer did she notice the detail that went into it.

The swirling bark for eyes and a nose. The gash where

a mouth would be. Bits of moss trailing down the trunk resembled hair and smaller twigs extending off branches suggested fingers. When she stepped before it, the tree ceased its display. Its leaves, which looked odd in the dead of winter, flashed like verdant blades and the tree pulled four limbs forward, ready to duel.

"We don't have all day," Morgane said.

Lily rolled her eyes, hefted the flanged mace, and charged toward the tree. Giving the trunk a wide berth, she made her move and lunged at the tree's side.

Bam!

A branch from the back flew into her gut, knocking the mace from her hands as Lily flew backward. She landed with a thunk. The damp from the grass seeped into her jeans, chilling her butt and legs.

Lily shook her head, retrieved the mace, and charged. And again. And again. It was exhausting, and she landed on her rear too many times to count. Eventually, she connected her mace with the tree's bark, resulting in a tiny gash on a limb, which promptly had her flying through the air.

Thank the goddess. Lily picked up her mace from the ground. It felt a million times heavier than when she'd started.

"Nice work, Lil! You have the basics of handling down; now we need to build your upper body stamina.

Does Brigit have weights? That could help," Morgane asked.

When no one claimed to have seen a single weight in Fern Cottage, Morgane volunteered to bring her own next time she visited, a promise that shocked everyone.

"Until then, use your body weight. Push-ups and plyometrics work wonders," Morgane instructed and turned to Evelyn. "You're next, sunshine."

Evelyn's lips flattened and she moved toward the tree.

"No! Not that. Mary, could you make a bubble of air? A hard one? We have to mix things up."

Mary obliged and soon Evelyn was battling a large bubble of air much like Lily had with the tree but to greater comedic effect. The bubble, guided by Mary, dodged and swooped over Evelyn, patting her on the head and blowing a whistle of wind in her face. Both shenanigans elicited a scowl from Evelyn and had her swinging her hammer with renewed vigor.

"Sorry, Evelyn, couldn't help but get a little cheeky with it," Mary laughed, when they were done.

Sara was up next, fighting a new tree Gwenn grew from the ground. Her stiletto was a weapon unsuited to fighting four-foot-long branches. The tree tossed her on the ground a few times before Sara wised up and flung the small dagger at the bark. Everyone's mouth dropped as it hit dead center.

"Lucky shot, but if magic was an option, I would've let it fly on a current of air, taking out the guesswork," Sara said.

"Amazing work, girls!" Morgane roared. "Now, it's time for a little payback. Let's help your aunts practice a wee bit, then everyone can have one more go, and we'll call it a day?"

"I call air with Mary!" Evelyn rushed to her water mentor's side, a sly look on her face.

Mary's tinkling laugh filled the field. "I sense the payback brewing already."

Gwenn wrapped an arm around Lily. "You and Sara can gang up on me. I haven't been around as much lately, so I need all the practice I can get. Come on, I'll teach you how to enchant a tree as I did. The spell for animation isn't hard, but making the tree look real is. I'm sure you'll get it and have me huffing and puffing in no time."

Lily grinned and allowed her aunt to guide her to the edge of the field, intending to do just that.

Siren vs. Incubus

Evelyn

Lily burst through the cottage door. "They're here."

"Is he—?" The rest of the question lodged in Evelyn's throat. *If he had any brains at all, he wouldn't dare get on a plane.*

Lily, who had been outside performing plyometrics to take her mind off Alfred's departure, nodded.

Evelyn shot up and grabbed her jacket.

Sara mirrored Evelyn. Her hand flew to the mala necklace she wore and ran up and down the beads. "Should I get Mom?"

"Get whoever you like," Evelyn replied, her tone short. She winced. Sara had done nothing wrong, but Evelyn couldn't help it. Tension had plagued her all morning as she anticipated Roman's arrival. "Sorry, I mean it doesn't matter who's there. It won't change my reaction."

Sara darted down the hall to their mother's bedroom to inform her company had arrived.

Evelyn turned back to the door to find Lily standing in her way, her lip white from where her teeth dug into the tender flesh.

"Don't worry, I won't kill him. I'll just make my feelings clear."

Lily considered what Evelyn said for a moment before stepping aside. "Fine, but don't hurt him too badly. I'm free of patients and would like it to stay that way."

"Nothing you can't reverse with a few spells." Evelyn pushed her way past her sister and into the downpour outside.

Evelyn opened a hand to accept the raindrops falling from the sky and turned them into projectiles. It was as if nature was conspiring with her. She could hear the delegation approaching, their laughter and conversation lively as they walked through the orchard.

Gwenn appeared at the edge of Brigit's garden first, then Jane and Shefali. Two other women Evelyn didn't recognize followed, meeting her eyes questioningly. Only Gwenn saw the missiles in Evelyn's hands.

"I'd stand back if I were you, ladies," Gwenn said.

Then Roman was there, emerging from the trees in all

his roguish glory. The same tousled blond hair she'd run her fingers through, now sopping wet. The bright blue eyes that had engulfed her, glued to the ground. His hands were clenching and unclenching, a nervous tic. Roman looked up as the women quieted. His eyes locked with Evelyn's and tingles shot through her before she squashed them forcibly.

She hurled the first water missile at him, then the second, third, fourth, and on, until she lost count.

Roman stood stock still, staring at her as each hard ball of water hit its mark.

How long she launched water at him, Evelyn would never be sure. All she knew was her shoulder ached and her anger had not subsided one bit. She sucked in a breath, strode up to Roman, and connected her hand with his face in a loud slap.

The surrounding supernaturals sucked in a collective breath, but none of them stopped her.

"How dare you?" Evelyn screamed.

The incubus flinched though he remained still, taking what Evelyn gave him even as welts formed on his skin.

"How dare you stand where you stand? You should be *on your knees!* Do you have any idea what I went through? What that monster did to me? Didn't you know I loved you?" Evelyn's ability to control herself dissolved in a haze of adrenaline and words rampaged from her.

Words she'd kept to herself these past few weeks, allowing them to simmer and fester inside her. Lily gasped and the clicking of mala beads through Sara's hands grew louder. The other witches shuffled nervously.

Roman dropped to his knees. His face screwed up as his eyes met Evelyn's. "I know what I did was terrible. I've thought of you every day since."

Evelyn stiffened. She hadn't expected this—an admission of guilt. Clear remorse. She expected a reasoned argument. Fine, a reasoned argument that escalated into a screaming match. Screams tossed back and forth in the desolate countryside. Debates on how one could put a *loved* one—because she was sure he had loved her, too—in danger. She expected a screaming match because it's what she would have done, had she been in Roman's predicament. Anger flared in her again, not willing to be pushed aside so quickly.

"Volavari," she growled.

Roman's repentance morphed into shock as he rose ten feet in the air and flailed among the orchard treetops.

"Birarazi," Evelyn said.

Roman spun like a top, arms and legs going every which way. A tiny cry escaped him.

"That's nothing," she said and Roman stopped spinning abruptly. "Inruo ego," Evelyn screamed and for the first time since that fateful day Aoife had shown the

Evelyn huffed air from her nostrils. "You didn't answer my question."

"I'm not a great spy," Roman admitted. "They keep me around thinking I may be able to seduce you again. It goes to show how little they learned about you during your imprisonment. To be honest, I haven't heard much, but I know your family is right in thinking there's a main camp, the human zoo. I'm not so sure about the rest though, like what they're doing with the people they claim."

Evelyn glanced over her shoulder and caught him shaking his head. She rolled her eyes. "They're using them as slaves, exactly as they planned all along." He quieted and she let the consequences of what they were dealing with sink in.

"Have they mentioned Empusa and Amon?" Evelyn broke the silence as they completed their first lap.

Roman walked side-by-side with her now and his mouth tightened into a thin line. "There has been talk. Mostly from the vampires' children. They want your family dead, but Noro has forbidden anyone from killing you and your sisters. He commands they take you alive." Roman's hand shot out, grabbing Evelyn's forearm.

A familiar jolt of electricity ran through her. Evelyn yanked her hand back. A reprimand was on the tip of her tongue, but Roman's eyes were wild and she stopped herself.

"I would die before I ever let Noro take you again."

Evelyn took in his solemn expression, his fierce eyes. Her heart softened, but she bit the inside of her cheek hard to remind herself of the pain she'd experienced. That she wasn't ready to forgive. She opened her mouth and suddenly she was babbling.

"Make sure you pitch your tent on the side of the house closest to the orchard. We train on the field, so you'll want to be out of the way. Plus, my window is over there and I don't want to see it." She paused. "If you'd like your tent heated, ask Aoife or Sara. They'll charm it so it stays dry and warm." With that, she turned and strode back toward the cottage as fast as possible without appearing to run.

An Army of Zombies
Macha

Macha flew for two days, stopping only to rest in the bodies of a snake and a badger. Both creatures fought her possession and the break had not been restful. Not when compared to Evelyn's body—the body she'd grown used to, even loved, despite the young woman's mood swings.

However, rest was the last thing on Macha's mind as she inched through the Vincennes Woods on the outskirts of Paris, searching for fata.

She needn't look far. Five minutes and she was there, flying through a rippling wave of magic, a ward to deter humans. Macha passed beneath a rotting Asian-inspired portico and gazed upon a decrepit replica of an Indonesian pavilion, the most intriguing of the abandoned buildings left to rot when Paris grew ashamed of its past.

The fata were there, too, dozens of them.

And we brought them all over, Macha thought, hidden in an overgrown thicket.

A fata flew in front of her. It was bright orange, indicating its full vitality—so unlike herself, who needed a host to recharge. A fact she was ever aware of, else she'd be lost to the ether.

They were not exaggerating. Noro and his seven have figured out a way to become powerful much faster than my sisters and me.

Macha lurked at the edge of the zoo. Jumping from tree to tree for cover, she examined the camp the fata had made. It seemed they'd resurrected parts of the overgrown buildings Brigit had shown the Ireland clan on the internet. Cutting back the vegetation and piecing together metal, wood, or stone with magic, they had built a sanctuary where the new fata could rest and hide.

People milled about, too, in and out of buildings, their cheeks sunken and eyes glazed.

Something pulled Macha to fly closer until she was ten feet from a man who she imagined was usually twenty pounds heavier and far more vibrant looking. *Enchanted and dying. But why would they bring dying humans here?*

She flew on, staying clear of any bright color or flying body. Macha rounded the next bend with care, unable to recall from the online photos what was behind it. She froze.

Fata, well over two dozen of them, were floating in an open area dotted with downed statues. A human sat or stood on the ground before each fata, all with the same glazed appearance. Wisps of white light floated from the person to the fata hovering before it. Macha witnessed a pale yellow fata's color brighten as a strong stream of white light flew from the human into the fata's core.

They're harvesting the humans' life forces. This explains the disappearances. It's much faster than waiting for Earth's magic to set in. Instead, Noro, clever Noro, elected to use creatures native to the earth, use their readily available life force to hurry the accumulation of fata power along.

Macha touched her limb to the space between her eyes, her third eye, the same spot she'd activated on Evelyn. *I must inform the girls. The more humans they harvest the sooner, the fata will be ready to fight.*

Macha opened her third eye and took in her surroundings like a video camera. She was still filming when a troop of fifty fata flew by and she started. *Fifty fata?*

"Where did they all come from?" Macha whispered.

"A fair question." A deep voice boomed at her back.

Macha stiffened. She would know that voice anywhere.

She dared not turn around, intent on recording the

scene for as long as possible. From what she'd seen so far, the witches would need every advantage they could get.

"Why don't you answer it then?" she asked.

Noro chuckled, a deep yet airy laugh. "Do I need to? You already know, my love."

Macha closed her eyes. She did know. The fata before her were stronger than she'd ever seen them on Hecate. There had to be a couple capable of opening a portal. Especially if they kept leaching life force from the humans for power.

"Then there's no need to pursue the triplets anymore?" Macha asked her tone careful, curious. A stretch of silence opened between them until finally Macha was compelled to turn and face Noro.

Her ex-lover floated, strong, more powerful than he'd ever been and more sure of himself, too. Macha couldn't believe she'd turned against her sisters for this creature's approval and a pat on the back from her father. *How stupid I was.*

"I loved you, Eve—"

She cut him off. "I go by Macha now, and strangely enough, I believe you. However, you didn't love me as much as you loved yourself, or my father's favor. The latter, I can't blame you for. It was my vice as well."

Noro shook his head. "Macha? So, I was right to fear you all those years ago. Claiming the name of the

Morrigan is a powerful thing." He paused and stared her straight in the eye. "You know better than to ask me to spare the girls. Your sisters betrayed our kind, us, and they live in those human shells. I will use those girls as I have been forced to use some of our kind, for the greater good. They will bring fata to Earth whether they want to or not. No matter how long it takes. After all the fata on Hecate call Earth home, their fate will be mine to decide."

"Use our kind?" Macha tried hard not to dwell on what fate Noro might decide for Evelyn, Lily, and Sara.

"To bring others over. The ratio was poor at first, and we lost a few in the portal. However, by harvesting humans, a group of fata managed what only you and your sisters had before. Albeit, poorly. It would take them years to create portals stable enough to bring over the entire population of Hecate. I see no need to wait that long when I have other options."

I have to send what I've seen to Evelyn.

Macha shot left, hoping to catch Noro off guard, to gain time. She flew through the trees, high into the sky, before darting low again, skimming the dirt to shake Noro.

The rustle of leaves and branches exploding off trunks came from behind, followed by a menacing, airy war cry.

It's All a Practice

Sara

THE AROMA of mint conditioner and hot steam filled Sara's lungs. She'd never been so sore or tired in all her life.

We're getting better, she thought as the glorious replay of working with Lily to trap Evelyn with air magic just hours before ran through her mind. Only days ago, maneuvering air with the dexterity and skill to best Evelyn—hell even forming it into a wall—would have been nothing more than a dream. Then again, just weeks prior Evelyn could barely walk. Sara wasn't sure which feat was more astonishing.

The only thing she was sure of was that both changes hinged on Evelyn, and while Sara remembered her status as most powerful triplet fondly, currently she was just happy Evelyn had been a good enough teacher for her to get the basics of air down.

Baby steps, start with baby steps. After that, practice makes improvement, Sara thought, changing the final word from "perfect," the word her adoptive father had always used as a weapon when he thought Sara hadn't been working hard enough to meet his high standards. Standards she'd never managed to meet, despite her many accomplishments, and which had only served to strain her connection to those parents further.

She shook her head, trying to keep the memories from her previous life, a life of isolation and not-good-enough, at bay. They were feelings Sara hid behind a calm, collected, bookish exterior, always filling her mind with knowledge so as not to have to examine what was already there. But feelings from her past had been popping up more often recently and Sara suspected she knew why. Now that Sara no longer was acting as a peacekeeper between Lily and Evelyn, Fern Cottage was more peaceful than it'd ever been. Only conflicts of the heart existed, of which Sara had many.

It seemed now was the time to finally convince herself she deserved to feel loved, entirely included, and worthy. It was something she'd even told Lily she wanted, but the actual act of believing she was enough was much harder.

Especially considering all her sisters had sacrificed that she hadn't.

Sara showered quickly so Lily would have hot water and dressed in record time, desperate for a distraction from her thoughts. Steam flew out of the bathroom as she opened the door to come face to face with Lily leaning against the wall in her bathrobe, waiting. The sisters' eyes locked and they high-fived, celebrating their earlier victory yet again before Lily disappeared into the bathroom.

Back in her bedroom, Sara found Evelyn wrapped in a Nordic-patterned cardigan staring at her altar. Since the New York witches had arrived in Ireland, the cottage had become more cramped. While most of their members volunteered to camp outside with Roman, Jane and Shefali were staying in Evelyn's room. Hence, Lily and Sara's room was now Evelyn's as well.

"Hey." Sara pulled thick socks from her dresser and perched on the bed. "Did you take a power nap? Looks like you just woke up."

Evelyn shook her head. "Spacing out. I feel a little weird . . . twitchy. I'm not sure why."

"Maybe you're hungry? Or exhausted?"

"Maybe," Evelyn agreed. "I'll go to bed right after dinner tonight. It's only going to get worse with the group arriving tomorrow, isn't it?"

Sara was sure Evelyn was right. Alfred had found air witches in the city in addition to other witches, wizards, and supernaturals who wanted to join them. Most of the volunteers were werewolves intent on avenging Caleb's death. The air witches were arriving the next day. Initially, Sara had felt sorry for the people destined to stay outside, until she poked her head into a tent one day. With the heating spells, thick air mattresses, flannel blankets and jarred candeo charms for light, the tents were homey.

And as warm as in here. Sara shivered despite her thick long underwear and sweats combo. "Speaking of dinner. I'm going to go help Mom and get as close to the fire as possible. You coming?"

***

FORKS CLANKED onto plates and chatter filled the cramped cottage from all corners. The cottage smelled of coconut and cooked onion from the meal, a vindaloo prepared by Shefali and Jane. Sara licked her lips, savoring the unique spices and flavors. She hoped her mother had gotten the recipe. Sara could get used to more spice in her life.

She leaned back in her chair, the fire burning hot at

her back. Sara claimed this seat as often as she could and no one, except Aoife, fought her for it.

Across the table sat Evelyn, chatting with Jane and Mary. Sara studied her sister. She looked more awake, though the way Evelyn kept placing her hand on her stomach told Sara something was still off. She wondered if that was where Macha had often lived in Evelyn. Maybe it was like when women become pregnant and touched their belly more? She'd always wondered how much of the gesture was subconscious. She was sure her sister had no idea she was doing it.

Sara shoveled another forkful of spicy vindaloo into her mouth and Nemain fluttered upward. Glancing at the clock Sara saw to her surprise it was nine. Most days Nemain would have asked to be let out two hours ago, though since Macha had left her pneuma had become more lethargic.

You ready to come out?

Nemain fluttered harder.

Sara put her fork down, gulped water to clear her mouth of any debris, and turned away from the others to face the fire.

"Caeliter," she murmured.

"Many thanks," Nemain said, appearing from Sara's lips. Her airy voice almost covered up Jane's gasp of surprise at Nemain's appearance. The New York witches still weren't used to the sight of seeing a pneuma pop out of the triplets' bodies.

"No problem. I'm surprised you didn't want out sooner."

"Badb and I have been traveling farther afield since Macha left. Keeping an eye out for an air witch performing magic in the dark of night. I need longer to recharge because of it. We hope to—" Nemain's black, round eyes widened.

"Nemain?" Sara waved a hand before her pneuma, who remained stiff, immobile. Her blood froze. Something was wrong. A glint of metal flew past Sara's shoulders, and a fork landed in the hearth, scattering embers and sparks. Someone gasped. Sara whirled around to see a plate fly as Evelyn pushed herself back from the table. Her chest was heaving, the space between her eyebrows glowing a brilliant, sapphire blue.

A heartbeat passed, quiet and calm after the panic. Then, Evelyn opened her mouth and screamed.

The Third Eye
Macha

DARKNESS WAS Macha's ally as she swerved through branches. She sensed Noro gaining on her as she flew for her life.

An airy limb flew up to her head, touching her third eye. It was hot, so unlike her chilled, energy-depleted body.

I must get higher. I need a clear shot for my memories to travel.

She soared above the trees, above the stench of exhaust and humans shrinking as small as ants. One hundred feet higher than any building in Paris. A mile, then two.

She surged upward, knowing without a shadow of a doubt this would be her last act. Noro would catch her before she reached her zenith or after she completed her task.

Let it be after.

"There's no point in fleeing, Eve. I can sense how weak you are. I'll catch you," Noro called after her, his voice full of glee and vigor.

He was strong, but Noro didn't have what Macha had. He'd never had a reason beyond his own pride to fight for others.

Macha, however, did: The centuries she'd lived with humans, deep inside them, pressed up against their own souls. Most never knew she was there, nestled next to their thumping heart. A few, such as the human she'd lived with when she was the Morrigan embodied, had embraced her. They'd welcomed a being once hell-bent on enslaving their entire race, all for the love of two creatures. Two selfish creatures who would never see the goodness of humans as Macha had. She hoped Noro and her father would meet their end on this planet.

The air thinned as the fata chased the pneuma to where the atmosphere of earth met the heavens—closer than they'd been to their home planet in centuries—in the space between Hecate, their old home, and Earth.

She halted. Her third eye burned on her face hotter than it had ever been. The time was now.

"I told you I'd catch you, Eve."

Macha did not hesitate. She pressed her third eye, opening the connection between her and Evelyn in a way she'd never done before. The information flew from her and she willed it to move fast, pressing harder into her body, providing as much energy as possible to the connection between her and Evelyn.

Noro's eyes narrowed. "I think not, my love. This is where your connection to those creatures ends forever." He touched her.

She screamed. His hate was almost too much for her, a repentant, pure soul, to bear. Still, she held strong, pressing harder into her scorching third eye, willing the information across the miles of land and sea.

Then, Noro did something unlike himself. An act that lacked bravado. He uttered a single word. A word reserved for the worst of their kind. A word there was no coming back from. And a word that meant instant death.

With that word, Macha's third eye stopped burning and she dissolved into the surrounding atmosphere.

A Bend

Evelyn

Evelyn wrenched her eyes open as the screaming inside her head ceased. She flinched. A dozen eyes were on her. Lily and Sara were at her side. Holy basil filled her nostrils and Evelyn turned to find Gwenn hovering behind her. Concern filled her aunt's moss green eyes and a calming spell pooled in her fingers, waiting.

"Evelyn. What happened? Are you OK?" Lily asked as one would speak to an injured child.

She furrowed her brow. How did they know about her vision?

Sara elaborated. "You were screaming."

I was screaming? No. Macha was . . . oh . . . Macha. Evelyn's heart plummeted at what she'd seen as the reason Macha had created the third eye connection between them clarified. *She expected something like this to happen.*

A pit of emptiness expanded inside her. A pit no being would ever fill. She pulled the sides of her cardigan closer, covering her torso.

"Our sister is gone, isn't she?" Nemain asked.

Evelyn nodded, unable to find the words for what she'd seen.

"What?" Lily asked, her tone bordering on frantic. "But how? You three . . . well, you aren't really alive, are you? How can she be gone?"

Badb's black eyes leveled not on Lily but on Evelyn. "It is true, not being able to sustain ourselves indefinitely, we are not truly alive. For us, disappearing into the ether is analogous to death. A pneuma that survives their fata body's death is still susceptible to puncture injuries from air and iron like when they were whole-bodied fata, especially if the air is administered by a knowing fata. Although something tells me neither air nor iron had anything to do with this. And Macha would not commit suicide by failing to seek a body to recharge in, especially considering the importance of her mission. Am I right, Evelyn?"

Macha's memories, a jumbled mess in Evelyn's brain, were unscrambling, assembling themselves into the story of the last hours of her life. Evelyn saw, with vivid clarity, Macha possessing a badger and a snake for hours at a time.

Evelyn nodded her head, not wanting to speak in case it halted the visions.

Nemain's limb flew to her mouth. "That means her death—"

"Her murder, you mean," Badb corrected. "There is only one other way we, both fata and pneuma, can die and cease to exist forever. Noro did this, didn't he?"

Evelyn nodded again, watching the reel of memories replay in her head: Macha getting caught sneaking around the zoo and flying high into the sky, away from Noro. Terror hammering through Macha as she fled. The sense of purpose until her last second.

"What is it?" Sara whispered.

"A curse." Nemain's voice echoed off the stones of the cottage as all fidgeting and breath stilled. "Fata, like some rare witches, do not need spells to work magic. They can make anything happen by willing it. What Noro did to Macha, however, is different. It is the single act in our culture where the caster needs to say it out loud and be touching the object of their curse. In that way, it is clear they mean it. It is often used as a punishment for a fata who committed a heinous act."

Her voice had thinned as she spoke, and Nemain took a moment to composed herself. "He sent her pneuma, which is to say all that remained of Macha, into the ether by force."

"But," Lily's tone was high, disbelieving. "Are you sure she hasn't gone to Earth to wait for a new human to live in?"

Badb shook her head. "Noro spoke the curse, didn't he, Evelyn?"

Evelyn replayed the end of the reel, seeing the memories Macha hurled through the emptiness of the sky a second before Noro spoke a single, bone-chilling word. The word that caused Macha's sapphire shimmer to evaporate into a white mist.

"Yes," Evelyn croaked. She cleared her throat. "He said Arimegin."

Badb and Nemain winced, and all the witches and wizards in the room gasped.

"Did anyone else feel that?" Brigit asked holding her chest, her brows furrowed.

Murmurs and nods of affirmations rose for a moment before falling back into silence as everyone turned to the pneumas for an explanation.

"The curse is the worst our kind has," Badb's tone was solemn. "Irreparable. None of us taught it to our children, your ancestors, to ensure the curse did not spread to Earth. Though it seems a part of you, deep within your genetic code, recognizes it all the same. It is unclear if this curse would work on a human soul. It would not be wise to attempt it."

A hushed silence fell over the room as each contemplated a curse so terrible a soul could not come back from it.

She's all alone now. Another wave of sorrow for Macha hit Evelyn.

"Macha died trying to protect us all and didn't deserve a traitor's death. She won't go unavenged." Evelyn swallowed loudly. "Macha saw things I need to tell you about."

Macha's revelations stunned them all.

"They're using humans not as slaves, but as food, sucking their life force out to gather power quickly," Aoife growled. "This changes things, doesn't it?"

She glanced around the room her gaze landing on Jane. "We must mobilize faster. The papers keep reporting people missing. By now there could be hundreds. Stockpiles of humans waiting, being held captive for the fata to come and suck out their vitality when they make their move."

"Not only that," Jane cut in, "but they're growing strong enough to bring over more fata. The cycle will only persist. You're right, Aoife, we need to mobilize."

The next ten minutes were a maelstrom of logistics.

Jane decided more supernaturals from her coven should make the trip to Ireland. Shefali called her many friends and family in India. The other New York witches phoned or texted covens around the globe.

Mary hung up her cell phone. "Morgane's calling some old friends."

"Hopefully they're younger than her," Gwenn teased, and a few people chuckled.

Evelyn couldn't. Her head still spun. It was too much. The loss of Macha, whom everyone else seemed to have forgotten alongside the fervor of planning. She had to get out of there. As she stood, Sara and Lily, who hadn't left her side, tightened their grips on her shoulders.

"What do you need?" Sara asked.

Evelyn exhaled. She was glad Sara hadn't asked her if she was OK. She wasn't up for lying.

"To be alone. Go outside. Tell whoever cares they can use my family's jets if they need to. Dad's number is in my phone. The password is 3333. You should call him, he likes you. Tell him it's an emergency and we may need to rent more planes on the company account. I'll take care of the rest if need be when I get back."

Sara nodded and loosened her grip. Lily followed suit.

"I'll be fine," Evelyn reassured her. "I need a minute alone."

The rain was coming down in sheets when she

stepped outside. *Arma.* Evelyn, swept her arm above her head, creating an umbrella-like shield, and trudged to the edge of the lake.

She's gone. Forever.

While everyone else in Fern Cottage seemed to consider Macha's death a side effect of the war Evelyn felt the pain as if it were a knife to her heart. Macha was the first person, being, she'd lost. And while they'd just started getting along, it was as if a sister Evelyn had known all her life had died. Beyond the emotional turmoil this put her in, she worried for practical reasons, too.

What will this mean when we face the fata?

It'd been so clear before. Lily, Sara, and Evelyn would train under their pneuma and then the six would enter the battle. Old and new, teachers and students, the Morrigan and the triplets united against one common enemy. But now she would be alone, with no pneuma, no integral but separate part of herself to fight beside. The magic of what she'd imagined as their indisputable victory had died with Macha.

She sat on a wet rock. Good didn't always triumph over evil. Why had Evelyn been stupid enough to think it did? Because she'd always gotten what she wanted? Because she got saved?

She ripped a handful of sopping wet grass from the ground. Dirt from its roots flew up and splattered her hand. Evelyn tossed the grass into the lake and leaned over to rinse her hand.

"Aren't you cold?" A deep voice cut through the wind and pounding rain.

Evelyn stiffened, her hand still immersed in the cold water. She'd forgotten Roman took his meals in his tent. In fact, the last thirty minutes were the first time since the incubus had arrived that she'd forgotten about him. Despite her militant efforts to avoid him in the days since he'd arrived, all of which were successful, Roman's playful eyes haunted her dreams.

I should have run to my room.

"I brought you a blanket."

Coarse fabric grazed her back. Her maternal grandfather's old sleeping bag. Brigit had lent it to a witch who soon complained that the fabric was too rough. Roman had switched with her.

Evelyn turned and saw Roman's careful eyes, the proffered sleeping bag already unzipped so she could slide it over her with ease. "Thank you," she said taking the bag and wrapping it around her shoulders. She stopped shivering, something she hadn't been aware she was doing.

"You're welcome."

She would have turned back to the lake but Roman stayed rooted in place, his eyes darting from her to the ground.

"Is there something else?" Evelyn sighed.

"What are you doing out here? It's freezing and you're alone. I can see Lily being out here, running or doing some crazy exercise, but if you're out here, something is up. Is it me?"

Evelyn snorted. He was right about one thing. Lily ran around in weather like this because she was an exercise nut. Besides the hours they spent outside for lessons, Sara and Evelyn preferred to cozy up beneath a blanket.

Roman quirked his head at her response.

"It's not you. You've actually done a great job of staying out of sight since you've been here."

Roman flinched. "Oh. That's good, I guess."

She bit her lip, regretting her words. "No, I'm sorry. That was cruel, something the old me would have said and meant. But if there's anything I've learned these last few days, it's that we can change. Macha—" Her voice cracked and Evelyn turned away, looking out onto the lake.

"Your pneuma?" Roman inched closer and sat a respectable distance outside Evelyn's shield spell on the damp grass. "Did something happen to her? I know I'm the last person you want to talk to, but once you shared your feelings with me. I hope you feel you still can."

A yearning rose in her at his words. A craving for the

way things used to be between them. When she could tell him anything and everything. Tears flooded her eyes.

"Oh crap. Please don't cry, Evelyn. If you want I can go get Lily and Sara? I didn't mean to offend you."

"Stay." Evelyn flicked her wrist, extending the shield out to cover Roman.

He glanced up; his eyes widened at the clear invitation before returning to her.

"They won't get it. And neither will you but," Evelyn turned to face him, "you'll listen. And you owe me so I don't feel bad making you sit in the cold."

Roman's lips twitched, but he remained silent, waiting.

"Macha died."

His blue eyes widened. "I'm sorry, Evelyn. I—I didn't even know that was possible."

She shook her head, and then she told him everything Macha had revealed to her. All they'd learned about the fate of the disappeared people and what fata were using them for. How they were preparing to fight, and soon. And worst of all, how a few fata had become strong enough to bring more over.

"That's insane," Roman whispered when she'd finished. "I mean, I never saw any of the fata, but I heard they were super weak."

"It's all my fault." Tears rushed down her face as

Evelyn spoke the words she thought every time she looked at a paper to find another person missing. "If I would have resisted, none of this would be happening. People all over the world are suffering because of me. People's life forces are being sucked out. Their families and friends are worried that they're gone."

"No way." Roman grabbed her hand and a shock of electricity shot between them.

Evelyn gasped. It was the first time since the day he'd returned that they'd touched.

Roman dropped her hand, expecting her to lash out like she had that day. "I apologize. I overstepped, but I can't let you continue on like that. If anything, all this is my fault." His spine straightened. "Which can only mean one thing."

Roman stood to tower over her, a determined glint in his eye. "I have to go to New York and take Alfred's place in rounding up as many supernaturals as I can. He's a better fighter and his talents are wasted trying to convince people to come here. Alfred can help train them while I motivate people to join."

He glanced around the massive field surrounding Fern Cottage. "I'll go talk to your mother about inviting people here. We'd be at an advantage if we trained together before attacking. If we can infiltrate the main faction, the one where Noro and Dimia are, then we stand a chance. Want to join me inside and deliver the proposal?"

Deliver the proposal? Evelyn choked on his business-like language.

"You realize this isn't a business negotiation, right?" she asked though she'd already thrown off the sleeping bag.

He held out his hand, and she took it without thinking. "I wasn't envisioning a boardroom. I was envisioning a war room."

The Air Witches
Sara

"Alfred's here!" Lily leapt off the sofa overlooking Brigit's garden. The door slammed shut behind her as she darted outside.

"Did she just run outside barefoot?" Brigit asked, her tone high with disbelief.

"I've said it before and I'll say it again: Girl's got it bad," Evelyn said, not bothering to glance up from her phone.

"Goddess be, I'll get a towel. As if I don't do enough mopping around here with dozens of people tramping around day in and day out." Brigit shook her head and disappeared down the hall.

Sara moved to the window and watched her sister rush across the garden and into Alfred's open arms. Though they'd only been together a little over a month, they'd been through so much already. It was impossible to imagine one without the other. Alfred thrust his hand into Lily's long, brown waves and Lily pulled his lips down to meet hers as if she needed Alfred more than air. Sara turned away, her face hot.

The front door opened and wind rushed in, raising goosebumps on Sara's skin. Gwenn and Aoife followed the gale, shaking the rain from their gear and kicking off their boots. Two women and three men followed.

The air witches.

"That girl ran right by us like we were chopped liver," Aoife muttered.

"No shoes or jacket either," Brigit walked back into the room and tossed the towel at Aoife. "Put that right inside the door. I don't want Lily's mud prints all over."

Gwenn laughed, then turning to the air witches and wizards pointed to the jacket and shoe racks. "You can put your stuff there. We'll set up tents for you outside after everyone eats a hot meal."

The newcomers obliged and walked into the living room, eyes wide and mouths hanging open.

"This place is straight out of a storybook," a willowy, black-haired witch a couple years older than the triplets said.

Sara smiled. "We had the same reaction when we first

arrived. Well, that among many others. I'm Sara." Sara held out her hand.

The black-haired witch blinked. "The fire witch?"

Sara nodded.

"Hmm, thought you'd be more intimidating and edgy. I'm Kim Wei." She took Sara's hand.

The others introduced themselves. There was Sasha Mendoza, Tim Tuala, Chase Kiser, and Denzel Strom, all air witches and wizards. Aoife volunteered to make tea and everyone settled in.

Sara eyed the group. She knew Alfred had found each of them in low-income areas of New York or New Jersey. If there was a common theme in her PhD studies, it was the history of witches and wizards as people on the outskirts of society. Often, they were poor or minorities, which seemed to be the case here, too. She sighed. It was a fact that had always bugged Sara and she hadn't let go of it, despite her months living as a witch and learning some could still live a good life on the perimeter of society. Still, she wished the stereotypes of her magical ancestors didn't hold true today.

Lily and Alfred walked through the door, water cascading off them.

Brigit pointed to the towel. "Wipe your feet."

"Thanks, Mom," Lily muttered her face flushed.

Alfred didn't bother with blushing. He looked jubilant to be back.

Sara's copper eyes roved over Alfred. His gait was smooth once more and she guessed he was nearing a full recovery.

Lily introduced herself to the group of air witches before taking Alfred's hand and pulling him back to the sofa.

Sara scooted over to make room for the lovebirds.

"Hey, Sara," Alfred beamed. "Where are the others?"

"Mary, Jane, and Shefali are getting supplies. We have to go into town about every day to keep everyone fed. Jane figured it would be best for the new arrivals to get to know us first, listen to our story, and meet our pneumas before meeting everyone else. The rest of your coven returned to New York with Roman to increase the efficacy of getting as many people here as soon as possible. Getting people up to speed quickly is imperative if we're to save the people Macha saw." Sara whispered Macha's name.

Though Evelyn was holding herself together, Sara noticed the sad gleam in her eyes every time Badb and Nemain were released. As if she'd developed sympathy pains, Sara's stomach had been testy since Macha's death. Sharp pains unrelated to food or actual illness plagued her every day. Sara knew her body was trying to tell her something, she just didn't know what.

Alfred's mouth tightened at the mention of Roman. "I heard his reunion with Evelyn was interesting. Anything changed since then?"

Sara shrugged. It wasn't her place to tell Alfred that the only person Evelyn allowed to comfort her over Macha's loss had been Roman. She wasn't sure it mattered. He had, as Evelyn told it, forced himself into the situation. "Too soon to tell. She said goodbye to him but they're not exactly chummy."

Alfred nodded as he took in the new information. "Sending Jane and Shefali to town for a few hours was a good idea. Most of the air witches and wizards were wary when I told them I was part of a coven." He glanced at the air witches and wizards chatting with Brigit and Gwenn. "Thankfully, your family can warm anyone up as long as Aoife isn't the one doing the talking. She's great for motivation but small talk is not her thing."

"I heard that," Aoife said, rounding the hearth, a tray of mugs brimming with steaming cinnamon tea in her hands. "Lucky for you, I take it as a compliment."

The next half an hour was spent listening to the triplets' story. *I can't believe so much has happened in such a short time,* Sara thought, listening to Brigit tell the tale.

Judging by the looks on their faces, the air workers seemed to agree. It was only when Brigit brought out the musty-smelling Hypatia's book and the other physical evidence Mary had acquired over the years that their expressions softened.

It's almost time, Sara thought as Brigit reiterated what the girls' pneumas had told them. That air witches were special and would be key in the fight against the fata.

"This is all good and well." Tim gestured to the book. "I'm open and the evidence you've supplied is convincing, but I'm having a hard time with this whole pneuma thing."

Mom called it.

"Caeliter." Sara opened her mouth wide for Nemain to fly out. There was a shimmer of red as Sara walked toward the group with Nemain floating at her side. Brilliant green appeared in Sara's periphery, Lily releasing Badb.

"Holy shit," Sasha whispered, her dark brown eyes wide.

"Seriously," Denzel echoed. "Do you do that every time you're trying to get someone to believe you? Because it works."

"Not until now," Lily answered. "But seeing your eyes I'm considering using Badb as an icebreaker at parties."

"You'll do no such thing," Badb said. The air witches jumped at her wind-laden voice, but neither Badb nor Nemain seemed to care. Instead, they stared at the new witches, black eyes round as ever. "You five will be of great help to our side if you stay. Which I hope you will."

"This is the most exciting thing that's ever happened in my life," Sasha exclaimed. "I'm in a new country for the first time, for shit's sake. And I'm about to battle aliens? Hell yeah, I'm in."

Kim, Chase, Tim, and Denzel each nodded their agreement.

We have air witches.

Sheepskin and Chocolate

Lily

LILY'S SHOULDERS relaxed as they drove across the perimeter of Mary's protective enchantments, one of the precautions Brigit insisted on when Lily requested a night alone with Alfred. A night Alfred would have been happy to wait for, but not Lily. Time was too short and their lives could end any minute.

I don't want to die a virgin. Not when I've found this amazing man. She grabbed Alfred's hand as he swiveled the wheel into a parking space behind the inn.

Alfred turned to look at her, his velvet brown eyes burning with desire. "We're here."

"We are," Lily agreed, leaning over to kiss him.

They grabbed their bags from the trunk and made their way into the inn.

"Wow," Lily said, as Alfred held open the door. "This is all ours."

The aroma of smoke from the hearth and wood polish enveloped her. A few chandeliers hung from the ceiling and the dark wood and red upholstered furniture were more elegant than she'd expected.

"You must be Lily and Alfred." An old man appeared from a room behind the front desk, his eyes glazed over courtesy of Aoife's ceremens work.

It had been no easy feat bewitching the proprietor and organizing other inns in town for his guests to stay in. Still, the McKays deemed it necessary for Lily and Alfred to have the entire inn for the night.

"We are." Alfred stepped forward to shake the man's hand.

"Good. Let me show you to your room."

They climbed two floors of creaky wood steps and stopped at a door at the top of the stairs.

"Penthouse suite." The old man chuckled at his own joke, unlocked the door, and pushed it open.

Lily's breath caught in her throat. The room looked like an old English hunting lodge with thick curtains, velvet chairs, and a massive canopy bed. There was a fire here, too, already filling the room with warmth. An over-the-top but luxurious white sheepskin rug and a box of chocolates lay sprawled before the flames, no doubt courtesy of Evelyn.

"It's beautiful," she murmured.

"I'm glad you like it," the innkeeper said. "Would someone show me to the door?"

Alfred nudged Lily.

"Oh! Right! I will," Lily said responding to the mental signal Aoife had planted in the innkeeper's head. The man was to leave them with the keys so Lily could seal the charms Mary had set with a locking spell. They walked back to the front door and Lily took the keys from the old man's dry, trembling hands before he faded into the dark night.

"Serostium," Lily whispered, turning the key in the lock, locking them in physically and magically. She was about to climb up the staircase when she realized the downstairs fire was still burning.

I should put that out. Explaining to the innkeeper why his inn burned down is expecting too much of Aoife.

"Eginura." Lily stood before the burning fire and water shot from her hands. She marveled at how the water came almost naturally. Before it had taken great concentration or a spike of adrenaline, like when she pushed Amon off of her in Alexandria. Lessons with Evelyn were paying off.

She stood there, watching the fire die, listening to the

sounds of sizzling and Alfred moving above her, unable to pull herself away. *Am I stalling? Am I actually ready for this?* Lily bit her lip and her chest seemed to freeze over.

As if in response a door creaked above.

"Lil? Are you alright?" Alfred's warm voice traveled down, thawing any doubts she had.

"Just putting the fire out. I'll be right there." She found Alfred standing before the large windows, flung open wide, allowing the chilly night air to seep into their cozy room. "What are you doing?"

"Come see."

Lily wrapped her arms around herself, more out of nerves than actual cold, and went to him.

His strong arms folded over her. "Look," Alfred whispered and pointed up with a single finger so as not to let her go.

Her eyes followed his finger from the woods behind the inn upward. Lily gasped.

The night sky shone above, ludicrous with starlight woven with dancing green waves. The northern lights. How had they missed them on the drive in?

A red beam shot through the green dispersing its own wavelike pattern and glimmering prettily. Lily laughed. It wasn't the northern lights at all. It was Badb and Nemain, doing their part to make her night with Alfred magical.

"They're putting on a show for us." Alfred squeezed her tighter.

Lily's nerves dissolved.

"Don't they know we can put a good one on for ourselves?" she murmured and turned to unbutton his shirt.

LILY FELL BACK onto the sheepskin rug and sighed. *Thank the goddess Evelyn had this rug put here.*

She ran one hand through the soft fur as Alfred rolled onto her other arm. The heat of him, the fire at their backs, her blood hot and full of desire running through her body made Lily's head spin. She closed her eyes and smiled, savoring the moment. The moment that could only happen once in her life.

It was perfect.

"Are you OK?" Alfred asked propping himself up on his elbow and staring down at her. Sweat glistened on his chest, which heaved with the exertion.

"OK? That was amazing. *You're* amazing. I'm . . . great." Lily pulled his face down to taste his lips once more.

They laid there silent, basking in the glow of the fire

and the love they'd made. Lily didn't want to be the first to break the spell.

Luckily, Alfred moved first. He lifted himself to kiss her once more and stared down at her. "I have something for you. A surprise I've been saving for a special occasion. Stay right here and I'll get it." He folded the rug over her, engulfing her in cozy fur, and inched the chocolates closer so she barely needed to move her fingers to pluck one from the box.

Lily popped a chocolate into her mouth. Its smooth, refined flavor exploded on her tongue as she watched Alfred walk away, the muscles of his tapered back traveling down to a tight rear. A flashing image of Alfred's sunshine yellow body moving with hers in perfect harmony resurfaced in her mind and she licked her lips.

I never thought of yellow as a sexy color but he proved me wrong.

Across the room, Alfred unzipped a side pocket of his duffle and plucked out a small blue box adorned with a white ribbon.

Lily stiffened.

Unable to hide the box, Alfred made his way across the room quickly, kneeling on the rug beside her and holding it out. "I know we haven't been dating long, Lil." His voice was thick. "Still, I want you to know from the moment I saw you I thought you were special. I wanted to give you something to show that."

He pressed the box into her hand.

Holy shit. Is this what I think it is? What will I say?

She'd never seriously considered being engaged or married. Hoped . . . one day it would happen, but even with Alfred being as wonderful as he was, she'd often been too preoccupied with other matters. Lily untied the ribbon and paused.

"Are you going to stare at it or open it?" Alfred teased.

She lifted the lid. Inside, was a ring Lily was familiar with, though with a modern twist.

"A Claddagh," she breathed, marveling at the modern gold and silver spirals around a heart that was encircled by hands and topped with a crown. A small emerald lay in the center of the heart, glittering up at her. "My mother wears one."

"As a wedding band; it's what gave me the idea. I realize we haven't been dating long and I come on strong. I told you the day we met, I see someone I like and I tell them. I knew you'd probably freak if I proposed but I thought it could be a promise ring? One that honors your heritage. If it's too soon I understand, but I liked the idea of announcing we're together to the world."

A lump rose in her throat. Warmth welled within her, though something else, something aching was there, too.

Only then did she realize she'd actually hoped Alfred was proposing. She slid the ring on her right hand and smiled wide to hide the disappointment. "My mother's ring was from my father. Thank you for considering where I came from. It's lovely."

Alfred cocked his head.

"Alfred, I love it. Thank you." She pulled him close and their lips met, hot and needy once more. Though when they pulled away, she found his eyes probing hers.

"But what aren't you saying? I can sense you're holding back something, babe. I don't like it," Alfred whispered.

Was she being silly? They hadn't been together long, and they were young, but there was no denying they'd been through so much already, life-changing scenarios most people could never even dream about. If she was being honest with herself, Lily knew she rarely felt so sure about people, certainly not people outside her family. That was telling in itself, but more importantly, the truth was that she loved Alfred and never again wanted to be separated.

Heat burned across her cheeks as Lily, aware of Alfred's velvet brown eyes on her, gathered her courage and cleared her throat. "I'm not sure. I guess I want you to know if you do ask me to marry you, I want to use the same band. I want to adhere to the traditions of my blood and slip this ring," she touched the Claddagh, "onto the other hand. Whenever that time may be," she added, hoping to the goddess she didn't sound as needy as she felt.

Alfred leaned forward, and Lily drew closer to him instinctively. He took her hand in his, slipped the ring off her finger, then set her right hand down and took the left.

"Is that time now?" Alfred whispered.

Tears she hadn't realized were brimming in her eyes fell down her face and Lily nodded. "It's now."

The ring slipped onto her left hand.

Clinging to Happiness

Sara

THE COTTAGE DOOR CRACKED OPEN.

Sara glanced up from her paper to find Lily at the door, an impish grin splitting her face. Alfred was right behind her looking, for once, more sheepish than his partner.

"It looks like someone had a good time last night." Evelyn put down the paper she'd been reading and wagged her eyebrows.

"As a matter of fact, yes." Lily glanced back at Alfred. "Thanks for the rug and chocolates, Evelyn. It made the room so cozy." She pushed her long brown hair, sopping wet from the rainy walk to the cottage, behind her ears and took off her rain jacket.

Evelyn sat up straight. "No freaking way."

Lily's grin grew wider.

Sara's brows furrowed. *Did I miss something? What's happening?*

Her head swiveled from sister to sister. Lily lifted her arm slightly. Light played on her hand and a glint of gold caught Sara's eye. Her mouth dropped open.

"You're engaged!" Evelyn roared. She jumped up and hurled herself at Lily who let out a squeal of delight.

"Look! It's a Claddagh! Like Mom has," Lily said as soon as Evelyn released her. "Didn't Alfred pick out the perfect one? It's so modern and chic!"

"He did a damn good job," Evelyn confirmed.

Alfred blushed. He looked as though he wanted to sneak into the cottage and sit quietly on the couch.

Good luck with that. Sara shook her head and made her way over to her sisters, still flabbergasted. That something so joyous, so fun, and so life-affirming could happen at this point in their lives did not correlate with her day-to-day activities.

I've become too used to thinking about the news and our challenges—my issues—not what may come after them.

"Let me see." Sara leaned in between her sisters. Their long blonde and brown hair tickled her face as she admired Lily's engagement ring. "It's beautiful. Alfred, you chose well," Sara said, and she meant it. She, too, would want a Claddagh ring, if she ever got engaged.

"You know what this means, right?" Evelyn sang out

each word louder than the next. "We get to celebrate!" She pumped her hands in the air and everyone around her laughed.

"Celebrate what?" Brigit asked, peeking out the bathroom door her towel turban leaning to one side of her head.

In answer, Lily lifted her left hand.

"Goddess be!" Brigit squealed, and barreled out of the bathroom, tightening her robe as she walked. "You're engaged! Oh, my! How wonderful!" She pulled Lily close, eyes brimming with tears. "You, too, young man." Brigit let go of her daughter and tightened her grip around Alfred, who looked equal parts astonished and pleased. "You're a wonderful man. I'm happy to welcome you into our family."

"Thanks," Alfred said, his face redder than Sara had ever seen it. "Maybe we should shut the front door? I'm freezing."

"Yeah, let's move this party inside! Sara, can you help me move all the papers and books off the coffee table? I'll need the space to make notes. We have a party to plan and I crown myself lead planner!" Evelyn bustled back into the sitting room before Sara could answer.

Lily looked as though she was trying hard not to laugh. "I didn't expect this exuberant of a reaction from you, Evelyn. I never pictured you planning a party. Hiring someone sure, but planning it? Where has my heiress sister gone?"

Sara had a sneaking suspicion she knew why Evelyn was so excited about planning the party. An engagement party meant a night of letting loose. It also meant that between their lessons during the day and planning a party at night, Evelyn's mind would be occupied. Sara had plenty of experience with keeping her mind busy so she didn't have to deal with the hurt and isolation inside. It was one of the extremes she used to self-medicate, meditation being the other. Neither ever fully made her feel whole, loved, an integral part of something.

Planning a party meant Evelyn wouldn't have to think of Macha or deal with her feelings for Roman. Sara's gut clenched and twisted. She took a deep breath to quell the pain she'd been experiencing since Macha's death, then pushed it aside, not willing to let the sensation steal the moment of joy.

"Probably missing all the New York social affairs and desperate for a party. This soiree will probably be the best one either of us has ever been to, Lil. Let Evelyn do as much as she wants."

"I second that. I should always be the boss," Evelyn agreed.

Lily laughed. "I don't know, you guys. The commune threw great parties. That reminds me, we still have to call them! It will be late in Oregon but Rena may still be up. Do either of you mind if Alfred and I use our room? I want to talk to Rena on speakerphone."

"Go for it," Evelyn and Sara said in unison and the newly engaged pair disappeared down the hallway.

The rest of the day passed in a whirl of congratulations, lessons with Badb and Nemain, and a welcoming of more newcomers from New York. They were a mixed group of supernaturals who had decided not to wait for Roman to fill up the Locksley jet and flew themselves over with Celestine as a chaperone.

Lily glowed as creatures congratulated her. Everyone, no matter if they'd known her and Alfred a minute or for years, seemed genuinely happy for the pair.

Surety of the future is fleeting so people will cling to their happiness.

Sara shook the dire thought away. Why was she being so negative? Even Aoife, normally so on task and gruff, was enjoying a second glass of champagne to celebrate the engagement. Her gut twisted and Sara flinched before pushing it away yet again.

Vicarious Living

Evelyn

Evelyn jotted another name down on the guest list. She was planning on calling the village's only caterer that day, so they would have plenty of time to prepare for what was sure to be the largest party they'd ever catered. She'd have happily flown over her favorite chef for Lily and Alfred's engagement party, but Lily had put her foot down when she offered.

"Use the caterer in town Mary mentioned. This party will be extravagant enough, what with people flying in from across the world."

I suppose she's right.

"Actually, I've been thinking," Lily handed Evelyn a mug of coffee before sitting down in an armchair. Their bodies were used to the early morning sparring sessions and had woken up without the help of an alarm, despite the long night of celebrating. Only Sara had slept in, a fact that did not surprise Evelyn, who was now sharing Sara's queen bed. Her bedmate had been up tossing and turning most of the night.

"I'm happy with a family party," Lily said. "You don't need to go to all this work, planning for people we barely know. As long as Rena, Annika, Selma, and you guys are here, that's all I need."

"No way!" Evelyn hissed. "You're engaged! This is huge, and you deserve to be celebrated."

"But it looks like so much work." Lily gestured to the piles of paper before Evelyn. The caterer info and menu, the list of guests, the closest rental for a porta-potty, which with all the new people arriving to train they'd need anyway.

It *was* a lot of work. Evelyn found herself thinking she should have paid her event planners much more. She waved her hand in denial. "It's fine! I like doing things like this. It's like I'm back in the corporate world, in charge."

Lily chuckled and turned to face the fire, a serene smile on her face. "Well, thanks again. It's nice to bask in the glow of being engaged without worrying about logistics. It's a pleasant change of pace."

"Speaking of basking in the glow. How was your night alone with the sunshine daemon?" Evelyn pulled her gaze from the guest list and sat up. She doubted she'd hear intimate details as she would with Vicencia, but she had to live vicariously through *someone*. At the very least, sex talk was a welcome distraction.

Lily pinked, reminding Evelyn of the first time she saw Alfred and Lily together. Her sister was such a schoolgirl.

"Don't tell me you didn't go through with it? What about your 'I don't want to go into battle a virgin. What if I don't make it out?' speech?"

Rising from her chair, Lily peeked out the window, apparently checking that Alfred, who had joined the rest of the supernaturals outside in a tent, wasn't listening. Her eyes locked with Evelyn's as she lowered herself back down and leaned forward.

"We did. And it was ah-may-zing. I wasn't joking when I thanked you for the rug. That was like—whoa. He proposed on it." Lily paused. "Can I keep it?"

Evelyn rolled her eyes. "Like I want your sex sheepskin rug! Consider it a deflowering gift."

Lily continued to chat about her night with Alfred, focusing on what they said, how she felt when their eyes met, and how their magic had played off each other. Evelyn found the last detail riveting. The only time she'd slept with another supernatural she'd been suppressing her power.

What would it have been like if I hadn't? Maybe it

would be different anyhow because Alfred is a daemon and Roman is an incubus? If his touch made me feel the way it did . . . ugh, stop thinking about him like that, brain! She pushed Roman, the thought of whom confused her all too often, from her head and focused on Lily.

"That sounds perfect," Evelyn said when Lily finished.

"It was. I'm so glad I waited for him." Lily leaned back in her chair, content to stare into the fire.

Evelyn, however, knew silence would bring thoughts of Roman or Macha, and wanted neither. "So, when do you think your family can make it for your party? I want to call the caterer today and give them a solid date, so they can plan when to shop for food."

"Oh! I forgot to tell you. Mom—Rena—texted me last night and said they bought the first tickets they could. They'll be here in two days and will stay for a week."

Evelyn marked down the dates. "Sounds good, I can't imagine a caterer in this tiny of a town is busy this time of year. I'll ask for three days after Rena, Annika, and Selma arrive and make it worth her time if she complains about the short notice."

Lily bit her lip. "Thanks again for doing this. I want you to know, I don't have a job now, but I'll pay you back for the party expenses when I do."

"Nope," Evelyn said, her voice hard and serious.

"Mom and our aunts have already taken over paying for half. They want to so don't try to convince them otherwise. I would have covered the whole thing if they'd let me. Consider it our engagement gift to you."

"First a deflowering gift and now an engagement gift. I had no idea the New Year would bring me so many presents."

Evelyn sighed. "If there's one thing I've learned recently, it's that you never know what the day will bring you. Enjoy the good as it comes. You never know when it will disappear."

Spreading

Sara

Tents littered the field outside Fern Cottage. Sara poured her coffee, emptying the carafe and made a new pot, knowing someone would venture in from the tent village soon to fill a thermos or make breakfast. It was the new way of things.

Though the newcomers tried to stay out of the main house as much as possible, Fern Cottage had transformed into a hub of activity. It acted as a community bath (every other day people were allowed to shower), kitchen, and meeting area. Sara imagined the cottage as a village train station with people coming and going all day long. She didn't mind. With every new arrival, she saw another soldier against the fata, increasing the likelihood they'd all survive the next battle.

She grabbed a paper waiting on the dining table. *Only three today. Mary must be busy this morning.*

Sara wondered if her aunt had a birth to attend to. Her schedule had been hectic these past weeks as Brigit opted to stay at home with the triplets rather than act as a midwife in the family business. Sara wondered if Mary used magic to ease the babies into the world a little faster as she still made it to most of their practice sessions, helped supply the cottage with food, and brought a cheery attitude to the cramped quarters.

And brings me my papers. It's astonishing she hasn't run herself ragged.

Glancing down at the paper, Sara saw the usual headlines dominated the first page: An economic crisis, a bombing in the Middle East, a shooting at a mall in the U.S., and the recent scandal in the White House.

Would any of these be issues if the wider world knew what they were doing? Sara doubted it. The papers would be filled with headlines of magical aliens and the atrocities committed against humans. Perhaps there would be a few articles of people and countries long at war banding together to fight. One could only hope.

She sipped her coffee, flipped the page, and nearly spit out the hot liquid. "Oh my goddess," she whispered, though not quietly enough. Lily and Evelyn stopped what they'd been doing in the sitting room and rushed into the kitchen-diner.

"What is it?" Lily whispered. There were still six sleeping occupants in the cottage—one of them being Brigit, who deserved her sleep after cooking, cleaning up after, and helping to train an entire camp of people. The other three were Selma, Rena, and Annika, who'd arrived late last night after many airline delays to attend the engagement party. At Jane and Shefali's insistence, the Terramar residents had taken Evelyn's old room, while the New Yorkers moved onto cots in Brigit's room.

Sara pointed to an article that took up half a page. It was the largest one yet that had to do with the fata, though of course they were not mentioned. The article proclaimed half the population of a small town in England had come down with the same illness while another quarter had gone missing. The unaffected quarter consisted of the elderly, babies, and the sick. Not people the fata would consider pulling life force from as it's already depleted. And they probably wanted babies to grow so they can harvest them later. They're becoming more tactical. A chill swept over Sara. The journalist joked that the quarter of the population who had gone missing may have run away, not wanting to catch whatever illness was afflicting their neighbors.

"Where is the town?" Lily asked.

"Here," Evelyn pulled out her phone and pointed to a spot on the northwest coast of the island. She clicked a link and a webpage appeared. "There are less than a thousand inhabitants, but still, that's almost five hundred the fata are sucking the life from, the most yet." Evelyn's face tightened.

Sara's stomach twisted at the pained look on her sister's face. She was sure Evelyn was reliving the vision Macha had sent her.

"They couldn't all stay in Paris," Evelyn said finally. "I bet their human advisors told them to move to avoid attention."

"Sounds very Nora." Lily's lips pursed in disgust.

Sara had to agree; their mother's ex-best friend undoubtedly had a knack for manipulation. "I think we should act soon. It's best if we're at the advantage, attacking them before they're fully ready or too many leave the main camp. That is, if we aren't already too late." Her heart sank at the idea of having to chase fata around the planet.

"I agree, but are *we* ready?" Evelyn asked.

Sara knew what she meant. Most of the new recruits were even worse with air magic than the triplets were when they'd first started. Even with the addition of one more air witch, bringing their grand total up to six, it seemed unlikely they were prepared to fight an army of fata and the Acolytes of Hecate.

At least we've gotten stronger. Mom and our aunts, too.

Sara thought back to the group lesson last night, where Aoife and Gwenn had wowed everyone with their manipulation of air walls, pinning Jane and Brigit to the ground as if they were fata. Evelyn and Mary were beyond their level. Sara and Lily were improving. Sara tried not to think about the new recruits arriving with Roman that day.

Hopefully, they'll be fast learners. We can't wait much longer.

"OUT OF THE WAY!" Sasha, the air witch from the Bronx, screamed.

Sara whipped about and saw a wall of air hurtling toward her. She flung herself to the ground and a whoosh of hardened wind swept above her. Her arm hit a rock as she landed and a yelp of pain escaped her.

"Sorry!" Sasha called and Sara waved her off with her good hand. There was no way she could be mad at a wall like that.

A swishing of material and the scent of jasmine filled

her nose as two feet materialized before Sara. "Are you OK? Those were some quick reflexes. It's obvious you've been sparring for a while."

She glanced up. Kim, the other air witch from New York stood before her, a hand held out to help Sara up.

"I'm fine, thanks." Sara took Kim's hand. It was soft and warm, so unlike Sara's own hands, which ran cold unless she was playing with fire.

"My sisters and I have been sparring every day for the past two weeks. Evelyn's gotten good, so you could say I've gotten equally good at getting out of her way."

"Don't be so modest. I've seen you practicing. You're the strongest fire witch I've ever met." Kim grinned and Sara looked away, flustered as she usually was when Kim paid her notice. Which, as it turned out, happened often.

"Well, like I said, we've been practicing a lot," Sara mumbled. A low swirling in her belly told her Nemain had awoken and was having a laugh at Sara's awkwardness. Sara scowled; she wished her pneuma would have stayed asleep. As if Evelyn's teasing wasn't bad enough, now she'd have to hear Nemain's, too.

"Did I say something wrong?" Kim asked, her brows furrowed.

"What? No! I'm sorry. My pneuma woke up. I should let her out, she's being—persistent. Excuse me, I'll go over there so as not to gross anyone out." She walked about twenty feet away.

"Caeliter," Sara said and opened her mouth. Nemain appeared an instant later with a wide smile on her face. It was, Sara realized, the first smile she'd seen from her pneuma since Macha's death. Her annoyance lessened a touch.

"You should talk to her," Nemain said. "It's obvious she likes you."

Sara shrugged. "I like her, too. She's cool, smart, and powerful but now is not the time. My sisters are wrapped up in their own relationship issues. One of us has to have a clear head."

Nemain shook her head, clearly disappointed. "You don't have to act the martyr, Sara." She turned and surveyed the scene.

As if not being in a relationship even counts as playing the martyr. Sara recalled Lily's loss of Em, Evelyn's torture, and Macha's death. She'd had a few scrapes, but nothing compared to them.

"You started air practice early. Why did the schedule change?" Nemain asked.

"We have a lot of people who are behind and wanted to get them started right away. We planned on waking you and Badb up soon. Roman and Morgane should arrive any minute with a bus full of more people. We'll need you guys to give the witches and wizards the tutorial. We'll be practicing or fitting the non-witches and wizards with weapons. Roman said he had a very mixed bunch." She puffed up her cheeks and let out a long exhale.

Nemain's dark eyes ran over Sara. "You rarely look this tired from sparring. What's on your mind that I missed?"

"I read an article in the paper this morning. The fata have taken half a town in England. They're getting bolder and we'll have to act soon. It's stressful, trying to get everyone up to speed so fast."

"Well," Nemain shook her head, "That changes things. I—" She stopped short, her eyes trained on the orchard behind Sara.

Sara turned to find a massive group of people emerging from the trees and stiffened. She relaxed only when she spotted Roman off to the side leading the crowd toward them.

For a second there I thought we were being infiltrated. She shook her head. That was impossible. Brigit had spelled Fern Cottage so heavily, not even the security at the White House could compare.

"It's Roman and his recruits," Sara said, seeing her pneuma rise higher in the air and puff herself up like a peacock.

"Oh. Right, I see him now," Nemain floated back

down. "I should have a word with Badb. Our job just became much more difficult." Nemain soared off.

Those performing air magic, or trying to, wound down their spells and the two groups walked toward each other.

There must be over one hundred people. Good thing we aren't staying here much longer. Mom would eventually flip out. Even with the conscious decisions of many to go into the village to eat or stay at the inns, the stress of hosting was getting to Brigit.

"I hope Roman told them to bring tents," Lily said sidling up next to Sara with Alfred. "We've cleaned out the nearest sporting goods store."

Sara scanned the new recruits as they drew closer, wondering what kind of hidden powers they'd find. Someone bumped into her. Sara turned to find Kim.

"I recognize some of them," Kim said, her voice low and eyes narrowed into slits. "A couple are air witches. Powerful ones, too. I used to practice with them but never on a schedule or at the same place twice. They're paranoid as hell and don't like to be affiliated with other groups. You said the guy's name you sent back to recruit was Roman?"

Sara nodded.

"Well, whatever this Roman guy said must have been super freaking convincing."

Sara turned back to face the group. She agreed with

Kim. You don't convince that many people to drop their lives and run into a battle without having a damn good argument.

"He's a businessman, a damn good one at that. Plus, he had a good incentive to bring us an army," Lily said, raising her eyebrows. "What do you say we go meet the newbies?"

All I Wanted

Evelyn

Evelyn's mouth gaped as Roman crossed the field with an army at his back.

I brought them all for you, his smoldering gaze said, loud and clear.

And in case she wasn't catching his drift, Roman strode through the torrential rain to the giant shield they practiced under and straight up to Evelyn. He inclined his head, as reverential as a full bow, practically screaming to everyone around them he'd found an army, for her.

It's not enough, but it is a step in the right direction. Evelyn's eyes locked with Roman's.

"Welcome back, Roman," Gwenn came between them, making it clear she had this under control.

Evelyn's shoulders relaxed. She hadn't realized they'd been so tense.

"Thank you. As you can see, I've brought a little extra company this time. Don't worry, I purchased a bulk order of tents before we left the city. They're on the bus."

"We appreciate your foresight," Gwenn said. "Did you happen to stop at the grocery on your way in?"

Morgane popped her head through the crowd. "We loaded the bus with supplies! Don't you worry! I spoke with Brigit already. I'll be taking twenty to Nora's house. We'll use her kitchen there. Use anything we want, really. Trash it. Throw a rager, as the kids say." Morgane raised her eyebrows. "Hopefully Nora doesn't want her home in one piece whenever she gets back."

"Wonderful," Gwenn said. "Now, what do you say we learn what the lot of you can do?"

FINALLY, Evelyn understood all the creature types called out from the crowd. It was a relief to not feel ignorant any longer. She caught Lily nodding her head as each person classified themselves and Aoife placed them in a training group. Evelyn recalled her sister's main gripe after they'd entered Peacock Manor to save her.

"It was like we were oblivious about creatures other than witches and vampires."

That's no longer the case. We're a part of this world now.

A young woman with dyed gray hair stepped out from behind Eros, who'd returned to Fern Cottage with Roman. Evelyn did a double take. She knew that girl.

The girl glanced back at the person behind her and Evelyn's eyes widened.

Goddess be, him, too! I used to see them at clubs all the time! Holy crap. My old world is following me into my new one.

As if the girl had heard her she turned her head, caught Evelyn's eye and waved.

"Friend of yours? Or are you checking out Eros? He is the picture of a perfect elf, isn't he?" Roman's scent of cloves preceded him as he appeared out of nowhere.

Evelyn gave him a withering look and shook her head. "So smooth. And no, I'm not checking out Eros, though you're right about him being the picture-perfect elf. Have you seen him fight? He's *inspiring*." She breathed out the last word like a teenager swooning and bit back a smile when Roman's lips turned down. Served him right, trying to woo her in front of everyone.

"I was actually noticing the girl behind him. We used to see each other at clubs. Kind of played off each other for attention; we even took a shot or two together. I never knew—" She paused holding back the words that were too stupid to utter. Of course she hadn't known the girl was a supernatural—she hadn't even known she was one.

"She's a witch, too," Roman supplied looking relieved not to have to compete with a dreamy elf. "An air witch. You had one under your nose the entire time. Her boyfriend is an earth wizard. Neither belongs to a coven to better keep her identity secret. I bet, back in the day, she was drawn to you, without realizing why. I found her through sheer luck. Literally walking down the street and caught a whiff of a witch. Followed her for a while and saw her play with her power, manipulate the wind to retrieve a piece of paper that had blown away. Confronted her right then and there."

Evelyn's eyes widened. "That was ballsy of you." A laugh overtook her. "I guess I can't say I'm surprised. You were assertive during our courtship too." As soon as the words left her mouth, she wanted to shove them back in.

They fell into an awkward silence and Evelyn allowed her attention to wander back to the army before them. One more person declared himself an air wizard, bringing their grand total up to nine.

Roman did well. Everyone here looks strong-bodied and able. The fata are only expecting us and a few others. They'll be blindsided when we show up with a two-hundred-person army and air witches.

"Evelyn?"

"Hmm?" Evelyn hummed, lost in her own thoughts.

"Where are we now? Like how much do you still hate me? You don't have to tell me but I'm curious if there's ever a way—"

"Don't you dare ask me to forgive you." Evelyn closed her eyes for a moment, begging for the strength to repel him. "I'm not even close to forgiving you yet. I thank you for bringing all these people and showing up again. You could have stayed in the states where it was safe. At the very least, you returning here and bringing an army leaves me with no doubt you're on my side now."

Roman nodded. "That's all I want, to be on your side. By your side." He let out a long sigh. "I'll go bring in the tents." Roman turned and walked through the trees toward the hedge.

Evelyn watched him go, her heart thumping traitorously hard in her chest as the distance between them increased.

Engagement Party
Lily

THE WIDE-LEGGED pants of her jumpsuit billowed as Lily spun at Alfred's behest. A faint aroma of grapefruit lifted off the fabric. Lily pictured Mary doing the same move years earlier.

"Not at all what I pictured you wearing but I love it. Come here, babe." Alfred held out his hand and drew Lily in so the faux fur stole she wore grazed his cheeks. Their lips met and Lily melted into him.

The outfit was not what Lily would have chosen for her engagement party either, but Mary insisted Lily try on the keepsake she'd been hanging onto for years. While Lily balked when Mary first brought the jumpsuit over, she had to admit, she looked pretty rocking in it.

"Things always come back into style," Lily quoted Mary.

"Anything you wear would look stylish."

Lily smiled. If he could utter obvious untruths with such devotion, she was with the right man.

"Hey, lovebirds." Evelyn sidled up next to them. She looked regal clad in a long-sleeved, black velvet dress. "Sara and I can only hold your guests off for so long while you two make out. Everyone wants to talk to the couple of the hour."

Lily's lips turned up and she stared out at the scene before them. Lights dripped from the trees in the orchard, proclaiming the outside boundaries of the vast shield the witches and wizards had charmed to keep the wind, rain, and cold out. Glowing balls of fire encased in breathable protective bubbles floated around the party providing light and warmth. The beat of the music was fast and merry. Food and drink were everywhere. Savory aromas of mulled wine and roasting meat overwhelmed the garden's typical floral and herbal notes. People milled about, enjoying the time off from training to relax.

"They definitely throw a good party," Alfred said following her gaze. "Your family never does anything halfway."

"Nope. We should mingle like Evelyn said." Many people were stealing glances at them.

"Al!" A burly man with a barrel chest and blond beard

called out. "Can we steal you from your bride-to-be for a minute?"

"Who's that?" Lily asked.

"Zed, werewolf and childhood friend from New York. I saw him in the crowd Roman brought but we haven't had a minute to connect. Do you mind?"

"Go on," Lily said, catching sight of Morgane at the edge of the crowd nearest the lake. She hadn't spoken with the old witch since she'd arrived, busy as Morgane was shuttling people to and from Nora's house, making grocery runs, and training. Lily inched her way to Morgane, stopping every few feet to say hello and thank someone for coming.

"Come to me, my pretty!" Morgane cackled once Lily was within earshot.

Lily snorted as the group she'd paused to make small talk with turned to stare at Morgane. "Excuse me," Lily said. "She's going a little senile."

Looks of understanding dawned and the group of well-wishers urged her on.

"Thought you'd never make it." Morgane took a sip of her drink, permeating the night air with whiskey fumes.

"You and me both." She wrapped her arms around Morgane. Her old bones stuck out, but there was hard muscle there, too. She might look frail and she couldn't move that fast, but the old woman was anything but weak.

"Congratulations on your engagement. Happiness won fairly after such hardship." Then Morgane's hazel eyes drifted into the crowd and locked on Evelyn. "Is she OK?"

"Better. She's strong now. I'm convinced her weakness had as much to do with clearing the air with Roman as it did with gaining physical strength back."

"Lovely men. Yours and Evelyn's."

"Thank you. But Evelyn and Roman aren't together."

Morgane shrugged. "He could have fooled me the way he talked about her." She turned to face Lily full on for the first time. "Things have changed with you three, too. I see it in the way you talk, how you hold yourselves around each other."

Morgane was the woman who first saw the triplets together after a lifetime apart. When Lily thought back to the first day she met her sisters, she couldn't believe the changes either. Sara and Lily had gotten along well enough right away but Lily and Evelyn's relationship was like night and day. She was glad they'd found their way from that tense ride home, those cutting remarks, and shared glowers.

"They're my bridesmaids," Lily said, still giddy from the memory of asking her sisters and their enthusiastic response that morning.

A smile split Morgane's weathered face. "That's wonderful."

They chatted a few minutes more before another group of guests called Lily over. She milled about, smiling and laughing as the night stretched on. A song she recognized blasted out of the speakers and a sudden urge to dance overcame Lily. She excused herself from the group she was chatting with to find Alfred.

She needn't look far. He'd been waiting right behind her.

"Care to dance?" Alfred asked, a twinkle in his eye.

"Are you sure you aren't a ceremens?"

Alfred beamed, exposing his dimples and making her heart skip a beat as he swept her to the center of the crowd onto an impromptu dance floor.

They swirled and twirled. Bodies moved around them, some in harmony and others—Morgane and Mary— to their own rhythm. It didn't matter; every face wore a smile. Alfred dipped Lily, and she caught sight of Sara dancing tentatively with Kim. She bit the side of her lip and grinned. There was no doubt Kim was into her sister. Or that Sara was the one hampering any feelings that might develop between the pair. *She needs to loosen up.*

The music slowed and Alfred pulled her in close. Lily spotted Evelyn dancing on the other side of the impromptu dance floor. Her partner was a handsome werewolf who looked thrilled to have the witch in his arms. Lily couldn't blame him. Evelyn looked radiant. No one who saw her would have ever thought she was having anything less than the time of her life.

Unless they saw how Evelyn's eyes drifted to Roman every few minutes.

"They'll figure it out, babe," Alfred said, kissing her cheek.

"How did you know what I was thinking?"

"When you're thinking about your sisters or anyone you love, it radiates off you. It's one of the things that draws me to you the most."

"I want them to be happy like we are. Sara needs to let herself and Evelyn . . . well, I won't pretend to know what she needs, but I know what she wants."

Alfred said nothing, simply held her tighter. Too soon, the song stopped and instead of flowing into the next tune a magically amplified voice rang through the field and garden.

"Good evening! I hope everyone has been having a good time."

Lily's heart warmed at the sound of her birth mother's voice. She found Brigit standing on the lowest steps leading up to Fern Cottage. Brigit's sisters milled around a step below and next to Brigit was Rena.

The crowd nodded and murmured their thanks. A

few people hooted and hollered, and two women shrieked with laughter at a shared joke.

"It's nice to let loose after all our hard work. And I don't intend to keep you from your fun for long. However, Rena and I wanted to pause for a mo' to toast the engaged couple. Lily and Alfred, could you come up here, please?"

The crowd parted before them, allowing them a direct path to the steps of the cottage. Lily's cheeks pinked as she walked through the masses and became aware every single eye had been on them.

Alfred, sensing her discomfort, placed his hand on the small of her back to guide her forward. They were with her family in an instant, gazing into a sea of people before them. Lily took in all the faces, searching for familiarity. She found Sara and Evelyn standing together, front and center, smiling at her. Selma stood at Evelyn's right, the pair shoulder to shoulder. Annika peeked out from behind the siren pair, white blonde hair shining brightly in the night. Tension seeped from Lily.

With them by my side, how can I be nervous?

"I promise I'll make this short," Brigit said and shifted so that Lily and Alfred stood between her and Rena. "This amazing woman here before you is my firstborn. It took me far too long to be able to say that. To admit it to the world. I'm so glad I can now."

She gripped Lily's free hand, tears shining in her eyes.

"None of this would have been possible without Rena, Lily's other mother. Rena took my daughter in and loved her like her very own. While I was envious of Rena at times for getting to witness all of Lily's firsts, Lily was meant to be under her protection."

Brigit shot Rena a grateful smile. "I'm so happy Rena, myself, and Lily's family and friends are here now. To witness her relationship with Alfred and partake in their rites of engagement and marriage. When I first met Alfred, it was clear he was special, kind, and good. I never dreamed that he and Lily would end up together, but apparently, Alfred did."

Alfred bobbed his head up and down and the crowd chuckled.

"I'm glad the lad had the foresight I lacked." Brigit lifted her glass. "To Lily and Alfred. To the joining of families and friends. May this couple always know they have a community behind them. May they know honor. May they know a love blessed beyond any other."

"Blessed be," the crowd sang out and sipped from their glasses.

"Thank you, Brigit," Rena said, taking up the mantle. "I remember the call that day when Brigit asked if I would take in her daughter. Hide her, love her, teach her the ways of witches covertly so she did not draw attention to herself. Brigit says I did her the favor in caring for Lil but really, she did me the favor. It was an honor to love and care for Lily and I'm thankful every day I got that chance. She's a remarkable woman and Alfred is a remarkable man. I'm grateful they found each other. That we all found each other." Rena choked out a sob and Lily bit her lip.

"I just want to say, thank you all for gathering. For loving this couple even if you met them yesterday. For being willing to love the entire world enough to drop your lives and rush over. It takes a certain type of person and that's exactly the person I want in my girl's corner. To the couple, everyone here wishes you all the happiness in the world." And with that Rena, uncharacteristically, burst out into tears.

Lily's hand flew to her mouth and the crowd lifted their glasses one more time.

"All the happiness in the world," they chanted. Glasses clinked and neighbors hugged one another.

Brigit stepped forward. "Please continue to have fun! We've set up silencing charms around individual tents in case someone needs to sneak off early. If not the music will be—" She stopped short as the ground beneath her shook.

What the hell? The trees in the orchard swayed and Lily leaned against the cottage only to jump forward in shock. Fern Cottage's stone walls trembled like a leaf in the wind. A roar like thunder but certainly not from this world shot through the night.

Badb flew into Lily's throat and she coughed.

"Goddess be," Brigit muttered.

Lily followed her mother's gaze to the massive shield above and the crack slicing it in half.

Party Crashers

Sara

A WHIMPER SHATTERED THE SILENCE.

They're here. Nemain whirled within Sara, frantic.

Sara spoke the spell to release her pneuma and opened her mouth wide. Not a second later, Nemain rushed out. Her black eyes were round and searching until they latched onto Badb emerging from Lily. Unspoken words transpired between the pneumas and Nemain sprang into action. "Follow me."

Sara grasped Evelyn's hand and pulled her sister behind her. By the time they made it to the cottage steps, the two pneumas had formed a psychic consensus and were already translating it to Brigit.

The crowd was erupting into quiet hysteria.

The fata are here. Whispered words from the crowd

echoed in Sara's head. She shivered and imagined she could smell the terror, striking and pungent.

Brigit took control, amplifying her voice magically. "Attention everybody! Look up here!"

Aoife flung a display of fireworks in the air, shutting people up.

"If you have guessed that the fata are here, you would be correct."

A collective cry sounded and Kim, who had appeared at Sara's side without her noticing, released a howling gale of wind. Everyone's mouth's snapped close. "Shut up and let her talk!"

Brigit nodded her thanks to the black-haired wind witch. "There's no use panicking. They are here and intent on getting in. I assure you, they have not breached the strongest enchantments on the property. Those should hold long enough for us to prepare."

"Why'd the shield crack?" a woman with bright orange hair yelled, her voice wobbly.

"That shield was created to withstand wind, rain, and cold, not actual magic. My stronger charms on Fern Cottage, however, *are* tailored to ward off magical attacks. Still, they are in the process of breaking. A strong spell may have slipped through or been sent through the earth to crack the shield above you. We shouldn't waste time. Change into something you can move, run, and jump in. Grab a weapon and meet us at the lake to fight."

The crowd dispersed, some sprinting toward their tents, others standing before the triplets and company blinking in disbelief.

"I'll round up a group to head them off," Alfred said. "The Acolytes who can't fly must be coming from the roadside, using the hedge to hide until the wards break. The woods are too vast, and we'd see them approaching from the adjacent field."

Bless that hedge. Sara recalled the day she first walked through it. It had been annoying then, but now, it was a barrier from war.

"Good idea. Get a large, varied group of creatures. I doubt the fata are coming in that way. Once my enchantments break, they'll have a more direct route." Brigit looked up into the night sky.

Sara followed her mother's gaze searching for specks of light in the black that would give away a flying fata's position. Only darkness covered them. "Looks like we're safe for now."

"No, your mother is right. Do not be lulled into a false sense of security. They may still be up there," Nemain said. "Fata can dim their luminescence. Remain alert."

Great, we'll be fighting flying, nearly invisible, powerful aliens soon.

"Be careful. I love you." Lily flung herself into Alfred's arms and kissed him so deeply Sara felt compelled to look away.

Why didn't we expect this? Macha told us they were growing stronger and Nora knows where we live. It's a miracle she hasn't led them here earlier.

As if she'd heard Sara's thoughts Brigit spoke once more. "We had more time than we should have expected with Nora's betrayal. Let's go get changed so we can meet the group by the lake and plan our defense."

SATIN AND VELVET rustled down the hallway as the women retreated to their rooms to change. The triplets shut the door to their room and rifled through drawers.

"We wanted you to know we won't be with you the entire time." Badb's voice cut through the sounds of clothes hitting the floor. "You three can take care of yourselves, especially if you stick together. Your army, specifically the new recruits and non-witches, however, are quite vulnerable."

Sara's blood froze. It was true. The newest recruits had only been there a few days. *What were we thinking bringing people here? Letting them stay? If they'd stayed in town, they wouldn't have to be fighting when they weren't prepared.*

"Where will you be?" Lily asked.

"We'll try to stick with the non-witches, the ones who can fight the Acolytes but will have difficulty with fata," Badb replied.

"Difficulty is an understatement," Nemain murmured and Sara's gut, perpetually queasy the last few days, tied into deeper knots of guilt.

"If possible stay away from Noro; he's the strongest fata. Stay alive and together. Tackle the other fata. Even Dimia is fair game, but the air witches are your best chance against Noro. Or Badb and I—unlike Macha, we're charged and prepared to fight. It doesn't have to be one of you acting the hero." Nemain's bottomless black eyes locked with Sara's as if she were speaking only to her.

Why does Nemain think I want to attack him alone? Doesn't she remember what happened last time Noro cornered me? I froze. She opened her mouth to ask Nemain, but Evelyn cut her off.

"If anyone has a right to go after Noro, it's me. But even I'm not that stupid to go at him alone. With help, maybe, but even then it seems foolish."

"Good. Badb and I will try to find him before he comes looking for you three. No doubt he will hide from us. He has eluded us for centuries." The cottage shook from its foundation to the roof and a round of other-worldly thunder rolled outside. Nemain's eyes flickered closed. "Stay safe and know we believe in you."

Then they were gone, two beacons of green and red, flying away into the darkness.

THE CROWD WAS ALREADY GATHERED before the lake, huddled together for reassurance, when the witches arrived. The shield conjured for the party looked like nearly shattered glass, a million thin cracks covering its surface. All it would take was a moderately strong offensive spell and it would shatter. What would it take for Brigit's greater enchantments to break?

Jane stood before the crowd, a mint green headscarf confining her dark, wild curls. "I've already told people to buddy up with a supe whose powers compliment their own, not mirror them. They are to keep with that person as best they can," Jane spoke to Brigit as they approached.

Brigit nodded. "It's the best we can do. Large groups make little sense here. With foes who can fly, grouping together would make it easier to take out many people at once."

Brigit tapped her throat, imbuing it with the spell to amplify her voice. The crowd quieted at the gesture. A hum of nervous energy fluttered over the field, energizing the air and creating ripples on the water.

A thin man in the back waved his arm for attention. His voice cracked as he looked out over the sea of heads, almost two hundred people, before him. "Before you amp us up, I'm compelled to point out that we need something to identify us as friends. I don't think I'll be able to recognize everyone here and I don't want to hurt anyone on our side."

"A conclusion we came to as well," Brigit said and she, Aoife, Gwenn, and Mary swept their arms wide in unison. A wave of magic crawled over the crowd and glowing bands of light appeared on everyone's arms.

"They will make you easier to spot in the dark." Aoife's spicy scent was intense, vibrating off of her. "But they may reduce the chance of friendly fire hitting you by accident. As we have the greater numbers, or at least we think we do, we figured it was a fair trade."

Many nodded. Some, including the man who'd asked for the identifier, appeared skeptical, perhaps wondering why he'd asked to become a glowing target.

"The enchantments I set twenty-one years ago are weakening," Brigit's voice boomed forth. "They will break at any moment. As Jane instructed, stay with your buddy. One supernatural born of Earth is no match for a strong fata, but with greater numbers, we can defeat them. A task force is already at the hedge fighting off Acolytes. Protect yourself, protect each other, and fight for our world. This may be our last chance."

Sara shuddered. Their mother was right. It felt like the finale. All these months—the sorrow, the pain, early mornings, sleepless nights, confusion bordering on madness, and most of all the love they'd found—had all led up to this moment. They would come out of this victorious, or slaves.

Sara flexed her hands before gripping the cold stiletto sheathed on her hip. Practicing with it had always been secondary to magic but still, its presence on her, its solid deadliness, was reassuring.

The ground shook and squeals flew up from the army. Footsteps followed, slapping on the wet grass and mud. Sara turned to see Alfred, glowing bright yellow, sprinting furiously out of the orchard, leading a small team of supes. Beams of light and spells flew at Alfred's team from behind. Lily's hand gripped Sara's, and she squeezed it tight in response.

The Acolytes had breached the hedge.

Alfred was almost to them now, his mouth wide open, his ragged breathing amplified.

A spell shot past him and Lily gasped.

"Fighting position, Lil. Protect him," Evelyn growled.

He was there seconds later. His team members shot

past them, joining the Triplet Army line behind the McKay witches.

Aoife, thinking quick, shot a spell behind her. Alfred's team members' arms lit up with bands, marking them as friendly.

Alfred gulped air as he stared straight at Brigit with wild eyes. Finally, he caught his breath. "They broke down the hedge. All of them came through that way. They weren't even trying to break your other enchantments."

Ice flew through Sara's veins.

They're caging us in. Mom doesn't have time to undo all the enchantments fully. Unless we can get to the main road, we're trapped. We—

Her thoughts short-circuited to nothing when suddenly, a horde illuminated by colorful glowing ghosts rushed out of the orchard.

The First Fallen
Evelyn

"To the other side of the lake!" Evelyn screamed and pulled her sisters with her, desperate to put a physical barrier between them and their adversaries.

"Wait! Alfred!" Lily cried.

Evelyn glanced over her shoulder. Alfred was holding his ground with a group of other supes—Aoife, Jane, and Mary among them—as a small contingent of Acolytes raced forward ahead of the bulk of their army. There was a tug at Evelyn's hand as Lily whirled around to help her fiancé.

"No! Look at me, Lil!" Sapphire eyes caught emeralds and held them. "You can help him more if you have his back. We stick together, remember? Alfred signed up to be the front guard."

"And is already doing a fantastic job. Look." Sara murmured.

Alfred, glowing sunshine yellow with the errant magic he'd picked up, was flying, one hand equipped with cold, hard steel, the other grasping a burning ball of energy. A werewolf with gray fur and feral eyes had broken ahead of the Acolytes' front line and leapt to meet Alfred. The two collided in midair, a mess of glowing yellow and fur. The werewolf snapped his long, sharp teeth, trying to clamp down on Alfred's arm as they fell to the ground together, but the daemon yanked his limb back just in time. Retaliating, he flung his ball of energy at the werewolf. A howl ripped through the night. The were retreated and rolled on the ground to quench the burn of Alfred's magic.

Evelyn's eyes followed the werewolf rolling on the ground, catching his momentary, clever transformation back to a hairless human. *Felix.* Her jailer at Peacock Manor. One of the most terrifying creatures she'd ever met. Her heart stopped. Her chest tightened.

Noro enlisted the help of the werewolf pack again. He must be paying them well with money he stole from my family.

"Let's move." Evelyn continued around the lake, wanting to put space between herself and Felix.

She'd gone only a few more feet when an unexpected

orange flash to her right sent a ripple of goosebumps up her arms. Finding the source, Evelyn breathed a sigh of relief. Brigit had pulled a few fire workers out of the herd running around the lake and was directing them to unleash an inferno. Their combined fire melted the recently frozen lake ice within seconds, thereby giving water workers an easy source to weaponize. She thanked the goddess for her mother's quick thinking, and no more than a minute later they were in position.

"Sara and Lil, use the water to make air," Evelyn said. "Don't waste your energy right away going straight for air. Leave that to the air witches." *And me,* she added mentally, already pulling air together at the center of the lake.

Lily and Sara nodded, each with their eyes locked on the battling front lines.

Kim joined them. "I've already told the air witches on this end to be at the front. We'll attack together, take out as many fata as we can early on. We'll only have the element of surprise once. As soon as they know you've recruited us and some have learned how to fight with air—"

"They'll be more careful," Sara finished Kim's sentence.

She's right, Evelyn realized. They only had one chance, and they had to make it count.

The fata flew above the bulk of the Acolyte army across the field, always in perpetual motion and occasionally swirling in and out of the dark orchard behind them, making the fata impossible to count. The Earth-born supernaturals were easier to assess and Evelyn guessed there were near one hundred Acolytes.

We don't have as much of an upper hand as we thought.

A familiar voice barked orders further down the lakeside. Her mother, shouting something to the crowd behind her. Witches and wizards gifted with air or water stepped forward.

Following suit, Evelyn took control of her end of the Triplet Army. "Air and water workers, begin assembling an offense. Walls, bullets, lances—whatever you can manage. Fire them at the fata in the crowd. The more we take out now, the better we'll be once they approach."

She pulled air together, forming a wall with ease. Then she pushed harder. Using a technique Kim had shown her, Evelyn drew the molecules tighter and tighter together until the wall morphed into a long lance. Concentrating hard on keeping the lance in place, Evelyn created a bed of wind for it to rest on. She hoped her plan to keep control of the lance, to not only spear it through one fata, but a dozen in one go, would work. Beside her Lily and Sara went through the slower, energy-saving steps of transmuting water into air and finally into thick, protective walls.

Sensing someone's attention on her, Evelyn glanced down the lake's edge and caught her mother's eyes. Brigit held up three fingers.

"On three we fire," Evelyn called out. The surrounding air pulsed with magic and she knew those who could contribute had heard her.

"One. Two. *Three!*" Evelyn screamed and hurled the air lance through the sky.

<hr>

SHE WATCHED, breath held tight as her lance flew through the sky on a current of air. Her aim was on point, and it soared straight for a fata who hovered motionless above the army as if it didn't know what air was yet. *It will soon,* Evelyn thought seconds before the lance sunk into the fata's chest.

Airy howls filled the starry night as other lances and air bullets hit their targets. A handful of fata fell to the ground.

"Surprise," Evelyn whispered, her lips turning up in a grin.

Noro roared, and Evelyn had never heard such fury in his tone. She stiffened as the fata's shimmering, navy body barreled out from the cover of the trees. The mark on Evelyn's inner thigh burned and a beam of light flashed from her pants, marking Evelyn's location. She cupped her leg, trying to keep the light in as Noro altered his course, heading straight for her. *Keep calm and gather more air,* she thought instinctively leaning back into the crowd behind her as Noro narrowed the distance between them.

He was magic and fury embodied, and nearly upon her. Evelyn sucked in a breath, preparing to battle, when suddenly Noro veered into the front line of fighting supernaturals.

What the—?

Noro swept his amorphous limbs wide and soared through the battling crowd. Metal glinted in the moonlight as Mary swung her dagger through the air at Noro. Jane followed suit, brandishing her mace and hurling it at the fata. Noro dodged, swept his arms in a brutal slash, and pulled up, out of reach of the witches' next assault. A geyser of blood followed and Mary and Jane collapsed to the ground simultaneously. Noro's dark eyes turned to find Evelyn's once more. He smiled.

Her heart stopped. The air she'd been collecting flew away in a jumble of particles. A scream climbed up her throat, like vomit. A bellow of horror to Evelyn's right ripped through her and she knew without looking it was her mother.

Jane . . . Mary . . . Instead of killing Evelyn, he'd gone for the aunt she favored. Her mentor. The one she resembled so closely it was impossible not to notice. Because Noro didn't want to end Evelyn now. No, he'd draw it out, use her, make the end long and painful.

I'll kill that bastard.

Noro spun, intent on slaying the other three in his range, but Aoife sprang into action first.

"Arma," she cried, hurling a shield in front of everyone, protecting them.

Then, before Evelyn knew it, a spray of air bullets filled the space between Aoife and Noro. It was unbelievable that none of them hit the navy fata as he retreated, soaring back across the field in seconds. Aoife and Alfred picked up Jane and Mary and fell back to the other side of the lake.

Evelyn, Lily, Sara, Gwenn, and Brigit met them halfway. A moment later Morgane joined, her wrinkled hands shaking.

"Is she? Are they—?" Brigit croaked. Tears streamed down her face as she took in her vivacious sister and Jane, the leader of the Sisters of Salem.

Aoife's face said it all.

Brigit's knees buckled beneath her and Sara steadied her so she didn't fall. "Mar . . . Jane. No . . ."

Gwenn squeezed her eyes shut as if by not seeing her sister's body the horror of her death would disappear.

But Aoife had no time for weeping. "Take their bodies over there." She pointed to a group of tents a quarter mile away on the edge of the forest. "If anyone fights in that direction they're trapping themselves in a corner. Their bodies should be safe from desecration." Her gravelly voice squeaked and two were men broke from the army line, hefted the women's bodies, and ran off with them.

A deafening roar hurtled across the field. Evelyn tore her eyes from the retreating body of her aunt to find the Acolytes were on the move.

The creatures were closing in.

Follow the Leader

Sara

SARA WAS HAVING trouble keeping her guts in place—they were twisting so violently. She would never again hear Mary's spirited laugh or the stories she'd promised to tell. Smell the fresh scent that was quintessentially Mary.

Her body shook. "Hey!" Evelyn demanded. "Snap out of it. We have to move."

Sara blinked. The Triplet Army, all except the air witches, was making its way into the woods.

"Keep up shields if you can! They're effective against fata magic. Otherwise use trees, bushes, whatever you can find as barriers," Aoife's scratchy voice sliced through the din of hysteria.

"Follow me," Lily said, and she took off. Alfred, still glowing bright yellow, was quick on her heels as Sara and Evelyn struggled to keep up.

A gust of hurricane-force wind burst past Sara. She glanced back to see a rainbow of fata approaching as one, overtaking the front line of supernatural Acolytes to descend upon the Triplet Army. Her eyes locked on Kim, black hair whipping in the tornado of air bullets that swirled around her body. At random a bullet would peel off and fly straight for a fata. Two, then three fata went down as Kim let her bullets fly.

The other air workers were taking a more universal approach: Forcing great gales of air at the encroaching army to hold them back so the Triplet Army had a chance at retreating into the trees. Sara wanted to vomit.

Goddess please let me see her again. I can't bear it if she sacrifices herself for me.

"Sara! Come on!" Evelyn screamed from inside the tree line.

Sara wrenched her eyes from Kim and followed her sisters into the woods. She didn't bother to wonder where Lily was leading them. Lily knew the woods best, having run through them often. There were creatures all around, some hiding, some preparing to fight.

A few stood out, their daemonic skin glowing as they waited for the wind witches to thin out the flock of fata. Eros the elf was visible a short distance away. A tornado of air flew from his head to knock out what appeared to be a couple witches or vampires. He then hunched over his opponents and a spray of liquid flew up as Eros dealt the final blow.

Sara shuddered. She wondered where her mother and aunts were. Were they a victim or victor? Had they stayed back with the air witches and wizards to fight? She hadn't noticed.

Evelyn, three steps ahead of Sara, let out a shriek.

Alfred's shining body flew to the side as a blur of gray rushed him. Snapping jaws and glistening teeth were at Alfred's throat as a familiar gray werewolf with bits of burnt fur tried to pin him to the ground. The daemon, unprepared for the attack, shimmied out from under the wolf and crab-walked backward as fast as possible.

Lily shot a spell at the werewolf who leapt out of the way and rounded on her, teeth bared. The werewolf charged and Lily threw up a massive shield, protecting her and Alfred. But the were kept coming, straight for Lily.

He'll knock himself out. What an idiot.

Unexpectedly, defying logic, the werewolf ran straight into the shield and using his powerful haunches rebounded off it to fly straight at Evelyn, his body now a missile of teeth and claws. The were's trajectory was true, and he crashed into Evelyn, tossing her against a tree. A heartbeat later he hunched over her, his paws rooting her arms into the ground, disabling her, his teeth an inch from her neck as he sniffed. The creature's menacing eyes projected a humanness a real wolf could never possess. A growl that turned into a chuckle rumbled out of the creature and he dragged his wolfish tongue from Evelyn's collarbone to her lips.

"Lotu." Sara lowered into a squat and aimed at the were's underbelly, his most vulnerable side, while she could still take advantage of his fascination with her sister.

The were's body stiffened and tipped to the side.

"Fuck you, Felix," Evelyn said, yanking her hands out from under his paws and grabbing a handful of the werewolf's fur. "Volavari."

The werewolf rose ten feet in the air, rigid from Sara's body bind spell, only his eyes moving, darting from side to side.

Evelyn's hand lifted. "Pream."

A fantastic display of blood and guts filled the night as Felix exploded above them.

"What the hell was that? Why didn't he go for your neck?" Sara asked, rising from her crouch once the innards and blood stopped raining down on them. She wiped a bit of warm who-knew-what from her shoulder, trying hard to pretend it was dandruff, despite the slimy texture.

"That's not Felix's way. He likes to terrorize his victims. Must have forgotten that now I can actually fight back." Evelyn wiped a hunk of bloody fur from her blood-stained cheek. "Plus, Noro wants us alive. The worst Felix would have done was disable me. Would have been a dream come true for him."

"We can talk about creepy werewolf motivations later. Let's go. We have to get to the unbinding site. It's our best chance." Lily, who thanks to her shield had avoided being splattered with blood and innards, took off at a sprint.

The unbinding site . . . yes! We're connected to the site. Maybe we'll have an advantage.

They ran as fast as they could, pushing through the soggy undergrowth, their weapons bouncing and clinking at their sides.

Snippets of fighting flashed between the trees in the distance. Sara shot off a spell when she could—usually a shield charm to allow a member of the Triplet Army a reprieve.

Suddenly, Lily hurdled over a log and let out a yelp before continuing to sprint. As Sara hopped over the log she discovered why. The log wasn't a log at all.

It was a body, a dead body with eyes open wide staring up at the starry night above. Even in that brief second, Sara recognized the woman as one Roman had recruited only two days prior. Anger flashed in her before she hit the ground. Her hands burned red hot, ready to unleash the flames begging to burst from her fingertips.

Her eyes bounced around the woods hoping to catch sight of a foe.

And she was in luck. Human and wolf silhouettes moved in the distance, no band of light circling their arms as they waited for a Triplet Army member to stumble across them.

"Flampila." A riot of fireballs exploded from Sara's hands. She didn't see the fire catch although the howls and screams vibrated in her ears.

Evelyn, a few feet ahead, shot a glance back. "Watch this." She pointed the opposite direction at a creature glowing dim purple. A daemon, hiding behind a large tree in wait.

"Argibeltza," Evelyn cried, projecting her arms at the purple figure as she ran.

Alfred stumbled mid-step. He whipped around in time to catch Evelyn's black light curse swallow up the other daemon's power.

"Nice one," he gasped, staring at the now powerless daemon with a smirk. "For a second there I thought someone was after me."

A ghost of pearly white appeared through the trees, swooping down on them.

"Down!" Sara screamed and dropped to the earth.

Evelyn and Alfred followed her lead, instinctively

flinging themselves to the ground, but Lily, who hadn't noticed the other three had stopped, kept running.

"Lil! Down!" Sara screamed but Lily was too far ahead to hear.

Before Sara could blink, her sister was in the fata's clutches, one hundred feet in the air, above the trees.

"Holy shit," Evelyn breathed. "I had no idea he was able to do that. The last time I saw him he—"

"Who was that?" Alfred scrambled to his feet and ran to Evelyn, his dark eyes wild with fear.

"Dimia. The king. I only ever saw him through Macha's eyes. He looks much stronger now. Before he was weak, sickly looking."

Alfred's eyes widened at Evelyn's assessment. "We have to find Lil. If you were close enough to her, could you latch onto her thoughts?"

Evelyn bit her lip. "Probably. When she freaks out, she loses all her guarding mechanisms."

"Good." He extended his hand to Evelyn and pulled her up. "You lead."

The Gap

Lily

THE WIND WHIPPED around Lily as she soared one hundred feet above the earth. Limbs, transformed into crude human hands, gripped her. The sensation reminded Lily of the time Noro caressed her face, like tiny tornados pressing into her skin.

Below her, flashing by like ants, small fires burned and great gusts of wind whipped over the forest she loved. Yellow beams of light cut through the darkness—daemons, maybe Alfred, fighting. She wished the fata who'd captured her wasn't moving so fast.

Her stomach lurched as the fata plummeted. Lily wrenched her eyes shut, sure she was about to collide with a tree. A minute later her feet touched down on earth and she opened her eyes. Tall oaks and blackened, scorched ground surrounded her. An aroma of magic, familiar to Lily as her own body, filled the air.

The unbinding site? Is this fata trying to help?

Lily took a step forward and smashed into a hot invisible barrier. "Shit!" She jumped back and gripped her knee where it burned.

A film, like oil on water and cloudy white, flowed before her on all sides, enclosing her in a cage. Lily touched the white film with shaky fingers. A searing sensation, hotter than before without the protection of her jeans, ran up her nerves, forcing her to pull her hand back. Where she touched the film, hazy particles of air swirled around the opening before sealing the wall. A heartbeat later the cage shrunk in on itself an inch.

"A precaution," a fata's airy voice boomed, all pomp and vigor. "In case you, too, have learned to use air against your kind, daughter. Your touch will cause the enclosure to constrict and burn."

Daughter. Crap. Dimia.

Lily pulled herself up straighter. "I'm not your daughter."

Dimia looked unimpressed. "You, like all magical creatures of this planet, are my kin. And you, more than most, are my daughter. Now, where is Lilith?"

Her blood ran cold.

"I realize she's not inside you. I've sensed her, flying

about, murdering her own kind in these woods to defend other creatures." Though Dimia did not use human facial expressions as the triplets' pneumas did, there was no misunderstanding the displeasure in his tone.

"I don't know," Lily said. "And she doesn't go by Lilith anymore. Her name is Badb."

"Her name," Dimia bellowed, "is whatever I want it to be. I am her father. Her king. The King of Hecate and Earth."

"A truer title I've never heard spoken, your Majesty," another unctuous voice said from high above.

Lily looked up and gasped.

Noro was descending to the ground with Brigit, loose-limbed and slack-jawed. When he was low enough, he dropped her lifeless form to the ground.

"What did you do to her?" Lily screamed wanting nothing more than to punch a hole in the air cage and cradle her mother's head.

"Nothing she won't live through, unfortunately." Noro replied before turning his attention to Dimia. "The rest should arrive at any moment."

Does he mean the Acolytes? Fata? Someone trying to save her and Brigit? I have to get out of this cage to help.

Stealthy, Lily shot a tiny fireball into the cage wall. A hole appeared in the cage large enough for a fist to fit through. She waited. Ten seconds passed and still, the hole remained open. Reassured, Lily stuck her fist through.

As if waiting for her act of rebellion, the cage sucked itself closed and bubbled around her wrist, searing her skin. She yanked her hand back inside and her top layer of skin ripped off like a band-aid. A cry of pain tore from her lips and she fell to the ground.

"Idiot girl," Dimia drawled, not even bothering to look up as her cage shrunk in an inch.

"Like her sister," Noro agreed, and the two switched to a tongue Lily could not understand.

Shit. Shit. Shit. Lily shook out the pain and took the burnt hand in her good one.

"Salus," she whispered hoping the cage would only constrict if magic was used against it, not in it. A moment later her burnt hand had grown a thin, pink layer of new skin. It was tender and not as sturdy as the skin that had been there a minute before, but it was better than open flesh. She shifted her weight to rise, and her shoes squelched in the mud beneath them. An idea sparked and Lily gasped, looking down at the damp earth beneath her feet. *I'll dig under!*

"Ah! There you are!" Noro boomed.

Lily's eyes shot up from the ground to lock on two dozen fata staring down at her, their eyes wide open and curious. One, a fuchsia fata, cringed back into the darkness.

"Yes, Master. We're all here, and the others will be soon. They're quick on our tracks. The magic of this place is strong. Many creatures will be drawn here. It will be of great help when you bind them to you." Nora emerged from the trees and gave Noro a soppy smile before turning her gaze to Lily. "Hello, Lily. I met Rena in the woods. She likely won't be joining us after our little encounter, but it's good to see you once more."

The ground beneath Lily trembled in response. "I can't say the same."

"I hope nothing I said upset you. It would be a crime to upset one of the chosen ones."

Nora's mocking tone set Lily's teeth on edge and she wondered how in the world anyone ever trusted such a traitor.

Rena never had. Somehow that made her feel better— that someone saw past all the bullshit Nora spewed to the evil woman beneath.

"No matter, say what you like to her. The sisters had options, and they selected wrong. Hence they will become slaves like the rest of humanity, ours to command once we bind them to myself and Dimia. I thank you for telling us of this place, Nora. You were right; the magic here is strong. Perfect for such a ceremony." Noro's voice boomed with bravado as he flew toward Nora and wrapped a limb around her shoulder.

Nora beamed with pride.

"And the troops?" Dimia asked.

"They are already in place, Your Majesty." Nora gestured to the woods and Lily's eyes followed.

In the dark, at the end of the clearing farthest from Fern Cottage, dozens of glowing eyes stared back at her. *If they come to rescue me they're going to be so outnumbered.*

"Can't argue with you there." Nora smirked.

Lily slammed down her mind barriers and scowled.

Then, a sound came dancing through the trees that made her blood freeze. She recognized the voice she had grown up with. The voice that taught her how to charm men, or at least had tried. The voice that soothed her when Rena's advice was too rough. Though the ethereal voice was different, she still knew whom it belonged to. Selma was singing her siren song, attempting to disarm Acolytes in advance of the Triplet Army. And with her song, would come Selma herself, defenseless, especially around the fata.

Lily poured magic into the earth below. There was nowhere to put the displaced earth in the cage of air unless she wanted the enclosure to keep shrinking in on her. Lily would have to widen the ground beneath her by literally pushing the earth far enough apart so she could climb in and dig her way out.

The song boomed louder with every heartbeat, every note, and already Lily trembled with the effort of her exertions. Despite her physical body telling her what she was trying to do was impossible, Lily knew better. She'd seen her magic crack a fissure in the earth ten feet wide and toss chunks of ground into the air the size of a small car the night of her unbinding.

I have to try harder, she thought, thrusting another swell of magic at the earth with vigor. An inch-wide crack formed and Lily sighed. *Much harder.*

Something moved on the outskirts of her vision. Lily stiffened. A man, likely a wizard, shuffled around twenty feet behind her, glazed-eyed and limp-limbed. Selma's song was affecting him. Lily glanced around. Ten other men and a woman looked similarly disengaged.

Selma was close.

Not close—the next second Selma was *there,* walking through the woods. Pure magic flowed from her lips, her face contorted in rage. Two other creatures followed: a white werewolf, its fur standing on end, and Shefali, Selma and Mary's old friend.

Mary. The name rang in her head, tinkling like her aunt's generous laugh. The loss hadn't even settled in yet, and now she faced another. *I have to get out of this cage.*

But she was too late. Nora knocked Shefali to the ground in a body bind curse before Shefali could even get her hands up in defense. In the same instant, Noro swept his arm across his body.

Lily saw it as if in slow motion. Her beloved Selma flew backward and collided with the werewolf. The thunking of skull on skull, the collapse of the wolf, and the crashing of Selma into its big, white body, stopped Lily's heart.

Noro soared to loom above Selma, who somehow was still conscious. "I'll admit, I saw no use for a siren. Now I recognize how wrong I was. How any supernatural, any line of the fata can be valuable against the inferior race of men. I regret I never came to you when I heard so much of your line, Selma. You see now how superior our forces are, how superior fata are. I don't blame you for fighting—it was the noble thing to do—but now that you have seen what we can do, I ask you to join us." Noro extended his arm.

Lily gawked with disbelief. He's not killing her right away. *Please, Selma, play along.*

Lily's hope dissipated the moment Selma lifted her gaze. Her brown eyes were aflame with anger, with pride dissatisfied by a few hastily given, flowery words. Selma yanked an iron dagger from her hip. She flailed, at a disadvantage in position and likely still dizzy from colliding with the wolf, before hurling it haphazardly at Noro. It missed.

Noro's arm flung forward to smack Selma across the face.

"No!" Lily screamed, "Don't hurt her."

Noro paused and in that instant, Lily realized she would have done better to keep her mouth closed. To hide how important Selma was to her. Noro's black mouth widened into a round fata smile.

"On second thought, I shall keep you around anyhow," Noro's voice boomed above the silence in the clearing. "If only for persuasion purposes." He waved his arm and Selma lifted in the air, her feet dangling above the ground, and a cage of air like the one around Lily appeared. "Careful not to touch the sides," Noro sneered.

Lily's jaw loosened. *Selma's alive, for now.*

"Or this will happen." Noro grazed the side of Selma's cage with his limb and the cage constricted, catching a bit of Selma's arm.

Selma's scream tore through Lily, who used all her might to thrust her magic into the ground.

The gap beneath her widened an inch.

An Unlikely Rescue

Evelyn

Screams and groans and, worst of all, occasional silence flew by Evelyn as her feet pounded the forest's uneven terrain. As when Noro tortured her, it was the stillness, the seconds when only her own breath filled her ears that scared Evelyn the most. The flashbacks were coming faster now, insistent under pressure. Her breath was short and ragged. Evelyn shook her head to expel the horrors and something whipped her in the face.

"Ahh!" She whirled around, searching as she cupped her injured cheek with one hand and extended the other for protection. A whip-thin branch swayed harmlessly from where her face had struck it. Evelyn sighed with relief.

"Are you alright?" Alfred asked, appearing a short distance away through the trees.

"Fine. All the fighting and sounds are churning up memories. Then I whipped myself in the face with that branch and freaked out."

"Do you want me to lead? You can call out directions."

"No, it's fine, really."

Sara finally caught her breath. "Did you lose Lily's trail?"

Evelyn closed her eyes and searched. She had, in fact, let go of Lily's trail when the branch slapped her, but that didn't mean she couldn't pick it back up. She flung her mind out, searching for the imprint of her sister. There was nothing. She inched out further, then to the end of her range and still came up empty.

Fuck you, branch. Evelyn opened her eyes and clenched her jaw.

"I've lost the thread."

Sara bit her lip. "What do we do now?"

"I'll tell you what you're going to do," a seductive voice purred from above and the trio stiffened. "You're going to meet our master."

A vampire and a daemon hurtled toward the ground with beatific smiles.

Sara threw three balls of flame in the air. All missed. The vampire touched down and lunged at Sara, who summoned an expert gate of flame from the earth. The vampire changed tack, turning to Evelyn while the daemon took on Alfred, who darted deeper into the trees to lure the daemon away.

"Flampila." Evelyn shot a perfectly aimed fireball at the vampire before hurling herself at Sara's flame gate, toward her sister, knowing they were safer together. The vampire veered at the last minute and the fireball slammed into a tree, burning the bark. Sara's gate fell, and the sisters stood back to back, prepared for the vampire's next move.

The vampire was a machine of the deadliest sort. She bounced from tree to tree, leaping and running around the sisters' circle of fire, distracting them, trying to catch them off guard.

"Are you going to keep running around for hours? Or fight us? I'd prefer the latter; I have a sister to save," Evelyn said, unsheathing her war hammer and lifting it to bait the vampire.

"The witch who killed Amon will die," the vampire shrieked. "Our master promised us." The vampire darted forth, straight at Evelyn, but changed direction at the last minute, flinging her fist at Sara. Knuckles hit skull with a sickening crunch and Sara cried out in pain as her knees buckled.

Evelyn dropped the hammer, which thudded to the ground, and caught Sara one-handed. She kept the other extended toward the vampire who had closed in. Her mind flailed, her heart thrummed.

Noro was going to kill Lily? Was this creature lying? Was *Noro* lying to his followers? It wouldn't be the first time. "Noro will kill her then and use us? What if we're not enough? The prophecy said he needs all three."

The vampire shrugged. "Our master no longer seems to think so. He believes the tiny one is all he requires to let the rest of the fata in. Though from the looks of her she can't take much, can she?" The vampire charged again, long fangs flashing in the moonlight.

Evelyn called a ball of fire in her free hand, aimed, and prepared to hurl it at the vampire. Hoping she wouldn't miss, that the vampire's honed reflexes would miraculously be off, that the beautiful and deadly creature wouldn't be upon them in seconds. She only had one shot.

Suddenly, the vampire halted mid-step.

A familiar sensation of electricity shot through Evelyn and her shoulders loosened.

Roman, stepped out of the trees. He ran to Evelyn's side and took over Sara's weight. "Don't let me stop you." He gestured to the ball of flame in Evelyn's hands. "She's under my command."

Evelyn strode up to the enthralled vampire, whose mouth was hanging open as she stared at Roman. "Please tell me I never looked like that."

"You? Never. You were always cool about every-thing." Roman reassured her with a small smirk.

"Naturally," Evelyn said, dropping the ball of flame on the vampire's head and watching her explode into ash.

A grunt of pain sounded thirty feet away. Alfred was still battling the daemon. He'd sustained a gash across his cheek and the other daemon was bleeding profusely from his shoulder. They spun and parried in rapid motion, beacons of yellow and green in the darkness, never staying in one spot for more than a second.

There was no way Evelyn could fire off the only spell she knew to disarm a daemon of his magic without a good chance of hitting Alfred, too. And they would need his power later. Evelyn considered wafting her siren magic over to the daemons but nixed that idea.

What if it hits Alfred, and he goes all goo-goo long enough for the other daemon to do him in? Lily would kill me.

Then, she had an idea so simple it may just work. Evelyn readied her hands, aiming them at the malicious daemon. She waited until Alfred's back was to her and then she screamed. "*Down!*"

Alfred, as he had when Sara yelled it earlier, acted on instinct and flung his body to the ground.

"Argibeltza!" Evelyn shot the black light curse at the other daemon, who stood ludicrously with his hand out in a jab that hit only air. Her curse struck the daemon straight in the chest, sucking his green glow, all the magical energy he possessed, out of him.

Alfred leapt up and slashed a knife across the daemon's neck.

"I OWE YOU BIG TIME—THAT daemon was strong. May have ingested vampire blood before the battle," Alfred admitted when he made his way over to where they stood. He was drenched in a mixture of sweat and blood. His eyes latched onto Sara, who was still unconscious.

"The vamp punched her in the head. She's knocked out, not dead. The vampire told me Sara is the only one Noro wants to keep alive at the end of this."

"What?" Alfred's voice broke.

Evelyn shrugged. "I don't get it either. Maybe Noro was lying to appease them? Maybe not. But knowing his plan doesn't change our goal. We have to wake Sara and get to Lil as soon as possible."

"Noro took her?" Roman asked.

Evelyn, unconcerned about the particulars of Noro versus Dimia, nodded and moved to place a hand on her sister. She'd never done even a general healing charm, but she'd heard Lily do them plenty of times.

"Salus," she said, her hands cupping Sara's head.

Sara stirred, her eyes fluttering open and falling closed again.

"Why didn't it work?" Alfred's mouth narrowed into a thin line.

"Because I'm not even close to being a healer. I've never used that spell before and all spells take practice for your body to feel and perform them properly," Evelyn snapped.

Alfred held up his hands, "Sorry. I just want to get to Lily. We don't even know where they took her." He sounded more dejected than Evelyn had ever heard him sound, including the time he had gallons of blue pus seeping from his body.

"I get it."

"You guys are sure Noro took her?" Roman shifted Sara in his arms.

"Dimia," Alfred corrected.

"OK, I think I know where they are."

"What? How? You haven't spied on them for weeks." Alfred's dark eyes narrowed and his hands flared yellow.

"Chill, Alfred," Evelyn leaned back and stared into Roman's blue eyes. "But seriously, how would you know?"

Roman shifted Sara, freeing one of his hands and pointed to the sky.

Evelyn's gaze followed his fingers and saw nothing. "I don't—"

"Wait for it," Roman instructed.

Her mouth narrowed, and she waited, ten seconds, then thirty. She placed a rigid hand on her hip. A minute passed. Her annoyance was peaking when suddenly a flash of shimmering orange flew up into the sky. She gasped.

A fata!

"That's the fourth one I've seen. All different colors. They're gathering in that direction—which means there must be something or someone important over there."

Sara groaned and Evelyn cursed. "You're right, but Sara can't walk yet. I'll try the charm again, but I don't dare do it more than twice. I've never seen Lil do that in such a short period and she's much better at it than I am. That's assuming mine is even working."

"We'll carry her. Roman and I will take turns. Evelyn, keep alert for ambushes. I'll take the first shift. Roman, you lead the way." There was a menacing undertone to Alfred's voice. A warning that said *you better not be leading us into a trap.*

Evelyn performed the healer's charm one more time before Roman handed Sara over to Alfred and the incubus led the way into the dark unknown.

Covered in Red

Sara

A FLASH of brown and green flew by as Sara's eyes fluttered open. Was that the ground? A hard thump pounded in her head and she groaned just as something hard shifted against her belly. Sara yelped as hands, *large* hands shifted their grip on her calves.

Someone's carrying me. Someone took me! Adrenaline flooded her system as Sara's heart rate spiked.

"She said something. Should I put her down, so you can take a look? We could try the charm again so she can fight when we get there?" A voice Sara recognized dimly said. It wasn't Alfred, but another man she'd talked to before. Why was his name eluding her? And what was wrong with her head?

"Good idea. We'll be as fast as we can be, Alfred, I promise. Let me put up a couple shields in case of another

421

ambush. We'll need Sara's help when we find the fata. Lean her against this tree," Evelyn instructed.

What the hell happened? Sara reached back into her memory.

Fangs. Superhuman speed. An evil cackle. A fist hurtling toward her and then, black.

Sara was laid down on a damp patch of moss and her torso leaned against the rough bark of a tree. As she settled, two light blue orbs stared back at her. Not Evelyn's eyes; these eyes lacked the dark depth of her sister's. Still, she knew those eyes . . . dammit, whose were they?

She clenched her teeth, trying to focus, though her head still pounded. Roman—the name came to her an instant later, slower than she'd like, but assuring her that whatever had happened to cloud her head, the effects weren't irreversible.

"She's awake," Roman said. "You took quite a wallop to the noggin back there. Evelyn's been trying to fix you up with a healer's charm. We're not sure if it's working, but she wants to try it again so you can help us save Lily. How do you feel?"

"Not great," Sara croaked. Considering a vampire had punched her, she supposed it could be worse. The vamp could have punched her so hard her head flew straight off.

"The vampire wouldn't have hit you that hard."

Evelyn sighed squatting down next to Sara and murmuring the healer's charm once more. "She made it clear Noro wants you alive. Not me and Lily, though."

"What happened?"

"Roman found us, enthralled her, and I finished her."

"Are we still following Lily's thoughts?"

Evelyn shook her head. "Roman saw a few fata flying high over a part of the forest. At first, I didn't know where we were going, but now I do." Her dark sapphire eyes leveled at Sara. "They're at the unbinding site."

That made perfect sense. A place already riddled with power those capable of working magic could harness. Where Lily had been leading them to use that same power. Where their magic had been unshackled, unleashed, and finally returned to them. Where Badb had finally spoken to Lily. A place of deep magic. No doubt Nora had told them about the site and Noro had chosen it symbolically.

"The nerve, right? That's our turf." Evelyn took her hands off Sara's shoulder. "Can you walk? The guys can take turns carrying you if you need it."

Sara shook her head. It would be better for everyone to have their hands free. "I can." She pushed herself up, not without effort and sighed. "You know this is a trap, right?"

The other three nodded.

"OK. As long as everyone is aware. You guys lead. I'll holler if I fall too far behind," Sara said. Roman took the lead, Alfred followed the incubus, and Evelyn brought up the rear. Sara smiled at her sister's protective gesture.

"I'll slow us down," Sara insisted.

"Doesn't matter as long as you make it there. If what the vampire said was true and Noro only wants you, you may have to bargain for all our lives."

A shudder ran through Sara at the thought of facing Noro, but she did as Evelyn requested—taking deep breaths and trying to center herself. They walked softly to mask their steps. The forest somehow seemed blacker than before. In a few hours, the sun would rise. The day would gain light, not darkness. Or so Sara hoped.

A twig snapped in the dark.

Evelyn threw up a shield and both daemon and incubus shifted into protective stances.

More sluggishly than she would have liked, two fire-balls appeared in Sara's hands.

"It's us," a gravelly voice called out of the forest before the strong scent of ginger and pepper mingled with holy basil.

The fire extinguished at the familiar tone.

Aoife and Gwenn appeared a moment later with Kim and Celestine trailing behind. Blood covered them, its metallic aroma mixing with her aunts' scents. Celestine's blonde hair was matted with a dark red liquid and dried brown trails ran down her chin from the corners of her mouth.

Gwenn's eyes filled with tears at the sight of them.

"Celestine smelled you," she gestured to Sara and Evelyn "We've been tracking you for the last ten minutes." Aoife paused and looked around. "Where's Lily?"

"Dimia snatched her. We're heading to rescue her," Alfred answered.

Aoife bit her lip. "Noro took Brigit, too. I assume you lot are heading to the unbinding site?"

Unsurprised by Aoife's uncanny assumption, they nodded and set off together without another word.

Leaves and needles crunched delicately underfoot as they walked. Only Celestine made no sound as she glided through the woods. Sara estimated they were less than a half mile from the site, although what gave her such certainty, she wasn't sure. She'd only been there once yet she felt the aura of the place—a sensation both welcoming, like coming home for Christmas, and repulsive.

Not that different from our actual unbinding.

Sara recalled the ring of fire that cut them off from their aunts. The evil green flames that almost devoured their mother. Rocks and boulders the size of small cars flying high. The unstoppable and terrifying tsunami. And yet, until now, she'd never dreaded being there again. In the place her magic had knocked her unconscious and into a new life. A life she'd never dreamed of.

There's no way Noro is taking this life from me. Sara clenched her fists.

A breeze blew past, ruffling her wildly grown-out pixie cut. The hair tickled the cartilaginous tops of her ears and Sara shivered. She'd meant to make an appointment to get her hair cut for weeks, among many other things she needed to do but kept forgetting. Her to-do list seemed suddenly laughable, and she smirked, unable to help herself.

"Finally, a smile out of someone. I don't know if I could have managed such a feat." Kim drew up next to Sara and jasmine flowers enveloped her, warming Sara to the core.

"It was more a grim smile than happy," Sara admitted.

Kim shrugged. "I'll take it."

They walked in silence for a few minutes before the question simmering inside Sara burst out. "How many fata did you guys kill before they—?"

"Stormed the forest? A dozen or two? There's still a lot of them, and they've repaid us. Hence all the blood."

Kim gestured to her shirt covered in red and bits of things Sara didn't want to think about. "I'll spare you the details but there's at least fifty still alive. Only one air witch, Sasha, sustained injuries, possibly died, I'm not sure. Fiona dragged her to the side of the property and tried to revive her. But then I saw Fiona running through the woods later. I assume that means Sasha didn't make it. The fata made short work of the ones unable to defend themselves at all. Or at least Noro did. Some fata flew on by. Maybe they can't fight yet. Let's hope so."

"Noro did most of the damage?"

Kim nodded. "Him and his seven riders of the apocalypse. There were others fighting but not with the same vigor."

Sara gulped. "Where are the other air witches and wizards?"

Another shrug. "In the woods somewhere. Fighting. Hiding. Trying to stay alive. None deserted, but we didn't stick together. I saw Badb and Nemain fighting with some Earth witches, too. They were amazing, slashing and using their magic like—actually, I've never seen anything like it. They killed a few more fata, though I saw more flying away from them than trying to engage the pneumas."

What a grim conversation, one of the few Sara had hoped never to have with the girl beside her. She shook her head. *How can I even be thinking about a relationship right now?*

As if in answer, Kim grabbed her hand. It was warm and clean compared to Sara's cold, dirt-covered hand.

Sara bit her lip but did not pull back.

"WE'RE GETTING CLOSE," Aoife murmured ten minutes later.

Celestine nodded, "I scent an earth witch in distress."

"Did you four have a plan?" Aoife asked the witches, daemon, and incubus gathering around her.

"No," Alfred answered, his voice grim.

"We didn't either. Not knowing how they would surround the site made wasting time concocting a plan seem a bit daft. So far, it seems like most of the 'em are inside. Whatever we do, I don't think we should split up. We're outnumbered, no doubt about that."

"Noro wants Sara. We should stick by her," Evelyn said.

Aoife nodded. "We go in together. If by some grace of the goddess you get a clear shot when we peek through the woods, take it." Aoife leveled her copper eyes at Kim, who nodded.

"Step lightly. Any advantage means lives saved," Gwenn said.

Sara's breath was thin from fear, though miraculously

still smooth, as they trudged ever closer. *Years spent sitting on a cushion controlling my nervous system—was it all leading up to this? To the moment when I'd have to defend and possibly lose those I love?*

Tears pricked in her eyes and she wiped them away with her filthy sleeve. A soft murmur came from behind her. Sara turned, thankful for the distraction of having others around. Her eyes widened.

Roman and Evelyn were walking side by side, his arm wrapped around Evelyn's shoulder, whispering as she stared at the ground.

She's not pushing him away. I guess the strong likelihood of death will have people forgiving anything.

Sara glanced at Roman, the way he bit the side of his cheek, the earnest look in his eyes. Sara believed he was sorry. She hoped Evelyn did, too. No one should go into battle having things left unsaid, feelings untold.

Soon the light of a fire, burning hot and bright in the center of the clearing ahead, came into focus. Sounds shot through the trees, slamming together in discord. Nora's abrasive laugh; Lily's screams; the sudden ceasing of a gorgeous, otherworldly song.

"A siren song," Evelyn breathed. Her posture stiffened. "Selma must be in there."

Selma. Sara's senses spiked as she recalled how Lily had been after Em's death: despondent, broken, a shadow of herself. Sara would do anything so that Lily wouldn't experience that sort of pain again.

"It looks like the way in from here is clear." Aoife rose from the squat she'd been in. "Let's get into formation. Sara and Evelyn in the middle. Kim and Celestine, you're in the front with me. Alfred and Gwenn, you take the side, and Roman, the back. Roman, we know there's at least one traitorous bitch in there. Try to get your hooks into her and any other women fast."

"My pleasure." Roman grinned a grin that should have been on the cover of a magazine. Sara knew no matter how good a witch Nora was, she could not guard herself against Roman's thrall.

They moved as one, a flock of supernaturals, drawing ever closer to the fire. Sara heard more subtle sounds now: crackling logs, the scurrying of feet. A flash of navy followed by pearly-gold caught her eye. The next second they were there, walking into the clearing.

The laughing, the screams, the sound of an unintelligible language from above ceased.

A chill swept through Sara as she stepped out of the trees.

Stand Off

Evelyn

EVELYN HELD BACK the growl vibrating at the back of her throat.

There floated Noro, thirty feet ahead and smiling straight at her.

That fucking bastard.

Evelyn tore her eyes from his sickly smile to take in the odds. Lily stood, immobilized in what looked like a cage of air swirling around her, her eyes wide, her stance awkward.

Why is she standing like that?

As if in answer, Lily's eyes darted from Evelyn's to the ground, back and forth.

Only when Evelyn followed her sister's gaze did she understand. Below Lily was a crack in the ground a few inches wide. Lily was not able to break out of the cage, so she was trying to dig below it. Judging by the exhausted and defeated look on Lily's face, however, it wasn't working out. She needed help, and Evelyn thought she knew just how to bust Lily out of her cage. Evelyn nodded, showing Lily she understood and Lily's shoulders softened with relief.

Eginura, Evelyn thought, but instead of pushing the magic out of her hands she sent it down. Releasing water into the dirt below to carve a pathway through the earth and break her sister free. Having done what she could for Lily, at least for the time being, moved on.

Selma, too, was in a cage, her face set in hard, unattractive lines Evelyn never would have thought the siren capable of. A wolf was sprawled on the ground two feet from Selma, and Shefali lay near the forest's edge, bound in vines and unconscious.

Finally, Evelyn moved to the last body and sucked in a breath. Collapsed on the dirt neither bound nor guarded was her mother. A fata hovered over Brigit and a faint mist passed from Evelyn's mother's body into the fata. A mist Evelyn had seen before through the eyes of Macha when fata were draining human life forces. Her fists clenched.

"I see you found us," Noro boomed, his smile wide.

"Allow me to introduce you to King Dimia, first of his name, ruler of Hecate and Earth. Eve—or shall I call you Evelyn now?

Evelyn's fingernails cut into her skin at his mocking tone that made light of Macha's—his Eve's—death.

"Anyhow, it matters not *your* name. Only your king's. You never met your ancestor's father while we were together. There was never the right moment. I'm sorry to say this has to be it, for there may not be many more."

Creatures behind Noro nodded, their expressions gleeful.

"Can we kill the caged one now, master?" a vampire with black hair and brilliant black eyes asked.

"Patience, Acolyte." Noro's bottomless black eyes probed past Aoife, Celestine, and Kim, then sidestepped Evelyn to land on Sara. "I need her first. Seraphina, will you not make this easy? Come to us. You have seen how you are outmatched. How I alone can cut down the best among you in a second. How you can save many lives tonight by submitting." Noro beckoned Sara with a wave of his arm.

Sara stiffened.

Evelyn recalled Lily's story of how Sara had reacted to Noro at the Battle of Peacock Manor. How she'd frozen and whimpered.

"He won't take you," Evelyn whispered.

Everyone around them shifted and reached for their weapons.

Sara softened and muttered something unintelligible beneath her breath. Her hand lifted an inch.

Evelyn looked down. Small amounts of air were already accumulating there in tiny, jagged shards that almost resembled the clean bullets Kim and Evelyn produced.

Good thinking. Evelyn set about doing the same, calling air to her and compressing it into neat bullets.

Noro took Sara's silence as it was meant to be taken. A denial. "I see you three are still set on doing this the hard way. On denying the inevitable. Have it your way." His navy color deepened with his frustration.

"Forward," Noro bellowed.

The wind kicked up, and from the woods behind Noro appeared dozens of earthly creatures—wolves, witches, wizards, two daemons, and vampires.

Evelyn sucked in a breath, her gaze darting up. The fata floating above weren't moving. Apparently, Noro had decided to use flesh shields before endangering his kind further. Evelyn wasn't surprised, but still, this changed her tactic. She released the air she'd been building in her palms, freeing the dozens of bullets back into their molecular form. Fire flashed in one hand as she gripped her iron hammer with the other.

She turned to her sister to urge her to do the same just in time to see Sara fling her shards of air high into the sky straight for the fata.

Incendiary

Sara

Five shards of air hit their targets and five corresponding fata fell to the forest floor. The rest fled into the trees, terror in their black eyes. A painful bellow rang through the clearing. The hoard of vampires streaked their way across the opening, heading straight for their small contingent of the Triplet Army. They'd be upon them at any moment.

Fear spiking, Sara called air again. *Elkartaire. Come on . . . elkartaire.*

The air failed to pull together, failed to create the hazy film between her hands that signified the particles were close enough to become solid and deadly. Sara bit her lip.

"Shit," Evelyn murmured.

Sara glanced up to find the vampires had company.

Noro was charging at them now with werewolves only a few feet behind.

"Skirt the trees. Save Lily. It has to be you three. We'll hold them off," Aoife instructed.

Kim pushed Sara out of their protective circle—the circle their adversaries were heading straight for. "Go," she hissed. "We've got this."

Kim molded massive torpedoes of air in her hands with ease and flung them straight at Noro as Aoife, almost in perfect unison, hurled fireballs. Celestine and Alfred surged forward to meet the oncoming vampires while Gwenn rushed to free Brigit from the fata sucking out her life force.

Evelyn sprang into action and Sara followed. They'd made it halfway to Lily when a vampire jumped in front of them. Her teeth snapped and eyes gleamed for a terrifying second before glazing over. Her arms fell to her side, limp.

Sara's eyes darted around. All the women in the field had similar glazed looks. Even Nora hovered docile over an unconscious Brigit. Still, there was motion, fighting everywhere, blood and ash flying through the clearing as the men continued to fight.

"It's Roman. Come on! If someone takes him out, they'll come to their senses." Evelyn tossed a small ball of fire, little more than a candle flame, at the vampire in

Roman's thrall. The vampire went up in a puff of ash and Sara blinked as Evelyn, not wasting a second, kept running.

Sara followed and zoned in on Evelyn's breathing, loud, frantic gulps of air, at her side. She shot a glance at her sister. Evelyn's palms were pointed at the ground and shaking. Sara sensed her sister was performing non-verbal magic to free Lily but could not tell what.

"Hit the cage with fire," Evelyn panted.

Sara directed her palms at the cage. "Flampila!" A ball of fire grazed the top of Lily's cage, which shrunk before their eyes forcing Lily into an awkward crouch.

"Shit," Evelyn muttered, then her eyes widened. "I feel a mind. Watch our backs."

"You got it," Sara said, shooting a glance behind them. The hair on the back of her neck stood up as she saw the creature Evelyn referred to, close enough for Sara to see the whites of his stunning, vampiric eyes. Sara aimed a fireball at him and the vampire exploded into ash. Five thundering heartbeats later, they were at Lily's side.

Evelyn's plan became clear immediately as Sara stared down at the gap, seven inches wide and six feet deep beneath Lily. Water welled from the depths of the earth, hollowing it out before their eyes. They only needed a few inches more for Lily to escape. An idea hit her, and Sara eyed the crack before aiming her hands at the ground on the other side of the cage.

"Pream." The earth exploded, and water sloshed out the other side revealing an opening.

"Again," Evelyn directed, still panting.

Sara took careful aim, fired, and a tunnel opened from the gap Lily and Evelyn had created to join Sara's coarse explosion site.

Lily hopped into the water and ducked beneath the air cage, which thankfully had not lowered to fill in the crevice in the earth. Once on the other side, Sara and Evelyn yanked her up. Lily shivered as her wet clothes met the cold winter air.

"Flamarba," Sara commanded drawing a line of fire around her sister.

Though her clothes remained wet, Lily's shivering stopped. "Thanks. I thought the damn cage would keep getting smaller and smaller until I burnt alive in there." Lily held out her arm, which bore blisters wrought by the air cage. "I tried to heal myself a few times but it's never as effective doing it yourself."

"Let me," Evelyn stepped forward. "Salus." The skin tightened, and the redness faded.

Lily looked impressed.

"I've had a few practice attempts. Sara got knocked out by a vampire earlier. Speaking of which, we should be helping turn a few vampires to ash." Evelyn's hard eyes swept the scene.

Sara's gaze followed and she exhaled. Fiona, a few of the New York witches—two of them air workers—and werewolves with a glowing band around their paws had arrived. Aoife, recognizable only by her blur of red hair, fought with fire blazing all around her. Kim was battling two fata at once. Celestine, Alfred, and Gwenn each grappled two on one, blades and canines flashing in the moonlight. From the sidelines, still holding as many females in his thrall as he could with his attention split, Roman circled what looked to be a fae gifted with water magic. He'd picked up a sword from somewhere and was brandishing it with surprising speed and agility.

Noro was nowhere in sight, nor was Dimia, though a handful of other fata remained to fight. Sara peered into the trees behind them and saw a half dozen glinting, black eyes shining in the dark. They caught her gaze and dissolved. Fata still in hiding, waiting until the coast was clear.

Probably the weakest ones—crap!

A shimmer of navy flew into Sara's peripheral vision and she whirled about to face it. "Arma!"

Noro zoomed by, his blob-like arms morphing into sharp blades as he flew. He slashed through the air and his arm nicked Evelyn's upper thigh seconds before Sara's shield materialized.

"Evelyn!" Lily cried, catching her sister before she fell to the ground with a grunt of pain.

Suddenly, Badb was there, her green shimmery body hovering over Evelyn. "Run!" She ordered the triplets.

Evelyn staggered to her feet, wrath in her narrowed eyes. "No freaking way. I'm with you. You two, get out of here."

Lily, too, shook her head. "I'm staying."

Noro was circling back on them now, both arms transformed into razor-sharp blades, rage written plainly on his face.

Evelyn shoved Sara back and threw up a shield, blocking her from the fight. Protecting Sara. "You're the one he wants. Go!"

Sara slammed her fist against the shield, not wanting to be the triplet who, yet again, was left out or needed to be rescued from Noro.

Her sisters did not see her rage. They were busy fighting. Badb's green magic was lighting them up as they spun, deflected, slashed with iron, and hurled weaponized air at Noro.

Sara glanced down the shield and saw it expanded only to the edge of the clearing. She whirled about, intent on running around it to join her sisters, and came face to face with a werewolf, his teeth bared, rancid, metallic breath heaving from his open mouth.

She jumped to the side as the wolf snapped his jaws. Adrenaline spiking within her, Sara sprinted for her life. The wolf charged after her, the heft of his paws hitting the earth an anthem to her terror.

"Pream!" Sara screamed shooting the spell behind her. She glanced to confirm an explosion of blood and guts filled the space where the wolf had been. *That was close.*

The unbinding site was turning into a massacre. Everywhere she looked, Sara saw bodies she recognized. Members of the Triplet Army she barely knew laid open on the ground, spilling their guts and blood, moaning, their faces covered in a mix of sweat and tears. Others battled with all their might. Eros tossed a lasso of air at a fata even as he doubled over in pain. Gwenn and Aoife circled a crimson-faced vampire. Morgane battled a muscular wizard as she hobbled, clearly injured, back into the woods for cover. Celestine was a blur of motion, attacking and killing anyone without a band of light on their arm.

Only we can end this.

Vomit threatened to climb up Sara's throat and her legs burned as she pushed into the fray. Fire pooled in her hands without thought and she shot off fireball after fireball at any foe she saw. Another snarling werewolf sprang into her path. She blasted him with a steady stream of fire and a yelp rang in her ears as the wolf incinerated before her eyes.

"Flamarba," Sara muttered, her arms flung out as she ran, flame gates trailing behind her, giving the witches a slight advantage over the vampires, who could not cross the fire.

A fata flew before her and she acted on instinct. "Homaire." The wall of air formed with ease. The fata was undeterred, swooping down to engage her. "Murr," Sara growled. The wall shot at the fata, crushing it against the ground and trapping it. She approached the being, the creature wanting to take over her planet, her life, and hurt those she loved.

Sara felt no remorse at shoving her iron stiletto in the thin crack between the air wall and earth, straight into the creature's shimmering skin. The fata deflated before her eyes and a justified sense of heat rose within her. Any remorse for taking life vanished. Fury and fire reigned in its place. Her insides were burning, clarifying everything around her. Evelyn's words from when Sara woke after being knocked out ran through her mind again.

"The vamp wouldn't have hit you that hard. She made it clear Noro wants you alive. Not me and Lily, though."

Sara stiffened. *I'm the one Noro wants. The one who started it all by refusing to bend to his will years ago.*

Nemain's warnings against looking for trouble suddenly made sense. She had known Sara would see the writing on the wall, eventually. Knew that once she did, she'd seek to finish it. She'd do it for those she loved. For those that had already sacrificed so much. Lily and Em. Evelyn with scars marring her body and mind. The death of her best teacher.

What had Sara sacrificed? Mary? She loved her aunt, but Evelyn and Mary had always had a special bond. Mary was not only Sara's loss.

I have only one thing that's mine to sacrifice. Myself. I'm the one who needs to finish this.

The knots in Sara's stomach released for the first time in days and she had her answer. Sara dropped her hands to her side and fire poured down. It stayed near her heels at first, until Sara coaxed it away, blew a little air out to feed the flames so they crept like spiders across the expanse of the clearing, devouring everything in their wake. Creatures picked up their fallen allies and ran. The vampires darted into the woods, away from the fatal flames. Across the clearing, a flash of shimmering crimson caught Sara's eye. Nemain had spotted Sara and would be at her side soon. She'd try to talk Sara out of the act she herself had committed as a young fata.

Martyrdom.

Sara pushed harder, the fire flowing from her shaking

palms like a waterfall. She pinpointed areas of the flames to control, building a moat of fire around herself, cutting herself off. Spelling a shield around Fiona, who was tending to Brigit, and manipulating the flames to allow the Triplet Army extra time to move from the lashing red tongue of fire. The rest she let ravage anyone and anything in its path.

Above the dancing red, Aoife rushed over her copper eyes—so like Sara's own—were wild, full of fear. There was a dimming of flames. Aoife was trying to control the fire Sara had let go of, allowing it to do as it wished. But Sara couldn't have that. She needed total destruction to draw Noro's attention, to make him leave her sisters and seek her instead.

She surged her magic at her aunt and Aoife tripped backward. Aoife shook her head and Sara sensed her aunt knocking to be let into her mind, to convince or even control her. Sara gave her aunt a small smile, shoved thicker barriers down and pressed the flames forth harder than ever before. For the first time, Sara was sure Aoife could not stop her. Not when she had discovered a way to end it all.

"Even when I told you not to."

Sara turned to find Nemain floating in the center of a blazing hurricane with her.

"You told me not to because you knew he would want

me. That I'd be the perfect bait. And now that you're here, you may as well help. Tell everyone to run and hide far from here, protect the ones who won't. Tell Badb, too. If this works, I won't be able to control what happens." She paused, not wanting to voice her next words. "I may not make it out, but I'll be sure to take Noro with me. That's all that matters, right?"

Nemain stared at her. They both knew fata domination would be impossible without Noro. He was the mastermind, the one with a true vision of fata ruling over humans. After years, he'd finally earned his reputation as powerful, irreplaceable. She sighed. "Five of his seven disciples have already fallen. You are correct. No other fata is strong enough to challenge your army, not without guidance. He must fall."

Their eyes locked for another second and then Nemain soared over Sara's flames toward Lily and Evelyn, who were inching their way closer to Sara. Noro was following them but being thwarted by Badb every step of the way. *Thanks for showing him the way, sisters, but I only want one creature near me.*

Sara surged the flames wider, higher, and saw her sisters jump back, looks of astonishment in their eyes. Sara stared at them and shook her head.

"Run," she screamed as Noro broke loose from Badb and shot a beam of magic at Lily. Nemain intervened at the last second, shielding Lily with her body as Badb blasted magic at Noro, shaking the ground of the clearing. Despite the narrow escape, Lily tried once more to get to Sara, but Evelyn, ever the practical one, grabbed her older sister by the wrist and pulled her down a path through the flames Sara created for them.

Sara watched, relieved, as her sisters disappeared into the woods. She urged Nemain and Badb to follow, to warn the army far away from the clearing. Her family, Kim, and whoever else was still fighting in the woods would need the pneumas' protection more than her. As if they'd heard her wishes, the pneumas disappeared into the trees leaving Sara with Noro, whose black eyes glinted with confusion, surely wondering why she was alone, so weak and defenseless. Why they were handing over exactly what he wanted.

We'll see about that.

Sara flung the flames higher, creating a large dome of swirling heat and furious orange above her with only a small hole at the top. A hole starlight shone through, perhaps the last she would ever see.

It was a show. A beacon of power Sara hoped Noro couldn't resist. Yelps and grunts filtered through the crackling fire. Fighting was still happening in the woods, but it would stop soon, once their general and true leader fell. All she needed was to lure him in.

"I thought you wanted me?" Sara screamed. "Here I am. Come and get me!"

A flash of dark light cut through the flames and a second later Noro appeared at the entrance of Sara's flame dome, his black eyes glinting with glee.

Dome of Air
Lily

THE PINK and blue fata who had assaulted Lily and Evelyn as they ran from Sara's inferno disappeared in an instant. Lily's head spun, and she gripped her mace tighter as she tried to discern where their fata opponents had gone.

"Noro is gone, too." Evelyn's mouth, tinged gray from the smoke filling the clearing, flattened. "He went after Sara. I bet he called those fata to help."

Lily's heart clenched at the thought of her youngest sister up against three fata. Three *strong* fata. There was no doubt in Lily's mind that the ones they had been fighting seconds earlier were two of the fata Eve brought over years ago.

"We need to get in there and help Sara." Lily hung

her mace on her hip and stared up at the thirty-foot-high dome of flame. The fire and smoke tickled the tops of the trees surrounding the clearing. Nothing outside the clearing had caught fire yet, though the tiniest surge of magic from Sara would change that. Lily had never seen anything like her sister's display and wondered what Sara was playing at.

Evelyn shook her head. "Sara planned this. She won't let us in. Not unless something goes wrong. Lotu." She shot off a binding spell, catching a werewolf attempting to sneak up on them between the eyes and binding his wolfish limbs together. The werewolf fell to the ground with a pathetic whine.

"OK, so, Sara claimed Noro, but if their king is alive after all this the fata still have a rallying point. The next logical step is to find Dimia." Lily pivoted to scan the forest.

Two Acolyte females, still entranced by Roman, sat docile at the base of a tree not twenty feet from them. Deeper in the woods, beams of light were discernible between the trees and screams filtered through the darkness.

Lily's heart soared as a jet of bright yellow light followed by a fluid shimmer of green flashed briefly in the night, assuring her Alfred and Badb were still fighting. For once, she wasn't pulled to join Alfred. Finding Dimia was her priority.

Mayhem surrounded them. The air stank of kicked up dirt, metal, and fear. Bodies littered the ground, some corporeal, others—like the fallen fata—resembling shimmering jellyfish. Lily's fingers itched to touch one, and she approached the closest, a brown fata a few feet away who would have been well camouflaged in the forest.

"What are you doing?" Evelyn asked as Lily squatted down and took the deflated fata flesh in her fingers.

Memories of the night Noro had touched her face spun back to Lily, his flesh like tiny tornados hovering over her skin. Dimia's touch had felt the same, but dead fata flesh was different. Feather-light, it felt like silk if silk were a material lighter than air itself.

This body housed a living creature. The corpse slipped through the cracks in her fingers like water from a colander.

"How dare you touch your fallen kin? I command you to stop at once." A voice bellowed in the dark.

Evelyn scurried forward, kicking up rocks and dirt, filling Lily's nostrils with the scent of wet earth. Their eyes met and Lily knew they were thinking the same thing. There was no need to find Dimia—he'd already found them. She rose from her crouched position and gazed into the darkness, waiting.

"You used to be the favored child, Lilith. How did this land taint you so?" Dimia's voice wove through the trees once more, though his body remained obscured. "And you, Eve. I am quite *displeased* with your choices."

Lily got the impression that vexing the king would have been enough for Eve to yield and do exactly as Dimia said. Unfortunately for Dimia, that was no longer the case.

"We're not them. You can't control us with old guilts. With us, there's only one way this will go. Come out and fight," Lily said, her tone even and calm. *Three battles in and I've finally found my feet.*

"As you wish, daughters," Dimia hissed and through the trees, the pearly fata emerged with Nora at his back.

LILY BLINKED at the smirk on Nora's face. The same treacherous woman Lily had spotted Gwenn leveling earlier. How was she still alive? *Gwenn is the better witch. How did Nora get away?*

Even as Lily considered the questions she knew why Nora was still here. Her mother's ex-best friend had been a part of the fabric of their lives for decades. Killing her would be like killing a sister, a traitorous sister but a sister, nonetheless.

Capitalizing on Lily's shock, Nora shot a body bind curse her way.

Lily leapt out of the way just in time and thrust her hand out, launching a stunning spell at her adversary. "Dionean!"

Nora advanced, facing off with Lily as Dimia went for Evelyn. As much as Lily wanted her sister by her side, she realized it was meant to be this way. Nora, the woman who had betrayed her, the reason Em was dead, was finally hers to deal with. Not even the healer within her argued otherwise. And Dimia, the father Eve—Macha—had loved so much she'd been willing to give up an entire species, was fitting as Evelyn's adversary.

A nefarious nudge caught Lily's attention. Nora was trying to enter Lily's mind. She slammed down her mind barriers hard, shaking out Nora's magic, and narrowed her eyes.

"It's about time you managed to keep your mind on lockdown," Nora sneered.

A gust of wind swept by, knocking them both off their feet. Lily lifted herself onto her forearms, searching for the source.

A protective tornado spun around Evelyn, whipping her long, blonde hair to the sky. From her thin barrier she beat back Dimia's blade-like arms by swinging her war hammer pick-side out. All the while, inside the tornado

Evelyn was pulling bullets of air together, the tornado and flailing iron simply a distraction for Evelyn's greater plan.

A spell scorched the ground near Lily, landing inches from her elbow and yanking her back to the moment. She shot onto her feet and charged straight at Nora.

"Islatu! Abbero! Arma!" Lily reflected, deflected, and shielded herself from Nora's onslaught of charms as she drew closer.

Nora's veneer of confidence was slipping with every step Lily took, the realization dawning on her that Brigit's eldest had progressed farther than she'd expected. She turned and ran into the dark woods to save herself.

Lily put on a surge of speed, intent on catching Nora before she disappeared, slithering away like the snake she was. "Lascero!"

The traitorous witch shrieked as Lily's spell hit her. She clutched the small gash on her side, leaving her defenseless to Lily's tackle. They landed simultaneously, Lily on top. She heard the wind fly from her opponent and seized Nora's second of defenselessness. "Lotu."

Her adversary's arms and legs snapped together, leaving her helpless.

"Quite the predicament you got yourself into, isn't it?" Lily smirked. "Not at all what you were expecting, me kicking your ass?"

Nora's brilliant blue eyes narrowed to slivers.

"Oh, that's right. Evelyn told me she couldn't talk when you put a body bind curse on her. That's alright, you've done enough talking for a lifetime." Blood dripped from Nora's wound and, shoving aside her healer's instincts, Lily pulled up the fabric and shoved her finger into the laceration.

"For all the times you lied to my mother." Lily dug her finger deeper. "This one's for Em." An inch further. "And this is for all the other people you betrayed." She ripped her hand out and blood sprayed everywhere.

Nora's eyes were watering and her body, though bound, appeared to be vibrating in agony.

"You didn't expect *me*, the healer, to best you—but shit has changed, hasn't it?" Lily studied the traitorous witch before her. It would be easy to end it here, to grow vines from the ground to strangle Nora, but Nora wasn't Lily's to finish. Only her mother, the person Nora had hurt most deeply, had the right to do that.

"Herbcapto." Lily waved her arms over Nora so that the grass grew and bound her to that spot. Once secure, she wove a shield around the woman and stood. "Now, if you'll excuse me, I have to go help kill a king. Don't worry, though, my family will come back for you."

Evelyn's face lit up at Lily's approach. Her tornado

and air bullets were gone, spent. How had Dimia dodged them all? Suddenly, there was a gentle nudge as Evelyn tried to talk mind to mind through Lily's mental barrier. She let her barriers fall.

I have a plan, Evelyn said. *Do you trust me?*

Lily nodded.

Keep him occupied. I need a few minutes. And be careful, he's quick.

If Dimia hadn't swooped down upon them brandishing arms transformed into sharp swords at that exact moment, Lily would have rolled her eyes.

Keep him occupied. Like I have any choice.

Lily thrust her mace in the air, its sharp spike pointed right at Dimia, allowing Evelyn to dart a few feet away, outside Dimia's grasp, and spell a shield around herself. Dimia howled and pulled up, rage clear in his dark features. Then, unexpectedly, as if just realizing something monumental, his expression smoothed over and he paused. The next thing Lily knew, the fata king was floating down to the ground slowly.

"Some things never change," Dimia said landing ten feet from Lily. "Even now, years and bodies later, your sister saves herself first. She never changed. Don't you see how easy it would be to return to how our relationship once was, too? Father and favorite daughter, adventuring in this new world together."

Lily cocked her head and the grip on her mace tightened. *Does he even hear himself?*

"That must be how it all began? You spread discord among your children, pitted one against the other. I bet once Eve did what you wanted you called her the favored child. Manipulative is an understatement."

Dimia swiped his arm to the right, and Lily dropped her mace as her guts twisted in on themselves. She trembled as her torso crunched in, trying to quell the pain that brought her to her knees.

"It's a shame you three seem to have grown savvier with your lifetimes. Closer, too," Dimia growled, his face alight once again with the rage he'd shoved down in a half-hearted attempt to sway her.

Lily wrenched herself out of her crouched position. "Pream!" She watched in horror as the spell hit Dimia in the center of his body and rebounded back at her. Lily flopped to the ground and her spell hit a tree behind her, exploding it into a hundred pieces.

Right, only air. Evelyn better hurry her ass up.

She tried to stand and collapsed with a groan, her intestines still twisting inside her.

Dimia rose, his white-gold coloring luminous against the velvet-black sky as he prepared for the final pounce.

Lily cringed and readied herself to toss up a shield when suddenly Evelyn was screeching in her head.

Lily! Look up! I need help. Complete the wall.

Going against every instinct in her body Lily glanced up at the fata king, looming above her.

There, behind Dimia, was a gentle swirling of air and bits of dirt caught in a vortex as Evelyn's wall rose like a hood of earth and wind over his head. The wall was the largest Lily had seen, level with Dimia, twenty feet in length and height. Evelyn was taking a page out of Sara's book and creating a dome. A dome with which to capture Dimia.

Genius.

"Elkartaire," Lily panted, trying her hardest not to pass out from the pain as the air in front of her constricted. "Homaire," Lily said before all the air constricted. She didn't have time for pretty. Her intestines twisted again and spots swam in her vision. She could black out at any moment. Faster than she'd ever managed before, Lily's wall pulled together. It was a mere five feet across compared to Evelyn's twenty, but it would have to do. *All I have to do is keep the wall up and stay conscious to bait him.*

No! Make him angrier. We need him ten feet lower to trap him. We need the walls to meet. Evelyn's voice rang through Lily's mind.

Lily's jaw tightened and her guts heaved as she forced herself to her feet. Her eyes hardened on the fata king hovering steady, like a bird of prey above a trapped mouse. She trembled violently. There was no way she could lift her mace. Instead, she flung her arm out to the side, where a jumble of rocks she'd pulled from the earth the night of her unbinding stood.

"Volavari." Twenty small boulders arced high in the sky, heading right for Dimia, who darted through the earthly projectiles with grace.

"Stupid girl. Noro was right. All the human breeding has made even my closest descendants inferior to the weakest fata."

"I'm not sure where Noro comes off calling anyone stupid." Lily jerked and winced with each word, so great was the pain Dimia was inflicting on her organs. "He's been stuck here alone for millennia, too weak and dumb to figure out how to bring the fata across." She tilted her head to the side for added effect. "Almost as dumb as you were for believing his plan. How on earth do you expect the fata to follow you when your own daughters didn't?"

That did it. Dimia flew at her, his arms once again sharp blades. He was not going to spell her. No, Dimia desired to take out his rage upon her human body.

Lily remained in place, shaking, sweating, and holding her small air wall between her and Dimia. She sent up a prayer that Evelyn would get the timing right. Fifteen feet, a single shaky breath, then five feet were all that remained between her and the fata king. There was a thrum, a vibration of air meeting air and finally, the walls knit together. Evelyn yanked Dimia back, away from Lily in her fluid net of air.

Dimia roared. The sound was terrifying as it resonated over the forest, mingling with other screams and shrieks.

"Murr." The word slipped out of Evelyn and the massive dome of air shrunk smaller and smaller until Dimia hovered in a cage barely larger than himself.

"Karma's a bitch, isn't it?" Evelyn said, pressing forward to face the fata king, whose eyes were wide with disbelief.

"Release me at once," Dimia commanded.

"You know, I don't think I will. Your little lackey kept me in a cage for a while. I was lucky to escape, but I doubt you'll be able to do the same." Evelyn removed her war hammer from its loop at her side. Turning it around she aimed the pick at the cage and smiled a wicked smile.

Lily gasped as her intestines finally untangled and the agony receded.

Dimia cowered before them, his full focus now on Evelyn. "I didn't mean what I said earlier. We shall still make room for humankind and you three in particular. My offer stands to allow you your own stable of beings to do with as you will."

"How kind," Evelyn purred, but the smile had dropped from her face. "I wish I could say the same for you." Evelyn struck, her hammer crashing down on the air cage, shattering it to pieces, and sinking into Dimia's airy flesh.

Tome of Fire

Sara

Sara's flames faltered for a heartbeat as two more fata joined Noro, their colors startling shades of pink and electric blue against the inky sky above.

Noro's smile expanded, sensing her weakness, but Sara recovered, arching the flames high above the fatas and sealing the tomb of fire. The sounds of battle deadened inside the inferno, a void filled only by whispers of the crackling flames and the shifting of Sara's stance. Blisters bubbled on her skin where the flames danced too close. Tightness crept through her jaw.

I only need to last a few minutes.

The infamous navy fata floated before her as if he were the king of the fata himself. "Once again, it comes down to you and me." Noro glanced at the fire, unconcerned. "It makes sense. The strongest of the three against the cleverest, strongest of fata. Imagine if we had joined forces? The greatness we could have accomplished."

Sara's teeth ground together. The fire tomb constricted an inch in all directions.

Noro released an airy, cruel laugh. "Fire cannot harm me. Why you have cloaked yourself in flame is a mystery to me, though truthfully, one I do not care to discover the answer to. I have other questions though." A hard slap whipped across her face as Noro's magic lashed out at her.

She gasped. The razor sharp shards of air she'd been cultivating behind her back slipped back to molecular form. *No!* Sara hurried to recollect them.

"Where is Seraphina?" Noro's eyes darted around the circle as if Seraphina—Nemain—would appear from the flames at any moment. "Gone, I see. Left you. Pity you did not inherit her knack for escape."

Searing pain came with a twitch of Noro's arm, radiating up and down her every nerve. Sara squeezed her eyes shut. *Breathe through it, breathe through it,* she repeated again and again.

Electricity pushed her heart to thump erratically. Her blood swirled in unnatural patterns within her, reversing and resuming its normal flow with sickening rapidity. Noro was playing with her, exhibiting his power over what he deemed the weaker species.

But she wouldn't let him win.

Behind her back the air remained, her small armory growing larger with each second. Heated to extreme temperatures, the frenzied molecules of air flocked to her call with ease for the first time. They acted like all things in nature, congregating around the easy, free energy she provided.

The second she released her fire tomb the air would disperse and ripple out from its source, her, with the new energy it collected. Each hardened shard would be a missile, bursting forth, injuring, if not killing, all within its wake. There would be no controlling it.

She constricted the tomb another two inches, willing the air particles to take the energy she gave. Her backside burned as flame licked her body and she bit her cheek.

Finally, Noro let up on his assault. "That is merely a taste of what I can do." He turned to his minions. "Take her. I will deal with her sisters." Noro's black eyes sought Sara's, glinting with the promise of the atrocities he'd commit.

But Sara would not allow them to cart her off. She needed to remain in the fire. The air in her hands was vibrating, nearly ready for release, but she needed more. More energy to ensure this battle was the last. Catching her breath, Sara lifted her head, looked Noro in the eye, and spit on him.

"You impetuous fool," Noro growled and the fata behind him roared with displeasure.

Sara shot ten feet in the air.

"What happens when fire meets fire?"

Elkartaire. Elkartaire. Elkartaire.

Sara repeated the spell over and over as she rose higher, rushing to collect as much air as possible. The particles of air flocked to her and she shaped them as fast as possible into projectiles. She glanced down to see if Noro had noticed the air collecting behind her through the smoke and flame. Despite the heat, she shivered. His eyes trained mercilessly on hers, black to copper. He didn't want to miss a second of her pain.

"Don't worry, I won't kill you. I just need to know this time you'll cooperate." Noro flung Sara into the flames above.

Her hair caught and the sickening scent of burnt hair engulfed her. Smoke filled Sara's mouth as she screamed and fire ran down her face.

Elkartaire! She thought the words one last time, a last-ditch effort to shape as many projectiles as possible. The air pulsed with life behind her as her head drooped. Sara couldn't hold it together much longer. She simply had to hope she'd allowed the air to absorb enough energy so that it could explode forth with the force required.

She had to act.

Flipping her hands to the front plane of her body, Sara aimed her shaking palms and projectiles at Noro and his cronies. The fata took her in gesture, their amorphous heads tilting in unison as they worked to discern what she was doing through the clouds of smoke. Finally, she released her flame dome.

The fire surrounding them fell to earth, and her handfuls of projectiles followed, expanding like a ripple. Through lowered lids, Sara caught the blacks of fata eyes as they grew round, recognizing the haze of weaponized air too late. The first projectile hit and shock swept across Noro's face before his amorphous body fluttered to the earth. Blurs of pink and blue fell behind him.

As Noro's magic died with him, the weight of Sara's body returned and she careened thirty feet to the ground, her head still aflame.

Is It Over?

Sara

Sara screamed. The adrenaline of falling teased her back from the brink of passing out. The ground came at her, seemingly faster with each foot. Pebbles grew and Sara wrenched her eyes shut as she braced for impact.

Suddenly, she slowed, caught in a strong gust of wind and lowered to the ground with a heavy, but not bone-shattering, thunk. Hands were upon her a second later, patting her head, dousing it with water, putting out the fire.

"What the hell kind of crazy stunt was that?" Evelyn choked out.

Strong, gentle hands—Lily's—pulled her up. "Salus, salus, salus," the healer didn't even take a breath between spells.

Sharp pains receded. Sara lifted her hand and gently trailed her fingers over her head. She exhaled when she felt only tender, slightly damp skin. No blisters, no outpouring of blood or even raw skull, as she'd feared, thanks to Lily.

Her eyes floated to Noro's corpse and Sara stiffened before swiveling around to take in the rest of the forest. The fata king still lived, and she'd just killed his best seneschal.

Evelyn touched her arm. "It's over. Lil and I killed Dimia. We were just coming to help you when you fell from the sky. It took all we had left to push enough wind to catch you."

"I knew I liked you when I first saw you, but I never expected to find gallant acts of heroism so hot." Kim's voice preceded her out of the trees. Kim was a mess. Spattered in crimson with a wide, congealed gash across her chest and still, she smiled at Sara.

Tears pricked Sara's eyes and a wispy, yet guttural noise escaped her throat.

"It'll be her windpipe," Fiona said, from behind her. "You can't put yourself in the center of an inferno and expect no damage from smoke inhalation."

"M—Mom?" Sara croaked and tried to peer past Fiona, to where Brigit lay.

Fiona nodded. "Alive. Noro was not gentle with her.

It appears she took quite the beating before arriving in this clearing but I've healed what damage I can from here. We need to be getting all the injured back to the cottage. Thank the goddess I've been stocking up on supplies. I only hope I have enough."

"Can you walk?" Lily asked.

Sara nodded, sure she could despite her tender, aching skin. She didn't want to pilfer aid from those who needed it more.

"I'll walk with her," Kim offered.

"That would be a great help. Lily, I'll need your assistance to perform general healing so people don't bleed out as we make the trek to the cottage. Evelyn, Roman is with Brigit. Help him carry her. Be gentle," Fiona instructed, and the triplets split off.

Sara's eyes flitted once more to the corpses beside her, navy, pink, and electric blue all resembling large, wet plastic bags lying on the ground. Noro and Dimia were gone. Many other fata, too. The battle was over. No more screams, cries, or sounds of bodies hitting the dirt.

Her gaze moved to the trees around the clearing, taking in the deep gashes in their bark, the divots, like bullet holes in the ground. Her jagged shards of air hadn't just finished off Noro and his cronies, they had mutilated everything in their path.

Thank the goddess Nemain and Badb got people out of the way.

"Wild, isn't it. It came on so fast and now it's over?" Kim spoke the word like a question and Sara felt the weight of it.

Was it over?

Aoife appeared out of the darkness of the trees, followed by Gwenn and Alfred. All three looked terrible, particularly Alfred, who was bleeding profusely from his right leg, but they were alive.

"Lily is over there," Kim pointed, understanding the frantic look in Alfred's eyes, and he ran to find her. Aoife and Gwenn remained.

Sara met Aoife's eyes. Her aunt winced and turned away. Sara sensed something terrible, more terrible than what she'd already seen, had happened. Her mind raced, thinking of all the people she'd met over the past few days. Hoping Aoife would not whisper any of their names.

What happened? She projected mentally, knowing Aoife would hear her.

Before Aoife could open her mouth to answer Celestine appeared, the body of Morgane limp in the vampire's gentle arms. The witch who had found Sara, who had brought her to Fern Cottage, Sara's first link to the magical world. A woman Sara loved as a quirky grandmother.

Tears stung and Sara squeezed her eyes shut as if doing so would make it go away.

When she opened them once more Morgane's wrinkled, kind face was still there, her hazel eyes staring blankly at Sara as wide open with wonder as they'd been the day they'd met.

Extended Hands

Evelyn

Hours later, Celestine and a werewolf known for his exceptional sense of smell proclaimed the forest clear of creatures.

"Now we know exactly what we're working with." Lily was all business, her hair sticking out of her ponytail at every angle, the blood of others smeared across her shirt. She was kneeling once more near Rena and Annika, both of whom had sustained vicious slashes all over their bodies, courtesy of Nora. Selma assisted, applying salve to her friends and running back and forth from the cottage to fill water cups.

And it's a lot. Evelyn gazed out over the makeshift hospital they'd constructed outside Fern Cottage by stitching shields together and casting warming spells. A few cots created an askew row but most of the injured lay on the ground atop their sleeping bags or blankets.

Fiona and Lily were a whirlwind, directing others to help, concocting salves and potions on the spot, and filling the air with a mix of herby scents. They performed countless healing spells and although one spell was enough for a few people, most needed more. Cloves tickled her nose and pulled Evelyn from her musings as Roman arrived at her side.

"Alfred, Eros, and I put the bodies on the far end of the orchard. No one will stumble upon them there," he said. "We'll need to bury or move the unclaimed ones soon. Aoife and Gwenn are spelling a shield over the bodies to stop the animals from scavenging, but it won't control the smell. Considering the number of injured, there aren't that many dead. Twenty-five from our side. Almost double from theirs, not including the fata we found. We were lucky to have the advantage in numbers . . . " Roman trailed off. "I'm so sorry about your aunt, Evelyn. Mary was always kind, even when your family was interrogating me."

Tears welled in her eyes and Evelyn looked down at the frost-covered ground. She was sorry, too. Sorry that Mary—good, quick to laugh Mary, the woman she had the most in common with at Fern Cottage, her water mentor —was dead.

"Thank you," she managed. "I appreciate that. Could you ask Lily or Fiona if they need any more help?"

A light hand caressed her shoulder. Familiar tingles rushed up her arm and then Roman was gone, back to work, for there was still much to do.

She looked around the controlled chaos wondering where she could best be of service. So far, the most helpful thing she'd done was listen to a patient who'd wanted to thank one of the triplets for releasing their pneumas.

Apparently, Nemain and Badb had made themselves most useful during the battle, protecting many of the less powerful members of the Triplet Army from vengeful fata. Evelyn hadn't had the heart to tell them that it hadn't been her pneuma, or her *doing* at all. Instead, she just listened, missing Macha more every second, until the patient fell asleep. She really didn't want to go through that again.

Suddenly, Sara's bald, burned head popped up in the sea of people and Evelyn, unable to locate a task in close proximity, made her way over to her sister.

"How is she?" Evelyn asked. Brigit's comforting cinnamon and lavender scent filled her nostrils as she drew closer to where Sara cleaned their mother's wounds as Lily had instructed her to.

"She's been in and out, said most of her pain was

internal. Fiona ran inside and put a cauldron of something on to help. Hopefully it's ready soon."

Evelyn knelt next to her mother and grasped her hand.

Brigit stirred at the touch and opened her eyes. "Hello, my darling. I'm so relieved to see you unhurt."

The words broke Evelyn's heart. "I'm fine, Mom. A couple scratches and bruises, that's all." She was thankful that she'd changed out of her bloodied pants and her mother could not see the angry slash on her leg that the clean, baggy sweats covered.

Brigit managed a smile and Evelyn could not help but ask the question burning inside her since they brought the injured back. "What should we do with Nora?"

Her mother's eyes hardened. There was a moment of silence before she let out a long sigh. "I was hoping someone else would finish her, but I should have known better." Brigit shook her head and winced. "How many Acolytes remain here?"

"About a dozen who were so injured they couldn't escape. Witches, wizards, a fae, and a daemon." Sara readjusted the pillow beneath her mother's head. "No fata, vampires, or werewolves. Those still alive managed to escape."

Evelyn bit her lip. How many fata were still here?

Another sigh escaped Brigit. "Well, we can't kill them.

It's against the law if it's not self-defense, like when they breached my wards. However, we can do the next worst thing without repercussion from any ruling magical court: take their magic. The witches and wizards we can handle ourselves. We'll need a fae, Eros if he'll agree, and Alfred to help with the fae and daemon. It won't be pleasant."

Evelyn's blood chilled. Take their magic? She hadn't even known that was possible. Binding, sure, but take it completely? Something in her rose up to fight and Evelyn wrapped her arms around herself, trying to calm her own magic.

No one is taking you, she thought, and the magic calmed.

Though she'd only known she was a witch for a few short months, it seemed the worst punishment possible. "They don't deserve pleasant," Evelyn said finally and all the women nodded in agreement.

"I'll take care of Nora as soon as I can stand by myself," Brigit said.

No one argued. Evelyn stroked her mother's hand as Sara cleaned her wounds. They sat in comfortable silence until, suddenly, a scream tore through the calm commotion of the makeshift hospital. Evelyn shot up from her crouch. Sara followed suit.

"Look! They're still coming!" A young man sat up in his cot and jabbed his finger toward the woods.

What the hell? Evelyn spun around and gasped.

Emerging from the woods was a small army of fata.

SHE SQUINTED at the colored creatures flying toward them, no more than a dozen, two of them more transparent than the rest. *Is that Badb and Nemain?*

Cries of worry and terror sounded. Some with grievous injuries tried to lift themselves from their bed while a friend or healer pushed them back down.

"Nemain and Badb," Sara whispered.

Evelyn nodded as another familiar figure came into view alongside Badb and Nemain. "I recognize that fuchsia one. I saw her on Hecate, through Macha's eyes. It's the one that looked scared."

An uproar surged behind them. Creatures grabbing iron weapons. A whirl of wind sprang out of nowhere as Kim, the only air witch still able to stand on her own, armed herself for another fight.

Nemain, despite still being an entire field away, picked up on the change in atmosphere and zoomed toward them.

"Stop!" Sara screamed. "That's my pneuma! Don't hurt her!"

Kim stopped whipping air around her and other faces softened from terror to uncertainty.

"What are they bringing them here for?" someone asked.

"We'll find out," Evelyn answered and she and Sara ran out to meet Nemain.

Lily caught up with them before they were halfway there. "What the heck are they thinking?" she asked, vocalizing the question all three were asking themselves.

They were there a minute later. "What's going on?" Lily, as the only one of the triplets able to form complete, wheeze-free sentences after their sprint, spoke for the triplets.

"Don't attack. They come in peace. They want to talk."

Talk? Why didn't they run? No one would be able to catch them, at least not tonight.

Evelyn sensed her sisters' eyes on her, urging her, the one who had brought the fata over, to take the reins and speak. She felt the weight of that responsibility.

"OK," she sighed. "We'll talk, but they have to promise not to use magic on anyone over there." Evelyn gestured back to the crowd in front of the cottage. "We promise the same. Give us five minutes."

Nemain nodded and in a flash, she was soaring back toward the fata on the edge of the forest.

Not everyone agreed to the parley, at least not until shields stood before what remained of the Triplet Army, particularly the injured. Only a few stood unprotected, the McKay sisters, the triplets, Shefali, Kim, Alfred, and Roman among them. Brigit insisted on standing, albeit assisted, with her daughters at the forefront.

"A unified leadership," Brigit had called it, sending a thrill through Evelyn at the word, leadership. Until today, she hadn't considered herself a leader in the magical community—more like a child's toy boat in rough seas—but her mother was right, they'd become leaders that day.

Nemain and Badb approached first, their familiar faces comforting despite the squadron at their back that made the hair on Evelyn's neck stand up.

"As you know, though Nemain and I were once true fata, we are no longer. Therefore, a representative of fatakind would like to speak to you if you will allow her to approach." Badb kept her airy voice measured, belying no sway.

"One, and only if Kim may have air at the ready," Lily said.

Apparently, Evelyn wasn't the only one who felt as if they'd grown into their leadership roles.

"Agreed," an alien voice, unversed in the intricacies of

English, said. The fuchsia fata Evelyn recognized floated forward, locking eyes with her.

She recognizes me, too.

"Allow me to introduce myself. I am Aphra, scribe to the late king of Hecate. It is in this way that I know your tongue as well as the king and Noro. My other kin, however, do not. Hence, I speak for my kind. No need to introduce yourselves. I am familiar."

Members of the Triplet Army nodded.

"We, the fata of Hecate, are aware we have caused much devastation. Many are dead on both sides. The kin behind me and myself are all that is left of the fata on Earth. We have been speaking with Badb and Nemain and realize your stance is that humans not be made to serve the fata. I'll admit, it is a new idea to us. Dimia and Noro claimed it was humankind's rightful place to be beneath fata. Many fata believed them. However, seeing you with all your power, how you fought for a planet of beings, I know this cannot be. A majority of those behind me agree. I regret we believed those lies. Please, accept my apology on behalf of my kind for the threat we caused and for your lost loved ones."

Reflexively, a lump rose in Evelyn's throat as Mary's tinkling laugh played in her mind. A strange, guttural sound came from Brigit. Evelyn wasn't the only one thinking of Mary.

"We appreciate your condolences," Sara spoke in little more than a whisper. "Now, did you come to apologize or to ask something of us?"

Aphra hovered, silent for a moment as if weighing her thoughts. Then, she bowed. "I request the fata who are here remain. That we may work on bringing our kind over ourselves and not be persecuted for those actions. Some of us, perhaps most, will perish in the act and that is our burden to carry. We may even fail, but if we succeed I request you allow us to stay here, on your home planet. Our planet, as you know, is dying. We cannot thrive there. Many of us had lost our gift of magic before you brought us here."

The fata nodded at Evelyn, who lowered her eyes to the ground. "Since then, some have regained a semblance of the magic Hecate once gifted us. We vow to never attempt to reign over humans or any other creature. We only want a home and a way to regain the part of ourselves we have lost."

The sound of breathing and rustling of wind through the grass crushed in around the delegation.

They're asking to stay. For a home.

The concept was not one Evelyn had considered, not when Noro was alive, intent on gaining power any way he could.

"Before you answer," Nemain spoke now, pulling

forward to face the triplets, her black eyes locked on Sara, "please consider that not all fata are as cruel as Noro or my father. That some, Badb, myself, and even Macha once she repented, loved humans and the magical creatures of Earth. We lived in harmony with them for many years. Badb and I truly believe these fata plan on doing the same. Speaking only with the supernatural community, of course."

She's right, it happened before.

"I say yes." Sara, in what Evelyn considered true peacekeeper fashion, stepped forward and stuck her hand out to Aphra. The fata glanced at it with curious eyes.

"We shake hands when we create a binding agreement on Earth," Sara explained. "That is, as long as my sisters agree. We are, after all, the ones known as the saviors. We'll decide, and we'll live with the consequences as will the fata living on Earth, should there be any issues in the future. If there are issues, the fata will not fare well. Do you take my meaning?" Sara's copper eyes leveled with Aphra, who nodded her understanding.

Brigit smiled a small, proud smile.

Lily nodded without hesitation.

Evelyn, however, hesitated. She thought of all she'd been through at the hands of the fata.

One fata.

The memory of Aphra's terrified gaze when Macha

soared through the Crystal Palace came charging back at Evelyn. Aphra had been as scared of Evelyn as she'd been of Noro.

And fear is an emotion that can go on forever. But it doesn't have to. We can break this cycle. Create a new reality.

For the first time in weeks, something lifted in Evelyn. A lightness poured through her and a flutter tickled her stomach. Though Macha had been distinctly absent since she'd dissolved into the ether, Evelyn felt her now. Some would call it intuition, a gut feeling, but Evelyn knew what it really was.

Macha was giving her a nudge, informing Evelyn of her wishes, trusting that Evelyn would listen. And because it was Macha, once Eve, the fata who had made more poor choices than anyone could imagine and altered the course of human history, she would. Because Macha had seen it all—the evil, the ignorant, the bullhead, the naive, and the good. Macha, more than anyone, knew the range of emotions fata were capable of and Evelyn would trust her. Evelyn sucked in a breath and gave the final, sealing nod.

Sara turned back to Aphra. "The fata are solely responsible for bringing more fata over. You will assert no authority over humans as none of the magical species of Earth do. I should add you will report to the Supernatural

Union, our ruling body, which you will need to do sooner rather than later to explain all these dead creatures."

Aphra studied Sara, her black eyes giving no hint of what she was thinking. Then, she stuck her limb out.

Evelyn's eyes widened. Aphra had transformed her noodle-like appendage into the shape of a human hand.

The fata and witch shook, ushering in a new age of magical creatures on Earth.

Magic Lost

Lily

Two DAYS later they released the accused from their cages. Hands tied with magic behind their backs, the guards accompanied the Acolytes of Hecate to face their punishment. The daemon and fae had been taken care of the day before by Alfred and Eros. They were released back into the world, looking stunned by their lack of magical spark, their utter humanness.

As Lily watched the witches and wizards tread the garden path, she was reminded of those from centuries past. The accused, marching to their deaths.

Is it worse? To lose your magic but keep your life?

Nora walked past Lily now, tears falling fast and free down her dirt-smudged face. "You can't do this! You wouldn't! Brigit, think of our years of friendship."

Brigit shook her head in disbelief at Nora's pathetic bargaining. She did not dignify the witch with a response, only stared her down, waiting for her friend to stand before her.

"You should have thought about that before you sided with evil. Our Mary died because of you. There's no way you're getting out of this. If Brig can't do it, I will," Aoife, Nora's guard, growled and shoved the bob-haired brunette in the back, urging her toward her fate.

Nora whimpered, and Lily realized then how pathetic she was. The glamorous exterior, the chic style and ostentatious laugh she'd marveled at when Nora picked her up at Terramar to meet her birth family had been a ruse.

Nora had had everything: a family, great friends, and prodigious magic. All tossed aside for a chance at power. Lily shook her head; she'd never be able to understand Nora. Not when she'd lost Em and worked so hard to integrate her Terramar family in with the McKays. The family Nora had thrown away.

The accused were before their enforcer now, Nora facing off with Brigit. Nora looked as if she were about to try reasoning again when Gwenn spoke, her voice clear as a bell among the mumbles and whimpers.

"You fifteen stand before us accused of endangering the human species, of attempting to throw off the natural order of Earth by allowing magical creatures to reign above us all, and of starting a magical war. Do you deny it?"

Lily gaped as the accused shook their heads.

"If they deny it, we have to take them to a real supernatural court. If they're found guilty there, the penalty is death. A slow one," Sara whispered an explanation for the quick admission.

"As you all admit guilt, the following punishment shall be enacted immediately. You will forfeit your magical essence, your spark, to the being before you, one you have wronged on some level. You shall never get it back and will live out the rest of your days ostracized from the magical community." Gwenn paused and only the sobbing of the accused filled the silence.

"Enforcers, as you're ready." Gwenn exited the end of the line of enforcers and accused, her part as the official in this macabre ceremony completed.

Lily inched closer to her mother, hoping to provide support should she need it. Steps followed. Sara and Evelyn were close behind. She reached her mother and stood behind her, Nora's once attractive face staring back at her. The stench of dirt and sweat clung to her trembling body.

"Brigit, I beg—"

"Stop." Brigit held up a hand.

From all around yelps, screams, and wails of other witches and wizards losing their magic sounded, their enforcers not bothering to wait a minute longer than necessary. Notes of rot with a hint of something innocent and good—jasmine, warm summer nights, and a first snowfall—filled the air. Magic, pure in its essence, leaving the bodies of those who had turned dark.

"How dare you ask for forgiveness?" Brigit said. "My sister is dead because of you, Nora. You endangered the lives of my *children*. You know how much I gave up to keep them safe. And that's not even considering the rest of the world, the chaos you would have caused." Brigit's voice was level, though Lily heard the fire behind it, so different from her mother's usual grounded tone.

Nora blinked. "I—it was so hard being your friend, Brig. I loved you, still do, but living up to a McKay, being your best friend . . . please understand! I was unworthy, jealous. If you let me go, I'll spend the rest of my life making it up to you."

"As if you could. You'll never be able to make up for what I've lost. No, you'll be serving your penance living as the beings you developed a contempt for." And with that Brigit held out her hand and whispered an enchantment Lily could not hear. One she never wanted to hear.

Nora collapsed in on herself, her body vibrating, her eyes dimming as a soft white glow emerged from her heart center. Nora screamed as Brigit ripped the magic out of her and hurled it into the sky, where it disappeared forever.

Into the Ether

Sara

A PERSISTENT FLUTTER in her chest woke Sara from her afternoon nap. Sleep clouded her brain as she rose to lean against her headboard. The last few days had been packed to the point of mental and physical exhaustion.

Their army had returned home with the bodies of those they came with. As for the dead Acolytes, Brigit would not abide them being buried on her land alongside Mary, a werewolf, and witch in the triplet army no one was able to speak for. Hence a team from the Supernatural Union was called in to deal with their bodies, take them to their families, or bury them where appropriate.

Digging the graves for the fallen of the Triplet Army had been backbreaking work, though Sara wouldn't have it any other way. Each shovelful of frozen dirt felt like she was honoring the fallen, a penance for living when the dead had given everything they had to save them.

A separate funeral was arranged for each and as Selma spoke the final words at Mary's, Sara's strength finally cracked. She'd been crying on and off ever since, much like the rest of those in Fern Cottage. Sara glanced at the clock and saw it wasn't just grief messing with her. Nemain usually didn't request to be released for a few hours.

"Caeliter," she said and Nemain appeared, bright crimson and smiling.

"Is something wrong?"

Nemain nodded, looking joyful. "Never been better."

The human phrase hit Sara's ear in a strange way. She cocked her head. "So why did you want out two hours early? I'd think after the last few days you'd want your rest."

"I'll need the extra time, to say my goodbyes."

Sara sat up straighter. "What?"

"The day has come for Badb and me to leave you and Lily. Our journey together is over, our task complete."

"Bu—but . . . *no*! You two can't leave. You'll die!" Sara's fingers trembled, begging her to lift them, to pull Nemain back inside, and keep her there forever.

The red pneuma lowered her weightless body to Sara's

bed, her features shifting from joy to compassion. "Yes. I will die. I am at peace with that fact. I've lived a long life, many lives, failed and finally succeeded in not only protecting humans but also ensuring my original kin a safe home. I am ready to disappear into the ether, to be free."

Sara bit her lip hard. She wanted to deny Nemain, to tell her what she was saying made no sense, but that would be a lie. It made perfect sense. And there was nothing she could do anyhow. Outside her body Nemain was her own being, a part of Sara but separate all at once. "How long have you been planning this?"

Nemain shrugged. "Since you released me the first time. Or since you and your family allowed the fata to stay. I can't say when the thought bloomed. I think I've always known I'd leave at one point. I brought it up to Badb yesterday, and she agreed. It is the natural conclusion of our life cycle to follow our sister and disappear into the ether." She waved her arm. "Into that which is everything and nothing all at once. So, I'll be gone but not. I'll be around."

Sara's lips curled up in half smile. Nemain made it sound so pretty. Dying. "What if I can't live without you?"

"You will be fine, Sara. There's only one of us that won't live through my departure and it isn't you. I promise, you still have your own soul and as someone who lives inside you I can assure you, you are healthy."

"When are—?" But Sara's question was cut short by shouting coming from the sitting room. She sat up straighter trying to hear but all she could discern was Lily's voice, high and frantic.

"We had bets over who would make the bigger ruckus. It seems like Badb wins again. Should we go join them? Make this a family chat?" Nemain asked, clearing up Sara's confusion.

Sara nodded and lifted herself from her bed.

***

THERE HAD BEEN no convincing Badb or Nemain otherwise, and hence, they held another ceremony. A shotgun funeral of sorts, though no one wanted to call it that.

Sara preferred the term exodus—a leaving, but not specifying how, or the fact that Badb's and Nemain's leaving meant they would be lost forever.

No matter what they called it, the witches still lit candles and prepared a simple feast filling the cottage with the timeless aroma of roasted meat, potatoes, vegetables, and fresh bread. They ate around the flaming hearth. Two bowls, one filled with water, the other with black earth, were nestled next to the flames. A tribute to their pneumas. They gave thanks for Badb, Macha, and Nemain, their teachers, for all their work and their commitment to saving humanity.

"I hope we can rise to the occasion like you three did, if we ever need to again," Lily said as the group walked outside hours later for a final goodbye.

"I have no doubt about it. We were separated by millennia, but I see my sisters and I in each of you." Badb smiled at Lily.

Sara approached Nemain one last time. "Thank you for everything. Teaching us, protecting us, being there for us and those who came to our aid." She dropped her head. "You've always been a part of me even if I didn't know you were there. Once I got over the shock it was nice. Like I've always had the family I wanted nestled inside me. I just didn't know it."

Nemain's crimson arm lifted Sara's chin and her black eyes stared into Sara's copper. "It was an honor to share your body. Thank you for allowing my kind a place to live. I will never forget it. As for being a part of a family." Her eyes lifted and darted around the room at the other witches. "You always had a family and now that you're all together—well, I'd probably have a better chance at turning purple before anyone in your clan left the other. And I'm not joking when I say I'll be here."

Nemain placed her limb over Sara's heart. "You'll sense me from time to time."

Sara hoped she was right.

Nemain nodded to Badb, and the pair waved a final goodbye before vanishing into the starry night.

Epilogue
Sara

Sara smiled as she walked down the aisle, jasmine flowers adorning the bouquet clutched in her hands reminding her of her girlfriend's scent.

Evelyn was waiting for her at the end, along with Alfred, Roman, Alfred's younger brother, and Gwenn as the officiant. Kim winked as she walked by, sending shivers up Sara's spine.

Their last six months together had been nothing short of magical. As was tonight, with the fairy lights twinkling from the great fir trees, the luminous glass ornaments decorating the spaces in between, and the sun lighting the sky behind the hills of the Columbia River Gorge.

There was no denying magic existed at Terramar commune tonight.

Sara took her place next to Evelyn, who grinned and gripped her hand. Beneath her sister's smooth touch Sara felt the knobs and thin skin on her own hand. It was the one part of her body Sara denied anyone from healing magically. Without the help of Fiona or Lily's witchy salves, the burns on her hands from the night she killed Noro weren't healing fast, but Sara insisted it be natural.

She wanted to bear a scar from their final battle at Fern Cottage. A reminder of the lives saved and lost the night she and her sisters made a choice and altered the course of life on Earth for good. It had been an abrupt decision to allow the fata to stay, but to Sara, it had felt right. So far, the magical alien race, now led by Aphra the scribe, had upheld their half of the bargain. Sara hoped it was a peace that would last forever.

Annika's plucking of harp strings changed tune. Guests stood and waited. Tears pricked in Sara's eyes and she bid them back, not wanting to mar the makeup Selma had applied.

Brigit and Rena were already weeping buckets in the front row. From the scrunched up look on her face, Aoife would be there soon, too. Sara pictured Mary's cherubic cheeks alongside them. It used to bug her that her mind did this, interposed Mary into a family scene, but now she considered it an homage to an aunt, sister, and friend lost.

Everyone gasped when Lily appeared at the top of the

aisle. The Irish blue lace of her gown deepened the green of Lily's eyes.

Alfred is a lucky man.

Sara stole a glance at her soon to be brother-in-law, standing tall and proud at the end of the aisle. The corner of her lips lifted as Alfred's eyes began to mist subtly.

He knows it, too.

The vows were short and sweet, which was for the best as the bride and groom could not stop crying. The handfasting was traditional, performed with the same cloth which bound Brigit and Aengus, throwing everything that occurred this last year into motion. The kiss was hungry. The crowd cheered as the couple broke apart and Gwenn pronounced the daemon and witch as husband and wife.

An upbeat tune, this time from a guitarist at the side of the audience, rose on the wind.

Evelyn brushed a kiss on Roman's cheek before taking his arm and intertwining her hand with his. The couple, incubus and witch, swept down the aisle beaming, their free hands pumping up and down in ecstatic celebration.

Sara chuckled and looped her arm with Alfred's brother's arm and, following Evelyn and Roman's lead, they performed an awkward little jig for the amusement of the guests.

Lily and Alfred followed last, the most radiant creatures in the forest as all three sisters danced forth into their new lives—together.

Hawk Witch, The Bonegates Series, Chapter 1

"SERVES THE OLD BUGGER RIGHT!" Branna Penny, the "it girl" of Dublin, shrieked with delight as she took her turn to cover the ex-provost's eyelids with a lurid shade of red lipstick.

I watched as other graduates climbed the stone statue of George Salmon, itching for their turn to deface the slimy bugger. Though it pained me to agree with Branna, this time we were of the same opinion.

"Aren't you going to join in on the fun, Lan? If I were a Trinners girl, I wouldn't want to miss a chance to get back at the spiteful fart."

My best friend—my only friend—Finnegan Fairchild appeared at my side, bringing with him whiffs of leather and moss that mingled in the crisp November air. He grinned as he took in the graduation ritual he'd explained to thousands of tourists as a Trinity College tour guide.

Young women in line for their turn to deface the statue turned to stare. Finn, well versed in ladies' stares, winked.

A couple swooned on the spot. Gag.

"Right," I scoffed. "You know I'm nothing like them. They only ever want to talk to me to get closer to you. You're why I have no girlfriends."

"So why do you have no guy friends? Besides me, of course. That's obvious. Who wouldn't want to be my friend?" Finn raised a playful eyebrow before pressing on. "Have you brewed up one of your witchy potions to keep the lads away?"

I swatted his well-muscled shoulder. "Oh, shut it! You know I don't brew up potions. I'm no healer. I suppose I'm too awkward for them. Or I give off serious daddy issue vibes."

Finn shuffled his weight and frowned at the mention of my father. Silence descended, and he turned to stare at the riotous scene before us. Not wanting to make him more uncomfortable, I turned, too.

Lipstick graffiti caked the provost's face now, and shades of red bled down his neck. By the time the queue finished, George's socks would be crimson. It was the provost's penance for shouting against women entering the college, even while he unwillingly signed the admittance papers. A humiliation his likeness suffered in accordance with Trinity's staggered commencement ceremonies year after year.

"You know, Lan, those girls shouldn't have used you to get my attention. It was a foul thing to do."

Finn never knew what to say when I spoke of my father, even peripherally, so he often changed the subject. Not that he hadn't listened to me in the past when I'd brought my father up, wondering where he was, what he'd be like, and what of myself I'd find in him. Finn *had* listened. Probably for longer than most people could bear, but the guy could only take so much.

The idea of a man abandoning his child made Finn profoundly uncomfortable. Despite the death of his biological father before Finn's birth, my best friend had grown up with a stable family.

For me, abandonment was a confusing and painful fact of life that most people thought I should be over by now. Then again, most people didn't have issues with magic *and* social anxiety.

"That's not fair now, is it? I've used you nearly all my life to pass as normal." I attempted to swing my arm over Finn's shoulders. Even at my above-average height, it was a stretch.

Finn bent his knees obligingly and an uncharacteristic

splash of pink stained his high cheekbones. "That's different. We're best friends. You can lean on me whenever you need." He slithered his arm atop my shoulder, and I laid my head there.

From the top of the statue, Branna and two other girls paused in their selfie marathon to stare me down. I sighed, recalling how they had asked me to coffee our first year at Trinity, and for a few weeks, I'd thought I'd made real girlfriends. Soon enough, it became clear they only talked to me to be around my best friend. When I mentioned their behavior to Finn, he dropped them straight away. They still hadn't gotten over the burn.

At least I wouldn't be seeing them again after today. They were all staying in Dublin and working the fancy jobs they'd acquired between term ending in the spring and graduation in the fall. Though attending university in the city had been fun, I missed the countryside. I couldn't wait to get the hell out and doubted I'd return soon.

A LOUD SCREECH filled my ears as I opened my car door.

"I'm coming, Naela," I yelled, my mouth spreading into a wide smile.

The screeching paused for a heartbeat before

sounding again, more insistent this time. My bloody bird was a diva sometimes.

Grabbing the bags I'd packed so I could stay at Finn's flat the night before graduation, I ran to the front door and pushed it open. I threw everything on the floor.

"Mam! I'm home!"

"Hi, darling!" My mother, Aileen Shea, appeared from her room. Her dark brown hair was up in a ponytail and only half her face was made-up for her shift at the hospital. Mam's gray eyes, eyes I'd inherited from her, popped against the red, puffy skin beneath them. She'd been crying.

"You all right?"

Mam made her way down the hall to take me in her arms. "I'm fine, darling. Just got a wee bit emotional on the drive home from your ceremony. Graduating from uni is a big accomplishment. I'm so proud of you. Gran would have been, too."

My eyes traveled past Mam to the other presence I felt whenever I entered our house. A photo of my gran was the first thing anyone saw when they walked through our door. Her familiar smile, the long gray hair, and her eyes that sparkled with mischief always tugged at my heartstrings. It was true she would have been proud. Gran had always been proud of everything I did, no matter how average.

"Thanks. I thought of her, too." It had been impossible not to think of Gran. I felt her absence daily.

Mam pulled away, but kept a hand on my shoulder, which she squeezed. "And I'm so sorry I couldn't stay longer to celebrate after you received your degree. I'm working with Dr. Cannon today. You know how he is."

"It's all right, Mam. Your patients need you."

There was no use in making her feel bad for having to work when I returned home sooner than she expected. I'd just wanted to leave the ceremony as soon as I was given my degree. Home had been calling.

"I'm surprised you didn't go out with Finn. Did his father have other plans for him?"

Finn's upright, English stepfather was a man of many plans. These included plans for Finn, for Finn's younger sister, and even plans for me. It was only because of Mr. Fairchild's connections, and Finn's determination that we attend university together, that I'd been accepted into Trinity.

My short brown hair swished from side to side as I shook my head. "Finn snagged a meeting with the head of the history department after graduation. Did it all on his own, so he's quite excited about it. He'll come by this weekend to celebrate but until then, he's busy schmoozing."

Mam laughed. "Who would have thought Finn

Fairchild would straighten up so prettily? That one suffered from a double dose of original sin for far too long. It's good to hear he's taking after his stepfather a bit more."

I couldn't deny that my mate was a bit of trouble. Finn enjoyed shaking things up sometimes. Everyone knew it too.

She jerked a thumb down the hall. "I'll prep the spare room tomorrow. Will he bring Kane?"

"I didn't ask, but I hope so. Naela would love the flying partner. Speaking of Naela, I better see to her, so she shuts up."

I nodded out back where my Northern Goshawk had been screeching insistently for the duration of our conversation. Honestly, it was a wonder we'd been able to ignore her, but I supposed after living with a needy hawk for years we'd gotten used to it.

"Brilliant, darling. I'll finish getting ready for work." My mother kissed me on the forehead and disappeared down the hall.

I rushed out the back door. Two gold eyes latched onto me as Naela released her loudest screech yet. The bird was pissed I'd taken so long. She really was a pushy little thing.

"Sorry, Boss! I was saying hi to Mam."

The goshawk puffed up her feathers, annoyed at

being second fiddle. My lips twitched up at the reaction, but I suppressed the smile. I didn't want to annoy her more. She might drop a mouse on my head. It wouldn't be the first time.

I pulled on my protective leather glove and went to open the mew—the specialized hawk enclosure that kept Naela from flying off to who-knew-where while I was gone. The mew worked most of the time, though, once I woke to find Naela sitting outside my dorm window. When I called to tell Mam, she'd burst into tears saying she'd been searching everywhere for Naela. I'd been a bit annoyed, but more amazed that Naela had broken free and sought me out, instead of taking her freedom as many hawks would.

"You're right. What was I thinking choosing Mam first? *You're* the boss." I unlatched the cage, and Naela flew out the door.

She zoomed above the treetops, did a few flips in the air, and plunged back down.

My lips flattened as her gray and white feathers disappeared into the woods behind our house. I placed my fingers in my mouth and pushed out a piercing whistle. Naela came barreling back toward me with incredible speed, and I flung my sheathed arm out to the side, thumb up. Seconds later I took Naela's weight as she perched, one talon on my thumb, the other digging into the thick leather covering my forearm.

"Nice to see you, too, Boss."

Naela turned to look at me, a chattering sound escaping her beak.

"Ah, right. How forgetful of me." I strolled over to the cooler where we kept her meat. My nose wrinkled from the stink as I fished out a cut.

Naela took the morsel and gobbled it down. A pleased noise worked its way up her throat.

"That good, huh?"

The bird inched a little closer to me. In hawk terms, it was basically a hug.

"So, you all right? Anything new?"

Naela tilted her gray head and in the gesture, I read what I wanted to. *Fine, thanks. Better now that you're back for good. Your mam's nice but she doesn't quite get me, you know?*

"I understand. You and Finn are the only ones who really get me."

Naela stiffened and her gaze sharpened upon me.

"*Obviously,* you know me better," I said reassuringly, and her stance softened.

The back door opened with a squeak, and Mam peeked out. "She never looks like that when it's me and her."

I grinned. "You off to perform miraculous healing now?"

My mam wasn't just a charge nurse but also a well-regarded healer in the witching community. If Western medicine failed her patients, Mam always offered an alternative route. It was easier to pull off as a night nurse because of less supervision. And as Mam says, in the dead of night when they're all alone, people will try about anything to heal—even witchy remedies.

"I hope so. You off for a walk with Naela? Better take it in while you still can. The leaves will be gone soon."

I nodded, already eyeing the woods behind the house. It called to me so strongly that one would almost think I was a rumbler witch.

"All right, darling. How about we breakfast together?"

"Sounds perfect. Night, Mam." I was already envisioning the nice, quiet night I'd have after my walk.

Home had always been my sanctuary. Here no one could bug me or interrupt my peace. Of that much, I could be sure.

***

Start this series now!

Acknowledgments

Thank you to Kurt Leopoldt for always believing in me, and allowing the space and time to follow my dreams. You keep me thankful for your love, unyielding compassion, and support everyday. I love you babe.

I would not be where I am today without my amazing critique partners and fellow authors Kelly N. Jane, April Taylor, Susan Robinson, and Jaci Miller. You ladies rock and I LOVE talking books with you!

Jennifer Roop, my editor. You've brought my work to a new level and gave me valuable, constructive, and kind input when I needed it. You're the best.

A massive thank you to my beta readers, Charlie Knight, Marcy Ettlinger, and Tara Ruff for pointing me in the right direction. And to my proofreaders, Emily Tackitt and Nancy Wege, I am so grateful for your keen eyes on my work and that you always point out errors with grace and kindness.

Finally, I want to thank all my family and friends who have supported me, stood by me, and cheered for me in my transition to becoming an author. I started out a super newbie and have grown so much. Not every creative can say the majority of people in their life support them, but I sure can. There are honestly too many people to name here, but if you are reading this book, just know, I mean you.

All the magic,

Ashley McLeo

Also by Ashley McLeo

<u>Coven of Shadows and Secrets</u>

Seeker of Secrets

Hunted by Darkness

History of Witches

<u>Spellcasters Spy Academy Series (Magic of Arcana Universe)</u>

A Legacy Witch: Year One

A Marked Witch: Internship

A Rebel Witch: Year Two

A Crucible Witch: Year Three

An Academy Witch: Prequel

The Complete Spellcasters Spy Academy Boxset

<u>The Wonderland Court Series (Magic of Arcana Universe)</u>

Alice the Dagger

Alice the Torch

<u>Standalone Novels</u>

Stealing Maid Marian's Heart (Magic of Arcana Universe)

The Alchemist of Silver Hollow (Magic of Arcana Universe)

Fanged Fae Series - A Bonegates sister series

Blood Moon Magic

Faerie Blood

The Bonegate Series - A Fanged Fae sister series

Hawk Witch

Assassin Witch

Traitor Witch

Illuminator Witch

The Royal Quest Series

Dragon Prince

Dragon Magic

Dragon Mate

Dragon Betrayal

Dragon Crown

Dragon War

The Starseed Universe

Prophecy of Three

Souls of Three

Rising of Three

The Starseed Universe (five-book boxset, includes two bonus novellas)

About the Author

Ashley lives in Portland with her husband, Kurt, their dog, Flicka, and the house ghost that sometimes makes appearances in her charming, old home.

When she's not writing urban fantasy and portal fantasy novels she enjoys traveling the world, reading, kicking butt at board games (she recommends Splendor and Dominion), and frequenting taquerias.

For all the latest releases and updates, subscribe to Ashley's newsletter, The Coven. You can also find her Facebook group, Ashley's Reader Coven and join in on the fun there!